Amanda Minnie Douglas

Whom Kathie Married

Amanda Minnie Douglas

Whom Kathie Married

ISBN/EAN: 9783337366179

Printed in Europe, USA, Canada, Australia, Japan

Cover: Foto ©Andreas Hilbeck / pixelio.de

More available books at **www.hansebooks.com**

WHOM KATHIE MARRIED

BY

AMANDA M. DOUGLAS

AUTHOR OF

"In Trust," "The Old Woman who lived in a Shoe," etc.

BOSTON
LEE AND SHEPARD, 47 FRANKLIN STREET
NEW YORK
CHARLES T. DILLINGHAM, 678 BROADWAY
1883

ALFRED MUDGE & SON, PRINTERS, BOSTON.

TO MY YOUNG FRIENDS,

WHO,

HAVING FOLLOWED KATHIE THROUGH HER CHILDHOOD,

AND EXPRESSED FROM TIME TO TIME DEEP INTEREST
IN THE AFTER-DAYS OF HER WOMANHOOD,
WITH ITS DUTIES AND PLEASURES,

This Volume is affectionately Inscribed,

WITH THE HOPE THAT IT MAY ADD TO THE FRIENDSHIP
SO CORDIALLY BEGUN BETWEEN

AUTHOR AND READER.

1883.   A. M. D.

WHOM KATHIE MARRIED.

CHAPTER I.

"Then you think I ought not speak of this to Kathie?"

The fresh, young voice had an accent of entreaty, as if in hope the listener might relent.

Gen. Mackenzie was softly pacing the polished floor of the dusky, old time room in the Piazza di Spagna while his son sat leaning his arm on a small table, his face partially averted, bowed a little on his hand.

"My dear boy, you are both so young —"

"If you think I shall change or forget — " Bruce began vehemently.

"No, no, it is not that. I believe you know your own mind and will keep it. I should be sorry if I could think otherwise of your stability ; and it gives me pain to refuse you anything, — you must know that, my dear son. But for Kathie's sake — "

"I am sure she loves me. She simply does not understand ; but if she thought of it — "

"That is just it. Listen a few moments patiently, Bruce, remembering that there is no one in the world whose welfare can be of quite such keen interest to me. Kathie is still a sweet, innocent, unawakened child. You and she have been like brother and sister all these months, and she has not the slightest suspicion of any warmer regard on your part. It is not time for her to think of love. She ought to go on in this unconscious, untroubled way a

year or two longer: she has so much to see, so much to
learn, before she can even judge herself correctly. Why
should we lay a burden on her, confuse and trouble her
perceptions as to what is coming to herself?"

"A burden! As if I would make it any burden!"
with the confident ring of youth. "She need not be engaged. She can go on just as she is now: I am not a
jealous fool!"

"Bruce, a marriage engagement is too solemn a thing
to hold that way. Either one must be bound or free.
These half-measures place a girl in a very equivocal position. I should like to return her to her mother as simple
and childlike as she is now. She was intrusted to our
care, and you see it *is* a point of honor. If Mrs. Alston
were here to decide, or if Kathie were a year or two
older —"

"Still, I do not think Mrs. Alston would question your
judgment," returned Bruce, with pardonable pride.

"That is one reason why I am so scrupulous. Because
I might so easily take the right of deciding her child's
future, I do not want to feel that we hastened any change
in her. If she *does* care for you, your absence will help
her to find it out. She will contrast others with you, and
for this cause, as well as more personal ones, I want *your*
standard kept high and pure. Take the noblest, manliest
view of it, my dear son. Think of her for the next two
or three years, perhaps, living upon your letters, exagger-
ating, no doubt, the dangers to which you may be exposed, never feeling that she has the right to be quite care
free, denying herself many innocent pleasures through what
she considers her duty to you. Do you not see that it
would eat the heart and the sweetness out of girlhood?"

The young man was silent a moment, then he rose
suddenly.

"You think it would be selfish in me, I know you do;
and it *is*."

There was a new resolution visible in every feature, as he stood in the dying light by the western window. It was a noble face, full of health and energy, and a certain integrity that would command respect anywhere.

"I had not looked at it in that light before; I was thinking of myself and the fear of losing her. You *will* guard her for me?" And his tone was full of tender entreaty.

A softened commendation shone in the father's eyes, as he crossed to his son, and Bruce, linking his arm in that of the other, resumed the slow pacing with him.

"I will do my best, but," with a fond smile, "I do not think she will require much guarding. And I need not ask you to keep honorable in thought, word, and deed for her sake. You have passed through some of the perils of early manhood unscathed; but in the frontier life, to which you are going, there will be new temptations, and, not the least, the subtle ennui of idleness. O my boy, I should like to keep you with me always!"

Bruce pressed the hand he was holding to his lips. To the boy his father had been the ideal of all that was noble and worthy of admiration. The strain and peril of all those years of civil war had given his soul a larger growth than the tranquil times of peace.

"It gratifies us to see our sons and daughters taking their places in the great world, and yet it brings a pang of sadness. They can only be children of memory, and the after-friendship must be largely their own gift. We have been more than ordinarily near and dear, and, Bruce, it pains me to refuse you; but I have tried to keep to the highest right and sense of honor."

"I am not sure but it will be a better discipline for me if it has a little bitter flavor. It is something to strive for, to win. I shall try to make myself worthy of her, and to keep the respect and esteem of all whom I love. You will not blame me for placing *her* first?"

"I hold that a man has as good a right to strive earnestly for the woman he loves as for any other great prize of life; and often an aim of this kind is the best incentive for a young man, since out of it springs the wider duties of life and citizenship."

"It has been such a happy year!" Bruce said in a tone of lingering enjoyment. "I ought to be the more ready to go back after such a grand holiday; but there seems so little that is heroic in frontier life, so little to do, contrasted with the stirring years of the past. It is only the steady tramp, now."

> "'That all the good the past has had
> Remains to make our own life glad, —
> Our common, daily life divine,
> And every land a Palestine,'"

repeated his father.

"Brave, gentle Whittier," rejoined Bruce. "I will try to remember that among the many noble truths he has sung."

"We are so apt to think our own times prosaic; but occasionally the victories of peace are greater to a nation than those of war. Heroes are often called into being by the emergency of the hour, and there is an inspiration in being called upon to perform a great deed; but it often takes more real strength and principle to fulfil the daily duties that are demanded of every human being, both by God and his neighbor."

Bruce was silent: he had fallen into a revery. He had enjoyed being at West Point, and the prestige of his father's name had given him a leaning toward military life, yet he wondered if he would make the same choice now. He had no right to shirk: he owed his country her meed of service, even if it was guarding a frontier outpost against marauding Indians and affording protection to travelling traders. He had come to dream of home life, of daily love, of sweeter duties, and the other looked bald and barren. What was it he had read somewhere — about girding one's self like a good soldier?

" Bruce?" The elder paused, in a tone of soft, doubtful inquiry.

" I was thinking — of all the outlying things — shall I call them so? Of the years to come."

" I am glad you can look at it in that light," in a greatly relieved tone. "And you are not unhappy?"

" I cannot promise that I will not be unhappy when I am alone by myself, but I am not as wretched as I thought I should be an hour ago, when you asked me to — to sacrifice my own desire. And yet I am just as much in love with Kathie; and the horrible fear comes over me — what if I should lose her! At least you will let me write. My letters may come in yours, unsealed."

The father's heart was deeply touched.

" Bruce, in this matter I trust you unreservedly. And I think I can answer for the others, when the proper time comes."

" Thank you," with a warm, earnest pressure of the hand. Then suddenly, " We must have lights: I hear them coming."

There was a sound of footfalls and voices on the stairs, and before the apartment was really illumined, the door opened, and Mrs. Mackenzie entered with her niece. A certain matronly grace marked the changes the years had brought Aunt Ruth; but Kathie Alston, to stranger eyes, would have been an undeniable young lady. A fresh, fair, slender girl, with the delicate complexion of her countrywomen, and a charm that was not so much beauty, perhaps, as the candor, grace, and purity of childhood still clinging about her. Certainly foreigners who met her did not have to complain of aggressiveness or imprudent frankness. She was rather shy of strangers, but enjoyed everything in such a wholesome, happy way that tired eyes and weary brains sometimes watched her with envy.

" Oh," she began now with a bright little laugh, " you were sitting in the dark, telling secrets; but you will have to repeat every little plot and plan! O Bruce, I wish you could have been there and heard Signora Biondo! She has such an exquisite voice. Only, it was so queer not to ask any gentlemen."

" They might have frightened the young *débutante*," said Bruce, glad of the cover of a commonplace.

" She does n't look so *very* young, does she, Aunt Ruth? And she is n't beautiful; but I believe celebrities seldom are. She is going to Milan to make her *début*, and then to St. Petersburg."

" And then to America, that harvest for singers," rejoined Bruce.

" No doubt. Would n't it be odd to hear her there some time, Aunt Ruth? But it was delightful. And did you stay in all the afternoon? Were you planning campaigns with uncle?"

She turned her clear eyes full upon him. Bruce studied her face curiously in the softened lamplight. It was frank, friendly, tender with the peculiar sympathy of her nature; yet she did not shrink or color, or drop her eyes to veil any secret. She loved him very much, but she was not in love with him. The pleasant intercourse of the past months had made them friends, cousins, as Bruce had at first insisted; but his father was right, — it was not her time to love.

" Oh!" she exclaimed with a little confusion, " I don't want you to think — We are all sorry; *I* am sorry to have you go."

" Then you must be glad —"

" The sentences do not join properly." There was a little gravity in her tone. " But you *do* know."

" I think he does," answered his father, as a flush of color dyed his son's face for an instant.

Kathie began to take off her wraps. Yes, she should

miss Bruce every day and hour; and if the Merediths
were not coming, she would want to go back to America
herself: sometimes such a homesick longing came over her.

The tea was brought in, and the conversation was kept
to safe general topics. Then some American friends called,
and after a little they dropped into the silence of reading
and thinking.

Just as they were parting for the night, Kathie went
over to Bruce.

" I am going to tell you," she began in her soft, comforting tone, " how glad I am that we had Scotland and
England together, and the Alps, and that great, strange,
barbaric Russia, for at home we can go over the bits and
fragments of remembrance. You will be rea'y for a
vacation, — or a furlough, is n't it, — by the time we return.
And I shall not care so much for Paris and the rest."

He was glad she could not see his face in that dim light.

" And — you do not think — that I shall *not* be sorry
to have you go?" with a little falter in her voice.

" O Kathie, how could I think that?"

" You know it is as uncle said; there is no choice about
it. We *must* give you up for a little while, and I have
been trying to be brave and — "

" Oh, my darling, don't!" Bruce cried suddenly; " I
know — There, you are actually making a coward of me,
— a soldier and a soldier's son. I shall think of you often,
always; and you must send a little remembrance now and
then."

" Yes. Good night." She stooped and kissed him on
the forehead, as any sister might. He pressed her hand
to his lips, then let her go. It would be like caging a
bird in May, to speak, to bind her by any promise.

And yet he wondered. With a young man's jealous
fervor, he had a fear that whoever saw and learned to
know Kathie would want her. What if he should miss
the golden moment of her awakening!

Kathie thought the parting over sadly enough when her head first touched the pillow: it had been such a happy time, — all their foreign tour so far.

Mr. and Mrs. Meredith had gone over with them. The voyage had proved delightful, with only a trifle of seasickness. Kathie had been a little shy at first with her new cousin, but Aunt Ruth and her step-son were very dear friends.

The party had all gone up to London. There was so much to see and verify, so much of history and legend and song; so like home, and yet so different, the likeness being greatly the familiarity of speech.

Bruce and Kathie were out every day with the General or Mr. Meredith when the ladies could not go, — for the baby occupied Jessie a great deal, and Aunt Ruth was not strong enough to stand the fatigue; but there were stage-coach and railroad jaunts to pretty country places of note, ruined castles, and long-ago battle-fields.

"It makes it so real," Kathie said.

There were odd little bits, — provincialism, English quaintness, the greenery of gardens and fields, little towns with their narrow streets and old inns, peaceful rivers, peasants, and tidy maids. Gen. Mackenzie kept the young people away from the darker side, — the crowded cities with their streets of want and crime. Theirs was the pleasure tour of youth.

Then the party separated. Business called Mr. Meredith to Paris, where he was likely to spend the winter. The Mackenzies went to Scotland and spent the early autumn rambling about slowly as Aunt Ruth could take it. There was as much of romantic interest, in fact, more, I think, to the young people; and perhaps, too, there was more time devoted to it. There was some far-back ancestry that seemed to claim kinship, and Bruce hunted up all the places made famous by the hero from whom he had taken his name. There were other heroes and knights, haunts and castles, and Holyrood, with its sad story of a checkered life and tragic ending.

"It seems strange to think of Queen Mary as a pretty French princess, with life and love and the luxury of the time all before her, when you contrast with it her dreary prison years. I never can wholly approve Queen Elizabeth," said Kathie with warm resentment.

"I do not suppose there ever was any great event or dispute where one side was wholly right," said the General; "there were always partisans to inflame both queens, and to sow dissension between them. Elizabeth, we must admit, was suspicious and jealous, and poor Mary fell upon evil times, even if she were as fair as her best historians represent her."

"But the strange thing," remarked Bruce, "is the curious love and veneration the Scotch seem to exhibit about her now, and the hatred with which they pursued her then. You almost feel now as if she had been idolized."

"That is the romance of time," said his father. "I think they had a chivalrous love for their queen, while their rigid principles led them to distrust and despise the woman."

There was Abbotsford to be visited, and the young people evinced a sudden interest in Sir Walter Scott's novels. They found so many historic places, celebrated battlefields, and lochs with legends of song. "The Lady of the Lake" was exhumed, Bruce and Kathie taking turns in reading aloud.

Gen. Mackenzie had some governmental business at St. Petersburg, so they were to take Russia as their next abiding-place. At first Kathie had tried to write letters home and to the girls full of descriptions of the wonderful sights; but she found it was not possible to keep it up. Aunt Ruth considered it quite too great a tax.

"You will have all winter to get your memories into shape," she said. "You can see now, and write it out afterward."

" It seems as if I should see it always," returned Kathie.
" The pretty rivers with their still prettier names,— the Dee
and Tay and Ayr, — the firths and the lochs, and the
Minch, with its countless islands. I really could draw a
map from remembrance. I used to wonder sometimes if
many of these places were not put down for the bother·
ment of one's brains." And she laughed over what had
once been quite a trouble.

The travellers felt at liberty to diverge from regular
routes, and as Bruce had a great desire to see something
of Norway and Sweden, they took those next, and then
made a little stay at Copenhagen. Kathie declared this
was the first of their foreign tour where speech and attire
and modes of living were so different. " And we cannot
learn every language," she declared in dismay.

Bruce was a very good German scholar, and though
Kathie had been reading it for the last year, it was quite
another thing to converse readily.

" For there are so many different kinds," she said, sadly
puzzled. " Now one American always *can* understand
another."

" But we could n't understand all the English or all the
Scotch," returned Bruce. " And here abroad there have
been so many petty kingdoms and places, and different
tribes and nations getting mixed all the time, yet each one
jealous for its own nationality ; and then, as one has ab-
sorbed the other, there comes to be a sort of mixed dialect.
But it seems to me as if everybody would speak English at
last : foreigners acquire a little of it so easily."

Gen. Mackenzie was much interested in comparing
different forms of governments and their results, and
Kathie often spent a day with Aunt Ruth while they were
occupied with what Bruce called the weightier matters of
pleasure. · On such days she declared she studied German
and geography.

They went up the Baltic Sea and coast of Sweden as

far as Stockholm. Winter was coming on, and though St. Petersburg was their next point, it was a question whether the ladies could take any pleasure in so rigorous a climate; but Bruce thought half the delight would be wanting if they were not there to share it, and Kathie declared it would be a great pity to miss one of the grandest capitals in the world. They would be sure to take good care of Aunt Ruth, and she was not afraid of the cold.

They felt well repaid for their daring. The wonderful city filled them with amazement. Long quays of massive granite hide the marshy shores of the Neva, that must have looked formidable to even such a conqueror as Peter the Great. But he saw with the eye of genius that there was no other place so well disposed for both safety and menace, and he rescued the land from the grip of the sea, and laid a foundation of such durability that palaces, churches, bridges, and obelisks stand securely and bid defiance to the forces of nature.

Bruce and Kathie had many excursions to themselves, as the General was quite occupied at first. They never tired of the wonderful winter palace, the churches and obelisks, and the Hermitage, with its accumulation of pictures, sculptures, and gems; and though its royal founder, Catherine, had long since passed away, there were many reminders of her lavish expenditure.

"I think the term 'barbaric splendor' is just right when applied to Russia," said Kathie: "it is so magnificent, and it is full of Eastern luxury as well. But now we seem right in the heart of foreign travel, do we not?"

"You will seem almost in the heart of the East when you get to Moscow," the General returned. "St. Petersburg is quite Europeanized in comparison."

The Mackenzies stumbled over some old military men who had been through our own war. Bruce received several very complimentary invitations, and went with his

father to different places where it would have been incon-
venient for ladies.   But Kathie had a great deal of pleasure ; operas and theatres were extremely brilliant, and
the Kibitka sledging very exhilarating when it was not
too cold.   Aunt Ruth enjoyed the opera, and several dinners that she attended with the General, but most of the
out-door excursions were impossible for her.   She was
very happy, however, in the enjoyment of the young people, and proud of her fine-looking step-son.   Kathie and
he settled to very friendly ways, and occasionally some
one, in speaking of her, said, "Your sister."   ·

"I am not sure but I shall have to adopt you," the General remarked with a smile.

"I don't always explain," said Aunt Ruth : "it makes
such a little difference."

CHAPTER II.

IT was as the General said, Moscow seemed indeed a collection of cities, the past, the present, the old world and the new, and was like nothing, Kathie declared, so much as the "Arabian Nights." The Tartar impress seemed everywhere with its glittering crescent, the minaret, and the swelling dome. The muezzin still called to prayer from the roof of his mosque; but by its side were pagodas of China, Byzantine churches, and the triumphant Greek cross, Grecian temples, French palaces, Turkish bazaars and German beer-houses, every variety of costume and feature, bizarre and picturesque, every nation under the sun it seemed.

They soon became comfortably domesticated, and with the experience of the last two months quite prepared to feel at home. Gen. Mackenzie regretted they could not have had this part of their tour in the summer, when gardens and fields were in their glory, instead of continuous snow and ice.

But they had some gay times skating and sledging; and the Kremlin was a source of unfailing interest and wonder. They visited the point from which Napoleon's army advanced on the silent glittering city, shrouded in snow, with its mosques and minarets sparkling as now, but with the more subtle fire at its heart that was to subdue and dishearten its conqueror. Then they ascended the tower of Ivan Veliki, the great belfry, and had all of Moscow at their feet, with the Moskva winding in and out, and almost doubling upon itself.

2

The cathedral of St. Basil, with its many towers, each one enclosing a chapel, the cathedral of St. Michael, and the church of the Assumption held them spell-bound with dazzling altars and shrine pictures set with jewels. Then the grand halls, with their inlaid floors and the soft gleam of many tinted marbles, the jewelled thrones of the great Russian monarchs with their crowns, the treasures and emblems of conquered and subjugated kingdoms, the treasures that make the Kremlin, beside its historic associations, the Mecca of the Russians, for within it is gathered all that is most venerated in religion and the most cherished in historical tradition.

They remained so long in Moscow that they made some friends and began to feel very much at home, though it seemed to Kathie that they might go on making discoveries for a lifetime. But it was decided at length to go on to Warsaw, and from thence presently to Berlin.

After some months of pleasant wandering through German cities and towns, of studying picture galleries and churches, highways and byways, mountains and lakes, our travellers came on to Rome, where they were to meet the Merediths presently. Bruce's recall found them here, and as he had exceeded his year, it was deemed advisable for him to return. It would hardly have been possible for any young man of Bruce's tastes and habits of thought not to have admired his girl companion, and for the reason of the familiar association, Gen. Mackenzie distrusted a little the true temper of the regard : both were so young, and the intimacy had been that of brother and sister ; besides, Kathie certainly was unconscious of any warmer regard.

That evening he discussed the matter with his wife.

"I think you were very — shall I say heroic? Spartan-like is better, I believe." And she glanced up with a wistful smile. "Was it not hard to refuse your own?"

"You don't mean, Ruth, that—and it seemed like taking an advantage of your sister," he ended abruptly

"Dora would not have been displeased, of that I am quite sure. Still, Kathie *is* such a mere child she would hardly know what love meant."

"And it is not right to bind her by an engagement until she *does* know what it means. I think she would assent, and make herself at home in the new strange feeling, and come in time to love with her whole heart; but would it not be anticipating the bloom and newness of love, trying for it? And it would of necessity change the current of her thoughts, her enjoyments —"

"How odd that you should think most of Kathie's welfare, while I lean to that of Bruce! Yet I do not know as it would be best for either of them, and I am not much of a believer in children's engagements, only I have a woman's fondness for lovers." And she smiled softly again.

"Yet I do dread to lay a burden on her. To my mind she is still a sweet, innocent child, and as such she ought to go on for another year or two. Let them be friends, let them correspond as he proposes; and if Kathie's time of blossoming comes, let her feel the exquisiteness of a preference. Let her choose, as well as be chosen."

Bruce had a new interest in his mother's eyes the next day, although she refrained from any overt touch of sympathy that might betray her real knowledge. They were all to go to see him off, as he was to embark on a government vessel bound for home.

There was a quiet manliness in Bruce that surprised his father, who seemed to realize for the first time that his son had come to man's estate in every respect.

A sad and tearful good-by, — that was as a, matter of course; but there was something to occupy them immediately, a letter from the Merediths, asking them to find rooms, that they might be as neighborly as possible. So Aunt Ruth and Kathie started at once, since there were no vacant apartments at their hotel. It was quite a search,

and presently they were rewarded by a chance of two rooms
in an old palace on the next square, which an Austrian
countess had just left.   They all went to meet and welcome
them, and Kathie's parting thoughts of Bruce were very
much confused, since as yet she could not realize the void
made by his going.   But oh, how delightful the familiar
faces looked ; and Mr. Meredith's hearty, joyous voice
brought back old times to the child's heart.   There was the
pleasant tumult of greeting, of being packed in the *voiture*
and taken at once to the Mackenzies, while the luggage
was hunted up and despatched to the new domicile.

She was so glad to see them ! Jessie had changed
greatly.   There was a certain something her sister-in-law
would have called style and *aplomb*.   No one would have
ventured to hint that Mrs. Meredith was countrified now.
The girlish prettiness had merged into a matronly piquancy
and dignity that would be able to hold its own under the
most critical eyes.   Her dresses were exquisite, and her
gloves and bonnets truly French.

As for Robin, he was simply superb.   He had grown
so since Kathie had parted with him ; he could walk and
talk, and his French was the cunningest thing in the
world.

Their rooms were satisfactory, and they were delighted
to be with their friends.   Mr. Meredith remarked the
change in Kathie, — she was so much taller, even if she had
not outgrown the sweet child's face and unworldly air,
and the trick of being warmly enthusiastic.

" It was too bad that Bruce had to return," declared
Jessie.   " I am disappointed, for I wanted to see him so
much."

" We were all so sorry," said Kathie with unaffected
regret.   " And we have had such delightful times."

" I never knew one could become such an enthusiastic
Russian," returned Mr. Meredith, while Jessie was studying the fair girl-face.   " I did n't know but you would end

by taking some fierce count with an unpronounceable
name, and then I should have disowned you."

Kathie smiled a little at that. "Oh," she said archly,
"you know I was not out, had not been presented, and
all that sort of thing! And everybody thought I was
Bruce's sister; one lady even congratulated me once upon
my resemblance to him."

"I have heard of people living together until they grew
to look alike," said Jessie; and then she made a sudden
pause.

"I did have a fancy," she said afterward to her husband, "that something deeper than cousinly regard would
grow up between these young people when they came to
be daily companions. What French woman would trust
her daughter so unreservedly with a young man not her
brother! Yet I dare say the French maiden would give her
chances for matrimony many a thought, while the idea has
not yet entered Kathie's head."

"There is plenty of time for love and all that. For the
credit of my young countrywomen I am glad there is one
American girl innocent of matrimonial intentions, though,
truth to tell, I think it a libel. See how many American
girls we met at Paris intent upon their studies, and not at
all anxious about society. But how odd it would be for
some one to have a better right to Kathie than her friends
and relatives."

"Of course the relatives come last," laughed Jessie,
lapsing into thought and silence. Yes, it *would* seem unnatural for any stranger to win Kathie. And then came
a little wonder, as she remembered one to whom Kathie
had always been first and best. If this fascinating young
cadet had made no other than a cousinly impression —

"What conspiracy are you planning now?" her husband
asked suddenly.

"Oh!" Jessie turned scarlet. Not even to him — hardly
to her own soul — would she admit her thought.

" I warn you to beware of plots and plans in behalf of titled foreigners. Americans for the American, say I. As soon as I scent danger in the air, I shall whisk Kathie off home."

" To all of which I consent heartily," was her reply.

There was so much to talk over on both sides. Kathie had seen the most wonderful places ; but Jessie, too, had taken out-of-the-way journeys to the South of France, and embarked finally at Marseilles. Switzerland they would have together.

" What will you give me for my news ? " asked Mr. Meredith when he had received his first instalment of letters. " A surprise ! "

" Some one is coming out," guessed Kathie, glancing up from her romp with the baby.

" No. A marriage, without any foreign tour, of a once very fashionable girl ! "

" Oh, it is n't Ada ? "

" Yes, it *is* Ada. Her father is delighted with his new son."

" But who is it ? " asked Kathie. " I can't recall any one. But we have been away so long."

" Oh, I am quite certain you saw him at Dr. Markham's."

Kathie studied a moment.

" Don't tease her," begged Jessie. " Dr. Garnier."

" Oh, then Dr. Markham is pleased ! "

" Yes. He has shown it in a very substantial manner. He insisted upon furnishing their library. He had taken the young man under his wing before we left New York ; and I think it an excellent choice."

" Did Ada's mother like it ? " ventured Kathie, a little as if she was treading on dangerous ground.

" I think Ada could have pleased her better," said Jessie· " She was going into society again, and quite admired, I gather from other sources. I suppose her mother felt that she might do better, though Dr. Garnier cannot be considered quite as a 'poor but worthy' young man : he has bought a house and has a good practice."

"And the right side of Dr. Markham is the high road to fortune. I was afraid he would not suit Ada, being of the rather solid order. What an insufferable piece of vanity and self-complacency Ada would have become without any check! I think we ought to give you the most credit, Kathie. I really did weary in well-doing, and was discouraged with her. Kathie, you have been the salvation of us all."

"But I had mamma and everybody to encourage me. And I do believe Dick Grayson and Mr. Langdon helped that summer. It was learning how happiness could be found in little things."

"That is it, you wise honey-bee," laughed Mr. Meredith.

"But tell me all about her. This is the first real news I have heard in a long time."

"Well, they have been engaged about six months. I think by what George writes that her mother was a little disappointed, but *he* said he was glad to give his daughter to such an earnest, honorable man, though it was a great loss to him to give her to any one : she had been such a comfort to him. I do believe she has, and I am thankful that he has had this through his days of adversity. What selfish, useless lives a great many rich people lead! It does n't seem so to you as you are going through it, but when you look back at it — Help me out, Kathie." And Mr. Meredith laughed. "What was my text? Oh, Dr. Garnier bought a house, and they were to go to housekeeping. Ada's idea used to be the grand tour. But I think now, like the fairy stories, they will live happily forever afterward."

"Don't you hear from her, Kathie?" asked Jessie in surprise.

"She wrote to me early in December, and I am ashamed to say that I did not answer the letter for nearly three months. Now that I think of it, she has quoted a friend a good deal whose opinions seemed to have great weight with her. I supposed it was Mrs. Arde."

"There is a lovely woman," remarked Jessie, "who is doing a good work in the world, — a regular home missionary to the so-called better classes. She is in comfortable circumstances, accomplished and refined, and might be a star in society. Such women, pure and lofty themselves, *can* raise the standard of womanhood greatly among young girls. And I am beginning to think we Americans let our elders drop out of our lives too soon. The girls educated in convents come to have a respect for middle-aged women, are trained indeed to defer to them and acknowledge the stability of their position, while the mothers and elder sisters get rudely pushed aside at home, snubbed, and reminded in every way that their day is over. You see I am picking up some very useful foreign notions. When I go home I shall establish a circle or clique, and become a famous woman."

Soon afterwards Kathie's letter came from Ada, dated in her new home.

"I hope you will not feel hurt by my silence," she began, "or want of confidence, for it really was not that: I never seemed to have time to write all the explanations I wanted to make, and I wonder if you are sufficiently grown up now to understand. My impression of you, Kathie, is that you are still an innocent little girl, with a great deal of unworldly lore; and yet how many love affairs you have had right under your own eyes! Why you must have seen and guessed about Uncle Edward; and yet how reticent you were! I wonder if you forgave my foolish far-sightedness. O Kathie, I must have been extremely silly in those days! My only comfort in remembering it is that we did not often drop down upon sensible people. I can hardly believe now that I was the listless, useless girl you found one winter day, ruined in health, energy, and hopeless of the future. You would scarcely imagine that I could become interested in the every-day work of the world and like it.

"When you went away, papa would have strained every nerve to send me, and I wanted to go ; but I was ashamed to go with you, after your good lessons. I shall always be glad that I struggled against my selfish desires and stayed at home, for through it papa and I came to understand each other better, and love truly and fervently. He is very noble and self-sacrificing, Kathie, and I am not sure but I have as much of a hero in him as you have in your Uncle Robert. I began to care for his comfort, and found so many ways, and so much enjoyment in them. We shall always be much more to each other for this time.

"Mrs. Arde was such a lovely friend to me, and I *did* go into considerable society. I was proud of attracting such a man as Dr. Garnier, though I was not in love with him at first. He used to drop in now and then, and send me flowers ; but he had little time for party going and dancing, and he was not the kind of man to hurry one into a decision. There were several others ; one young man mamma favored a great deal, who was in very good circumstances, and his family were all extremely fashionable people. We went to Long Branch a month in the summer, and he was there. He *was* attractive, and I did like him, only I knew with him I should go right back into the old life ; and it did not look so inviting to me as it once had.

"After we came home he attended me to a party ; it was very gay, with an elegant supper and an abundance of wine and champagne. He drank until he became absolutely silly ; not more so than several others, but I was disenchanted with him, with the whole set. I found I was beginning to measure all men by Dr. Garnier, who is a *true* gentleman, gentle in his strength. And so the rest was easily settled. Our engagement was hardly six months.

We resolved to go to housekeeping in a pretty way, and Dr. Markham has been just delightful. I think he has adopted Philip in his brusque, generous way, and takes great pride in his success. And if you should be caught by some high-sounding title while abroad, I think I might displace you in his esteem.

"So we have begun life with love and home and an earnest purpose, but prepared for many failures. Papa is to be our frequent guest. Both boys have gone away to school, and Florence is in a kindergarten; so mamma will have it quite easy. Some day I hope to see you, and then we will talk over the things that cannot be written."

Kathie read most of this to Aunt Ruth, who warmly commended Ada.

This was followed by a letter from Mrs. Langdon. They hoped to be in Rome before long. They had gone first to Spain and visited the old cities of romance and history, finding wonderful things on every hand. They would spend some months in Roman wanderings, then take Switzerland and the Alps and a little of Germany, spending all of the ensuing winter in Paris.

"I wonder if you would like to have a winter in Paris?" Aunt Ruth asked.

"Mr. Meredith and Jessie expect to return in the autumn," Kathie answered, with a kind of wistful touch in her voice. "I should want to see Paris—"

"But you have a longing for home, is that it? Still, as we had to take the first part of our tour with reference to business, we can certainly devote some time to pleasure. I want to see Paris also, as it is not likely I shall ever come abroad again; but we will consider whether we want a whole winter of it."

The General and Mrs. Mackenzie had gathered quite a little circle of friends, foreign and American, so Jessie, who had grown much fonder of society, was at once taken in their midst. They saved up some things for Emma and

Mr. Langdon to enjoy with them, but there were lovely drives, churches and palaces to visit, until, as Kathie said, one almost had a surfeit of sight-seeing.

"And the comfort of it is to just stop and live somewhere," said Kathie. "We lived a little while in Scotland, and a longer time at Moscow, and now we are living here; all the rest is journeys between."

"You will be a noted traveller when you reach Brookside again," commented Mr. Meredith.

"And I shall be all the rest of my life getting things straight."

It was so delightful to see Mr. and Mrs. Langdon. They took them quite by surprise one morning, hardly an hour after their arrival in Rome.

"Oh!" cried Kathie, with her arms about Emma's neck. "You seem like a little bit of home. How good it is!"

"Surely you are not homesick?" inquired Mr. Langdon.

"It would be dreadful to confess it, would it not? We are not going to abridge our stay, but I do think Brookside will look just lovely to me when I see it again."

"It has changed so much you will hardly know it," Emma returned. "A new railroad touches it at the north side, and an immense factory is being built, to say nothing of several smaller ones. We shall soon be South-End people, the select aristocracy of the town. O Kathie! do you remember the old patrician days at school? I met Belle Haddon last summer in New York. She is divorced. Her father is very successful in some 'ring' again, and they are floating on the topmost round. It was a great pleasure for me to tell her you were in Europe with your aunt and uncle, Gen. and Mrs. Mackenzie. Several of the girls and boys are married, and hosts of new people have come in. Has your uncle told you about the improvements? They have straightened and widened all the drive along the lake, and cut through one place that makes it lead up to the heart of the town, and it is called Cedarwood

Avenue. The people who thought themselves almost out of sight are right in the midst of style and what will be elegance after it is finished. And there is going to be a town hall and a library. Mr. Grayson and your uncle and Mr. Adams have all taken hold of it. You will hardly know the place when you get home."

Uncle Robert had kept Kathie pretty well posted, but it was very enjoyable to hear it first-hand, as it were. Such entertaining little bits were always cropping out, that Kathie declared it was almost as good as seeing with her own eyes. And it was so nice to hear about the boys. Fred Lauriston had graduated, and gone to South America for three years; Dick Grayson had decided upon law; he and Rob and Charlie Darrell would graduate the following summer. Emma had seen them all during vacation. Sue Coleman was married and gone to Chicago, and one of the Gardiner girls was engaged to Henry Cox.

In fact, for the first few days everybody gave up the girls to one another for " pure gossip," Mr. Langdon said. He was very proud of his pretty wife, and took great interest in her talent, as one could plainly see. She was still girlishly slender, and seemed not to have grown a day older, while Mr. Langdon had that indescribable married air of supreme content. The gentlemen of the party fraternized admirably. Emma had been sketching and painting a little in Spain, and they had some beautiful views.

" They remind me of Moscow," said Kathie; " yet the two countries are so far apart and so different."

" Yet the same race and the same religion has left its impress on both," remarked Mr. Langdon. " Moslemism bid fair to overrun the world at one time, yet the Cross has triumphed over the Crescent, and will go on a great factor in civilization. How new it makes one feel, Meredith, to wander about places a thousand or two years old ! "

" And to think of all the mighty races that have lived and died, and left enduring traces of themselves. If we were bachelors, Langdon, I should like nothing better than a run through Egypt."

" Well, you can take us," said Jessie. " I used to think Egypt and Persia were the two countries above all others that I should desire to see."

" Yes, we might; but Kathie, you know, is homesick."

" I should rather take the rest some other time," she responded gravely.

CHAPTER III

If Kathie had been left quite alone with her aunt and uncle, to miss the absent one at every turn, to dream and brood, and hold intimate thought, communion, — conversations one really makes of it in solitude, — the result might have been quite different; but it was all active life instead. Gen. Mackenzie had been in Rome twenty years before, Mr. Meredith had run through it once with a party of young men; but to Mr. Langdon everything was new. There was a great deal for the gentlemen beside the picture galleries. Old roads, bridges, and ruins, old battle sites, and dead and gone armies with their heroic leaders. The start of a wonderful civilization that was destined to rule the world in various guises, the going-out into all the world of Christianity, that had left behind old and enduring monuments, and changed the face of the earth wherever it spread.

Kathie and Emma listened with deepest interest to these talks of matters they had just touched upon, it seemed, at school; or they lingered in churches, studying rare sculptures and wonderful paintings, that inspired them with a sacred awe. How much of human and idealized lives they represented!

"One could pass a lifetime here and never weary of the great work," Emma said, "if body and brain could stand the constant tax. I am afraid I shall never want to do anything but look."

"Rome makes you understand antiquity: it is such a gradual going back," rejoined Mr. Meredith. "Every

year is represented   There are no breaks.   Far beyond
the Christian era, every century keeps its own intact,
every ruin has its story to tell, with its date and name."

" And what stories they are ! " said Jessie.   " We were
through the garden of the Pincio yesterday and out to
the spot where Lucullus lived and gave his great feasts ;
and later on Messalina gave hers there, until she aroused
the tardy resentment of Claudius.   Was he noble, or simply weak, I wonder?   But her enemy triumphed over her
entreaties and her husband's forbearance, and slew her
when, less courageous than Cleopatra, she dared not com-
pass her own death.   What men and women there were in
those days !   I *do* think the world has improved."

" Yet I wonder if our growth in morals is to mark a
degeneracy in other matters?   We have no such sculptures to-day, no such bridges or palaces.   What work of
ours will last thousands of years?" mused Mr. Langdon.

Kathie proved quite a guide to her friends.   When they
were tired of journeyings they spent mornings in galleries,
Emma studying and sketching a little, and occasionally
meeting with an entertaining episode with some of her
own countrywomen.   Jessie was much interested in the
peasant women and children, the promenades and drives,
and the odd phases of Roman life.   Aunt Ruth introduced
them to inner glimpses of Roman society, and the days
were so crowded with enjoyment that they passed too
rapidly.   It was as Kathie said, they had to do the seeing
now, and the thinking afterward ; to store their minds with
the grand, the exquisite, the wonderful, to serve for after
feasts.

As soon as was practicable in the season they started for
Switzerland.   Of their journey over the Alps, of the lakes
and mountains, of passes wonderful and dangerous, of
Chillon, with its fortress of the cruel Middle Ages, of the
vale of Chamounix and Mont Blanc, and the hundred historical and romantic points, the world knows them almost by

heart, yet the great thing is to see them with our own eyes,
to linger breathless and awe-stricken, and feel that the half
had never been told, — the half that could not be told, —
but must be seen and felt, drop deep into one's soul.

When Kathie could stop she vainly tried to transcribe it
for Bruce, as she had promised. "If you had been here,"
"If you could have stayed," to see this or that, mixed with
Emma and Jessie and the wonderful baby, but not much of
her very self. There was no time in "marching on" to
think of one's self. That she missed him everywhere and
longed for him was but natural: any friend would have
done it.

They took a small corner of Germany in their way, and
then pushed on to Paris. Jessie was so at home here that
she proved an excellent chaperone. They soon domesticated themselves; they were all so accustomed to foreign life
that it did not take long.

"The shopping will have to come now," declared Jessie,
"and we must put it in by bits along with the sight-seeing;
but I made up my mind long ago not to overload myself,
and when I wanted again, to pay duty, patriotically."

Their first tour was to Versailles. The city was bright
and open and full of sunshine, and so clean in contrast with
many other places. There were the palace and garden of
the Tuileries; the slender, beautiful obelisk of Luxor, standing in what had once been the Place of Revolution in those
mighty times of terror; the broad avenue leading straight
out to the Arch of Triumph, the riverside, the villages with
their narrow streets and pretty gardens, the white-capped
women and peasant men in blouses, the contrast of the
beautiful carriages and their gayly dressed occupants, and
so on down the Boulevard de la Reine to the gateway of
the Trianons.

The place was full of remembered presences of dead and
gone royalty. Here kings and queens had played at grandeur
and at simplicity. Here had mingled joy, ambition; dreams

attained ; here, too. heart-breaks and sorrow. They lost
themselves in still lovely glades of greenery, they wandered
past fountains, they came to Marie Antoinette's Swiss cottage, with its overhanging gallery and latticed windows, the
dairy where she played prettily at butter-making ; then on
again through avenue and mall, through the court-yard to
the gallery of sculpture, with its glories, and then to the gallery of battles, that seemed to tell of themselves the
world's history.

Here, everywhere, it seemed, Napoleon the First had left
his impress. Kathie and Bruce had studied up his campaigns while in Moscow, — Bruce with a soldier's ardor for
a famous general. Now she paused before the great picture of the Coronation. All these shadowy kings and
queens still live in the great heart of the world that makes
pilgrimages from afar to see them. They went back to
their carriages too tired for even a word.

" We can talk it over in New York," said Emma ; " it
will seem more of a luxury then."

There was many a delightful but fatiguing day. Sometimes Aunt Ruth could not go, and Kathie was glad they
had left Paris to the last. " For it seems now," said she,
" as if we could go home and go to bed, and get rested
after it all."

" But I shall miss you so much," said Emma, regret-
fully.

" I have never had but one temptation to be jealous,"
confessed Mr. Langdon ; " and that is about Miss Kathie.
I think Emma spent a full month gathering up messages
before she left America, and it will take me a month to
comfort her after you have gone."

" I think *I* ought to be jealous as well. He has be-
wailed you every time he went to Cedarwood, Kathie ;
and he liked me first because he thought I resembled you.
Perhaps if you had been older, he would not have liked me
at all."

3

"That was a lovely summer, with so many young people at Cedarwood"; and Mr. Langdon sighed. "I really believe I would like to live it over again. And your invalid friend has married, Miss Kathie, as well as several others. I shall always count your uncle among my choicest *confrères*, and some time, when Mrs. Langdon has become a famous artist, we shall drift back and set up a studio or a country home or something charming, in memory of the old-time delights, and your uncle and I will come to be quoted among the solid men of the place."

"Langdon, you are sentimental"; and Mr. Meredith laughed; "though I think we all owe a good deal of what is best and happiest in our lives to its influence," he appended, in a graver tone.

Gen. Mackenzie glanced across at his wife, and she answered with a touch of rising color: so many ever-widening circles had evolved from that one centre.

Yet it began to be really sad when a time was appointed for the Mackenzie party to leave Paris: there were so many little last things and last visits.

"Though no doubt we shall be here again and again," declared Mr. Meredith: "people so often run over for a three months' tour; and you can do one or two places very thoroughly."

"And it is nearly seven months since we dropped down upon you at Rome. I can hardly believe it. You will see us back in New York in a year or two."

The last shopping and packing, and then a journey to picturesque Normandy together, — a kind of afterthought, to soften the parting, — then a brief sail across the Channel and they touched English soil and seemed almost home; but they must spend another week or two in London, looking about, and then the longer trip over the ocean, pleasant, with not a great deal of sickness.

Home! Yes, it was delightful.

"And you can only have one little place to really live

in," said Kathie. "I believe I would as soon have it Brookside as any other. Think of our pretty lake and Guilford River; and we have some hills — "

"But they will look very small after Mont Blanc."

"I should n't want to live in the shadow of Mont Blanc all my life: it would overpower me."

They had not sent word of the exact time of their return, but after reaching New York, Gen. Mackenzie telegraphed to Cedarwood. They were driven at once to a hotel, and were glad of a rest. New York did look strange after the Old World cities; still, to the elders it had a pleasant suggestion of home.

Kathie and Aunt Ruth went to bed to get rested up after the sea dizziness and confusion of the last day. Jessie was engrossed with looking after nurse and baby, who had thriven physically on his tour, if the remembrance never could be much to him. The gentlemen were very busy with the luggage, and considering what was to be done next. It was late in the afternoon, and no friends would be likely to come to greet them. Mrs. George Meredith was away on her summering, but the brothers met in a most cordial manner. George had aged a good deal.

"Old fellow, it will be your turn for a holiday next," Edward said with heartfelt regard. "I feel almost conscience smitten."

"But you never need, Ned. If you had not come to the rescue so nobly, I must have gone under. I have had a hard time, but we are on our feet again, and shall be fairly prosperous. The boys are bright and hardy, and Ada is very happy. I am down there half my time when I am alone. Garnier is a really splendid fellow. As men go, Ada has secured a prize."

His fatherly pride showed in his face.

"I am so glad," was the warm response.

"You can never know, Ned, what a comfort she was to me through some of the hardest. If my boys turn out as well — "

If Kathie could hear that commendation ; for surely it
was her hand that planted the good seed.   And a little
further back, had there not been something that set him
to thinking,— an influence a little different from any that
had entered his careless manhood up to that period?   If
he had married some worldly young girl, and repeated his
brother's life : but no wealth or elegance could ever make
Jessie frivolous.

Kathie did not even wake up for any supper, but slept
straight on in the restful slumber of youth and fatigue.
Aunt Ruth came and looked at her with a tender smile,
and then went down to supper.   Gen. Mackenzie had
brought in letters, among them one from Bruce.   He had
gone to his new post of duty and found it a great change,
of course.   He was not much in love with the surroundings ; indeed, he was fast coming to think that he preferred
the amenities of civilian life ; but he meant to stand steadily by his colors.

"Tell me about Kathie," he begged: "she says so
little of herself."

She came down the next morning bright as a rose,
rested and refreshed.

"It will be quite a reception day," began Mr. Meredith ;
"the world has all gone out of town, but what is left of
it will drop in and congratulate you on your safe arrival.
I suppose the next move will be Brookside, for I know all
the Darrell clan are wild to see their grandson."

Jessie colored with motherly pride as she bent to kiss
her little boy.

"I think the delegation will be up to meet us," remarked
the General.   "I am most anxious to get out of the heat
and dust ; but we cannot leave to-day."

"Do you really think Uncle Robert will come, and —"
Kathie paused with softened eyes.

"Mamma will be awaiting us at home," returned Aunt
Ruth, quietly.

"Is n't it just a little bit odd," began Mr. Meredith, "but the first time I saw you, Mrs. Mackenzie, and Kathie here, I was standing on the hotel steps? Kathie was a little, bright-eyed, country girl, looking like a field daisy or a wild rose ; and you brought a wonderful charm with you. I don't believe any one ever understood before how pretty they were, for the whole world has gone to wild roses and daisies since."

" Did I look so *very* countrified ? " inquired Kathie. " I felt as if I had gone into not exactly fairyland, but wonderland. And there were so many people, such a noise and confusion. and you just took me and Aunt Ruth's shepherd's-plaid shawl up-stairs ; and it seemed a palace to me, it really did," laughingly. " There was a great dinner afterwards, and a drawing-room filled with lovely women and brave men, and I felt all the time as if I was enchanted. Did I do anything very queer and awkward ? "

" Not a bit," declared Mr. Meredith. -

" It was one of my three wishes, you know. When Uncle Robert came home he gave me three ; and I always shall believe in fairy stories to the very end, for I had my three wishes, and they all came out splendidly."

" Which one did I come in ? "

Kathie colored.

" The very first," replied Aunt Ruth. " She wished for me, and we came to New York to see Dr. Markham about my lameness."

" And I seemed to have a pretty good share in that wish too," responded Gen. Mackenzie, with a smile at his wife and niece.

" Like the strawberry girl — ' me too, Katy ! ' " exclaimed Mr. Meredith. " We two," glancing at Jessie. " You never dreamed, Kathie, how many incidents and romances were to grow out of it."

" But if you had not been there ? " supposed Kathie, archly.

"I should have lost incalculably. Robin, nothing could
have made it up to us." And he took his little boy on his
knee.

A waiter entered with a card, — "Mrs. Garnier."

"Kathie, go first and try your enchantment," said
Jessie. "How shamefully late we are that Ada should
call before we are through breakfast!"

Kathie lingered, but Jessie and Mr. Meredith promised
to come directly.

Kathie smiled a little as she crossed the threshold of
the reception-room, thinking of the awe of that childish
time. Ada rose; the two years had changed her very little, except in the expression of content and satisfaction.
For a moment she glanced uncertainly, then her arms were
around Kathie; and if the embrace was more demonstrative
than the languor of the day approved, no one could have
questioned its genuineness.

"O Kathie! what a pleasure. I did not expect to
see you first of all. Papa told me last evening you were
all in, and that I must call upon Aunt Jessie, — as if
I had forgotten my manners in my new life. Oh, how
you have grown and changed, and," holding her off a
little, "how indescribably foreign you look!"

"Do I? I have a queer feeling as if I did not quite
know what I was, but I shall, when I get to Brookside
and mamma."

"Kathie Alston, I wonder if you will be *quite* content
there now? I do not want to stir up any longing or
desire, but Brookside *is* small, and there is no great variety of people or employment, or enjoyment for that matter. I have speculated a good deal upon it, and though I
am not as silly as I was a few years ago, it does seem like
burying your graces and accomplishments; for you *are*
stylish and pretty. and you could be quite a star in society,
with all your newness and freshness."

"I'm not going to bury myself, returned Kathie.
"There is too much real work to do. O Ada — "

" There, it was only one of the temptations. I could n't
help uttering it. I don't believe anything will ever spoil
you. What is it — this content in stillness and sweetness? this holding everything with reverent hands, as if it
was not really yours, and yet enjoying all things to the
uttermost? You see I am no angel yet, but full of questions and wonders."

" But happy?" Kathie asked, with a kind of jealous
longing for her friend.

" Happy? oh yes !" And Ada gave a smile of rare content. " When you come to know Philip, — and Uncle Markham and I have talked him nearly deaf, dumb, and blind
about you, — I think you will understand the sort of pro-
gression in me, for it is that which puzzles you. One can
desire to go on without being altogether dissatisfied with
the things that are, but you can't go on without questioning.
And I must go on to keep up with my husband. I can't
allow myself to fall behind, and so if I question you a
little and watch you — What a queer talk right in the beginning ! And I am so glad to see you ! Of course the
whole journey was delightful. Did you bring home most
in lovely laces and new gowns, or did you turn artist or
poet or novelist? Everybody writes a book now."

" I am the one girl without a genius," confessed Kathie
frankly. " I have learned a good deal, and seen until my
brain could not hold another sight; I am afraid it is yet a
chaotic mass, that I shall have to straighten out all the rest
of my life to get all the objects in order."

" But Mrs. Langdon is going to be a real artist, is she
not? I think she paints beautifully already. They spent
a winter in the city, and Mrs. Arde met them, — you know
she is always taking up special people and bringing them
out to delight the ordinary ones. And so I found in her
the Emma Lauriston of that summer at Cedarwood. One
of the girls said then that *you* always found so many nice
people, and I begin to think you and Mrs. Arde alike in
that respect. And she is crazy to see you."

The Merediths entered at this moment, and Ada's attention was directed to the new channels. Aunt Jessie was elegant, certainly, and the baby a marvel of prettiness, talking French as if it were his mother tongue. Kathie watched her friend with a curious feeling, as if again there was a great distance of years between them. It had never been, it would never be, a love friendship, as that between herself and Jessie or Emma Lauriston; yet there was a strength and determination in Ada's face, as if she had set out to reach some of the higher places. "And I shall know her better presently," Kathie thought. "It is like getting acquainted with a new person." Then she wondered, in a little dismay, if every one would seem so different. Perhaps the two years had changed her as well.

Dr. and Mrs. Markham were announced next, and it became quite a gay family party. Aunt Ruth came in for a large share of compliments, and Kathie began to realize suddenly that a great change had been going on with her most unconsciously. She had passed from young girlhood to womanhood. The eager child-life was a thing of the past, and at this moment of missing it Kathie stretched out her hands unconsciously, as if to implore it back again. Life suddenly looked large and sacred.

The Doctor came over and teased her. She was so tall and stylish, and had seen so much that no doubt her own country would appear poor and plain by contrast. Could she condescend to an old chap like him, who couldn't put a French sentence properly together to save his neck, and would she come down some time when the others could spare her and make *them* a visit, and talk over the wonderful things she had seen?

Some old friends of Jessie's entered presently, and the others went away with promises; then a telegram announcing the arrival of home friends at one, and Kathie's heart gave a quick, glad leap.

"Aunt Ruth," she began, when they were in their room, "have I changed very much?"

Aunt Ruth looked puzzled, then smiled.

"You have grown, of course, and — yes, I suppose you have. The rest notice it more easily than we do. What is there to look so grave about, my darling?"

"I wonder if I shall ever be quite the same to mamma and Uncle Robert?"

"O Kathie, to them, to us, there can be very little difference! The old love is the same. and takes no account of years or change."

She asked no further questions, but glanced out of the window, thinking. She must do something with her life, with the years to come : people always did when they were quite grown up. If she *could* be something, if there could be some aim, some purpose, and not all a simple going on of pleasure.

She had quite lost herself in a tangled train of thought when a voice outside somewhere said, "And Kathie?" The young girl sprang up and took a few steps forward, and was clasped in two strong arms.

"O Uncle Robert! Uncle Robert!" And hiding her face on his shoulder, she gave a little sob. She was home to her own again. There could not be any sense of change with him.

But he was not to have her all to himself. Right behind were Rob and Charlie Darrell. Robert, tall and erect, with a proud, masterful face, clear, frank eyes, and a line of dark mustache shading his upper lip. He really seemed stranger to Kathie than Charlie Darrell, who was not less manly looking if not so tall. There was a fine and spiritual expression in his face ; it looked like some of the pictures she had seen, — the indescribable indication of a life a little higher than the ordinary round.

Father and Mother Darrell had joined the party. There were some other grandchildren at a distance, but Jessie's

baby had somehow been a little different from the rest, —
perhaps because Jessie's marriage had been a little out
of the common order.

Rob said it again, " O Kathie ! how you have changed ! "

" And yet it is, it always will be, the same little Kathie,"
said Charlie Darrell ; and she felt strangely comforted.

CHAPTER IV.

"I HAVE brought her back to you, your very own, as I promised."

It was what Gen. Mackenzie said to Mrs. Alston on the great porch at Cedarwood, when the mother held her child again in her arms. To him it represented the sacrifice he had made in not taking her for his own, the putting off, the waiting that might have a little danger in it; for right behind was another to whom Kathie would be fair and sweet with the charm of womanhood.

Afterward they all talked at once. Kathie ran round to every place, and found there had been a great change. The child nooks did not fit her so well: she had outgrown them and come to the larger abiding-places. There were no children, for Fred was shooting up into a tall, slender boy, and Rob was a man. The days of frolics, laughing, and glee were over. How strange it was!

And yet the dear old house had not changed. She was so glad the rooms were large, the hall and stairway wide, and the porch room abundant. It would do for anything they might ever grow into. There had been a little refurnishing, but Uncle Robert told her they had left plenty of room for the treasures she had brought.

"Dear home! I am so glad to be here again. I think I was homesick two or three times, mamma. After Bruce returned, if Jessie had not come I should have wanted to end our lovely journeyings then and there. We used to wish for you so, Rob, when we were in Moscow, talking over Napoleon, who seems to have left footprints all over

Europe. And when we did start, when we reached the Channel to cross to England, it seemed as if I could n't get home fast enough, as if something would happen. And yet here we all are, and nothing has happened except just the right things, that always do happen, I suppose. Do you know, mamma, I never realized until yesterday that I was grown up, a young lady."

"Yes," Mrs. Alston said with a sigh. "I think I would have been satisfied to keep you by me in childhood for years to come."

Robert went round and sat on the step by his mother, Kathie being on the other side. Then Fred came and seated himself just below, leaning his arms on his mother's lap. It made a pretty picture.

"I wish I could have you painted just so," remarked Uncle Robert. "You own them all now, Dora."

"I and mine," she uttered with pardonable motherly pride,

"But Rob is going away," said Freddy.

"O Rob, where?" Kathie asked.

"Why, I suppose I ought to be looking out for my living somewhere," returned Robert. "You don't think I could stay here always, hanging on uncle, do you?"

"But what are you going to do?"

"Did you hear to-day, Uncle?" the young man asked, glancing past his mother.

Uncle Robert nodded. Then he said aloud, "Yes, that is one of the pains and penalties of manhood, — an old law."

Robert Alston looked straight before him, over the space of lawn and lake to the woods on the farther shore. There were old laws and old penalties, and no one could hope to escape them. Every error or carelessness or sin had to be paid for in kind. He would fain have made his mother's wish reality, — begun again at childhood. If one could retrace — if regret could undo !

Uncle Robert would not allow the conversation to drop to any saddened key just now of all times. It was right enough that Rob should strike out for himself; but if he could have elected to remain nearer home! Yet there was always a little roving tendency: was it in the blood? Even when he had started another topic, he kept a quiet side for his thought.

Indeed there was no chance for conversation to flag. Not an old friend or *protégé* had Kathie forgotton, though it had been impossible to keep up with them all. But Uncle Robert seemed to have a catalogue of them and the most important events that had happened.

Kathie found her own room refurnished and quite a marvel of beauty. The other belongings had been placed in a smaller room across the hall; and when all the pictures and bits of remembrance had been unpacked, it became a wonder to know what to do with them.

There was much going to and from between them and the Darrells, and after a day or two Cedarwood was besieged by old friends. It was still warm, being the first of September, and there could be a good deal of out-door living. The girls were all wild about Kathie; and there were compliments and exclamations enough to make her vain.

Rob had decided to make his business essay in Chicago; why, no one could quite tell, for his uncle wished him to take a situation in New York among friends. Through Mr. Meredith. Uncle Robert had found a nice position; but Mrs. Alston was quite disappointed at her son's preference for mercantile life. The offer had come, and now in a few days he was to say good by again.

His college career had proved very satisfactory on the whole. He had the Latin oration and had taken one of the prizes. There had been a good deal of rowing and pleasures of various kinds, and some boyish escapades, but nothing that had detracted from his standing. His mother had gone to commencement and felt duly proud of her son.

"Mother," Rob said the next morning, "I think we ought to give another party — a sort of welcome home to Kathie — to introduce her afresh to Brookside : so many new people have come in ; and then it is something to have a travelled young lady in one's family."

Mrs. Alston glanced up at her brother.

"I was thinking of that myself. I suppose Kathie will have to begin young ladyhood."

"Does n't it seem queer?" said she. "Will I have to drive round in a pony carriage with mamma, and keep my cards in her case, as they do in English novels? And I ought to have a white silk dress."

"Why, that would be a wedding dress," declared Fred.

"Not necessarily — in my case." And Kathie laughed.

"The party is a bright idea," said Uncle Robert. "We ought to set about it at once."

"Oh, do you remember the first lovely party we had here, when the house was christened? I don't believe I should ever want to go entirely away — to stay I mean : there are so many dear and delightful memories and joys. I seem not to have really *lived* anywhere but just here, only I have been out a-visiting a good deal," she said gayly.

"I hope to keep you for many years to come," rejoined her mother, with a tender kiss.

"Oh, you will be sure to! I feel as if I was just ready to begin some kind of living. I suppose I do not need to go to school any more?"

"Not unless you wish to study law or medicine," said Uncle Robert, with a dry sort of smile.

"I am afraid I have not sufficient application. And I have no genius. Mamma, will you be satisfied with a commonplace daughter?"

A glance answered the question. The every-day virtues and pleasures were not quite so commonplace as the world might think.

" Yes, I should like to have a party," Kathie began, " if the girls have not forgotten me, or gone away. A real American party again."

" We have quite a number of new neighbors," said Uncle Robert. "I have had to solace myself with some other young ladies."

" Then I shall be all curiosity to see them — my rivals," she exclaimed archly.

They all decided it would be quite the best way to announce Kathie's return. Uncle Robert began a list. Kathie listened to the strange names. There was a Miss Georgie Halford, who had been spending the summer with Mrs. Adams, their neighbor, and whose mother, now dead, had been Mrs. Adams's cousin. There were some new neighbors on the avenue, the Collamores, who had three delightful young people ; and as they went on Kathie exclaimed, " Why, I shall not know any of them ! It will be quite like a foreign party, after all."

" You will like the Collamores," said Rob. "And, Kathie, do you remember little Rose Gordon? She graduated this summer from some great school, and is just beautiful. I took a party of girls out rowing one day, and she amused them by telling of a wonderful snow-house we once built, and a fairy play we had. I 'd nearly forgotten about it, but it all came back."

" It was the winter before Uncle Robert came home. Oh, how strange it seems !" And a curious light filled Kathie's eyes.

" Now your friends, Kathie," said Uncle Robert.

"Let us invite the girls who were here so long ago ; at least, all we can. Oh, where is Lottie Thorne ? "

" Still here, still in ' maiden meditation fancy free,' " declared Rob, " but making big eyes at all eligibles. She would remind you of what Ada Meredith used to be, only she is sickly sentimental."

" Oh, have you seen Ada? She has changed, and she puzzled me a good deal."

" She is getting fitted into another new life," said Uncle Robert. " The past two years have been very hard for Ada. Mrs. Meredith will never be anything but a worldly wise, fashionable woman. What ' our set' thinks and does and wears is all in all to her ; she is surprised at having a daughter who does n't think like her, who feels that fashion may not be quite everything. I must commend Ada for trying to be a good daughter to her mother as well as her father. Dr. Garnier is an intellectual man, with a strong home side to his character : and now Ada is trying to adapt herself to a new sphere ; she has more real character than I gave her credit for."

" She 's grown a famous favorite with Uncle Robert," declared his nephew. " I can't get on with her any better than I used."

" Lucy Gardiner and Harry Cox are engaged. I heard that in Italy, — was n't it odd? I want the girls and Harry, and Sophie Dorrance, and — oh, I am afraid I shall forget somebody ! Mamma, do you ever hear about Mary Carson ? "

" She married very well last winter : her husband has a large iron interest at Pittsburg." And Mrs. Alston glanced questioningly at Kathie.

" I was n't going to invite her," and Kathie flushed ; " that is, we never were intimate, you know ; only at Rome Emma and I were talking over the strife between the patricians, and — But I think the strife was all on one side, — Emma was so stanch and loyal. I shall always love her."

" It was quite an experience. Of course you have heard from Sarah Strong ? "

" I always wrote to her when I could, for I knew just what would interest her."

" They have all improved greatly," said Uncle Robert;

" you see it in the farm as well. The son took some prizes at the county fair. Do you know, Kathie, I think it is a little leaven that will leaven the whole village in the course of time."

" Sarah loves teaching so much ; and she is studying the whole time as well. I believe I shall enjoy a talk with her wonderfully, and I dare say she will know as much about Europe as a great many who have been there."

So the party list was made out, and Uncle Robert wrote the invitations in Mrs. Alston's name. Brookside was beginning to take on quite a society tone, and wore a thriving business air on account of the new factories. It brought in many families of the poorer classes, for whom something was needed beside mere shelter. Mr. Grayson and Mr. Adams, who had considerable interest in the town, had aroused some of the most influential men in its welfare, and had begun a crusade against ignorance and intemperance. Beside the library in progress, there was a gymnasium and reading-room for the employés of the different shops, made contingent mostly on good behavior, as the fee was but trifling.

" You see, Pussy, after you went away I had to employ myself in other things," explained Uncle Robert as they were driving along.

" You have all interested yourselves wonderfully in the town," replied Kathie. " Why I never saw such a change ! Mr. Meredith insisted that the place would look so small and poor to me that I never could content myself here again ; but I fancy it was partly teasing. But travel does change one a little," she ventured timidly.

" It ought. That is what it is for : to give new ideas and improve the old ones. Well," with a rather roguish twinkle, " shall you be dissatisfied ? "

" Oh, no, indeed." And her little hand slipped in Uncle Robert's unoccupied one.

4

" Because mamma and I have counted upon you a good deal. I think she feels a little sore about Rob's departure."

"Oh, why does he go?" interrupted Kathie. "The boys are to be in New York, — and when he might have stayed there."

" Yes, Mr. Meredith would have given him as good a chance. I can't quite understand Rob's suddenly developed taste for business. He is very fond of chemistry and several scientific pursuits, and I thought he would choose among them ; but when I found he had made up his mind firmly, I gave in. Perhaps when he has tried it a year or two, he will not like it as well as he thinks : he has grown so much more quiet."

" Yes, I noticed that. And he is real handsome," said Kathie, with pride. "He compares very favorably with Bruce."

" Is Bruce your ideal? "

Uncle Robert seemed not to look at Kathie, yet he was watching her narrowly with drooping eyes that hid so much.

" Yes," she made answer tranquilly, without any rising color. " I don't mean that he is above and beyond all others ; Dick Grayson is as manly and noble, doubtless, and Charlie is — Well, he has what Grandmother Darrell calls the mark of the calling ; and you would never doubt his goodness. But Bruce seems to be made to go out into the world and *keep* his goodness and nobleness, and all that. And then he has so many little touches of tact and tenderness that you hardly look for in one who has always been brought up with boys, — knightly, chivalrous, express it."

Uncle Robert lapsed into silence. He, like the others, had wondered if Kathie would return with her deeper emotions unstirred ; but he understood at once how it had been. Or was Bruce in the too familiar friendly contact?

Her thoughts went back to the months of journeying.

"I am so glad you have seen it all, Uncle Robert," she

began presently. "It is such a comfort to preface a bit of anything with a 'don't you remember.' Through Germany there are so many little bits of villages with a thread of river winding around, and a range of mountains in the distance, looking so calm and peaceful, as if people could live there forever and be happy. And yet how many people in the world are stolid, indifferent! Education is a great help, after all. One has to learn how to appreciate."

"And you can still appreciate this?"

"It is like a picture, Uncle Robert; and the soft, hazy light is so lovely. I think," she went on slowly, "we are too busy to pause and take good long looks, as we do abroad. There you have the sort of holiday feeling. You come purposely to see. The primrose is something more to you; but maybe it is n't quite so much to them."

Uncle Robert watched her with a peculiar delight. She was still simple hearted. True, though she had gone out to some extent at Rome and Florence, she was not considered in society, and she had made few girl friends. All that part was yet to come.

Kathie showed herself an eager, pleasure-loving girl through the party preparations. It somehow became merged into quite a grand affair.

"You may as well give Kathie her social standing at once," Mr. Conover said to his sister. "She is to be the equal of the best here, both in wealth, accomplishments, and, we all trust, in character. But I desire that there shall be no question *now* as to where she belongs." And he smiled.

So the supper and the music were to be the best of their kind. Rob made the discovery that it would be full moon; and the weather was delightfully pleasant. There were to be colored lanterns on porch and lawn, and some out-door amusements. The most familiar of her girl friends had

dropped in, but after the invitations were out the others
waited.

Rob went to New Haven for a few days while preparations were going on, and immediately afterwards he was
to start for his new post of duty. Freddy developed a
boyish adoration for Kathie, and did not want to be out
of her sight a moment.

The day had been lovely, and the evening was perfection. When the house and lawn came to be lighted up
Kathie declared it looked like a palace on a small scale.
Her choice for a dress had been a pale blue silk, trimmed
with an abundance of Malta lace, which gave it a peculiar
delicate and airy appearance. Without being particularly
handsome in any respect, Kathie was a very pretty girl,
quite tall, and with a graceful slenderness. Winsome was
the word to apply to her. A freshness sweet and wholesome, a thorough enjoyment that somehow made the joy
sweeter and better for all around her.

She appeared exceedingly lovely this evening, as she
stood with her mother, being introduced and receiving
guests. Aunt Ruth, in purple velvet and soft laces, looked
as if she might have stepped out of a picture. Jessie and
Mr. Meredith were as much at home as members of the
family; and Ada had come out with her husband.

"I took him away from important cases and everything," she said to Kathie, "for I felt that I *must* see you
this night of all. He rarely goes to parties. How lovely
everything is; and you are simply perfect! Give me credit
for a great deal of self-control, for I am tempted every
moment to be jealous of you. Kathie, all the good things
of this life *do* come right in your way. You will be a little queen, with everybody doing you homage. Everybody
always did, for that matter. Why! It is one of the
grand puzzles to me, when the whole world, or at least a
great part, is striving continually —"

"As to who shall be greatest"; and the pause was

filled in by Uncle Edward. "'Seeketh not her own' —
is n't that the great secret? And then — 'all things shall
be added.' But we must not get into a weighty discussion
just now, for the young gentlemen are looking askance at
Kathie, and the music is inspiriting."

Dick Grayson came up to ask Kathie's hand for the first
quadrille, if she were not already engaged.

"What a handsome young couple!" exclaimed Ada.
Then, with a smile, "The next important question will be
who Kathie will marry. I opine there will be heart-burn-
ings and jealousy, even if she does not set up for a fashionable belle. But she has everything in her favor."

"Ada —"

"No, Uncle Edward, you need not begin a lecture. I
will admit that I have a curiosity to be Kathie just a little
while, to see how it seems. But I am not dissatisfied with
anything in my own life. I cannot imagine a husband
better or nobler than Philip." And a gratified smile lighted
up her face. "We have all we want at present, and some
time we shall go abroad, — when we are educated up to
the point of thorough enjoyment. And I am *glad* to be
through with the strife and the anxiety of choice, and all
that. So now I can speculate on the future of other girls,
and watch their mistakes, and their seeking after pleasures.
But the thing with Kathie seems to be this, she has had
everything just *in* the time. I was a young lady at heart,
thinking of lovers and marriage and dress, when I knew
her first. I never had any real childhood, — few girls do
nowadays. Hers was so perfect, so lovely; I think
of it often now. How happy they all were the summer I
was here! and they were only tasting the mere edges of
their cake. If they had run through it and found the ring,
there would have been nothing but the same old pleasure
over again — the crumbs. But see, the dancing is to
begin, and I am to take Dr. Garnier through a quadrille."

The band was stationed on the wide piazza, and some

of the younger people had proposed the beautiful lawn for a part of the dancing ground. The turf was short as velvet, and the evening an unusually dry one. Over all the moon wended her way royally, dimming the countless stars, silvering the outlines of the evergreens until they seemed alight with gems. Here and there a colored lamp toned the scene, giving apparent warmth and softened tint. The strains of music were enchanting, as they always are on the evening air.

Kathie and Dick led the quadrille in-doors. Rob and Miss Fay Collamore were *vis-à-vis*. Kathie had been introduced to both girls, and her first glance had been caught by the younger one, Louise, a bright, lively girl, not so tall as her sister, whose hair was still a mass of fluffy golden curls, and whose dark eyes gave her a piquant expression. But now, as she met the other face in crossing and balancing, an occult sympathy drew her to it. Like the pictured faces abroad of some of the saints, a pure oval, with the soft brown hair brushed straight across the forehead, and worn in a heavy coil of braids at the back, a mouth of tender sweetness, and eyes of resignation. There was something more in them when she turned them to Rob, — an expression that gave Kathie a curious little thrill, and that she found herself speculating upon afterward when she saw them together.

But her speculations were all fragmentary in that delightful whirl. There were so many new people, and the old friends had changed, — grown or stood still, — as Kathie began to realize that even the last might happen. When she was not dancing she sought them out, but the new claimants seemed to crowd in and bewilder her.

"I believe I *am* vain and frivolous," she confessed, pausing a few moments beside Uncle Robert. "It is all delightful! and the spirit in my feet leads me, — 'who knows how?'" smiling up into the fond eyes; "it is just a fill of pleasure!"

" My little girl, it is right to enjoy it all."

The supper was elegantly served, and the guests seemed to enjoy everything to the uttermost. The sweet and bright variety in bringing young and middle-aged together, the sympathetic pleasure, that gave a more personal tone to the intermingling, a delightful remembrance that each could take of a party a little different from the regulation affairs, having the best of them, and something better beside.

CHAPTER V.

KATHIE sat by the open window the morning after the party, glancing out in a dreamy fashion. There was a great mound of salvia resplendent in its September glory, and over a pagoda of lattice-work climbed in a luxuriant manner a gorgeous trumpet creeper. How the evergreens had grown since they first came here! and what a beautiful, cool, green shade tempered the brightness!

"Tired?" Uncle Robert sauntered up to her, and then dropped on the ottoman in an indolent fashion.

"Tired! oh, no," with a gay little laugh. "Do you suppose one party would wear me out? If so I must have climbed Alps and explored picture galleries in vain."

"But I thought you looked grave, and I wondered if your serene royal highness had found some dregs in your cup."

"Well, I have"; but she smiled as if they were not very depressing. "I was thinking how curious people are, and that I was no exception."

"So you have acquired that much worldly wisdom?"

"Do you call it worldly wisdom? I did not dignify it by so high-sounding a name, and I felt a little humiliated; for it seemed like fickleness on my part, or some sort of change, or outgrowing — "

"You are delightfully ambiguous."

"When I was a little girl I used to come to you with all my puzzles, you know. I have not had any of late; perhaps because I was changing about and enjoying myself, and did not keep to one range of thought or feeling."

"I shall be glad to take back my little girl"; and a tender light shone in his eyes. " You are grown so tall that I need some link or chain to bring you back ; so what is the puzzle?"

" Do you think I have changed very much?"

" I can hardly answer you yet. I believe I *was* a good deal surprised at first, for somehow I never tried to get the little girl out of my mind ; as to virtues and vices — "

" Oh, you know I did not mean that! It is — Well, I will tell you just what it is. You know how fond I was of the Gardiner girls? It seems awful to say it, but last night — " Kathie paused with a flush of embarrassment.

" You found a difference," Uncle Robert suggested, quietly.

" It seemed so strange. Of course I congratulated Lucy on her engagement, and we talked of the girls and the changes, and it appeared somehow as if we came to the bottom of everything so quickly, — were really aground, — and you could hear the crunching on the sand. Lucy is happy and content. Annie talked a little about Europe, as if it was a few towns and rivers and pictures and ruined castles. Then Lottie Thorne — not that she ever was any great favorite — talked as if it was all Paris and fine dresses and being presented to the queen. She seemed amazed that I was not at a drawing-room or a grand ball in Paris. And even Sophie Dorrance was n't— Well, it seemed suddenly to me that I had outgrown them all, and here, in sober morning light, I was trying to get the matter settled satisfactorily. Can I, ought I, to put myself back, or could I bring them up? It is no real lack of regard."

" No. It happens to many of us after a separation. One mind broadens, deepens, and another does not. But it will hardly do to dwarf the growing mind," with a shrewd half-smile.

" Then you do not think it wrong? " with a joyful sense of relief in her tone. " Or fickleness? "

"No. It is one of the inevitable laws of mental improvement. You have had a wider sphere and experience than most girls of your age. This is the thing we are all doing unconsciously, — outgrowing some one else; standing on a little higher intellectual plane. When we begin to be vain of our ascent, and despise those who are left behind, it is time to take heed of our ways. But the natural changes settle themselves. The Gardiners will always keep in a small round, and be very estimable women, not comprehending or longing for the greater knowledge. It is a wise providence of God that there should be a great many of these kindly, simple-hearted, easily contented people in the world. But those who have greater advantages are expected to use them."

"I may as well confess all my faults, since you are so lenient. Are you not partial, Uncle Robert?" Kathie asked archly. "I could n't help thinking that I liked the Collamores, in just one evening, better than the old friends; that is, I had the feeling that there were more real sources of enjoyment between us. But to throw over old friends—"

"You need not throw them over. They gradually drop out of themselves. I was glad to have you begin with the old and the new, that none of the old friends should feel hurt or slighted. Society does demand certain courtesies of us, and it serves to keep in check the selfishness of human nature. Many of these matters will be regulated by experience. Your life, your pleasures and enjoyments will take you out of the Gardiners' circle. They will have their own friends and relatives, whom you probably will care little about; you will have yours, among whom they would not feel at home. You will go on exchanging calls and visits at intervals, and both will recognize the fact that each has an interest beyond the other, and good sense will keep both parties from any imaginary injury."

"Then you think I may make all the new friends I desire to?"

"I do not believe it will be necessary to restrict you yet awhile. Dr. Johnson advised people to keep their friendships in repair; and I have found it very good counsel. You will make mistakes: young people always do, — older ones too, for that matter. Some persons will appear very charming at first, and you will soon tire of them; then you may discover a gem where you had not looked for one."

"I wonder if you will be surprised at my developing a taste for gayeties? I thought last night enchanting."

"My dear, it is the province of youth. There are pleasures then that we cannot enjoy later in life. I want you to be a happy young girl; not a pedant or a critical moralist. And now what does your ladyship propose to do this morning?"

"Oh, I did promise to drive over to the Darrells this morning. Ada goes at noon with Jessie and Mr. Meredith. How I shall miss them! Uncle Robert, I have a fancy that I grew up to them. I was such a little girl when Miss Jessie first liked me. But I must run away and change my dress."

She soon returned in driving attire, looking fresh and rosy, showing no sign of fatigue. Indeed, it seemed even now as if she could dance on forever. How lovely the world was! What a delightful thing it was just to live!

They were all delighted to see Kathie, from grandmother down to Robin. Jessie's trunk was packed and stood in the hall.

"The birds all fly out of the old home nest," said grandmother; "we can only keep them a little while."

"But they come back again," rejoined Mrs. Darrell, with her motherly smile. "It is the way of the world; and we are so glad to have Jessie near by once more."

"And to think of my having her all the time! I am so glad I decided upon the seminary, for now that Jessie is to set up her household gods in New York, I can watch the process of their being decorated with foreign gear and gauds," declared Charlie. "Kathie, pardon me," and he bowed very low. "I ought to have risen with the lark — does he get up early in September as well as June? — and made my party call. I had no idea that you would be out after such a night of dissipation. It was just splendid! but I can't imagine anything at Cedarwood being less than the most delightful of its kind."

"Highly complimentary!" exclaimed Ada, entering at that moment. "But I thought we should miss you, surely. Early rising is an old habit of yours, I believe."

"It was late this morning," returned Kathie.

"No need to ask how you are, for your face tells the story. It was a lovely party, and I think everybody enjoyed it. Please put me down for the next one. Even Dr. Garnier was n't a bit bored, and he is very shy of parties."

"I am so sorry to have you all go," Kathie declared, looking around. "Aunt Ruth and uncle are to start for Washington the first of next month, Rob and all the boys will be away, and I shall have to take to party going in pure self-defence."

"And visiting," said Jessie. "I do not mean to abate my claim. I shall certainly give parties, if that will be the way to beguile you; and Robin cannot be deserted."

Ada took her off presently.

"After all," she began, "you are a real young girl. I wanted to see what you did last night, — whether you were too grave for follies and pleasures, and meant to set us all an example."

"But Uncle Robert does n't think it wrong." And she glanced up with questioning eyes. Ada was difficult to understand.

"No one said it was wrong; and if one could map out one's life and find the true dividing line, and shun that

where pleasure runs into frivolity and where enjoyment
turns to envy and jealousy and detraction! But you *will*
have a lovely time, Kathie Alston, and why should you
not take the best that comes? There is no one to hurry
you into marriage, to hurry you into anything; and so
you can enjoy your pleasures slowly, thoroughly; and if I
can't give you a party when you come to visit me, I can
regale you with a choice little supper, and show you Dr.
Garnier at his best. You will never be able to slip quite
out of my grasp."

Kathie laughed a little, yet was not quite sure she
should elect Ada for a friend now any more than in the
past. It was one of the puzzles of life that was not comfortably settled for her.

Dinner was early on account of train time. Charlie
took out the light wagon to drive Kathie and Ada, while
the others and the trunk would occupy the family carriage.
They were all loath to spare cunning baby Robin; but the
good-byes were said presently, — they were only for a little
while now.

After they had watched the train out of sight, Charlie
helped Kathie back into the wagon.

"I am going to present a petition," he began. "I want
you to give me this afternoon. I shall go away so soon,
and I am not satisfied with bits and fragments. I want
one good long talk, that will keep in my mind until I see
you again."

"But mamma—"

"We will stop, so she need have no anxiety. I think
she will trust you to me," he said, a little proudly.

Kathie had been so used to guardianship that it seemed
odd at the first moment. Yet she and Bruce had gone
so much together; still, there was a little strangeness
about the young man Charlie, with his deferential courtesy,
quite different from the boy who had been her playmate
and champion.

Mrs. Alston had no objection. She was very fond of Charlie Darrell, and would have enjoyed a son of this kind, who never gave one an anxious thought.

They drove slowly through the old haunts, now and then greeted by a familiar voice. Here they used to go chest-nuting A great strip had been taken off for a street, the woods thinned and cleared up, the ground a mass of velvet turf and moss. Then they followed Silver River to the point where it met and emptied into Guilford River. Even the little straggling settlement of Guilford had improved and was brightened up by a paper mill. But they were not intent upon these signs of industry, so turned out of their course to beauty, softness, the tender touches of nature. Birds sang in the lingering tones of later summer, bees droned, insects crooned, and the sweetness of balsam, the resinous odor of the pines, and the wine-like fragrance of wild grapes filled the air.

They talked as young people will, — of the future and its promises, bright with hope and romance. old, old memories and interests. His were the dreams and the ambitions, tempered with the higher grace, of the great work to do in the world, of the poor souls that were to be raised, ennobled, saved, of the truth to be made manifest in daily living and work. He had an enthusiastic love and rever-ence for the calling that he had chosen, and it had not only the sanction of his parents, but their approval and sym-pathy.

Kathie listened with an interest that was very fascinating to the young man. All the delights and variety of the two years abroad had not spoiled her. She was the same honest, frank, tender girl, ready to take up her duties in life, ready for sympathy and earnest endeavor; and as he glanced at her fair face the half-formed dreams of boy-hood took shape, and he knew then what the hope of man-hood would be to him.

When she returned she found her mother and Uncle Robert ready for tea.

" Where is Rob ? " she asked.

" At the Collamores', I fancy : I saw the young people playing croquet on the lawn."

" How odd ! Rob did not affect croquet, as I remember"; and Kathie smiled. " I think he likes Miss Fay very much."

" I should be glad if he liked her a great deal, and she liked him," said Mrs. Alston.

" Rob has never been a very ardent lover of the sex," returned his uncle, " but I am glad in his first essay his fancies run so wisely."

" And I shall cultivate them," declared Kathie. " I liked them all so much ; but I believe I admire Miss Fay the most."

" You could not choose more agreeable friends," said her mother.

Aunt Ruth and the General entered, and they went to supper. Kathie begged to be excused and retired early, and scarcely had her head touched the pillow before she was in the sweet sleep of care-free youth.

Mr. Conover found his sister sitting on the broad step of the piazza after the others had left her.

" You are grave, Dora," he said, in a kindly tone ; " you must learn not to feel so anxious about Rob. There is not very much to fear, I think. He certainly has conducted himself very well through his college years ; and if he disappoints us both a little in his choice, we must remember, ' The thoughts of youth are long, long thoughts.' "

" Thank you, Robert"; and she motioned him to a seat beside her. " No father could have been kinder to them than you have been, or more patient. I am trying to resign myself to his going away, though I was not thinking so much of that now. If I could make a wish for him and have it come to pass " ; and there was a lingering cadence in her tone.

" What would it be ? "

"That he might love and marry Fay Collamore."

"Why, Dora! You have actually a longing to choose your son's wife. Mothers are not always ready to do that."

"I understand that I must give him up; that, however brave, manly, and successful he may prove, he will never be to his mother what some sons are; and yet I think he loves me better now than at any time in his life. But he has always been outside of mine, so to speak. It was boy friends and pleasures, now it will be men and business, and some time a wife. The wife may wean him away entirely."

"And if it were Fay, you know she would not."

"I should have another daughter. I am glad Kathie has taken a fancy to the girls; I hoped she would. Yet I think mothers have a right to feel as anxious over the marriage of their sons as that of their daughters; and an unfortunate marriage as surely wrecks a young man."

"I own I have felt a little surprised at Rob's evincing a preference for any one, and Miss Collamore's influence over him could be productive of good only. She is strong and firm, with all her gentleness; yet it would seem a little strange for any of them to marry: they are such children."

Mrs Alston sighed. Just then a step sounded on the gravel walk. Rob came up and paused before them, while they exchanged a pleasant greeting; then, as if obeying some sudden impulse, he clasped his arms around his mother's neck and kissed her fondly, and a moment afterward uttered an abrupt good night.

"I wonder if I ask too much?" the mother cried, in her longing, yearning soul.

The next day was Rob's last at home. He had said good by to the old haunts and friends, and he lingered about the rooms in such a melancholy way that Kathie rallied him on a newly discovered sentiment. He packed his trunk, talked a long while with Aunt Ruth, and even declined an invitation to go out driving with Uncle Robert. Late in the afternoon Miss Collamore came over with her sister to call on Kathie. The girls soon discovered similar tastes and fancies. Miss Fay painted considerably in oils, and had met Mrs. Langdon, whom she liked very much. Kathie pieced it out with bits of their adventures abroad.

"How delightful it must be to have her husband so much interested in her pursuits! I like to hear Mrs. Adams talk of them, and I hope to know her better when she returns, — and you two were schoolmates!"

"Yes," returned Kathie, "only you know she was much wiser in nearly every point than I, and she has a genius."

"I was wondering," said Miss Fay, "how it was you put your mark so upon people. Everybody seems to remember something. Why, at first, I supposed you a woman grown, and your uncle told me one day that you were only a child. You are not older than Louise."

Kathie flushed, but made no answer.

"And I was so afraid I should not like you. I wanted to so much; but sometimes, when you hear persons talked of a good deal — is it the perversity of human nature? — you can't or will not like them."

"I hope you will," Kathie said, in a sweet, grave tone.

"Oh, I do! I liked your face in a moment, — and the party was so delightful; but it could not be disconnected from you. It was not so much in honor of you as a part of you. Then your uncle had told me of a party you had when the house was christened, and that Mr. Meredith called it ' Kathie's Fairy Land.'"

"I used to be such a famous little girl for fairy stories," said Kathie, with a bright laugh; "and I like them yet; it seems as if a great many real fairy incidents had happened to me."

Mrs. Alston came out to announce that supper was

5

ready, and beg them to stay. At first they insisted they
had only come to make a call; but everybody overruled,
and they remained. After supper they had some very fine
music, and Rob escorted them home.

"I am to go over and see Miss Fay's studio," Kathie
announced; "and Miss Louise is doing lovely high-art
work. Mamma, I suppose I shall have to get at something. Shall I embroider, or paint, or study operas?"

"For a while you need not be distressed, I think."

"Can I spend my time in idleness, just enjoying everything and loving you? For mamma *mia*, we have two long
years to make up." And Kathie kissed her fondly.

The tears came into Mrs. Alston's eyes. Here, as in
the years gone by, she must find her greatest comfort; and
she pressed her daughter fondly to her heart.

Two days later Rob said good by and went to his new
path of duty. It was a promising position in an excellent
mercantile house, and on good behavior and business
capacity depended a series of promotions.

"You'll write often?" his mother had said; "and I
hope you will find a pleasant home."

"Don't worry about that, little mother. I hope I shall
prove no discredit to any of you, and I do mean some time
to be a rich man, to take care of you in your old days."
And he laughed, with an effort at gayety.

"I hope it may be so," she made answer; but there was
a tremulousness in her tone.

Uncle Robert accompanied him to the station. It was
a quiet drive, but, as they stood on the platform, Rob suddenly grasped his uncle's hand, and though his face was a
trifle averted, the husky tone betrayed how deeply his
heart was touched.

"No words can ever thank you, Uncle Robert," he said,
"for the kindly care you have bestowed upon me; but I
want you to know that I *do* appreciate it, that, as my
mother says, you have been more than a father to us, to

me, and I want you to feel sure, positive, that I shall not shame you in the new essay I am about to make. If I should ever be tempted to dishonesty, I will throw up everything and come back to you ; and I feel quite certain now that I shall never drink or drop into bad company. Trust me in all these things, will you, and comfort mother?"

" I will trust you, remember that, my boy ; and I think I could hardly care more for an own son."

He felt the shiver that ran through the boy's arm ; but the train came along with its rush, and their hands clasped tighter for a moment, then parted as if with a wrench. Rob entered, settled himself, but would not trust even a glance without.

Uncle Robert drove home slowly. There was some trouble, some lesson learned by bitter experience, some urgent need of money he guessed, and sighed to himself. Time would tell. He could trust him for the future.

CHAPTER VI

THERE was nothing but changes, Kathie thought. Aunt Ruth and Uncle Mackenzie went to Washington, and she had a promise of a few weeks if mamma could spare her. Mrs. Meredith had taken a house in New York, and as soon as she was settled Kathie must come and help her arrange some of the adornments brought from abroad; and at home every day seemed occupied finding the new level and adapting herself to it.

Hannah and Jane Maybin were still in service. Indeed, Jane had become so useful, so deft and ladylike, that Mrs. Alston gave up the care of the dining-room and sleeping-chambers almost wholly to her. She had gone more in society, and was enjoying some of her olden prestige. She was glad now that she had begun it, for Kathie needed a chaperone and friend. Mrs. Alston had no fancy for leaving her young daughter unguarded through her perilous years, and the little touch of deference to elders that Kathie had acquired unconsciously abroad was extremely grateful and pleasing to mother love. Indeed, it seemed almost like her lost youth returning, to have this tall, fair girl for her companion; and though she was very unlike Aunt Ruth, yet those days were suggested by so many incidents of the present.

Fred was giving very little trouble. A rather slow but indefatigable student, and evincing a passion for chemistry and all corresponding experiments that sometimes quite startled one's nerves. Uncle Robert had fitted him up a laboratory in the old play-room, and tried to keep an oversight on his doings. He developed an almost girlish fondness for his mother, and had little of Rob's rapturous regard for boys; but as little did he care for being a girl's favorite. To be let alone with books or experiments was his delight; and his passion was horseback rides on Jasper, who had now reverted to him.

Invitations poured in upon Kathie. Already quite a charming " set " had been formed, happily of cultivated people with some interest beyond the exciting one of dress. There were many out-door amusements, though the boat club was shorn of its glory. Archery had become a great favorite. Georgie Halford was queen here, and Mr. Adams had fitted up an admirable archery ground. Then there was a sketching club, that went out now and then to study nature. They were all bright with the dreams and hopes of youth, and tinged with the inseparable romance which lends to these early years its greatest charm.

They welcomed Kathie warmly. Uncle Robert had made himself an immense favorite with young people, and they all felt acquainted with her after the evening of the party. There were little teas and musical evenings, which often ended with some favorite quadrilles.

" How do you ever find time for anything?" she asked in despair, as she sat one morning in the pretty room at the Collamores', that was devoted to everything, Louise said, and in which one felt at home immediately. Fay had her easel in the bay-window, and Louise a pretty willow workstand, with her bright, soft silks and quaint embroideries.

" I don't know," and Fay glanced up with a quiet smile, " unless it is that we have settled, and you are still on the wing. Coming back has made everything new to you. Last summer mamma and I spent all the time in calls and company, it seemed to me, and taking our bearings, as a sailor would say. Lou was in school then; and I have a fancy companionship helps you along."

"Then I shall have to bring my work over here. Only what shall it be? I think it spoils one to go abroad. You buy such an endless sight of pretty things at such bargains; and I know I should never have the patience to work a set of curtains"; stooping to examine Louise's delicate embroidery.

"I am fond of sewing. I sit here and go over the old romances, — of queens with their maids doing marvellous handiwork, of ladies making colors for their true knights, who went crusading,—and it takes me back to the old world of chivalry."

"And Lou is romantic," declared Fay. "Now I should never care to sew unless I was in great trouble. It seems to me distracting rather than tranquillizing; and yet it is a pretty sight to see a group around a table, in the glow of a lighted lamp, the busy fingers sewing, while one reads aloud."

"Then Fay and I decided not to have the same specialties. Of course we both studied music, — that seems a necessity nowadays, — but I had no genius for painting, and I wanted some pretty house accomplishment; and the reason why I began curtains was that I was afraid I should get the house too full of tidies and lambrequins and banners, and this would last me a long while. So, Kathie, you can come over and read to us, or tell us of the wonders abroad : we may never go to Europe."

"I hope you will," returned Kathie, warmly. "Hearing is not quite like seeing; but I do not want to fall into the ridiculous habit of prefacing everything with, when I was in Rome, or, when I was in Paris."

"I think you are extremely modest, and I do enjoy your descriptions, they are so fresh and graphic. Sometimes you remind me of your brother. How you must miss him !"

"You see I never had very much of him. He was at school and college, and now I have been the truant. We should all have enjoyed his being nearer home; but then he was n't — I mean he never cared for girls."

Louise laughed at that.

"He used to consider us a great trouble, but I think he has changed somewhat." And Kathie flushed a little, while a look of fun lighted up her eyes.

"How fortunate young men *do* change!" exclaimed Lou. "Who is it says that some one else always has to find out how nice boy's sisters are? We thought him quite gallant; and papa praised the young men of Brookside without stint. Only it is remembered virtues, or blessings, brightening, etc., for they do seem to have taken their flight pretty generally. Eugene groans dismally."

"I thought it nice that some one should charm Rob out of his boyish indifference, to use the mildest term. He always admired men so much. Mr. Meredith used to be his ideal."

"I don't wonder, I am sure: he is a most delightful gentleman; and there is some one else I am anxious to see — Gen. Mackenzie's son — your cousin by courtesy. Do you suppose he will ever come back to Brookside? Your brother told us so much about him."

"You will like him," Kathie said, enthusiastically. "I don't know whether the government will give him any vacation until his three years are up, but I hope so."

"I do sometimes experience a little tinge of envy when I see you in all your glory, Miss Kathie Alston," began Lou, in a whimsical tone, when Fay interrupted.

"Here comes your 'loyal knight and true,' to spirit you away. It is like a story-book. Shall I wave my lily hand to him?"

Kathie glanced out of the window. Uncle Robert had the large carriage and a sudden thought flashed across her mind.

"I will run down a moment, she said, vanishing.

"Do you all want to go for a lovely drive?" he asked.

" We shall not have many such gorgeous days, for autumn is on the wane."

" Yes," answered Kathie, " I will gather up the girls."

They were delighted, and went to inform their mother and hunt up their wraps Mr. Conover was on very friendly terms with them, and he was the kind of man to prove an invaluable companion to young girls. They were too young to count on his marrying, consequently there was the charm of perfect ease.

Kathie resigned to Fay the seat of honor beside her uncle, and after they had turned on the lovely river road he gave Fay the reins; she was very fond of driving the ponies. It was a fragrant, dreamy, Indian-summer day, and made one feel luxuriously indolent.

" Oh, here is a letter for you ! " said Uncle Robert, hand-ing one to Kathie.

It was from Rob, as she knew at a glance. He was not a very diffusive correspondent, but quite exacting of late. " Tell me what you do, and where you go," he said; " I am hungry for home news, I did not think I should miss it so much. Do you see anything of Miss Collamore and her sister? Remember me kindly to them."

Kathie read the paragraph aloud. " How queer for Rob to long for home ! " she said; " and yet he seems a good deal interested in business "

" Tell him you *do* see us," said Lou, " and that we could n't live without you." Fay colored delicately and made a gentle inclination of the head. Was it the fresh, bright morning that stirred her with unwonted emotion? She could afford to give him, not one thought, but many,— the young toiler in a far-away city. There were pleasant walks still sacred to her, little bits and fragments of talk to which she had a half-fancy she held the key. He had never cared for girls before, but he had seemed much in-terested in them ; she would not detatch herself from her sister ; and she wondered if he would be back at Christmas, or another summer: there were so many pleasant things yet to discuss, so much of earnest purpose left unsaid.

Uncle Robert watched the wavering color. He could not know the thoughts that were bringing her nearer to him, but he speculated slowly upon what life would have in store for her The strange, sweet mystery folded deep within, like the frond of a fern, the joy or sorrow, or negative content of a young girl's life. No, it would never be the last. When nature was once roused, moved to its uttermost, it must be for joy or suffering,—something that involved her in the supreme emotions of life.

The two on the back seat laughed and chatted in gay unconcern. Their time would come later. How could any one help being joyous on this queen of days, in this air of heavenly content!

It was past noon when they returned. Dinner was waiting, and Mrs. Alston was going to the sewing society that afternoon.

"And I shall write letters every precious moment of the time!" declared Kathie. "How they do accumulate! Uncle Robert, do you know that I have been extremely remiss to an old friend? I have not been to see Sarah Strong. She told me she should not expect me until I had gone the round of the home friends, and was thoroughly rested. I have been home almost two months, and shall never get around, because the circle widens continually. I've been wondering if I shall feel disappointed in her."

"No," answered Uncle Robert decisively. "She has been going on as well as you. She is not of the stuff to stop while there is a next."

"Well, I am anxious to see her, even if I have waited. It was because I thought it best to go on Saturday, as she is more at liberty then; but my Saturdays have been so occupied. Suppose I promise for this week, — can you take me?"

" I am at your service," bowing.

" Thank you. Then I will write."

She settled herself to her proposed employment. A long, gossipy letter to Rob, but it seemed full of the Collamores. They had gone here and there, they had talked over so many things, and she liked them so much. " I suppose I ought to be fondest of Lou, because she is near my own age, and I do like her to be gay with; but if I should ever be in bitter trouble, with no mamma or Uncle Robert, I should go to Fay. Isn't it queer how suddenly and inexplicably you trust some people?"

" He will set that down as girls' rodomontade," she said to herself, with a smile.

Aunt Ruth, and then Bruce, to whom she sent all the news about the boys. I think the thing that comforted him the most was her naive admission that they had all gone, and Brookside seemed so queer without them.

It was dark before she came to the end of her notes, but she drew a long breath of relief, and resolved to keep them in better order in the future. After mamma's return came supper, and nearly all the evening Kathie sat at the piano and played soft, bewildering tunes. The night had turned rainy after the day of wonderful loveliness, and sometimes between the lingering chords one could hear the soft dripping without.

" Have I tired you?" She bent over Uncle Robert as he lay on the sofa, and kissed his forehead.

" Tired! my little darling, no. It is so seldom that I get you all to myself, unless I am taking you somewhere or bringing you home."

" I have developed into a sad run-about. You ought to have a great deal more of me. I am defrauding you out of your just dues."

" I must not turn into a selfish old fellow and shadow your brightness. I am so glad to have you happy."

" But, can any one be too full of joy, — too easily pleased? Am I not childish and frivolous?"

"I told you the other day you were to have your holiday of youth. Enjoy it and you will please me."

He watched her as she flitted across the room to her mother. These sweet, pure, transparent young girls' lives interested him so much, for he had reached a time when he could detect the false, and the true had become dearer to him. His little Kathie had grown into this tall, fair being, and stood on the threshold of womanhood. Some time — But no, it was pain to anticipate.

Saturday was fair and auspicious, with a rather crisp air after the storm. They decided upon an early dinner, and then Uncle Robert handed her into the phaeton, and tucked the soft robe about her. How pretty and refined she looked, with a little dash of scarlet in her soft, gray costume, and everything so exquisitely harmonious!

The road to Middleville had met with few changes or improvements, and looked rather cheerless, with its well-nigh leafless trees and yellow or brown stubble fields; yet Kathie enjoyed the drive, thinking how all the changes of the seasons contributed, each in its turn, a beauty and tone to the world; and this was like a plain dish the day after a gorgeous feast.

But as they caught sight of Farmer Strong's, they remarked a change. The trees were trimmed up, the fences in good order, and the fields had a cleared, tidy look, as if the harvest was finished and put away, with no loose ends or fragments left about. The house had been painted a soft, restful stone color, with brighter trimmings, and the old-fashioned door-yard still abounded in bloom. There were chrysanthemums of almost every color, some late roses, and clusters of geraniums. A porch ran across part of the front in place of the little stoop, and at one end a Chinese honeysuckle was timidly clinging, while a Virginia creeper had made bolder essays and was hanging out its scarlet sprays.

A figure flashed out of the door and down the walk.

Yes, the two years had done a great deal for Sarah Strong.
Kathie felt that she would hardly have known her the first
moment, and yet it was more the inward, spiritual change
manifest in every direction, than any purely outward alter-
ation. She was of medium height and rather stout, but
there was a compactness to her figure, a firmness and vigor
to her step, a character in the poise of her head. Her
hair had deepened in its color, though it was still red, but
its tint and abundance rendered it really beautiful. Her
clear, serious, gray eyes, her gracious expression and tender smile, made the face good looking in the truest sense.

"Oh!" she exclaimed, then paused suddenly, as if half
abashed.

Kathie sprang out and clasped her arms about her old-
time friend and admirer.

"How good of you to come!" Sarah cried, with a
long, struggling breath. "And oh, how — how beautiful
you have grown! I must say it; has n't she?" turning to
Mr. Conover. "I have thought so much about you, and
wondered, — and your letters were such treasures. But
there is nothing like really having you once again; changed
and yet not changed; but I don't believe anything could
spoil you."

"I don't know," returned Kathie, archly. "Praise
might."

"No, it would n't: you would know that the truth was
true, and the rest you would n't care for; and sometimes
people cannot help speaking out what is in their hearts,
sure that it will not be wrongly interpreted. But they are
all so anxious to see you, and yet they are afraid that you
are a great lady."

Sarah laughed softly, with a mellow kind of cadence,
and Kathie joined her, as the two walked across the porch
and entered the parlor.

Kathie recalled unconsciously her first introduction to it.
That too had been gradually toned down. And what

pleased Kathie the most was the utter absence of any
sense of newness, though she realized that it was Sarah's
parlor, for it had nearly all been refurnished. The carpet
was a rich deep brown, with here and there a dash of
crimson and olive green. A few easy-chairs and the sofa
she had once been so proud of acquiring, a pretty home-
made bookcase, with some jars and ornaments on the top,
and getting to be quite well filled; the melodeon, some
well-chosen pictures, and soft, drapery curtains in ecru,
that toned the white wall, which Mrs. Strong would retain
as a point of cleanliness. A cheerful fire was burning in
an open-front stove, and the air felt delightful after the
ride.

"No, I am not a great lady that any one might be
afraid of," said Kathie, with some amusement. "I feel
very natural in getting back to the old places; sometimes
it seems as if another Kathie had been abroad, until I
count up the changes."

"Mother!" Sarah said; "Cousin Ellen!"

Mrs. Strong entered, her own hearty self in spite of a
certain diffidence; and her delight was visible in every line
of her face. Beside Cousin Ellen, Martha, a tall, bashful
girl, seemed longing to hide herself, and yet a certain curiosity conquered her shyness; but in a few moments the
group seemed increased indefinitely, with almost every
child pushing forward, until Kathie stood in the midst, a
little princess with her loyal retainers.

Uncle Robert had driven down to the barn, as usual. To
the thrift here had been added a kind of sensible orderli-
ness. The farmers around rather sneered at the new-fan-
gled notions of the Strongs, taken out of books and papers,
but the result remained a source of astonishment, and not a
little secret envy. There were better crops finer fruit,
some successful ventures in new things; and the money
gain was the thing they could not well despise. Father
and sons labored harmoniously together. James had his

workshop and exercised his ingenuity on rainy days pro-
ducing some creditable pieces of workmanship. He had
decided not to go to the city for a trade, and add another
to the strugglers.

Within the house they talked and talked. Kathie in her
refinement, breeding, and culture was the same marvel to
them as heretofore. There was no condescension, no
standing a little apart, and yet they, by a fine natural consent, set her above themselves.

"Now, children," said Mrs. Strong, "come out in the
kitchen and leave Sarah and Miss Kathie to themselves a
little while."

The children obeyed rather reluctantly, but the two were
finally left for a girlish confidence. And there was so
much to say, — school, with its gradual advancement;
church, with its music and its grand lessons, a little society, even in that country place, and the work to do.

Sarah Strong said it with a glad, true ring. Work was
the thorough comprehensiveness of living. A plain, narrow place, but not small, only a little soul could contract
it. Everything she touched came presently to have a vitality of its own. She was not a nurse, she could not
pander to weakness; her theory must stand alone, robust,
far-reaching, and her practice must lead others to help
themselves. Yet there was no rudeness in all this, rather
a gentle firmness, that allowed no turning back, that pointed
out mistakes clearly.

As Kathie listened she wondered. What would Sarah
do with this life presently? Was she not needed out in the
great world? And how would she get there? And then
Kathie knew the God who had guided hitherto could not
fail or go wrong. Perhaps it was just here the work was
required. And she was holding herself steadfast, garner-
ing up the true content, staying here, but learning all the
time to go up higher when the true summons came, yet
not hurrying nor dimming the grace of the present by any
impatience.

"What a grand thing," she said, presently, "to have been in all these places; and the next best is to see through a friend's eyes. When I had your two or three letters from Rome, I knew you were looking at things for me. But further back, when you were in Moscow, you spoke of Napoleon, and we found two or three histories and read them aloud. James was so interested. Then we wanted to know about Russia and Prussia, and all these quarrels with kings and emperors. I interested the school children, and they in turn roused their parents. It is always the little leaven. And how can people shut their eyes and care nothing about the events outside their little circle? I always did want to know"; smiling. "When I find a child dull and ignorant, and am tempted to be impatient, I think of your goodness."

"But you were not dull," said Kathie. "Ask Uncle Robert. I believe his sympathy has brought about higher results than any act of mine."

"There was a step on the porch and Sarah started. It was too dark to see the quick color mantle her face.

"Kathie," she said, "I must beg your pardon for something I have done. I hated to lose even a moment of your precious time, but I read one of your letters to our minister, and promised him if ever I could arrange it you should meet; so father asked him down to tea. He is coming now. Don't feel annoyed, please."

Then she began to light the lamp. Martha opened the door and announced Mr. Truesdell.

Kathie rose. A grave, rather careworn man, not much beyond thirty, but looking old for his years, yet with a certain scholarly refinement and a gentle, almost entreating strand in his voice.

The moment after the "men" came up from the barn, and Mrs. Strong announced supper, — a generous country supper, with a table that would not have shamed more pretentious people.

Mr. Truesdell and Uncle Robert were acquainted, it seemed. Mr. Strong and James were delighted to see Kathie, the young man somewhat shy at first. It certainly was a pleasant supper, and Mr. Truesdell proved himself very companionable.

There was a bright moon, so the guests did not hasten away immediately. Sarah opened the melodeon and they sang a few grand old hymns. Some strange consciousness flashed across Kathie as they stood there, and it seemed as if her question about Sarah was answered.

But they had to say good by presently. Kathie promised to come again, and Sarah was to have a whole Saturday at the Palace Beautiful, as she called it.

"Well?" said Uncle Robert interrogatively, when they had ridden a long distance in silence.

"Uncle Robert, who is Mr. Truesdell? and has he been long at Middleville?"

"About a year, I think. He is an earnest worker, for all his quiet air, and a widower with two children."

"Oh! and Sarah will go to the very place she is so well fitted for. Did you guess or know — "

"I know that he cares a great deal for her, but Sarah is hardly conscious of its meaning. She likes him, but the cousin being there blinds her a little. How did you come to see such a thing? I did not know your eyes were so sharp."

"It was his tone when he spoke, and his look. I am so glad! What a strange thing that all her improvement should tend to this point! And she is such a sincere believer, such a noble worker, I feel quite shamed beside her. The pupil far exceeds the desultory teacher."

"I think it will be an excellent marriage. They are not the people to hurry Providence, but will go on tranquilly until some day when her eyes will see the truth and tenderness awaiting her. But remember, Kitty, that you have surprised the knowledge."

"Oh, I could never hint such a thing to her. Do not think that poorly of me. But you know" — and he understood the kind of tender amusement in her voice — "that I have been in the midst of a good many love affairs."

"Yes. You deserve credit for the judgment evinced, and I know you will not fail in this."

She was silent for a long time again, wondering, in an innocent, young-girl way, how this great mystery would come to her, — if ever it came at all.

CHAPTER VII.

KATHIE was rather quiet and thoughtful after her visit to Sarah Strong. Was she really idling away too much of her time? She could take up some study, a course of reading, or an accomplishment. She did practise her music, she was very fond of that; and she dropped in now and then among the old friends she had known, who were always delighted to see her. The Morrisons were still at the Lodge, and another baby had been added to the group. She used to talk over old times with grandmother, who was still hearty and cheery. Far-away Ethel and her father were doing well; and, though she realized more truly than ever that she had outgrown some of the girls, there was no need of any abrupt breaking off. As Uncle Robert said, these matters settled themselves.

Mrs. Alston wanted to go to New York, and her brother proposed that they should take a real holiday with Kathie, go up to the city and board for a month or two, shop and see pictures, and attend some operas, as there were several noted singers announced. Hannah would look after the house and Fred, and Jane would be glad to go home for a few weeks, as this was always considered a great treat by the Maybin family.

Kathie's new friends were in despair.

" I don't believe you ever mean to stay at home !" declared Eugene Collamore. " Here we are just getting in nice train for in-door amusements, planning a series of amateur concerts and a Shakespeare reading club, and now away you go."

"But I am only one."

"Every one counts, especially in the winter. Girls, let us try to persuade her."

There was such a very evident admiration in Eugene's glance that Kathie colored with a curious sensation not quite comfortable

"I have expended all my eloquence and all my reasons," answered Lou, "but the stubborn fact remains; and if I had so good an opportunity I should go. Perhaps we will for a week, Kathie; would n't it be jolly?"

"Oh do!" cried Kathie.

"Worse and worse. You set a bad example, Miss Alston, and stir up disaffection. If you could plead duty now, but pure pleasure — "

"Let us seek pleasure while we may," carolled Lou, gayly.

Eugene walked over home with Kathie; they, too, had become great friends.

"Eugene is regularly smitten with Kathie Alston," said Louise, after they had gone. "If they were older, one might wish — "

"But they are too young to wish about. I never saw a girl so innocent of love-making or marrying as she. I don't believe it ever enters her mind."

So they made ready and went to the city. Mrs. Meredith would not hear of their staying at a hotel. She was just settled in her lovely new house, as Mr Meredith decided that now they might safely purchase. It was but a short distance from the Park, and in a very select neighborhood. The furnishing was elegant and artistic, and Mrs. Edward herself a stylish and fascinating woman, with her Paris culture and experience. Her sister-in-law was amazed and a trifle envious. Jessie would never be a purely fashionable leader, — but one clique no longer ruled society: it was the thing now to have a specialty; and Jessie chose hers among the pleasures she really enjoyed. Ada was glad to be drawn into this delightful circle.

Kathie declared they did nothing but go and enjoy. Charlie Darrell was a frequent visitor at his sister's. Dick Grayson and some other student friends found a cordial welcome, and Kathie soon had a train of admirers. It troubled her mother a little at first.

" We shall not always be able to keep her a child," said Uncle Robert, smilingly: " young men will discover her charms."

" But I should be sorry to see her flirting or making a bid for admiration."

" She has little need for that.   And you know, Dora, she has been brought up with boys, as one may say, and is in a certain way used to their attentions. Think how Mr. Meredith and Mr. Langdon treated her two or three years ago, and she never overstepped the bounds of childish pleasure.   We will not trouble her with cautions until we see her on the verge of dangerous paths.   There is nothing so lovely as the entire innocence of a young girl."

" If young men do not mistake it.   The most finished coquettes of the day assume it as their strongest ally."

" There are no counterfeits on base metals," said Uncle Robert, with a pleasant laugh.

Dr. Markham had not lost his olden fondness for his favorite.   She took rides with him, and they had long talks about Ada.

" She has awakened to the true sense of living," said the doctor, " but she is grasping at too much. A man does n't expect to master all the knowledge of a lifetime in a few years. You have to try things, to sift and winnow, to hold fast of some truths not altogether palatable, to let others go that may be charming, but have no real place in your manner of life.   It is the fitness that makes symmetrical characters, not the many bits of knowledge pieced on.   Some time I think she will get things untangled, and realize that of this great mystery, life, we can only have one small piece here.   But she is making a better woman than I ever fancied she would. After all, I think it takes love and mothering to make true girls and women, — and heaven knows she had little enough of that."

"And I had so much," said Kathie, with a thrill of strange, secret joy.

Beside the operas and dinner parties, Kathie went to some quite gay entertainments, where she danced to her heart's content. Weeks flew by rapidly. Gen. Mackenzie was up once on business, armed with entreaties that Mrs. Alston and Kathie would spend the remainder of the winter in Washington.

"Well, why should you not?" asked Uncle Robert. "There is really nothing to confine you at home, and you are not so old as to have lost all zest for society. Ruth would be delighted, I know, and Kathie would have a glimpse of the most important men and women of her own country. Congress will be in session; and so many celebrities seek Washington in the winter to see and be seen."

Kathie was enchanted with the idea, and so the elders laid their plans accordingly. The Collamores were to come up and keep Christmas with some cousins, and they hoped Kathie would stay. There was shopping and dressmaking, and no diminution of enjoyments. Kathie was the same favorite here that she had been in childhood.

"I will tell you what I want to do Christmas morning, Uncle Robert," she said, her eyes softened with emotion. "Let us go to some quiet church for morning service. I want to think of the winter when I was here with Aunt Ruth, while she was being cured. It was so hard to stay away from you all, and somehow she and I both fell into the Slough of Despond, I believe"; and a soft, sad smile played over her face at the remembrance. "But Christmas morning brought great joy to our souls, and I would like to keep the feast reverently, thanking God for all the blessings."

It surprised all her friends that Kathie resisted the grand music and elaborate decorations of the great churches, and went off with Uncle Robert to a plain church to celebrate her festival. They could not understand what it was to her, but Uncle Robert knew by that how little the child's heart had changed, that under all the lightness there were deep soundings to be touched by the greater hand, and to answer in kind.

Eugene Collamore came up Christmas eve to stay over Sunday with his sisters, who were already very much at home at Mrs. Meredith's, and having no end of enjoyment with the young College Clan, as Lou called it. They were nice, jolly fellows, and Eugene had enjoyed Charlie and Dick wonderfully the summer before; but he soon made the discovery that *he* had not come to see the boys, and as for Kathie, one could never get near her any more. When she was talking and laughing with Dick Grayson he was very sure she liked him best, and when Sunday evening they were all singing hymns, as Charlie played on the organ, there came a rapt, heavenly look in their faces that seemed to make them so of one kin, of one mind, that Eugene turned sorrowfully away with a pang he could not fathom, something beyond boyish perception, yet very real and keen.

How often they said, "If Rob were here; if Bruce were here," and called up old and fond memories. Kathie wrote to them both, but she felt that letters were a poor substitute for this delight.

Mrs. Alston went home for a week, and then the party started for Washington, where Aunt Ruth received them with unalloyed gladness. Kathie recalled her first visit to Washington, but oh, how different everything was now! Aunt Ruth was the centre, one might say, of a very charming circle. Her husband's position, her own culture and recent travel, and perhaps the indescribable charm that goes by the name of fascination, filled her rooms with choice friends. She still looked very young, and her slight lameness seemed to give a touch of romance, an excuse for her husband's devotion.

Mrs. Alston awoke to a peculiar interest in it all. The war had not quite dropped out of everybody's mind, for the heroes were still honored, some of them showing scars or betraying the loss of a limb; and with it had developed a wider national life; denizens of other countries came to Washington to study and observe, and foreign ministers and their families added a piquant charm.

" It is almost like being abroad again," said Kathie.

There was this difference, she was regularly in society now. Young people were not long in finding her out. Her freshness and zest, her sunny temper and generous disposition, made her a favorite. Invitations piled up on her little table, and it was quite impossible to attend to them all. Uncle Robert was oftenest her escort; indeed, he seemed never to tire of taking her about and showing her the things she hardly dreamed of in her former visit. They attended congressional debates, and her bright face and interested air caught more than one eye as she looked and listened.

Of parties, dinners, dances, and drives she had a full share. Sometimes her mother became anxious lest she should injure her health or run into some danger. She was forced to admit that her little Kathie was a very attractive girl.

Perhaps it was the fact that Kathie had grown accustomed to a certain degree of approval from her boyish friends as well as the elders that led her to accept attentions with a winning grace quite removed from coquetry. Young men observed that much sentiment or blandishment was lost upon her. She often checked a fulsome compliment by merely raising her eyes to the speaker ; and she kept her delicate manner of reserve about her like a fine foil. It was with her the simplest truth and honesty.

On their return they made a short stay in Baltimore and in Philadelphia. It was quite a disappointment to Kathie that Bruce had not been able to make a flying trip to Washington, but he consoled her with the thought that he might spend a few weeks during the summer at Cedarwood, which would be ever so much pleasanter. While they were in New York, Uncle Robert took a brief journey to Chicago, and found his nephew and namesake giving entire satisfaction in his position.

Some great change had certainly come over gay, laughing, fun-loving Rob Alston. He looked older, with a settled, determined expression, as if he had already begun to fight his battle of life and did not mean to be worsted. He explained to Uncle Robert that he was living very quietly in the suburbs, but the two nights he spent with him at a hotel.

"Rob," his uncle said, "I do not like to see you taking life quite so hard, giving up the useful and innocent pleasures. There is only one youth after all, and if it is spent with a wise economy you lay up pleasant remembrances for middle life. Money is not quite all, my boy."

"I have been a good deal engrossed mastering the intricacies of business. The other will all come in time." And he gave a kind of half-smile, that seemed to lack heart

"You are going on very fast, Mr. Farwell informs me, and have learned more rapidly than any one he has had. It is high praise, Rob, but you must not neglect health, and some of the attainments acquired in the past. I think you do show your close confinement."

"Then I must take a course at a gymnasium, and the fresh spring air will soon tone me up. You are very good to me, Uncle Robert, but you need not be afraid of a great strong fellow like me working too hard."

It was a satisfactory visit in all respects save one. Was there not something kept back, some secret or perplexity?

All he could think of that seemed probable was that Rob had contracted a debt in the past and was working out of it himself, as a penance and a punishment. If so, it was brave and manly, and he would not interfere with the work of conscience. Yet it pained Uncle Robert to leave him toiling on alone, away from old friends, and making no new ones; it seemed unnatural for youth.

It was really delightful to get home once more and settle, Kathie thought.

"Now, mamma," she declared, "we will not have any journeyings or wanderings about in strange places, but just a little bit of home life and home people. It will take me ever so long to get my mind untangled, and know what of the past I want to keep and what I shall throw away, dismiss and forget."

"Then you think there will be some you shall not care to retain?" And her mother smiled. "It is a good thing to have a weeding-out process now and then."

The house was to be cleaned, the garden put in order, and taking up her old interests engrossed Mrs. Alston considerably. Kathie carolled about the place, joyous as a bird, her smile as bright as when in the midst of gayety. Clearly she had not yet been spoiled.

She stood by the open window one morning early in May. Oh, how fresh and fragrant it was with all this dewy sweetness! Birds were singing and darting hither and thither. Yonder a hen was clucking to her brood of downy chicks, and the ducks were swimming about in the lake. How wide and inspiriting after the narrow in-doors of pleasure!

Uncle Robert was sauntering slowly through the walks, surveying some improvements. The young girl tied back her beautiful flowing locks and ran down to him.

"Upon my word, Miss Kathie!" And there was a merry twinkle of affected surprise in his eye.

"You did not think I would be able to rise with the lark

after a winter of dissipation, did you?" she asked, with be-witching archness.

"Why, the lark has been up to heaven's gate and come back to her breakfast," he made answer, humorously.

"I have been almost up to heaven's gate, too"; and a sweet seriousness overspread her face. "I was glancing out over to the mountain, — hill I suppose we ought to say now, — and all the glory of the scene, the peace and brooding tenderness, filled me with gratitude. I have seen so much, Uncle Robert, and yet nothing seems bet-ter to me than Cedarwood, though many things are grander."

"My little girl, I am glad, yes, thankful, that you can enjoy it thus heartily. It seems to me, a true appreciation of what is lofty and great ought never, would never, I should say, lead one to despise smaller phases of beauty and excellence."

"I shouldn't want to dwell among the Alps," Kathie said slowly: "they chill me and leave a kind of awe-some admiration. I do not think either that I would care to live at Rome, among ruins and old palaces and pictures; yet I am very glad to have seen it all, and now I am con-tent and happy to be here and watch these lovely pictures that grow nearer perfection daily."

"So your winter's dissipation has not spoiled you?"

She laughed brightly.

"I do suppose you sometimes thought I might dance away my senses. It *was* lovely, Uncle Robert, enchant-ing." And she gave a graceful *pirouette* on the gravel walk. "Am I queer and changeable? But it is so delightful to be alive, to enjoy everything. How would it feel, I wonder, to be languid and bored, and have no emotions!"

"O Miss Alston!" exclaimed a fresh, young voice; and Eugene Collamore reigned his horse up to the hedge. "Must I wish you joy, or shall you wish me? It's such a rare delight to see you. And I have stolen a march on the girls. They were talking of you last night and will call to-day."

" I shall be glad to see them." And though the words were simply uttered, the earnest eyes she raised gave them meaning.

How beautiful she was, he thought, standing there in the sunshine, the wind blowing lightly among her curls, stirring them so softly they looked like a shower of gold.

" You have had a grand time at Washington, among the magnates and great people and everybody. I wonder if we shall not seem just a little commonplace, uninterest-ing?"

" Why should you not make yourself interesting?" And she glanced up archly. " You must not allow me to pine and waste away with ennui.

" O Miss Kathie, I don't believe you know what ennui is ! "

She surely did not look as if it had depressed her seri-ously. He glanced her all over in a quick eager fashion, even to the dainty feet that still seemed to take dancing steps on the gravel walk.

" No, I do not believe I ever suffered from it. I think it would be extremely ungrateful in me. What a pretty pony! Do you ride much?"

" Now and then of a morning. Fred and I have been taking constitutionals," with a laugh. " What a queer, old-fashioned chap he is ! O Miss Kathie, if you would go out some time ! Wouldn't you trust her to go with me, Mr. Conover?"

" Oh, he trusts me to ride alone," cried Kathie, with innocent grace ; " but I like better to have company."

" Will you go to-morrow, then? The girls nearly always drive in the afternoon."

" I could — " And she glanced at Uncle Robert.

" Of course," he said, consenting rather against his will.

" You must take good care of her."

Eugene promised in a delighted tone, and presently rode slowly away.

Was it best to utter some little word of warning? What could he say to his darling, with her fresh, pure heart, that would not somehow shadow it?

CHAPTER VIII.

KATHIE declared she meant to begin living in real earnest, and practised her music for an hour, then read with Uncle Robert.

"But it seems all for myself," she said. "Ought it not be something wider and better? Why, I used to be such a busy little girl!"

"I think you will find your hands full presently."

Indeed, just after luncheon, Mrs. Alston asked her to attend to some kindly errand for her, and when she returned Fay and Louise Collamore had come; so the girls had a chatty and delightful time, talking over all the happiness. They were very glad to get Kathie back again, and before their visit had ended, Georgie Halford came to insist that she should join the archery club.

No, the days were not likely to hang heavily on her hands. Eugene Collamore began to haunt her like a shadow. Their cousins came from the city for a fortnight, and there were teas, and discussions on needle-work and painting and music.

"If one could only tell just how much of one's life ought to be given to these pleasures," Kathie said to her mother. "It is so lovely to be flitting from one thing to another like a butterfly, enjoying all, and tiring of none. Do I waste my time, mamma?"

"My dear, there is a season of enjoyment as well as study and work. I think your mission just now is to make us all happy; and you do that."

"Thank you," with a fond kiss.

Then the invitations for Lucy Gardiner's marriage were sent out. It was to be in church. Harry Cox had a very nice position in one of the mills, and they were to have their house furnished and ready for living when they came back from their wedding journey. Kathie went over it with Lucy, and pleased the young girl by her ready admiration. It was neat and pretty, some of the furnishing Lucy's own handiwork.

"Kathie," she said, when they had inspected everything, "it is so nice not to have you proud and over-critical. You have seen so many beautiful and costly articles, and you can have almost anything yourself; and if you were going to be married there would be such a time."

"How odd to think of my being married!" And Kathie gave a wondering, incredulous smile. "I don't know after all, it is such a sacred, solemn kind of step, that it seems as if one ought to be grave and serious, and not think only of handsome attire or rich gifts."

"Well, you will have them all yourself, no doubt; but it is lovely in you to praise mine. You see Harry and I are not — not — " and Lucy flushed. "What I mean is, that we shall never be rich or grand, but we can be just as happy. And you will have plenty of other friends; but you won't let them crowd me quite out. We used to have such a good time at school, playing and studying; and you were so kind to us all when you first had your pretty pony carriage; and what lovely, lovely times we had at Cedarwood playing croquet and rowing on the lake. But so many new people have come in, — girls that I shall never know enough about to feel at home with, even if they cared for me, — and, Kathie, don't you think it best to be happy in one's own way? I really don't care for things that I can't enjoy, — well, like Italian songs, for instance. • I would so much rather listen to a pretty English ballad. And I don't know much about pictures or wonderful poems; I am quite sure I couldn't understand them: so I think it is best to keep to things I do understand."

"O Lucy, it is so much wiser and more sensible!" And it seemed as if all of Kathie's old regard for her friend came back. "I do think people often make themselves miserable in striving to be something they do not really enjoy. I am glad you are brave enough not to attempt it."

"Harry and I mean to be real happy in a plain way, and you must drop in and see us, and come to tea; for I think you will never quite forget the old times."

"Indeed I shall not," said Kathie warmly.

She talked the call over with her mother afterward.

"Lucy certainly has the right view of common-sense enjoyment," Mrs. Alston made answer. "I think many of the young girls of to-day do make themselves useless and miserable by attempting the things they cannot achieve; for the one grand life there are so many plain, every-day ones, that require household virtures instead of accomplishments. If one brings out his best, that is the true aim, and an excellence much to be preferred to any second-rate work."

So Lucy's marriage passed off very nicely, and the young couple came home bright and happy and began their new life with as much satisfaction, perhaps more, than many in a broader sphere.

It seemed to Kathie that she lived almost entirely in the lives of her friends. Perhaps it was the result of the lessons she had learned in childhood, — the continual outgiving of herself and the best she had. Her interests were widespread. Every one claimed her. Fay Collamore and Georgie Halford, dissimilar as they were, insisted upon her bringing to each a fond and warm sympathy.

Then Sarah Strong came down for a Saturday. Some letters had passed between them while Kathie was in Washington; but Sarah evinced a high delicacy in regard to Kathie. She was confidential in many things, and yet never dependent. Her trenchant sentences often brought to Kathie a kind of breezy freshness, as of clear mountain air. They never tired or depressed.

She wondered a little if the romance had gone on to fruition. Sarah seldom made any allusion to Mr. Truesdell, and then in the most ordinary way.

She was fresh and bright this morning as she greeted Kathie. Her clear eyes had a curiously limpid look, and a little something about her *was* changed. Kathie guessed, but held her peace.

"We are to have a nice, long day to ourselves," the young hostess said, as she led her up-stairs. "I have announced on the right hand and on the left that I am engaged."

"How good you are to give up all other plans and friends for me !" And Sarah turned toward her with an appreciative smile.

"There is n't much virtue in it when you are really interested yourself," answered Kathie.

"Sometimes it quite puzzles me"—and a dreamy look filled Sarah's eyes—"how it is that you can care, that others care." And a softened inflection marked the words. "If I could give you back a tithe of the pleasure you have given me."

"You have given me back an interest. One does tire of pure pleasures sometimes. I did last winter. I was really glad to get away from the gayeties, the round that never leads anywhere. And yet I enjoyed it. I really am afraid sometimes of growing quite frivolous ; but it has n't taken away my appetite for solid food. When it does I shall have to turn over a new leaf."

She looked so bright and enchanting that she seemed to Sarah, as she had more than once before, a denizen of a different world. Something beside wealth and culture had given her this. What was it? The glad heartsomeness that she put into everything, the truth that seemed better for being uttered in such a winsome voice.

" I should like to go to Washington just once," Sarah
began slowly. " Not for balls or parties, but to see the
capital of the nation, and the men who make and obey
her laws, the foreign ministers who come to us from other
great countries. Did you ever think that seems our widest
and greatest life? Then comes the State centre, then the
family, and it reaches out to every one ; we all have a part
in it, and it belongs to us just as truly as our own lives. I
don't understand how people can become indifferent ; and yet
nations do, and let themselves drop into decay. Individ-
uals do, as well. Little towns and hamlets seem to go to
sleep, and the slumber is dangerous. It is the old story of
the enchanted lands, and the lotus-eaters crying, ' Let
us alone.' "

" I think you could rouse some of them, the near-by
ones," said Kathie. " You make me feel as if I had been
lazy and careless "

" No one will accuse *you* " ; and Sarah colored a little.
" I think you have roused a great many, and what is better, you reach out your hand to lead them over rough
places. So many of them are like me, wandering about
unguided, and needing to be put in the right way. But oh,
there are so many things to see and to hear that I must
not keep the floor, and dream aloud ! "

Kathie thought how Bruce would enjoy a stirring talk
with Sarah. He seemed always to be the one she wanted
to share such things with.

" And now," the visitor said, quietly, " I want to see the
pictures and go on the journey with you. We did not
finish last time, you remember, and that is six months
ago."

" Then we shall have to go to the library." And Kathie
led the way.

Uncle Robert had arranged the photographs and engravings in portfolios, and the girls could sit at their ease
and turn them over as they stood on the low easel. The

7

library had taken on a deeper tone. It seemed to Kathie that everything had changed with her growth and development.

Their first journey with the pictures had been in Paris and Rome. They went through Kathie's Russian experience now, until luncheon was announced. Afterward they took up Scotland; and here Kathie was vivid and enthusiastic.

The day grew warmer and lovelier.

"We ought to go out and enjoy it," Kathie said, presently. "Let us save the others for the next visit, then you will be sure to come again."

"I shall want to come again, often: it is like a bit of fairy-land here; but I would like a walk down around the lake. Do you ever go out rowing now?"

"Not so much," returned Kathie. "You see the boys are grown up and busy or away, and there seem new pleasures. It is archery and lawn-tennis now; and I have a friend who is fond of painting, so we go out together sketching and studying up nature. Now and then Uncle Robert takes a row for exercise. How bright and happy it was!"

They turned into a half-shady path. The sunshine glimmered through the young leaves and sifted golden grains upon the ground until it seemed to quiver, a shining mass. The air was sweet with manifold blossoming, and the soft fragrance of a ripened spring, more delicate and fine than that of summer before the stronger and richer scents are blended.

Sarah put her arm around Kathie's slender figure and drew her nearer with a little pressure. She was hardly as tall, but her ample figure gave her a more matronly air.

"I ought to tell you something," she began, presently. "I want to tell *you* first of all, for it has come partly through you; that is, I should not have been fitted for it, and it would have passed me by. And it seems so strange to have a great and blessed thing come into your life, when you realize how easily you might have missed it, and gone hungering for something all your days, without ever being able to tell just what it was."

There was the faint tremulousness of deep emotion in Sarah's voice.

"You did not think — but how could you? — that —" Then her tone swelled to a certain joyfulness. "Kathie, some one loves me, has chosen me, and will set me in a blessed place. It seems so strange, unreal."

"Mr. Truesdell," said Kathie, softly.

"Oh! did it appear so back to that little visit when you saw him? I never dreamed — how could I? — that any one would ask me to share such a life. I don't think I ever looked on marriage as a thing for myself. I liked teaching, and it seemed quite reasonable to fancy that I should some time get into a larger sphere, go Westward, perhaps, and devote my whole life to the work. I used to talk it over with Mr. Truesdell. He was like you: he could understand and appreciate needs and desires; and so we grew to be friends. He did not come very often, but he used to stop at school now and then; and we took to reading the same authors. He sent me books, too; and he is fond of the same kind of music, — the strong and restful. There is nothing weak about him, Kathie, though he seems so grave and quiet."

"O Sarah! I am so glad for you!" And Kathie kissed her fondly.

"What led you to imagine? It surprises me, for it was only a month ago that he spoke."

"I do not quite know. I think Uncle Robert helped. Something in Mr. Truesdell: a man shows it occasionally; and perhaps men understand quicker, at least about each other. And you love him?" Kathie asked, with a kind of awesome timidity. She had never fallen into the habit of discussing love with other girls, trying on all its emotions beforehand; yet there was a delicate curiosity prompting her now.

"I don't dare to say all that just now," Sarah returned, reverently. "Can any one tell all about it at once? I am in a strange state of content, and ask myself whether I can, whether I dare, take the life. To be a mother to two children, — and yet I love children so, and his are sweet, shy little things. Then that larger life with its duties, — can I have something to give to that, and to him, out of my own small daily resources? Yet I feel that I would rather be with him, if it were a desert or a lonely island, or in trouble and toil, than take anything else, if I can be found worthy."

"It *is* the life for you," Kathie returned earnestly; "and yet you might choose an easier one."

"Do you think so? I wish there was something to give up for his sake. It seems such a large awaiting, such a daily reward for the work, as if he had so much for me, and I not enough for him. Can we live in earnest, and accomplish some heavenly work, — cheer the weary, fainting souls, lift others out of tangled paths and set their feet in a large place? I keep thinking it over. And you believe, Kathie, that I should be justified in taking it?"

A country minister's life, — there would have seemed nothing very large or grand in it to some girls; but Sarah was not looking at the food and raiment, nor the small daily round, — it was the higher life, the communion of saints, the nearness to God in this work, that glorified it for her; just as her single-hearted faith had glorified the work she had done thus far.

"Justified! If he loves you and you love him, ought anything to separate? And why should you not work together, when both are laboring for the same end? Oh, I think you will be happy!"

"I do not suppose God gives us life just for the happiness in it. Isn't it making others happy? When we reduce it to absolute self, we narrow it. God wouldn't have put the whole great world around us if he had meant us to look continually at one object; and this is why Mr. Truesdell's life satisfies me; he can never get it down to one small, objective point: it is always broadening."

Kathie was silent. Had her pupil so far exceeded her? Would she always be ready to take in the great world?

"We are going on just the same until school closes. I believe two or three people imagine it is Cousin Ellen; so you see I do not need to be called into question. And all this time I shall be getting used to the thoughts of my new work."

She did not say her new life. She could not bring it all down to the level of daily existence, as she would by and by, when the marriage was talked about.

They had to retrace their steps, for there was not much time to spare. The new railroad had a station near Middleville, and she was to go in the train. Kathie drove her down to the station, and though there were no ardent, girlish promises, each knew how warm an interest she held in the other's heart.

She was turning her horse slowly when some one spoke.

"Where are you going?" asked Eugene Collamore. "Don't you want to take in a stray?"

"You?" She smiled gravely, for she was in a serious mood.

"Yes, if I dared to invite myself. You and the pony look so tempting and so lonesome."

"Do we look lonesome? Now I thought Hero and I had a peculiarly companionable aspect. But we will take you in."

"Admirable condescension. See what an humble-minded adorer accepting the crumbs the princess flings out to him."

"I did not mean to *fling*, Eugene," she returned quickly, holding herself erect, with a sudden dignity.

"Oh, you know that was pure folly!" And with a laugh he sprang in.

They waited there for a train just coming up. Mr. Darrell drove beside them, and spoke to Kathie.

"I've come for my lad," he said. "I believe he has been studying overmuch again or else he is homesick for the sight of the country."

"Charlie? Has he been ill?" Kathie leaned over; was it the position. or some warmer touch, that flushed her fair cheek?

"No, not ill, only a little used up, and wanting a week's rest. There!"

The train came in, amid smoke and noise. When it had cleared away a little, the procession filed out. Saturday evenings always brought full trains.

Eugene took up the reins. "Wait," said Kathie

Charlie caught sight of her first, and smiled, then came around and held out his hand.

"See what a rival you are to old people, Miss Kathie; but it is the way of the world." And Mr Darrell shrugged his shoulders with a touch of humor.

"I am sorry you are not well," she said earnestly.

"It is nothing much; but I want to come in splendid a month later on, so I thought I would rest up a bit. Now, father. You may look for me to-morrow," he added, as he sprang into the wagon.

Both parties nodded an adieu. They could have taken the same direction, but Eugene turned Hero into one of the new avenues. Kathie made no comment. Already in her mind she had gone back to Sarah. There was a curious connecting link in her mind between the aims of the two; not that such dissimilar souls could ever come together on any but a broad general basis, yet there was the life, the work."

"How deadly solemn you are!" Eugene said presently. "I don't think Darrell looked — well — dangerous."

"It wasn't that —"

"You were thinking of him?"

" Yes, in a way."

Eugene Collamore bit his lip while his face flushed a dull scarlet. Charlie Darrell was very nice, no doubt, but why should he drop down upon them just now, when they were all going on so comfortably?"

"Let me drive you over home," he began earnestly. "The girls will be delighted, and I will bring you back after tea."

"Not to-night, thank you. I have had company all day and I feel now like being lazy and thinking"; and she smiled softly.

Did she mean, to think of Darrell? How pleasant and jolly they had been since Kathie's return, and now something had come to spoil it all. Why could they not have gone on just the same until — until —

"Here we are." And Kathie's voice roused him from his revery.

"Good night," he made answer, huskily.

CHAPTER IX.

It was very comforting to see Kathie's gravely sweet face at church on Sunday, and no Charlie Darrell. Eugene Collamore thought of her all service time; indeed he had thought of her nearly all night.

"There is a picnic for the Mission School and Orphans' Home on the carpet," said some one to Kathie as they all came down the church steps. "I wonder how many of you young girls could be counted on for the supper?"

"Why, any of us," returned Kathie at random; "all of us, I think," correcting herself.

"The committee is to meet after Sunday school: try and be present."

Some one was talking to her mother, so she crossed over to Miss Collamore, and made the announcement to her; and as they turned down the street Eugene took the outside of the walk, and constituted himself Kathie's cavalier.

A young man not to be despised, well grown and well looking, a little darker in tone than either of the girls, straight and manly, with a certain degree of character that spoke in his favor. His father was one of the partners in a very prosperous new mill, and Eugene was an only son, not foolishly brought up in idleness.

As they walked together they were a very pretty young couple; even Uncle Robert thought this.

He, Eugene, was so happy to be beside her, and listen to her bright talk. She was her olden joyous self; and the brilliant day served to clear up the clouds and forebodings of the night. If they could only go on this way until the right time came for a word to settle it all. If there were no other young men.

But the radiant morning did not end so brightly. The girls stayed, of course, to see the committee in the afternoon; and when Eugene sauntered out to meet them, Charlie Darrell had taken possession of Kathie. They were all deeply interested in the picnic. The Orphans' Home, one of the charities that always get merged into the larger asylum, had been undertaken by a kindly and benevolent woman. There were twenty children now. The mission school consisted of the poor that had been gathered in, and their scanty pleasures were of necessity provided by others. Now there was to be a day in the woods, with swings and other simple amusements, winding up with a holiday feast. The elders would take the charge, and do the hardest part of the work, and the young people must come in as assistants. They were willing enough, and talked it over in the interested, eager manner of youth

" It is such a nice plan to have it before one begins with company and all the grown-up pleasures," said Fay Collamore. " We had such a delightful time last year. You had a hand in it, Mr. Darrell. Are you going to stay long enough for this? "

" I think not. I shall have several very busy weeks before my vacation. I only wish I were; but I must get back the last of the week."

" Tuesday of the week after is the day settled upon."

" You must enjoy it for me, though I believe such things are often more work than pleasure. Yet we used to have some nice times in the old days, did we not, Kathie?"

" It will seem quite new to me again. Charlie, you must give me due instructions, so that I shall not make blunders."

They reached the place where paths diverged. The lawn lay in a flood of sunshine, but the porch was cool and shady. Kathie and Charlie turned.

Eugene walked on moodily. The sunshine had all gone out of the day. When they reached their own home, he went to his room and threw himself on his bed, and a flood of impatient, impotent passion swept over him.

Yes, he cared for Kathie Alston, was in love with her, he admitted quite frankly, and with the ready despair of youth felt that if he could not win her, there was nothing but blankness and bitterness left to life. They all liked her. There would be a warm welcome for her, from his father down. And she *seemed* to care for him. They had been such pleasant friends : they had so many tastes and fancies and aims in common ; and they could be so happy. Why should another come in between? What was the other friendship to his love?

" What is the matter, Eugene ? " asked Fay that evening ; " you were so bright this morning, and now you are all out of spirits."

" Am I ? " and he tried to laugh. " I believe I have a little dull headache. I am not very companionable, so I think I will take a stroll out of doors."

There was but one place to stroll, one face that he cared to see. Up the avenue a little way, across the lawn, as near the house as he dared, until he learned where the family were sitting. That was on the wide porch, in the sort of yellow twilight made by the lamp within. He heard her voice, — gay, sweet, contented. Why did she not have some presentiment? Could she not see that he cared, — that it was everything to him?

How foolish ! How could she know until he told her, unless she was a coquette, trying her arts? and that Kathie Alston was not. A word would explain it all, make his longing dream a reality. Why should he not dare his fate — win or lose it all? But oh, he could not lose !

Charlie Darrell was there, and it would be no real pleasure to join them, though, like most of the young people in Brookside, he had grown very fond of dropping in where he was always made welcome. No, he would steal back again and bide his time. To-morrow, perhaps, or some day soon. He could not wait with the great risk of losing.

But Kathie seemed engrossed every day and hour. He haunted the house; she was either at the Darrells' or there were visitors. The two rode out together; and when Eugene caught sight of them, his heart dropped like lead, and a shudder ran over him.

But at last his rival went away, lingering over the second Sunday, and keeping her so engrossed that she had not once called on his sisters. To be sure, there were committees and plans for the picnic, but she need n't spend all the rest of the time at the Darrells'.

Indeed, Charlie, with the languor of semi-indisposition, and his head full of Greek translations, church histories, essays, and poems, to which Kathie must listen and discuss and reason out with him, did claim a good deal of her time. It was such a pleasure to have her there just as she used to be in Jessie's reign, but not sharing her with brother Edward, or have him deciding on her ways and plans.

Yet he said, "What time will you come to-morrow?" or, "Come over in the afternoon, and when we get through with study we will go for a drive, and then I 'll take tea at your house, and we 'll get Uncle Robert to go over the Greek, or judge of the merits of this translation." She slipped so easily into all the arrangements. They were such good comrades, students, friends.

"You quite forget," said his mother, "that Kathie Alston is a charming young lady, and that the young men are all anxious to do her honor. Studious readings and scientific discussions may not have the charm for her that they have for you."

Charlie glanced up suddenly, and though his eyes rested on his mother, his thoughts did not go with them, but beyond.

" Why, mother," he returned, "you must see that Kathie
is different from other girls, and does n't — " There
was a long pause, rather curious to himself, even. " If
she showed in the slightest that any subject wearied her, I
should drop it in a moment. I could n't bore any one."

" You think she *would* show it?" And a sweet, motherly
smile shone in her eyes.

" Kathie is the soul of truth and honor. She would not
assume an interest she did not feel. And she brings such
a fresh, inspiriting vigor; her views are clear and crisp,
and she has a good deal of critical knowledge. Not one
girl in fifty gets such splendid training. I do think,
mother, her soul is the larger for having been so much
with men of the grander stamp. She never seems to think
of her dress and her hair, and if her dimple shows to the
best advantage, or her smiles are properly fascinating. She
enjoys everything so much, and she brings such a zest to
work, finding all the attractive points. She is like a glowing spring morning, and freshens you up in every pulse.
Why, I believe she has put more new ideas in my head
than I should have thought of in a month at the seminary;
and my headaches have quite vanished. As for honoring
her," — and his eyes kindled with pride, — " I have always
done that, and Kathie knows it. If other young men — "

Charlie walked over to the window. He had never considered other young men before. Kathie had in a sense
belonged to them ever since the day so long ago, when
Jessie had taken her and Aunt Ruth out in the sleigh.
They had just grown on and on into youth, keeping the
fine and pure regard untarnished; but other young men
might begin at youth and go on to something warmer than
friendship. A sudden flash of remembrance disclosed a
vivid picture, — Eugene Collamore, in all the frank allure-
ment of a cultured and attractive manhood, sitting in
Kathie's pony carriage and holding the reins, almost
with an air of ownership. It was like a sudden plunge
into an ice-cold river.

He turned with a nervous laugh, and did not meet his mother's wondering eyes.

"Other young men are not born blind, I suppose, and they will see that Kathie is attractive; but the old friends have the strongest hold, I think." And he sauntered out of the room.

He had felt quite certain of returning on Saturday, but he waited until Monday morning. Would young Collamore be likely to attract Kathie? It was a sort of mental problem that had to be solved outside of ordinary rules. There was family and position, and wealth, no doubt, but was the vital, underlying strength sufficiently apparent in his nature to influence a girl like Kathie, who had, as he told his mother, been the companion of men? Uncle Robert certainly was clear eyed: he would not let her fall into a mistake; and Kathie had no need to think of the future in the sense of providing for it. They would not want to give her up at Cedarwood. Yes, she *was* safe for the present.

Yet in less than a week Charlie Darrell had a new and uneasy feeling about her. Never before had the tranquillity of his regard been stirred. He was to finish his studies, to be ordained to his high and sacred calling with Kathie's clear reverent eyes upon him. Farther than that he had never gone; but out on that boundless sea stretched a man's life, with its wants and needs and dreams.

Sometimes a word or an incident changes the whole tenor of a girl's thoughts and carries her swiftly to the shore of womanhood. To a young man accustomed to sisters and real friends among those of his own age, as sudden an awakening may befall,—the time when the friend must be something more, or a new ideal is set in her place. In this instance it was the something more. He said to himself in his tender, poetical way, "Here, by God's grace, is the one soul for me"; and then resolved with an almost awesome reverence to win her for the life here; and what should part them in the life to come? He laid it up with a certain large awaiting, as one of the best gifts of a heavenly Father, — the thing that was almost certain. He would not allow jealousy to creep in and distract him. First, his duty was to be to his God, whose faithful servant he was vowed to his life's end, and then all these things were to be added.

But no such high and pure faith sustained Eugene Colla-more. He had the love and jealousy, the hope and despair, the madness, of a very honest, earnest, first regard. He had not flirted with girls to any extent only in the happy idleness when one gives and takes of the outward sur-roundings rather than the inward heart. And he had passed a very miserable week, losing both appetite and sleep. His mother believed him to be on the verge of illness. The girls were puzzled when they thought of it, but rather busy; and he kept pretty well out of the way.

The picnic party was to meet at the Home, and the children to march in a procession for about a mile, part of the way through the new end of Cedarwood Avenue, to a pretty clearing in the strip of wood that still remained. It was the loveliest of days in early June, and the children were wild with delight. The ladies of the committee and the teachers were to accompany them and spend part of the day in various entertainments. There was to be a simple lunch at noon, and a supper at four, quite in reg-ular order, and the return home shortly after. By a sort of tacit understanding, friends would be welcomed at the close of the feast.

" When we are fagged out and have lost our freshness," appended Georgie Halford.

Some of the mothers came too, with a baby in their arms, pleased to see their little ones made much of, and out on a holiday belonging to their very selves, — not shreds and fragments of some other pleasure. They sang their pretty, joyous carols, they marched in a circle, and then sat down to the abundant table.

The young men began to stroll in presently, — those who could get off for an hour or two. There was some merry jesting and serving, not quite to the manner born ; and some of them awkwardly helped afterward in the clearing-up. The wagon came for the luggage, the children formed again in a procession ; there was a vote of thanks and much cheering, and the day's delight was relegated to remembrance, to be enjoyed over and over again by the little ones.

"There is no use of our strolling through the town like a band of gypsies," said Georgie Halford, who had an admirer at her elbow. " Let us walk down the river road : it will be nearer for all."

"Excellent," declared half a dozen voices.

They paired off. Louise Collamore accepted an escort, and Fay, after a moment's wavering, joined her. Why it was she did not walk with Kathie and Eugene she could hardly tell; an intangible sign of preference in her brother's face and manner as he gathered up Kathie's parasol and pretty straw satchel with its blue ribbons, and slipped her hand through his arm. Somehow they always offered Kathie their choicest.

Eugene loitered behind. Kathie had been very busy and helpful all day, quite like old times, and yet she was as daintily fresh, with no sign of fatigue, as if the day had just begun.

Over on the little winding river the sun twinkled ; out on the lake it lay in a quivering sheet, full of translucent purples and greens, with a shimmer of gold. There was a fragrance in the trees overhead and in the turf under their feet. Here a wood-robin sang, and one over beyond answered. There was such a sense of richness, fulness, and life everywhere, that Kathie drew long breaths of content.

She glanced at Eugene, so unusually quiet, for ordinarily he was of the gay order of young men, always ready

to take his share in amusing and being amused. There
was a little shadow under his eyes, and his face had a
tense, set expression; the laughing lips compressed, the
eyes glancing straight ahead, as if confronting some vision in the glowing yet softened air.

The motion she made, slight as it was, roused him from
his revery. All day he had been dreaming over opportunity, and now it had come, to find him nervous and illy
prepared.

"Engene," she said softly, "something troubles you."

"Yes." His voice was husky, and he made quite a
pretence of clearing it. "Kathie, did you ever suppose —
do you think — any one might be unhappy about you?"

"Unhappy about me?" There was a touch of incredulity in the very sympathetic tone of her voice. "Why
should any one be?" as if not sure the thing was possible.

"But one might be. Can't you understand, Kathie?"
The dream girl of Eugene's love was to respond at a word,
and he seemed to himself, at that moment, like one on a
wide and lonely sea.

"What have I done?" pausing suddenly.

"You have made me love you; love you till I can think
of nothing else; till I long for you day and night, and am
jealous if any one comes near you"; his voice deep with
boyish earnestness, and his face scarlet, his eyes shining
almost to tears.

"Oh!" She faced him and saw all this, then she turned
her eyes toward the rippling water. The robin's song
smote her ear, the summer air seemed harsh upon her
cheek.

"Kathie, I love you so much, so much," lingering over
it as if it were sweet to say. "I know we are both young,
but they, mother and the girls, would be delighted; and
father will take me in the business, so I have something
to offer you. And my whole life, with all its aims, its
truth, its devotion, is yours. We could be so happy!"

It seemed to Kathie at first as if her lips were paralyzed, and would never move again. She shrank a little away, and he saw the motion. Holding out his hands he cried beseechingly, " Kathie, Kathie!" and would have come, would have taken her.

" Don't!" she cried in a piteous tone of regret. O Eugene! why did you care for me so? I thought we were only friends."

" You see it now. You know how, in what manner, I care for you. I shall always care just the same. I will wait. Kathie, you *can* learn to love me. Oh, say you *will* try!"

He seemed to put so much of his soul in the pleading, broken as the sentences were, that Kathie scarcely knew how to answer, bewildered by his evident pain, and a sense of something like remorse that she had so misled him, even innocently.

" Oh," she said, and her voice sounded as if a sob was back of it, " we cannot, ought not try, in such matters. I want to tell just the truth. I do like you very much, and it seemed to me we were pleasant and true friends. I did not mean to lead you to think of me in any other light. I did not dream it was possible."

" You love some one else."

" No, I do not love any one in that way"; and she raised her clear, frank eyes to his. " I do not think I understand just what such a feeling can be. I have never speculated about it"; and her voice sank to a tremulous sadness. " You see, I have been quite a little girl all along."

" Then you will let me wait"; and he raised his head with a joyful manliness, as if he had found a sure place on which to trust his regard. " I won't ask you to be engaged. All shall be as it was before, only — "

Oh, what was she to do? How could she make him understand that she should never want his love? It seemed so cold and cruel.

8

" No, it is better not. Let us try to forget it all. I cannot explain it very well, only I don't want you pained by any waiting in vain. You see I should feel all the time as if I ought to be trying — "

" You might, for my sake ; and if you could not, then — "

" Let us go on " ; and she turned back to the trodden path. " I suppose I have been very wrong somewhere, lead- ing you to love me, when I — "

" No, you have never been wrong." He would not have her blame herself any sooner than he would listen to any other person's censure of her. " You cannot help being the sweetest and dearest and most attractive of girls. Everything you do is just right. I mean one would not have you changed in any way ; and," with some warmth, " do you suppose everybody is going to be blind always? Other people will love you as well as I."

" Oh, I hope not" ; and she shivered. " I do not want any other life for a long while to come. I don't under- stand it. It seems like going out of the safe, pleasant places, and I do not want to go."

That struck home innocently. He turned too, — she was a little ahead of him in the path, — and walked slowly be- side her. For some moments there was silence.

Presently he began :—

" I suppose I blundered about it. I have not made you feel as if I was strong and reliant, and you could trust me for all time. I have not even made you understand how much it was and is to me."

" It is not that." She was crying a little now, just quietly, the tears dropping from her long lashes. " Can't you feel sure, Eugene, that if I wanted any happiness outside of my own home I should be brave enough and true enough to take it when it was offered? And if I wanted it I should know just what it was."

They were silent again. He could not reason it out. Kathie's exceeding honesty blunted his endeavor in some intangible way. He could only think how much he loved her, and wonder why she would not *try* to love him.

They came to the drive leading around the lawn to the house. She held out her hand for her small belongings. He gave them to her, but kept on beside her to the very step.

"Good night." She could not give him any word of comfort that would not be a word of hope as well, yet her heart ached to see him so sad.

"I shall think of you all the time: I cannot help it."

He walked slowly down to the street. She ran up to her own room, threw off her hat, and, dropping on the bed, all her courage seemed to forsake her. She could not even cry. Two or three dry sobs shook her frame, and then she put her hands over her eyes as if to shut out everything. Oh, if Eugene had not made them both miserable!

CHAPTER X.

SHE did not go down when the supper bell rang, for she could not see any one just then. There was a strangely guilty feeling at her heart as the words rang through her ears, "You have made me love you!" What had she done to bring about such a result? They were not on the same terms as — well — Bruce and she, or Charlie and she. It was a mystery she could not fathom.

"Miss Kathie, your uncle sent me up to see if you would not have a cup of tea," said Jane, pausing in the open doorway.

"Where is mamma?"

"Gone out to tea. Mr. Conover is down there all alone, for Freddy is at the Archers'."

"Tell Uncle Robert that I don't want any tea, but that I am coming down to the library presently, when I am a little rested."

For she must have the matter settled. She must know where she had been to blame. She could not go on being sweet and attractive and everything — making people care, and being so surprised if they did. There was a safeguard, an armor, that she must put on.

The lamp was burning low on the centre table as she entered the room, sweet with the dew and honeysuckle, and the breath of roses.

"You have tired yourself out." Uncle Robert crossed the room to meet her, and, sheltering her with his arm, drew her near him, as they both seated themselves on the tête-à-tête.

" No, it is not fatigue." Her voice was not quite steady.

" You are very pale." But as he looked she flushed deeply.

" Uncle Robert, will you tell me just what you consider a coquette?" she asked.

" Why, a woman who tries to win a man's heart, who makes a bid for his admiration, or who leads him to suppose she cares for him when she really does not. I might give you a more critical analysis." And he smiled.

" But if she did *not* try, if she did not even suspect that he cared."

" It has been the misfortune of some very fine and noble women to inspire a regard they could not return. Sometimes a better happening awaited them when the mistake was overlived, and both came to see clearer. But what has put all this into your head?"

" You think it ought not be there. I am more sorry than I can tell that it should have come to me. UncleRobert, I think I ought to tell you or mamma — and she will not be home until quite late, so it must be to you — that some one cares for me, and wanted me to be engaged." Further she could not go, even in her thought.

" Some one? Kathie, when did it happen?"

" A little while ago, — walking home from the picnic "

She hung her head with a child's diffidence, but he noticed her quick-coming breath, her evident agitation.

" Oh, I can guess. Eugene Collamore."

" Do you think, Uncle Robert — "

"My dear Kathie," — he wanted to smile, but he would not have wounded her tender heart for the world, — " do not distress yourself so deeply over it. I am extremely sorry it should have happened ; and Eugene is nothing but a boy with a first fancy. Such things will occur occasionally. What did you say?"

" I was so surprised, and — But I do not love him, and I tried to make him see, to understand. I don't want to marry any one. I don't want any real lovers, but just you."

He pressed her closely to his heart and kissed the dewy lips that were tremulous with nervous excitement. After all, it was a serious matter to her.

"Tell me all about it. What led to such a talk?"

"Nothing. We had fallen behind the others, and he suddenly began. He said I had made him love me, and that he was very unhappy. I like him ever so much, and we have had such pleasant times; but I never tried, because, truly, I never thought about it. He seems to me — like Charlie and Dick and the other boys."

"And he really asked you to be engaged?" To Uncle Robert there was a startling audacity in the young lover.

"Yes. He said they would all be so glad at home; and oh, what will they think of me now?"

"He did not say he had told them?"

"No. But oh, Uncle Robert, I can almost feel now that Fay *does* suspect"; and Kathie's face crimsoned to its utmost capacity. "Will they think I ought to —"

"They will have to think as they please, whether justly or unjustly. Since you do not care about the young man's love, the point is settled. He is too immature to know his own mind for manhood, and at his time of life love is merely ' blind contact,' not the stern necessity of loving. Any sweet, amiable, young girl with whom he was thrown a great deal would attract him."

"I wish it had been some one else," said Kathie with a sigh of regret.

Uncle Robert experienced a sudden check to his reasoning. There *had* been other girls. Georgie Halford, Rose Gordon, and several who had come before Kathie, and who were alike charming.

"My little girl, it is an unfortunate thing, but I hold you absolved from any real intention to lure him on to this step."

"O Uncle Robert," she cried, "you couldn't think *that* of me."

"I have just said I did not," he answered gravely. "Doubtless he believes now that he never can see any charms in another girl, or in the whole world; but he will get over this desperate state, and when he finds you are in earnest he will accept the fact."

"But what must I do? He said, the very last of all, just here at the step, he should think of me all the time."

"You must go on the same as before, or nearly so; and you must not allow yourself to be drawn into too deep a sympathy for his pain. He will suffer, poor lad; and our griefs and disappointments are as hard to bear then as at any later period, for in the after-sorrows we have more wisdom and endurance. I hope he will keep his own counsel. And Kathie, the wisest and finest of women learn to refuse their lovers beforehand, — to show them such a thing could never be."

"But I don't see how, when they do not know themselves what will be said. I hope never again to have any to refuse."

He smiled to himself: she was still a very child at heart.

"Well, the experience has come unsought, and your eyes are opened. I think you will understand it another time, though it may not always save you; and now do not worry. Time is the great rectifier of such mistakes. I cannot have you made ill for the sake of any young man."

"Mamma ought to know?" Kathie uttered it inquiringly.

"Yes; I think I will have a little talk with her first."

"Oh, thank you! Not that I am afraid, only I don't want to talk about it any more: it seems such a puzzle."

"Well, so I think I will dismiss you to bed: that is the best place for tired nerves. Sleep away your trouble, my little darling." And her kissed her tenderly.

He had treated the matter lightly because he did not want to deepen the impression she had already received; but he paced the floor softly now in an unquiet mood. When a man comes to middle life it is difficult to realize that the girl you have petted and tutored and kept free from care is a child no longer. He was a little provoked and a little saddened. The days of change were coming on so swiftly, — days of separation perhaps; days when important decisions must be made on which would hang the happiness of a lifetime. Was she prepared to meet them?

Kathie uttered a reverent prayer and soon fell asleep. The matter had not touched her with any keen, self-abiding pain. She was grieved, — sorry for him; but she had no glimpse of possibilities in it for herself.

As for Eugene, he went home feeling that he had pleaded his cause very badly indeed. He would fain have absented himself from the supper-table, but a certain consciousness forbade it.

"One can't eat after all that feasting," he said carelessly toying with his fork. "I suppose it went off satisfactorily?" nodding to Louise.

"To the children. Poor things, life with them is not a continual holiday; but they have had a grand one to-day. Papa, Mr. Hunsdon came over. He was asking about library stock — whether it was all taken, — and thought he would call and see you some evening."

"I shall be glad to have a talk with him. Hunsdon is a man I would like to get interested. Why, there must have been quite a gathering! I suppose Miss Oldham was as happy as any of her children."

"Indeed she was," returned Fay.

Eugene was glad to have them get off on these subjects, and when they left the table he strolled out on the porch, to nurse his trouble, — despair he would not call it yet. He would wait so patiently. They *were* young, and she said she did not love any one. Then of course she did not care

for Charlie Darrell in that way, either. It was a comfort
to him, and yet —

A long time afterward there was a step beside him
and a soft hand laid on his shoulder. He knew it was Fay,
and he pressed his lips to the tender fingers.

"Eugene!" She stooped and clasped her arms about
his neck with so sweet a sympathy that it brought tears to
his eyes. He had not meant to betray his sorrow to any
one, but it was his first grief and hard to bear. "Kathie,"
she whispered, just under her breath.

"O Fay, don't think me a baby, but I must tell you.
Did you guess I cared for her? No, that is n't the word;
I love her, and I was jealous and miserable, and I
could n't help speaking. But —"

"There is some one else. They have always been together."

"Oh, no, it is not that! She does n't love any one;
she told me so frankly; and she has a curious shrinking
from all these things. That is my great comfort. And I
am glad now that I did speak, for it will stay in her mind.
O Fay, I would wait a lifetime for her!"

Fay kissed him, but her heart was full of sadness.

"She knows we all love her, and that I _do_ mean to
wait. Of course we are both young, and she is so innocent. I believe she does n't really understand. Some
time it will come to her."

"O Eugene, I am afraid —" How could she shatter
his dream? Some womanly prescience seemed to forbid
all hope if Kathie had answered.

"Fay, I think you might find out a little for me; you
see so much of her. You need not really ask her anything,
you know, but girls _can_ judge each other more truly, I
think. And if you could impress her with the certainty
that I should wait always, that I should never love any
one else —"

His tone was so beseeching that it pained her keenly.

If there was anything she *could* learn to comfort him.   It
was that he longed for now ; he was not able to face with
any kind of calm or reasonable judgment the emotions he
took for unchanging verities, and that were in themselves
honest convictions.   Many a love has grown and strengthened on this soil, and become a worthy passion.

"You will *try*, Fay?   And you must go on just as before.   I don't want our nice social times spoiled.   I don't
want any one to feel hard toward her," he explained,
with a lover's loyalty.   "She is n't to blame, you know.
She has been friendly, and all that, not holding out a real
hope, or I should not have asked so soon."

"That puzzles me a little," Fay answered softly.   "If
you saw no hope — "

"You must understand that she was n't thinking about
such a thing, and how could she know I was, until I told
her?   I wanted a chance before she began to care for any
one else ; for she really does n't love any one."

Fay sighed.   She did not feel angry with Kathie, but to
her the case looked quite hopeless ; and she upbraided fate,
not knowing where else to lay the blame, that it should
have tossed Eugene's heart to the feet of a girl who had so
much love on every side that she could hardly esteem it a
treasure.

"I will do my best, but oh, Eugene, if nothing should
come of it ! "

"There must, some time," in a confident tone.

"Children," exclaimed their mother as she sauntered out
on the piazza, "are you not tired?   Fay must be, I know ;
it has been an engrossing day for her.   Louise has already
retired."

It was a gentle reminder, and not unwelcome to Fay.
Eugene was not in a state to be strengthened against his
own wishes.   She breathed a lingering good night and
slipped away.

Kathie wondered the next morning how she should ever

meet any of the Collamores. Fate ordained that she should not be kept long in suspense.

She drove in town with Uncle Robert to visit the library. Just as he was handing her out of the phaeton, Mrs. Collamore and Fay crossed the street.

" Are you going in to inspect the pictures?" inquired the elder lady. " Mr. Collamore told us they were hung yesterday. I am sure we are delighted to meet you." And she smiled winningly.

Kathie flushed with uncomfortable recollections. She felt, by some intuitive process, that Fay knew her secret.

The library building was quite an ornament to Brookside. There was a handsome, wide entrance, and a hall for concerts and lectures on the lower floor, while the library and reading-rooms were above. A very fair collection of books lined the shelves, and the arched windows, with stained-glass borders, gave it a rather antique effect. The long alcoves at either end were fitted up as reading-rooms, the tables filled with magazines and pamphlets, and the arm-chairs standing around with an aspect of ease and leisure.

In one of these alcoves the pictures had been hung. Quite a choice collection of steel engravings and photographs, some fine portraits, and a few oil paintings.

" I suppose you saw so many galleries abroad that this — shall I call it humble effort? — will hardly be a treat," said Mrs. Collamore, addressing Kathie. " I miss the city so much in this respect; still we have the beautiful, ever-varying world without.

" I do not believe my being abroad spoiled me for any true enjoyment," the young girl answered quickly. " And then," with a rather arch smile, " I am not a trained critic : the little things please me as well as the great ones."

" I am glad to have this place started here, and I hope the young people will improve it. I like to have them interested in something above the mere pleasures of youth.

It is laying a foundation for something that you can enjoy in after years, when dancing and lawn-tennis pall."

There was a soft rustle on the stairs and Mrs. Adams joined the party. Mr. Conover came forward to speak to her, and the three elders formed a group. Fay went to view a photograph of statuary, and as Kathie stood alone, her cheeks grew hot and her pulses throbbed with a sense of guiltiness. It was so unusual for them to keep apart, she was afraid Mrs. Collamore would remark it.

Could she go over to Fay? She made an effort, but her very step seemed to protest.

Fay acknowledged her presence with a little inclination of the head, then began to talk in the rapid way people often use to shelter an embarrassment.

"I heard Mrs. Langdon was to send a picture of her very own. When she comes home I am afraid I shall be ashamed of my small efforts ; only," with a nervous laugh, "they interest me and do not bore any one else, as I do not insist upon being admired."

"You will find an admirer in Mrs. Langdon I am sure, and you need never feel afraid."

Then their eyes met. There was a subtle consciousness, that could not be hidden by commonplaces. All the honesty in Kathie's soul rose to the surface. She could not afford to be misjudged. Reaching out, she clasped the soft fingers in hers, and with a tremulous whisper, whose very tone entreated, murmured her plea.

"O Fay, I am so sorry anything should happen when we were such good friends ! Are you angry ? " For Fay's coldness was a new experience. " He told you —"

" He was very unhappy, and sisters can divine changes, and regret — "

" Do you believe, Fay, that I would have won his regard purposely? I never dreamed of such a thing." And Kathie's cheeks glowed while her eyes were humid. "And," timidly, " I should like you to know just how I do feel. I cannot bear to deceive or hold out any false hope — "

" I knew it would be so ; and we all love you so much, Kathie."

There was a mournful half-reproach in the tone.

" I know." The tears overflowed Kathie's eyes now and beaded the long, dark lashes. " That makes it seem so much worse. I want to be true and honest. You would not have me give a half-promise that I could not keep?"

Fay mentally berated herself for being so poor a champion. She was not trying at all. It was a miserable, hopeless case ; and yet Kathie was so sweet. She did covet her for Eugene, for them all.

Kathie wanted to fling her arms around Fay's neck and cry, but she steadied her voice with a great effort

" Since I have given the offence," she said, " you must decide the rest. I should be sorry to make any change, but I know this hurts you as well as Eugene, and if you would like me to keep quite away — "

" No, don't let it make any trouble or break between us "; and Fay seized Kathie's hand. " They would all know something had happened. I think Eugene will get over it, and realize that if you could not love him it was more honorable to say so at first, — only it must be very hard, when you love any one." And Fay's Madonna face was pitifully sympathetic.

" It is very hard to refuse, as well. If it could be unsaid ; and if we were only on the safe ground of friendship, — since I care so much for you all."

Fay began to realize that the pain had not all been on Eugene's side. Kathie had a tender, generous heart; she could even imagine her giving the best of herself to save another pain. With her utmost endeavor she must still be impartial, understand intuitively that a space of this kind could not be bridged over.

" Let us go on as before," she made answer. " I cannot give up my friend, and the explanation would be extremely awkward. No one will understand just what has occurred except Eugene and you and I."

"Thank you," Kathie made answer gratefully.

"Well, young ladies, have you settled the merits and demerits?" asked Mrs. Adams, in her bright, friendly tone. "I think it quite a beginning. Miss Fay, you ought to send one of your flower pieces ; and Miss Kathie does a little in that line. We can afford to encourage native artists, as we have no picture galleries or bric-a-brac shops. And your audiences will be rather plain, uncritical people, who will delight in a rose if it looks like its sister rose in our gardens. Kathie, we have just had a letter from Mr. Langdon. They are in Rome again, but rather homesick. We shall see them back presently." And there was a bit of humorous triumph in her tone.

This monologue gave the girls a chance to recover their equanimity, and the conversation merged into a general talk as they continued their inspection. There were other subjects as well, — the picnic, the Orphans' Home, — and finally Mrs. Adams declared she had spent a most pleasant morning, and must go, begging the girls to come over, as Georgie was complaining of them.

Mrs. Collamore had a little shopping to do, but said Fay might remain if she chose.

Fay preferred to accompany her mother, and remembered an errand or two. They parted cordially, Mrs. Collamore begging that Kathie would not neglect them.

Mr. Conover bowed graciously.

"A rather fortunate *rencontre*," said he. "The sooner one gets over the awkwardness of such an episode the better. You and Fay had an explanation, I fancied. I hope the young man has not made it a family matter."

"Oh, no ! I am not sure but Fay has suspected for some time, — and it would have pleased her so," with a bright blush. "But I am very sorry. It is so hard to justify one's self."

"Do not discuss it any more than you can possibly help. I hope Eugene will use a little common-sense in the matter."

"But it is very hard for him."

"Be careful of too much pity, my little girl, if you do not intend to love."

It seemed to Kathie that the sky, heretofore so sunny and enchanting, was being dimmed by shadows.

CHAPTER XI.

EUGENE COLLAMORE was too manly to carry his heart on his sleeve. He knew that would not be the way to win Kathie's respect, — and win her he meant to do. In spite of Fay's gentle admonition, he would not admit discouragement, only delay; and, though both were rather embarrassed at their first meeting, they were too well-bred to suggest by any marked conduct that a secret was in their keeping.

As the season went on, gayeties increased. Georgie Halford took the lead in pleasures and was quite a belle.

Then the word came that Mrs. Meredith had a little daughter. Charlie was very enthusiastic, and Kathie took a trip to the city to shop a little, and be present at the christening. They had so many plans to settle. Everybody was coming home, — Brookside always stood for that, — Gen. Mackenzie and Aunt Ruth; and Bruce had applied for leave of absence; and the Langdons.

"And if we could have Rob, and Fred Lauriston," said Charlie, "the circle would be complete."

"We shall try hard for Rob," declared Kathie.

Some curious change had come over Charlie Darrell. The outer garment of boyishness had dropped off, and he was a man, gentle, deferent, and protecting, but with a strength that seemed to raise him to a finer height. At first it gave Kathie a little feeling of awe, then a touch of fascination.

One evening, as they were sitting together, she spoke of it. He smiled, while a bright tenderness irradiated his face.

"The old evolution, Kathie, that St Paul experienced among his many transitions. ' When I became a man, I put away ' or slipped out of childish things, — the unreasoning faiths, hopes, beliefs. Something stronger and higher comes to take their place. And when a man has chosen from all the great aims of the world that of a work for God and his fellow-men it does bring with it a more reverent seriousness. A true life of faith and service must make itself felt : the sincere desire to help, even if it be only in one little corner, cannot but ennoble any soul ; and I must try to do my part, not merely taking up what comes to me, but going out to find it."

"It troubles me sometimes" ; and Kathie glanced up in perplexity. "There is so much living without any direct aim, any appearance of being in earnest. How can we always remember ? And how much is to go to daily matters and pleasures ? "

His pulses stirred at the sight of the sweet, questioning eyes. Would it be his delight as the years went on to direct them ?

"There are so many phases of spiritual and material life that seem to clash, that fail to accord with our best thought of it ; and yet God is working through it all ; and as he sifts and winnows it, the golden grains shine out. Even when we do not stop to gather them, they are there, and God builds slowly with them. If we could remember that religion was the complete whole, the sum of life, instead of detached fragments, not to be garnered up in one season. We can give always without any lack ; and he accepts the least, the cup of cold water, in his name."

"You will bring great comfort," she said slowly, wondering how much she might take to herself. "Good tidings of great joy."

"As if all religion is not this, — a great joy here amid all the sorrows and perplexities, but the greatest of all in the other country, where all the mistakes are set straight,

9

all the tangles smoothed out. I think I like best St. John's portion, the religion of peace and comfort, and it shall be my highest endeavor to bring it to the worn and weary."

"I wish you and Sarah Strong knew each other real well," said Kathie: "you are both so in earnest; you both see so many things to do. It will be 'living in the midst.'"

"And you are not to be crowded out," he replied, with a sudden heart beat.

She sighed softly, yet it had no wider meaning than the very words : she was not searching for possibilities.

But to him it seemed very certain. While she waited all unknowingly the future was shaping itself about her. There was the stir and unrest of the transition period, like the quickening breezes of spring that shake wildly about all the early fragrances and leave them to settle later in summer sweetness. When she understood she would take it up reverently, gladly, just as she had accepted the truths of childhood and translated them into larger language.

He remembered with a thrill one thing she had said, — that he had changed. The few words uttered by his mother in that brief visit home, though with no direct reference to this result, had lain and brooded in his soul until crystallized into definite shape. Every day he was coming nearer the measure of a man, the self-knowledge of needs and capacities. He had never lived any part of life alone, but grown up in the centre of a family, with all the assistance and comfort of tenderest home life broadened by the most generous outlook. It was natural to imagine the years going on to the new centre, — dearest of all with the other soul in it. He was too refined and too reserved to give it any new name at present, but he lingered over it with the luxury of a gardener tending some strange and choice plant. It had absolutely nothing to do with passion ; and there was no touch of jealousy, no fear of loss, and no unrest.

By this new knowledge of himself he judged her. He put away the sweet, frank unconsciousness of boy-and-girl friendship, when a caress counts for nothing but the outcome of youthful gladness. She, too, was putting away unknowingly many little things. He had seen it all through the visit, — the fine sense of self-appropriation that dawns with womanhood; the intangible reserve of one's self, holding the sweetness folded instead of scattering it about. He had never remarked these fine and rare delicacies in her before, and took it for a sure sign. Not knowing the other episode, he interpreted the subtle change to mean what was simplest and most easily understood by his own soul.

" It was such a restful visit," Kathie said afterward to her mother. " There was no company and little going out, except delightful walks with Charlie ; and he is so serene. Carlyle, you know, bids people be thankful who have found their work ; and he has truly. It seems such a grand thing to have such aims constantly before one. As Grandma Darrell says, he does appear ' set apart.'"

" Yes."

There was a soft, motherly sigh as Mrs. Alston studied her daughter. This tranquil young life had always touched her with a jealous nearness, — a kind of coveting, as if she longed to take it in with her own rather turbulent boy. It might come in another way, — a sonship and kinship, dear almost as that of birth.

" I think it the noblest of all callings ; and he is peculiarly fitted for it. Being in the fold is the very heart and centre of the work for God and man ; and if one is heavenly minded there can be no conflicts. It is an every-day preparation for the other world," she continued.

A rift of softened light fluttered over Kathie's face like a cloud at daybreak.

" I can't imagine Charlie anything else, unless he were an artist like the old ones whose memory is kept sacred abroad, who painted Christs and Madonnas because their faith and fervor were so real: they never thought of money or fame."

"A letter for you"; and Uncle Robert entered the room.

It was from Sarah. She and Kathie were frequent correspondents in these days. The engagement was not declared as yet, though the marriage was to be early in September.

"It does n't seem quite true and honest to shelter myself under Cousin Ellen's wing," wrote Sarah; "but it does spare us both the comments and gossip of this small place. It is true that among the women here some one might be better fitted for the position; but after seeing and knowing them, he has chosen me. And why then should I shrink from accepting his love and his life, if I do it reverently, resolving with God's help to do the best I can? But it is the old, old story, — the pulling down instead of building up, the thrusting out instead of gathering in. I realize that Mr. Truesdell will be pitied for not looking higher, and that I shall be treated with a distant toleration, — as if I had climbed a social fence and entered a field in which I had no right. There will be plenty of work to do in the church as well as out. I wonder why religion must put on the garb of ungraciousness, for many of these people are really striving to do right in most things. I am afraid too often we make our own religion, instead of taking that of our Saviour. Can I live down the little stings, keep patient and serene, for his sake, and let my life show the manner of soul that is in me?

"This train of thought came from a disagreeable comment that was made about Mr. Truesdell marrying Cousin Ellen. And he asked me then if I would rather go to some other place and begin my life with him among strangers. It was very kind in him to give me a choice, was it not? What would you have answered?

"I thought of the time so long ago when the girls

laughed at mother, and you stood by your colors. If you had not taken me in hand I should not have been fit for this place, and no voice might ever have said, ' Friend, come up higher.' Perhaps there was some pride in it, and a touch of belligerency that took away the sense of being hurt and made me brave.

" ' We will stay here,' I answered, ' until you consider your work done. Since you want me in your life we will not worry about what other people think ought to be in it.'

" He smiled, and I think he was greatly pleased. ' A man of my habit and temperament,' said he, ' seldom takes a step like this without consideration, though I believe ministers' marriages always provoke criticism. I want your freshness and vigor and strength ; and the comfort of your love is like a late blossoming to my shady life. Yet even you might do better. When you are in the prime of life I shall be an elderly man. Never think there has been any sacrifice on my part. For myself, I believe what God has equalized in heart and soul and brain can never be subject to petty social distinctions ; but I want you to be happy.'

" And I am happy. There must always be a between and a higher round. But it seems so narrow and cruel to desire to crowd out your neighbors. O Kathie, are people always fighting their way up ? When will they be made welcome to a broad and generous level ? Do we not truly belong to the heights we can reach ? If so, no one has a right to pull us down.

" I think all this has brought us nearer. There must always be a solemn awe to a great and unexpected love ; but I am learning of how much service I can really be to Mr. Truesdell. I am so thankful for my health and energy, and the many things I have learned ; and I shall stand on one of the ' betweens ' with him and stretch out my hands to any one who will come. I have learned this one lesson never to forget."

Kathie read most of the letter aloud.

"I think it quite too bad and foolish!" cried Kathie indignantly. "Sarah is really well educated, and a good musician. In many places she would be a noticeable girl; and I do not believe many women in Middleville are better fitted for a clergyman's wife. It seems very unjust to be compelled to make a fight for respect when one is so worthy of it."

Mrs. Alston smiled a little. "No doubt there is some jealousy among those who do account themselves worthy of the position," said she. "A minister choosing out of his own congregation seldom fails to stir up strife and envy."

"Mamma, do you not think it very unworthy of women? Could they thrust another out and put themselves in? What would become of the preference of love? And Sarah *is* liked ever so much. You would be surprised at the nice invitations she receives. And the Strongs do live picturesquely pretty. The children are growing up quiet, and have nice manners, and Mrs. Strong's odd phrases and disregard of grammar have a quaint sound. She tries to please Sarah, too, only she never will be able to understand the harmony of colors" And a mirthful smile crossed Kathie's face.

"I think Sarah will conquer all opposition as time goes on. Mr. Truesdell is a brave man to take what he wants, deliberately, and let others see the suitableness at their pleasure. I am glad they have decided to remain and live down silly prejudices, though it seems to me he might have a more congenial place. Uncle Robert thinks him a very earnest and scholarly man. I almost wonder at his settling in such a little country village."

"His wife had just died, and I suppose he was full of trouble and grief. Then, mamma, the parsonage is a pretty old house, almost like an English picture, with a garden full of roses, and a great oak-tree right at the gate.

Sarah will make lovely living there, I know. I really long to see her its mistress."

Indeed, Kathie was so interested in the new phase of affairs that she drove up to school one afternoon and took Sarah out for a regular girl's confidence. Middleville was at its best estate. Farm and meadow lands were filled with promising crops, belts of woodland stood up straight and tall in their mingled shades of green, and the distant range of hills told of suggestive hollows and nooks of dreamy glory. The faded houses and barns were mellowed by shadowy lines and changing reflections, and occasionally through an open doorway one saw a bit of interior with the homely charm artists love.

Sarah was bright and joyous, though the day's teaching had not been all smooth sailing; but her vitality had the force of perfect health, and her employment that of satisfaction.

"How delightful of you to come!" she cried. "I am nearly always thinking of you, but I try to remember your many claims, knowing that you cannot divide and subdivide yourself, so the farthest must be content with an occasional ray."

Kathie studied the uplifted face with its clear, blue eyes, the masses of hair framing it in like an aureola, soft, shining, waving in loose, irregular lines upon the white forehead. Not a common face, even if it lacked the elements of beauty; for it had been glorified by the secret of true living, the companionship of broad and generous resolve, taking each day in a firm grasp and extracting whatever sweetness it held, with no fear that there would be a lack to-morrow.

"How happy you are!" Kathie exclaimed, impulsively.

"Yes, I am," with a confident and grateful ring to her voice. "And yet," smilingly, "did n't I write you a lugubrious letter? I was afraid afterward that you might think me weak to cry out at the first thorn that pricked."

"It is a pity, it is unjust, that there should be thorns of that kind," was the firm rejoinder.

"Yet the thorns may be set as a sign to make one go more carefully. I used to think at first that his life and happiness," with a tender inflection in her tone, "were the great things I had to consider. You see it seemed wonderful that he should want me, — that he thought me fit for the great highway where he was to walk. When you stand on the top of one peak and look over to the next, the glory touches you, kindles your love and fervor, and you realize that it is going down and coming up again ; and there are so many things to take hold of as you go, — blossoms and leaves and gems, maybe, to gather up, — and stumbles, and a little roughness, thorns perhaps, but all the time it *is* going on ; and you never do lose sight of the other great glory, towards which you are pressing. If there were no valleys, there would be no mountain-tops ; and could we always endure the level of the plain?"

"You are not afraid of the thorns now?" Kathie asked quickly.

"I shall be careful of them, but I am trying not to be afraid, nor to run into them heedlessly. We all know Mr. Truesdell might have paid more deference to position. I was born here, and ran about an ignorant country girl ; but when one fits one's self for something better, and it comes, why should one refuse it? Why should others seek to thrust you out of what you have won?" and her face flushed with emotion. "When he first asked me, I was surprised and overwhelmed with a strange humility ; and then I think some one might have pushed me aside for very fear. Then he showed me what I had to give, — health, energy, and spirit, help everywhere, at home, with the children, keeping a comfortable and restful place. That was partly your teaching. All the days will not be Sundays, even if we are doing God's work. He put the six days between, the six days of trying and the one of rest."

"O Sarah, you have gone far beyond anything I ever taught you!" cried Kathie in all humility.

"With two such teachers I ought to come to comprehensive knowledge"; and she smiled with rare sweetness. "At first I felt quite inclined to glorify my — Mr. Truesdell. I had never counted on marriage, or speculated about love, so it was very new and strange. It is odd to be asked to stop and rest when one has mapped out one's life as a continual march; not that we shall loiter very much," smilingly, "but we shall be among the wells of water and the trees of palm; and we have come to this freedom between us, — he is to tell me when I go wrong, when I do little things that might hurt or jar, and I am not to be troubled about what others say. I shall have his great love and the comfort he will take for my reward. I shall not go out to meet cares or phantoms, but stay in safe paths with him."

That was the entire faith of love. How could one be sure of the safe paths?

There was a slight bend in the road, and they came out by the parsonage. The little girls were playing tea under a great rose-bush.

"O Kathie," Sarah began, "I wonder if I shall always be just to the children and not try to crowd them out of their father's heart: they were there before I was."

"But you *do* love children, and you have been with them all your life."

"Yes, I could not teach if I did not love them, for children are often very trying; and some really good women fail of being good step-mothers. I wonder why? If we take anything else on conditional terms we try to respect the terms. So you see there will be many things to study, and claims to balance within as well as without. They are shy little things, and have never been to school. Their mother was delicate and refined, and I fancy rather proud of position, and all that. It is a pretty old house, is it not?

and yet it has always seemed a sad place to me, perhaps because I have always connected it with two motherless children. O Kathie, I wonder if I can win them to love me : step-mothers are always looked upon with disfavor ; and they are old enough to know.".

" Love you? They could not help it," cried Kathie, eagerly ; and as she looked at the earnest, glowing face, she felt if she ever needed some one strong and comforting in any great perplexity Sarah would be that friend.

" You are so generous : do you think me weak with the weakest?" and she gave a bright little laugh. " I shall tire you of myself and love ; but one comfort is that it is new to every one, just as is the dawn, though we see it every day."

" You could not tire me with anything you might say ; and I am so glad to have you happy. Yet when it comes to one's own self, what a solemn thing it seems, to say what can never be unsaid. If one *should* make a mis- take."

She let her thoughts revert a moment to Eugene Colla- more. No ; centuries of waiting could not make love on her part.

"I suppose one who realizes all the solemnity must have some fear and questioning at first ; but soul answers to soul. You could not receive an unwelcome or inhar- monious guest. It is the peace and the satisfaction that determines whether it rightly belongs to you. And when it comes to you I think you will know. You have been the dearest of friends and confidantes."

They talked a little of other matters and then lapsed into contented silence, just glancing and smiling at some lovely view, or a bit of bird song that broke the stillness. And all this had come from one small deed of kindliness : the drawing in instead of the crowding out. Why was she not doing something now, instead of idling away her days in pleasure? Then she thought of Charlie, and longed

for him with that curious sense of loneliness that sometimes
pervades the soul.

They said good by at length, and Kathie turned homeward. For days afterward she was haunted by a tender
gravity, far removed from sadness, yet it seemed to bring
her nearer to all who came in contact with her.

CHAPTER XII.

THE lovely summer day was on the wane. Lengthening shadows, a waft of cooler air, the long-cadenced song of a homeward bird, the tremulous, infrequent chirp of a hidden insect muffled in turfy fragrance were suggestions of coming evening. A perfect day, Charlie Darrell had said a dozen times.

He and Kathie had been spending it together. In the morning there had been a lovely drive; then after dinner she had swung in a hammock in a shady place, while he, stretched on the grass, recounted the last days of study, the examinations, parting with friends, and the sanguine plans of youth.

"I always tell you everything," he declared laughingly. "I wonder how I managed to exist while you were away! My remembrance of it is as a long, lonesome time."

"Thank you," gayly.

Kathie had been letting herself be quite free and joyous this day. For several weeks she had been on guard every moment, for she saw that, although Eugene Collamore held himself bravely, the fire still burned. He tried to be the same to others and chaffed gayly with Georgie Halford; but when his eyes turned to her, waiting and hoping were written in them.

A few days before he had started for Canada on some business for his father, accompanied by Fay. Louise had taken a new whim, — archæological studies with Mr. Hunsdon. Jessie and the children had come down for the two summer months. Mr. and Mrs. Langdon would be home in August, and Aunt Ruth also.

" We will not plan to go anywhere," said Kathie to her
mother. " I want a lovely old-time summer at home."

" We must write for Rob," Charlie had declared.
" What is he about? It is always business when he vouch-
safes a brief note to me."

" Poor Rob ! " Kathie had answered with a sigh, though
why, she could not have told, as the accounts were all to
his credit.

The letter was sent, and this day the work seemed all
done. They had ended their afternoon with a row on the
shady side of the lake, that dropped presently into a leisurely floating. They sang old songs, said over half-for-
gotten poems, and drifted into a subtle, mysterious sympathy. Kathie let herself rest in pure enjoyment : it was so
good to be at peace.

And now they sauntered up the lawn, she carrying her
hat full of fragrant pond lilies, and Charlie holding her
blue-lined parasol over her, that seemed to make a bit of
azure sky. Mrs. Alston watched them, — so young, so
pure, and sweet, and a vague desire ended in a soft sigh.

Charlie waved his hand gallantly.

" Come, truants," she said tenderly : " supper is waiting,
and I am all alone."

" Where are Uncle Rob and Freddy ? "

" They have driven over to Deerfield, and will not be
home to tea ; and I have heard from Rob, — he is almost
sure to be here early in August."

" Oh, how delightful ! " and Kathie's eyes sparkled.
" It will be quite like the old summer. Now if we can
hear from Aunt Ruth and Bruce."

" History repeating itself," rejoined Charlie ; and yet
would there be any days as perfect as this?

" Run up to Fred's room, for of course we cannot dis-
pense with you," said Mrs. Alston laughingly.

He was so much at home here, and " over at the Darrells' " was a second home to Kathie.

She soon returned, looking cool and sweet in her fresh, white dress.

"Come down here," said Mrs. Alston to Charlie; "let us be sociable, if we are few."

"How queer it seems to have such a small family! I shall be all impatience until the rest come. I suppose Bruce has changed."

"I am not to be crowded out of my place," interrupted Charlie; "mine is the oldest right."

"As if we could forget that!" Kathie turned her soft, clear eyes full upon him, and he felt a rift of color mount his brow.

Afterward they went out on the wide porch, while the summer twilight faded, and the moon came up amid her golden host. They sang two or three old hymns; they touched upon past memories, from whose simple beginnings so much had grown, drawing them nearer in the touches of sympathy and tender joy.

Somewhere along that mysterious kinship Mrs. Alston said "son." All boys were dear to her through her own; but Charlie Darrell especially.

It was not the first time she had called him that, but it came with a new and deep meaning. All day the soft light had moved and stirred his soul, until creation, new living, manifested itself to his thought a tender presence. He reached over and caught her hand.

"Mother," in the full, deep tone of a great emotion, "why should it not be? Will you give me the real right in the days to come? I have always loved Kathie; she is the other part of my new life, its completeness. I had not meant to ask so soon; but now, — now I cannot wait. I want to feel certain of my place in your midst. Kathie! Kathie!"

She sat as one in a dream. "The other part of his life, its completeness." She felt it in some mysterious way, as one may have visions of second sight.

"Kathie!" He drew her gently to his heart, and she felt it beat; his pure, ardent lips kissed the consciousness of his love into her soul. Was this what the happy day had presaged? She did not shrink from his tenderness: it seemed natural, right.

"She loves me; do you not, my darling? I think we have always loved each other; so there is no strange suddenness to make us doubt or question. You will keep her for me, mother, safe and sweet, like a cloistered nun, until we can begin our own life together. God knows how tender and careful I shall be of her, — how we shall go on our way doing his work all the better that he has given us so much; and, as he trusts us first of all with the best and choicest of human gifts, love, so we must work to win on every side love for him."

All the tenderness of Kathie Alston's soul seemed to culminate in the high tide that drifted her toward him. She was not thinking of time nor place. That there was anything singular in this confidence before her mother, first of all, never occurred to her. This was not a miser's treasure to gloat over in her secret soul, but something to be shared; something she could share, and was glad so to do.

"You give her to me?"

He took Kathie's hand in his and laid both, clasped, in Mrs. Alston's lap.

"She must give herself, Charlie; I can only ratify with a mother's love. There is no one with whom I would sooner trust her. Kathie, my darling?" in a soft, persuasive tone.

Did she love him? Honestly she thought so. There was no shrinking or reluctance. The life by his side looked so safe, so useful. There would be no perplexing questions of duty, — how much for God; how much for the world. She was in a curious state of exaltation, — the emotion that makes one heroic in deed; and yet she felt

exceedingly humble, — it was so great and sacred a thing
to her.

"O mamma, if I could be good enough!"

"The little violet!" Charlie laughed in that happy,
incredulous gladness. "You *are* good, Kathie; you
always were, — better than the lot of us, way back at
school. I think no one could ever be quite good enough
for you, when it comes to that, but I shall always try, God
helping me, to be grateful for this, his choicest gift. Let
this be our betrothal, under the solemn stars." And his
reverent tone was tremulous with happiness.

There was a silence of many moments, the three hands
clasped softly together. Presently he said, —

"I am glad it has come about in just this way. I have
been thinking of it for some time, but I had not meant
to speak so soon. I have another year before ordination,
and then I must find a home for my bonnie birdie; so it
must be quite a long engagement. But you know it all,
mother: we have no secrets from you."

"I could not give up my darling on a sudden notice,"
replied Mrs. Alston, kissing Kathie with all the fervor
of a mother's love. "I am glad to have it a long engagement: you are both so young; and time will bring you
wisdom to make the life what it should be. I think it
best — " And she hesitated a moment.

"Whatever you think best we shall do," Charlie said
with tender deference.

"I think it would be better for both of you not to make
any public announcement before another year: you have
your studies, Kathie has her home duties and young friends;
and the tendency nowadays is to leave lovers very much
to themselves. Let me have her yet this year."

"We will lock our secret in your safe keeping," he answered with a trustful inflection of tone; "and we will go
on just the same as before. We have always been such
friends that no one will question. And as I shall be away

another year, I should not want my darling embarrassed by the teasing of careless tongues. It serves to make it more sacred : just our own blessed knowledge."

The sound of wheels came crunching up the garden walk. Fred's soft voice sounded in a gay little laugh.

Mrs. Alston rose. They all came back from that enchanting love-land, and the summer night was the more beautiful for their sojourn.

" Have you had supper?"

" What! at this time of night, mother mine? Why, I should have been brought home a victim in my youth and bloom if I had not been duly fed. What a small conclave ! Why are not the neighbors sitting round? The porch looks lonesome, melancholy."

" If they came you would run away," said Kathie, brightly. " But you don't know the most joyful of all, — Rob will be home in August."

" Have you heard?" There was such a sense of relief in Uncle Robert's tone.

From this bit of news they dropped into general conversation. Charlie was in no mood for ordinary talk. A sweet, sacred spell enveloped him as a cloud ; he wanted to dream over his great happiness in solitude. He rose presently and wished them a quiet good-night. Kathie rose too ; was it the beginning of a new influence? She had often walked down to the gate with the boys, but now every pulse quivered with unwonted emotion.

" O my darling ! Can I ever thank God sufficiently for this great happiness?"

" You are quite sure I shall make you happy?"

She could not consider herself in this rush of tumultuous emotion. Indeed, when she came to think of it long afterward, she learned that she had not considered herself at all.

" Sure ! O Kathie !"

The gentle reproach pained her and settled her faith. She would never doubt again.

10

"We may not always desire what is best for us, but in this matter I think a man understands the blessedness of getting what he does want. There is nothing more for me to ask. Good night. God and his angels have you in their keeping."

When she entered the library, whither her mother and Uncle Robert had gone, there was a blessed content in her face.

"She is very happy," thought the mother, and was for herself entirely satisfied. Doubt and anxiety were over, and she would keep her darling a while longer.

Kathie could not sleep; yet it was no nervous restlessness that haunted her pillow. She lay quiet and serene, wondering that so great a question should be so simply decided. So brief a while ago she had shrunk from Eugene Collamore's pleading and declared that she wanted no change, and now for her the current of life had turned, still without any positive desire on her part. It must be the right thing, or God would not have allowed it to come in this way. A noble and serious life lay before her, with companion, friend, and guide, in the heavenly walk.

But she slept soundly and late the next morning as the result of her unwonted vigil. After breakfast, when they were alone, Mrs. Alston informed her brother of the engagement.

He was glancing idly out of the window, and for the moment felt strangely disconcerted.

"You surely do not disapprove?" rendered a trifle uneasy by his silence.

"I am surprised: Kathie appeared so utterly ignorant of love a few weeks ago."

"But it seems to me the most natural thing in the world," replied the mother, with some warmth: "they have always loved each other."

"And yet engagements rarely grow out of that kind of love."

"It is best and safest, much to be preferred to these hot-headed, imperious, exhaustive passions, that spend themselves in courtship, and make a barren waste of after-life. They have grown into it; and when the full time came it declared itself. O Robert, it is such a comfort to give her to some one you can trust thoroughly, — our dear, darling child! To see Kathie unhappy would break my heart."

"My dear Dora, Kathie's happiness is all I ask; and the lover is suitable in every way; but it seems sudden."

"It is hardly to be called an engagement this year. I could not have Kathie exposed to foolish girl-gossip; and Charlie quite agreed with me. Another year, when he is ordained, there will be a regular engagement; but I am to have her two years longer.

"I really could not think of her marrying just yet."

"We shall not have to think about it, or to worry over possible lovers. She will be of suitable age, and will have had a pleasant, happy girlhood; and, although I am not mercenary, I am glad Charlie will never be entirely dependent on his salary. Grandmother Darrell's will is made in his favor." And she paused with a slight flush.

"Yes, I think it is hard to accustom a girl to all the comforts and refinements of one station and then plunge her into a life of poverty and hardship; still, it has always been my intention to make some provision for Kathie, if it was needed. She should have had an unbiassed choice."

"You are so good and generous, Robert," she answered. deeply moved. "But I want you to feel quite satisfied"; lingering on the last word.

"I hate to think any one has a claim on my little girl. I am a selfish old fellow after all," he made answer, with a half-petulant shrug of the shoulders.

"It would come some time: marriage and a home *is* a woman's best and highest destiny, her most satisfying life;

and we do keep her a while. Could we trust any stranger as unhesitatingly as Charlie Darrell?"

"So that she is happy, my prayer will be answered," he replied gravely.

"There is every prospect of it."

He turned to leave the room, then paused.

"If you are writing to Ruth to-day, just mention it," he said abruptly; "but with that exception we will not let it go beyond family walls."

Was he annoyed? Mrs. Alston wondered. Men often hated to give up their daughters, and — Kathie was like a daughter to Uncle Robert. It might be that feeling of tender love that held him from welcoming any new tie. And yet she wanted him to rejoice in it as she did.

When Kathie came down-stairs eager and smiling, the faint misgivings she had been nursing vanished; so she poured out her full heart in the letter to Aunt Ruth, and felt in some degree satisfied. Surely no one could have Kathie's welfare more at heart, or dread a mistake more deeply than her mother.

Certainly the lover proved himself no laggard. Uncle Robert bethought himself of an errand as he walked out to the stable, and resolved to set about it instantly. He could not meet Kathie just yet, with her new happiness shining in her sweet face, so he ordered the horses and drove away to settle his mind to the fact.

He had not gone far when a pleasant voice called to him, and Charlie Darrell stood in his very path.

"Good morning"; and there was a flush of conscious pride on the fair young face. "I was coming over to see you. May I get in? I have something important to say."

He could not run away from it. Charlie Darrell's eager, pleading eyes would have disarmed a harder heart.

"Yes." And the young man sprang in, too happy to notice if the invitation lacked its usual fine cordiality.

But he was very much in earnest, and stated his case

in a manner at once manly and generous. He would not even ask for an engagement at present, but he could not go on a day without confessing his desire and resolve; his entire assurance that they loved each other.

What was there to do but consent? He made a few stipulations, feeling in his heart that Charlie's fine sense of honor would have led him to observe them, without any promise being exacted.

When he returned, about noon, the lovers were sitting on the porch in their olden friendly attitude, and Georgie Halford besieging for an afternoon at lawn-tennis, Dick Grayson and several others being promised.

"You see I mean to make hay while the sun shines," she went on, laughingly. "You young collegians will need plenty of out-door exercise after your months of close confinement. If Kathie shelters you in this palace of ease and indolence I shall complain of her; ought I not, Mr. Conover?" wheeling suddenly round.

"She ought not to frustrate your good intentions," he made answer.

"I shall be generous with everybody," said Kathie; "even Rob when he comes, and this afternoon I will be at your service."

"And I." Charlie Darrell rose and bowed in a most overwhelming manner.

"Now you ought to stay to luncheon," said Uncle Robert, "and some one will drive you back. The sun is intense."

"How charming of you! Kathie invited me, but she held out no such tempting inducement. Ask me no more; I yield!" sinking into an arm-chair with indolent grace.

So they had a gay little meal, and the three drove back. On Kathie's return there was company to tea, and some gentlemen to see Uncle Robert in the evening. As she was lingering about the hall he came out and gave her a good-night kiss, saying with fervent solemnity,—

"God grant you may be happy, my darling."

So Kathie's engagement settled itself very simply and naturally, and the days rolled on quite as before. Even if Charlie Darrell had not, in some degree, been put upon his honor not to compromise Kathie by ultra devotion, his own fine sense of delicacy would have restrained him. He felt sure of her; the rest could wait until the proper time of development.

The Darrells were all delighted, and welcomed the young girl so warmly that her heart was touched anew.

" But they seem like two children playing at love," Mr. Meredith declared in a rather dissatisfied tone.

" It is better for the present that they should play at love," returned Jessie. " I have always strongly objected to young men forming marriage engagements while at college; their attention is so distracted, their time so taken up with letter-writing and dreaming, that they are good for very little."

" How many college lovers did you have, pray, that you are so well informed?"

Jessie laughed.

" My feeling about it is that a man ought to wait until the right time and then make a regular business of it, — love with his whole heart and soul, even if his body be somewhat dilapidated." And a mirthful light shone in his eyes.

" I suspect there was, and is, a great difference between you and Charlie; and I should not like to see him engrossed, with a headlong passion just now. No, it is best as it is.'

" Well, I hope they will be perfectly happy when their time of awakening comes, for as yet they are only in a summer dream; and I *am* glad to have Kathie in the family. I feel as if I had some small, undisputed right to her. They have always cared for each other; consequently the regard is not so apparent. But after all,

> ' There 's nothing half so sweet in life
> As Love's young dream.' "

CHAPTER XIII

" DEAR Rob ! " Kathie cried joyfully as the young man strode down the platform at the station and caught both hands in his. Then she stood still with a touch of strange awe.

Yes, the old merry Rob was gone forever. This tall, resolute youth, older looking than his years gave him any warrant, with a determination in the eyes, and a compression about the lips that had laughed so easily, was a man with a man's future, whatever that might be, before him.

" O my precious little home daisy, how delightful it is to see you again ! It is really I ; you need not look so gravely questioning, as if you might be tempted to deny me ; and everybody is well ? Has Aunt Ruth come home ? "

" No ; you are the first of the long list of arrivals ; and they will be so glad to see you, though that goes without telling."

" It is good told, nevertheless ; and here are the ponies waiting for me. O Kathie, how many splendid drives we have had behind them ! "

He threw in his satchel and then helped her, taking the reins, while his face softened to a half-smile.

" We ought to have a good trot, for my blood rises with the occasion ; but they are counting the moments at home, and the trot can wait."

" How thoughtful of you, Rob ! " Kathie cried involuntarily.

"You do not take into account that the waif and stray might have a little longing for home and friends. But how Brookside changes, and how we have changed since Uncle Robert came home; and it seems to me that he has put his impress on the place. Kathie, there is no moving power in the world equal to a true, energetic, high-minded, honorable man."

Kathie's check glowed. If Uncle Robert could hear that tribute!

They turned into Cedarwood Avenue.

"Oh, how lovely! Even the very stones look good! It all grows more homelike with the mellowness of time. Oh — "

He reined up the ponies suddenly and sprang out, almost forgetting Kathie in the fond embrace of his mother. But her loyal knight was at her side.

"Fred wants the ponies presently, so we will let them stand," said Uncle Robert.

Rob walked up the steps with his arm about his mother. He was all hers; she felt it in that clasp of protecting tenderness, that indescribable air of affection. The quiver in his voice as he spoke touched her almost to tears. Yes, she had her boy back again with the man's heart.

He had not really grown taller, but it seemed so. He had filled out in chest and shoulders, and his voice had deepened, — lost the merry ring. There was a little look of care in his face, but his eyes were clear and honest, and his whole bearing proud and manly.

"Hillo, Traveller!" and Fred came flying through the hall.

"O mother mine, you have no more boys!" exclaimed Rob. "I suppose this is the way I used to surprise you in my annual returns. Why, Fred is nearly as tall as the rest of us; but oh, how slim and elegant! We shall have to send you out on the prairies."

Fred colored and laughed. "At least, there is a good

frame to fat up, you must admit. I have n't your knack of
growing both ways at once; my exceeding intellectuality
forbids that. I must run away for a half-hour, and by
that time you will have made acquaintance with the others,
and may find a few moments for me. Addio."

"Upon my word! You have style as well as beauty,"
laughed Rob to his mother. "I never quite came up to
that, did I?"

Something in the answering look said that whatever he
might have been she would hardly have had him changed.

"I suppose I can go up to 'our room'?"

"You are to have one all to yourself," said Kathie.
"Fred has turned his into a sort of museum, and you
might find a hospital as well. There are birds and beasts,
I believe, in every stage of dilapidation and recovery."

"'Pastime ere he goes to town.' Well, that is better
than —" But Rob did not finish the sentence. Taking
his satchel he followed Kathie.

"Here is dear Aunt Ruth's room," and he paused.
"The scent of the rose; you could n't take out all the
crimson tints, if you did bring in new lights. How lovely
we thought it at first, and what a gathering place it was!
We studied our lessons and had our talks and puzzles and
comforts, redeemed our stray articles from the inexorable
pound, confessed our sins, and nursed all our little aches
and pains here. Kathie, I think now no set of children
ever had a more delightful childhood! You are quite certain Aunt Ruth won't fail us? I 'm wild, too, to see
Bruce."

"We think she is on her way, as she has not written in
some time."

When Rob rejoined them again he looked fresh as a
rose. His year of hard work had not worn on his
physique, if it told in other ways. They went out on the
porch and talked over the boys, for Rob had not outgrown
them.

" Do you remember how eager I always was to set out
after them? " he asked. " Now I am going to wait for
them to come to me : one of the beneficent results of age
and experience. Hillo ! "

Dick Grayson vaulted over the side fence and came
striding up.

" How good it is to see you, old chap ! I was wondering when you would come." And the two shook hands
heartily. " O Kathie, the Collamores have returned ;
I met Louise down the street ; and the Langdons are
expected in the next steamer. Now for news about the
young lieutenant ! "

" We have not had any as yet."

" I shall never forgive him if he fails. I don't believe
we ever can have such a summer again. The cares of this
world and the deceitfulness of riches will be upon us all.
Have you found them heavy, Rob? You do not look
deeply careworn."

" The riches have not as yet proved a heavy burden,"
rejoined the young man, with a touch of humor.

Fred returned presently, and they kept Dick to supper.
Afterward Jessie and Charlie came over. Mr. Meredith
was up to the city for a few days.

" I don't know but we ought to give you a party, Rob,"
said his mother, " and ask all the young people over
here."

" You see, Kathie, my many virtues or my long absences
are coming to be appreciated," commented Robert in a
sort of humorously confidential tone. " You know, Dick,
all the great things used to be done for her. We were
bidden to feasts in her honor, we came at her command — "

" Not always," she interrupted gayly.

" And now you are come at my command. We will
not wait for gilt-edged cards, mother dear ; time presses,
and a fortnight is soon gone. Neither will we put off for
the laggards, though the loss can never be made up to

them. Just a jolly tea drinking, and a general state of
beatitude, mostly wandering about the lawn and talking
over old times. Why can't it be to-morrow or next
day?"

"Suppose we say Thursday, then?"

"Agreed. Charlie and Dick are invited; Mr. and Mrs.
Meredith and the rest we will look after to-morrow."

Rob and Kathie went out the next morning and had a
very pleasant time. She was secretly glad of this excuse
to call on Miss Collamore for many reasons. Fay was
delighted, and promised for the three, Louise being
absent.

They drove on silently afterward, Kathie revolving two
or three subjects in her mind. When she glanced at Rob
again a strange change seemed to have overspread his
face. It was stern and set, the lips compressed to a scarlet line. His eyes were bent upon the far distance, yet he
was not studying hill nor stream. Some occult link took
her back to Rome; the last night with Bruce. Of what
was Rob thinking? Were there some deep mysteries to
life that girls and women never knew? Did they live more
on the surface?

Rob's party resolved itself into a company of young
and middle aged, as informal gatherings were wont to do
at Cedarwood. There were a few games of croquet, but
that was on the wane, following the career of many displaced favorites. The evening was very pleasant, so they
interspersed it with singing until it became quite a little
musicale.

Mrs. Alston begged for a duet that Rob and Miss
Fay used to sing the summer before. Rob declared he
was all out of practice; but after Fay had played it over
several times, he joined her, and they succeeded so well
that the company petitioned for more. Fay played and
sang exquisitely. Then there were choruses and a few
pathetic old ballads, Mrs. Adams's delight.

It was quite evident to Kathie that Eugene had not made a very earnest fight with his fancy. In fact, he had not fought at all. During the journey Fay had gently tried to persuade, but her pity for him weakened her efforts.

"I must wait," he would answer bravely. "When she is convinced that I shall always love her, she may come to have some faith, some pity."

So Kathie was very glad to shelter herself under Charlie's wing. Eugene watching him and finding none of the heat and petulance of jealousy, none of the impatience of possession, decided that it must be merely friendship.

They planned some amusements for the next day, to end with a supper at the Darrells', Jessie's ovation to Rob, she declared.

"I shall save mine until next week," said Mrs. Adams, "but be sure you do not fail me, Robert. And, Miss Fay, I look for you and Mrs. Langdon to be warm friends."

Fay colored brightly.

Mr. and Mrs. Meredith made their little supper a charming success. There were so many old things to talk about. Rob entertained Fay with a graphic description of the first party at the Darrells', and Kathie's Cinderella dress, as he called it, and of his own boyish admiration for Mr. Meredith, and the episode of his going to war.

"I think them the loveliest of married couples," said Fay enthusiastically.

"That was Kathie's match making, I am quite sure, though she was such a little girl. And the Langdons; she was always going about with Emma and admiring her, and somehow, — I can't at all explain it, — but she always made you see the good and lovable points in other people, unless you were obstinately obtuse, as I used to be sometimes."

"And presently her hero will come," ventured Fay.

" Kathie's? She deserves the best and noblest of them all. I hope Mackenzie will get here this summer; I'd like you so to see him. I've always had a half-fancy, — and he's such a fine fellow, strong and brave and upright! Somebody said once that Kathie always found such delightful people. She met Gen. Mackenzie in New York when she was a little bit of a girl, and he liked her immensely, as everybody did. And that is all mixed up with the Merediths' romance, but the outcome of it was his marrying Aunt Ruth. She's just the sort of mother for a chap like Bruce Mackenzie. Oh, I remember thrashing a schoolmate once who called her an old maid, and she wasn't old, either!"

Rob laughed at the recollection, and then Fay must hear that story. Mrs. Alston watched them together, and her eyes grew strangely tender. What if this, too, should come about?

After they reached home that evening Uncle Robert took a note from his pocket.

" A disappointment from Ruth," he said. " I had not the heart to spoil our pleasant evening with it. They have decided to go on to California."

" Oh! " cried Kathie; " and Bruce? "

" She does not say a word about him. She does not even explain what has changed their plans. It is too bad! "

" I did so want to see Bruce," exclaimed Robert. " He was counting on it so much. Do you know I think Bruce is rather tired of soldiering. There isn't much fun in it now."

" Spoken like the old Rob," said his uncle.

Rob flushed and laughed.

" Or much glory, either," he added.

" No, we have come to the victories of peace; and yet sometimes the warfare is harder; the results more barren, or not so perceptible."

"And that is to our life's end." There was a sudden lowering in Robert Alston's voice, and, clasping his uncle's hand, he said good night abruptly.

Sunday was a lovely, quiet day. They "kept the feast" with each other. Even Charlie delicately refrained from coming over, for he judged they would like to have one day to themselves.

Many a time afterward Mrs. Alston recalled this day. Rob and she seemed to drift together, to get nearer than ever in their lives. Some strange charm woke a new chord whose refrain was tender to sadness. How could she spare him for a whole year when he had just learned to be companionable? What had brought about this marvellous change?

Kathie sat at the piano the next day, practising a few songs, when Jane paused in the doorway.

"Mrs. Langdon has come, Miss Kathie. Mrs. Adams has just sent over. I think they want you."

"Then I may go at once." And she sprang up in delight, her vague speculations giving way to active joy.

Mr. Langdon stood in the hall, when she reached the house, barricaded it seemed with boxes. He took one long step and caught her in his arms.

"My dear Kathie, how good it is to see you once more! Who was it said a man ought to take a journey for the pleasure of coming home? He was a rare philosopher. When I have shaken the dust off my feet and gotten the flavor of foreign languages off my tongue, I shall be a boy again. Has the lake dried up? Have the oarsmen vanished? Rob, I hear, is at home, a young man, and oh, you are all men and women!"

Some one came flying down-stairs before Kathie could reply. Emma had certainly grown more beautiful. She stood there in her radiant bloom, talking, laughing, glad to get back her girl friend, and charming her with every word.

" It is enough to make any one jealous," declared Mr. Langdon, " though I can't make up my mind of whom."

" Well, I shall carry Kathie up-stairs if she can climb over these boxes. I want to hear all about Brookside."

" What is to be done with them? And there are more at the station. Kathie, we have 'ransacked the ages and spoiled the climes,' and now we have an embarrassment of riches."

" We pass by boxes as a minor consideration," disdainfully. " Come, Kathie ; Georgie has gone out, and Mrs. Adams is lying down, so I can have you quite to myself. Oh, how natural you look ! You can't imagine how homesick I was after you had gone. I believe I should have begged to come home if I had not been ashamed, and thrown up 'fame and all.' But I went to work in real earnest, and Mr. Langdon was so good. But I am afraid marriage makes you lazy, or you get over the enthusiasm."

" I hardly think you have lost yours," replied Kathie, archly.

" Is n't it queer how we all want to come back to the home of our youth? Fred writes about it. He is doing so well, too, but he counts the months of his stay. We were all so happy, and yet we had our troubles, too," with a piquant smile. " I suppose Cedarwood is still the rallying centre for all the forces, with your delightful uncle in the midst."

" We do not seem to change much, only Freddy is almost as tall as Rob, and goes to college this fall."

" Kathie, what will your mother do without children? She is the most motherliest mother I ever saw. You will all have to get married and fill the house with grandchildren."

Mrs. Adams entered just then, and greeted Kathie warmly.

" How much longer does your brother stay?" she asked. " We must explain to Emma the cause of the tea

parties going round. Mr. Robert Alston has been the
hero of the occasion."

"He will have to leave us on Friday evening," replied
Kathie. "Why, the fortnight will seem like a dream."

. "You will have to rest up a little —"

"Oh," declared Emma laughingly, "I shall be rested by
the time Mr. Langdon gets the luggage stored away.
What a house we are making? And I must go and see
grandmother presently. I had only a ripple of sea-sick-
ness coming over, so I feel none the worse for my journey."

When Kathie started for home Emma put on her hat to
go to her grandmother's; Mr. Langdon would come to tea.

"And no doubt some 'spirit in our feet' will lead us
through Cedarwood on our return," she said with her
good-by to Kathie.

Sure enough it did. They sat on the porch and planned
pleasure enough to fill up a month.

"Brookside will become noted for its beauties," declared
Rob, "and geniuses, too. I expect next year I shall hear
of a certain Brookside Club that will immortalize the
place."

"Don't laugh at us, — at me," entreated Emma.

"I'm not laughing. You will find a rival in Miss Collamore, and you will both have to look well to your laurels.
Kathie's gift will declare itself next."

"I think it did a long while ago," replied Emma softly.

"Do you know," the latter said, a few days afterwards,
"I think the one who has changed most of all is your
brother Robert. He is so very different, so gentle and
almost grave at times. I venture upon a guess, that he
is in love with Miss Fay Collamore."

"I think we all wish it might be," Kathie made answer
in a curiously reverent tone.

Indeed, the young people had been thrown much together.
It would have been quite impossible to traverse Mrs.

Alston's quiet directing of events. But something struck
Uncle Robert that the mother passed by quite unremarked.
Much as he seemed to prefer Fay, he was more careful
than youth is wont to be, than he had ever been. It was
not coldness, but distance; as if there was some cause for
keeping himself well in hand, and, cordially sweet as he
had been with his mother and Kathie, he had not been at
all communicative about his inner life or plans. He was
putting away something with an unflinching resolution, the
old quality they used to consider stubbornness. He went
very little into society, belonged to a debating club, and
read a great deal; was taking quite an interest in some of
the political questions of the day.

He covered all this with a feint of business ambition,
but that was not the thing deepest in his soul. And
Uncle Robert came to have a misgiving that *tête-à-têtes*
with him were rather avoided, or at least not sought.
True, they were all occupied every moment with pleasure.
The days were crowded full. Dick Grayson had so many
plans to talk over with his old chum, there was rowing
after Mr. Langdon came, teas, music, two or three archery
meetings, and continual amusement. Yet at times it
seemed as if Rob's real soul was not in it.

The mother was so happy in her son's devotion that
Uncle Robert would not have disturbed her faith for
worlds.

What was there to dread? Some miserable entanglement, perhaps, formed in college. And yet he evinced no
special interest in New Haven; he had taken no journeys
thither during the year, and now was staying at home
until the latest moment. Uncle Robert observed narrowly,
but all his penetration was baffled. It was not a happy
secret, and it was something he was striving to thrust out
of sight, but to which, by some fatal enchantment, he must
return.

Yet it was a joyous fortnight, in spite of the disap-

11

pointment about Aunt Ruth. And now there was a general outcry.

" You are quite enough to spoil any one," declared Robert. " Why, did n't Kathie go to Europe and stay two years, and here I can come home two or three times a year! I am not so far away. And here is Fred going to college, and you will see but precious little of him until next year. It is the old marching orders. I don't believe you are as fond of soldiers as you used to be, Kathie."

Kathie was winking the tears out of her eyes. At least, she was not fond of partings.

Dick, Charlie, and several others came to see Rob off on his journey. To them it had the heroic side. So Uncle Robert could only say good by with the rest, and go home pondering the subject.

Ah, how lonesome the house was without him! Every one came to comfort Kathie, and pleasure flagged a little, but weightier matters started up for consideration. Fred's wardrobe must be gone over, and this would be quite a new parting, as Fred had never been away at school. He was to enter Columbia College, and there would be the " boys " to take him in hand, and Mr. Meredith's house as a second home. But the mother would be left nearly alone.

" We shall settle down into staid old folks, Dora," exclaimed Uncle Robert, " and we must both set up a hobby. They must be different, so that we can dispute about them."

" Fancy mamma disputing! " And Kathie laughed heartily.

Mrs. Alston gave a gentle sigh.

CHAPTER XIV

THE pleasures fell off a little after Rob went, perhaps because there was so much to do. Everybody was planning something, or growing toward it unconsciously. Louise Collamore had a drift and a leaning quite plain to see, now that the whirl was a little over. Mr. Hunsdon was gravely, carefully attentive. He was twelve years older than she, the proprietor of a chemical factory, a man of culture and rather curious tastes, with a great love for old-time adornments, which were now beginning to create a stir in every one's mind. "Fireplaces and candlesticks," Georgie Halford called them, and declared mirthfully that Louise had tangled Mr. Hunsdon in her embroidery silks, and would finally wind him up in a curtain and cover him with roses.

Several little incidents drifted Fay more toward Kathie. She was a connecting link with Mrs. Langdon, and the latter took a warm interest in Fay's pursuits, indeed, encouraged her greatly. Mrs. Alston drew her towards herself with a delicate, motherly interest, something indefinable, yet very tender and winning, as if a thought in her mind was sanctioned and settled, and, the path being clear, she had only to go on to fruition. She was very happy in these days. It seemed as if she could put her arms about the two she would have chosen out of all the world to place at her own fireside.

Dick Grayson seemed to vibrate between them all, with the longer stroke on Kathie's side. He liked fun-loving Georgie very much, and she managed to attract a crowd of young people around her who were always doing something or going somewhere just for the fun of it. A bright, beguiling girl, with no special depth or sentiment, or any defined purpose to life.

"She is one of the large tones of color," said Dick one day, as he and Kathie lingered in one of the shady lawn paths at the Adams'. "You want filling in and shading down, and the little bits, accessories, is n't it, to make the picture perfect? and I feel as if we were the little bits, the sort of neutral tints, the sky, and the water, and the hazy atmosphere. So it takes us all to get anything like a complete whole. Did you ever remark the tendency in so many people to make the world over just their way, to bring all to one method of thinking? Would n't it be queer to have no variety?" Kathie laughed at the conceit. They had many trenchant bits of talk together, but when Charlie came, Dick yielded the place of honor to him. Why he could not have told, except that it had always been so, and yet Charlie was the least aggressive of any of the boys. And so Eugene fell quite into the background, Kathie always sheltering herself under some half-defined influence.

Fay and Mrs. Langdon soon became very warm friends, with their sympathetic love between.

"No one can ever be quite what *you* were and are," she said to Kathie one day; "we seem to have lived through one of the infrequent experiences that never die out. But Fay is very charming, with her serene truth and quaint bits of humility, and, as you are never jealous, I shall take her up, make a *protégé* of her.

"I could n't be jealous of her, and mamma loves her so," returned Kathie.

"And if some one else comes to love her? One can't always help speculating, and then — Kathie, how do you keep fancy free amid all this adoration? Your loyal knights come ' two and two.' And I fancy not last, perhaps, that Eugene Collamore is rather hard hit, but the others do crowd him out."

"Oh!" Kathie's face was scarlet, sore against her desire.

"Then you have mistrusted? Kathie, you are discretion itself. I am sorry for the poor lad, only youth has many cures for heart-breaks; or they are not quite heart-breaks, I think. I suppose being used to older men; you know I grew up with the past generation." And she laughed lightly as a soft bloom overspread her lovely face. "Your uncle, and Mr. Meredith, and Mr. Langdon make the boys appear extremely young to me. Eugene and Charlie, and most of Georgie's admirers; Dick Grayson passes beyond them a little; he is going to make a fine man, Kathie, one of the kind who carry weight. And Rob seems so much older; he is not at all what I fancied he would be. I suppose young people are more difficult to guess about than we imagine."

"Why?" Kathie asked it in a breathless sort of way, as if a shadowy fear tugged at her heart. She and her mother were so thoroughly satisfied, but how did it seem to a person quite outside of relationship?

"Rob used to think always of the good times, of *his* good time. He had a fancy, unconscious maybe, of making every one over to suit himself, and now he is growing so like your uncle, trying to fit and suit other people. And how much he reads! We had several delightful talks. But why is he staying out there by himself? His heart isn't set on making a fortune, though he does talk about it."

"It was a very good business opening," said Kathie slowly.

"And I suppose people can't always keep together? But that season of youth was so perfect I'd like to live it over again and have my lover come so by surprise, and tell me he watched me first because I was so much like you"; and Emma laughed, with a lovely scarlet flush in her face. "Instead, I shall watch for your lover, only *he* will never compliment me so daintily; but I shall not be jealous.

Who knows but Providence is saving you up for Fred?
He will be home next summer, so you need not hurry.
You must have your choice of the flower of chivalry."

Kathie's heart beat with a curiously guilty feeling. It
had come over her more than once when some incidental
reference had been made to her future.

Another thought worried her more than she liked to
confess. She had been owing Bruce a letter a long while.
Ought she to write to him now, and what must she say?
There was a great confusion in her mind on the subject.

She tried to settle it that evening. She stayed to tea
with Emma, and several of the young people dropped in to
arrange about a sailing party. Charlie walked over home
with her. They reached the lawn path before she could
resolve upon the manner of presenting her perplexity.
Then she paused with a tremulous little "Charlie?"

"Well?" in the comforting tone that always seemed so
restful.

"I want to ask you — about — writing to Bruce. I owe
him a letter. He was so sure of coming when he wrote,
and I waited to hear — "

"There certainly has been enough disappointment
expressed to make your letter entertaining, to say the
least."

"But — "

"O Kathie, you don't mean — that I am selfish enough
to keep you from — anything?" And his quick tone made
the hurt manifest.

"I want to do just what is right, proper," trying to
steady her voice that *would* tremble. "It is so strange to
think of anything different."

"But you and Bruce are — Well, it *is* a relationship,
after all. Kathie, I think I have been the least bit jealous
twice. When I came home last spring, and saw you
and Eugene in your phaeton; by the station, you remember. I did n't understand just what it was. Then mother

made a comment one day to the effect that other young
men might find you sweet and attractive, and it came to
me that my regard was something deeper, warmer than
friendship. And then, the night I spoke you had been
showing such joy at the news of Bruce's return that I
wanted to feel quite sure. And now that I am sure, the
little social demands cause me no uneasiness. There
always seems to me something cruel and uncalled for in
jealousy. If you have entire faith in a person, as I have
in you, surely I can trust you to decide how much is owing
to the ' small, sweet courtesies of life'; if I had not faith,
— of course I can't imagine so monstrous a thing, — it would
be better to give up the thought of love. There *must* be
confidence to hallow it. I could not take the shell without
the substance, as love would prove without faith. And I
am always at rest about you. Besides, this year I shall
be away so much that I want you to go on with all the old
friends and have all the happiness that comes to you.
Your own soul will teach you what to reject. You and
Bruce have been dear friends, and there is nothing to be
rudely broken up. You will meet each other at intervals
all your life. I should like to count Bruce Mackenzie one
of *my* choice friends, our welcome guest in the time to
come. So write to him just as usual, you dear, conscientious little body."

She wanted to ask another question, but was it courage
that failed? And yet he partly answered with his next
remark.

" You know we are only half engaged." And by his tone
she understood the sweetness of his smile that she could
not see in the dusk. " Next year I may claim more, but
I hope never to forget how sacred a trust you are."

He kissed her softly on the forehead, then walked up to
the porch steps with her, and said good night.

And yet the question was not wholly solved. How
much, how much? seemed to float through her brain. She

could tell with Eugene, it must be nothing, for even tender sympathy would be cruel ; she could tell with Dick, for he asked only interest, but what puzzled her so about Bruce? Ought she to tell him just how matters stood? How could she? Delicacy seemed to revolt at the thought. And all the others, Emma, Fay, who were so unconscious of any stronger interest!

She was driving up to Middleville one afternoon with Uncle Robert, who watched the shadows come and go on her fair face, and the perturbed little lines that settled on her brow and compressed her soft red lips.

" Well, what is it?" he asked, presently.

Kathie colored a vivid scarlet, and her eyes blurred with a weariness near to tears. The utter joyousness that should be in the day and in her soul was not here ; there was a vague sense of disturbance, as if something not quite true in the relative adjustment of atoms had strayed in and the currents were displaced.

" You know," very tenderly, " that I have always been your father confessor."

" Yes. I wish *you* understood without the telling. It is so tangled."

" We will straighten it out, then. Have you and Charlie found — "

" Oh, it isn't Charlie, Uncle Robert! He is always generous, and sure, and untroubled. It is because I don't know and can't tell how much there ought to be ; where the lines should cross sharply, and where they should run parallel. I wish — it had all been left until next summer."

" I wish so, too, my darling. But you know how often visions vanish when you put forth your hand boldly." And he smiled, with the persuasive light of sympathy in his eyes.

" I want to be entirely true. No one dreams of my being not quite free. Emma was talking a few days ago of the future, and balancing claims, as it were, and when she

spoke of Charlie as one of the — the improbable ones,"
and Kathie gave a little ghost of a smile, " it seemed not
quite fair. Was it just to him? No one appears to think
we are any more than friends."

" Well, what would you like? to have the engagement
announced?"

" Oh, no! " A little sort of shiver ran over her as if
she shrank from that, and her uncle remarked it with dismay. " I must be unreasonable, am I not? I don't understand myself. And I can't have the un-knowledge, can
I?" smiling again faintly. " But here is what puzzles me
most: I want to write to Bruce. Ought I to tell him?"

" You want to write to Bruce? " Uncle Robert repeated the works in a curiously emphatic manner, not
turning his eyes on Kathie, but noting every movement
of her face, nevertheless.

" Oh, I asked Charlie if he would rather not have me,"
she answered quickly, but with no show of emotion. " He
considers it foolish to — to crowd every one else out Then
he wants to be friends with Bruce always. He likes him
so much, even if he is not as enthusiastic as Rob about
him. He likes all brave, manly, earnest men, and he is so
earnest himself, so quick to give of his best. And he said
we were in a way related, which is true, but — I can't help
it, I *want* Bruce to know just how it stands. I am quite
sure he would tell me of such an event in his life."

Was that all her reason for wanting him to know?
Uncle Robert studied the fair face, whose color fluttered
under his watchful eye. There was " no part of the
price " kept back now, or, if so, it was done quite unknowingly, in bravest innocence.

" Yes, I should tell him."

" But how? " She blushed distressfully. " It would be
so queer to blurt it out — "

" You are not much given to ' blurting out,' Kathie,"
he answered gravely. " It would be like telling a brother."

" But we did n't even tell Rob. Mamma was afraid he might tease a little or be not quite discreet. But Bruce is so far away, and Aunt Ruth will know. He might feel hurt."

Was she in love if she did not even know how to confess her lover?

" It is best that he should know. About the others, Kathie, I think you had better settle to a wise silence, and then put it quite out of your mind, as Charlie's secret, if you please, which you have no right to make known at present. I think you have been nursing a little ultra conscientiousness, and the end would be a wretched state of indecision. There are times in life when we just go forward, as the children of Israel were bidden to do. It is very reprehensible to deny an engagement, as I have known girls to do, but simply to keep silence when no one questions you is not a matter of deception. I want you to be happy, content. Remember that this is in some respects my year as well, that I shall have to give you up in many ways, hereafter, and so we must take comfort together."

She smiled through her tears. Yes, there were other duties and loves. Had she not been rolling up a mountain to overshadow herself?

They had reached the Strongs' by this time, and Sarah was doubly anxious to see Kathie. The marriage had not been announced, but just suffered to be made known, and had created more than a ripple. Perhaps at the bottom it traversed too many secret hopes to be cordially received.

The grave, quiet man, rather shy of ladies in general, and shutting himself in his study when meetings were appointed at the parsonage, had so held his even tenor that no one could justly take hope. Even after the surmises there was a great amount of incredulity, and now it was shown in the utter lack of cordial welcome, except among Sarah's young friends.

" We are to be married in church, at ten in the morning," said Sarah. " There will be a kind of general invitation," and she smiled rather archly, " so no one can really slight us if they desire to remain away. I wanted to be married at home, but Mr. Truesdell was not willing, and I think now his way is best. Then we shall go away and forget all the dissatisfaction for some happy days. After that, trying to do our duty, and living in peace so far as we are allowed."

Kathie added her little gift to the simple and becoming wardrobe, which had been selected with excellent judgment.

" And I shall have some pretty articles for my new home," said Sarah, with pardonable pride. " I want to make the old house look homelike and enjoyable. James has been making me a really beautiful easel and a set of pretty shelves, a sort of cabinet. Since I have known you I have been collecting pictures and books, and doing needle-work, so it will not seem strange over there to see some of the familiar reminders. It is so gray and barren within, yet I think it might be made a lovely old place. Only once in a while it comes into my mind, what if they should n't want Mr. Truesdell to remain afterward? "

" Oh, they could n't be so hateful! it would be just that! " cried Kathie indignantly. " Why, if you are good enough to sing and play in church, and to teach their children, and visit them — "

" But all that is not being set over them. It does appear narrow and foolish, does it not? And yet in country places party lines are very strong. We shall just trust and work, and endeavor to make our lives larger. I am beginning to think the victory worth trying for, at any rate. And what shall separate us from that larger Love? "

" Not powers or principalities," said Kathie, softly kissing the glowing cheek; " or things present."

" And we must in some degree determine the things to

come, but not by impatience or self-assertion. Oh, I wonder if I can always! I shall have to hold close by the
great truths, the greater love."

Cousin Ellen, too, had a confidence for Kathie, when she
could be spared.

"I suppose this all looks like a very foolish fuss to you,
Miss Kathie," she began, "this barring out and putting
up social fences. I wish it had been Sarah's lot to marry
differently, but they love each other, and it has so come
about. In some other place they might be very happy,
but here it will be continual warfare, and no foes are so
cruel as those of man's own household or his church. I
wonder sometimes how much good religion really does us,
or rather how we can take in so much and get so little of
the true spirit, the divine wisdom! But I did n't mean to
preach a sermon; I had a favor to ask, instead. I am
afraid there will not be any real hearty welcome for the
poor girl when she comes home, and I am thinking of fix-
ing up the old place a bit, so it will look cheery. If you
could come up one day and give me a few hints, after her
belongings are taken over there."

"Oh, I should so like to come, even if my hints should
not be of great importance!" Kathie answered eagerly.

"There's a parlor, study, and sleeping-room on one
side of the hall. The paper is very dingy, and James and I
have decided to re-paper the study and chamber. I wonder where I 'd be most likely to find pretty paper! Those
two rooms will be so much to her."

"Suppose I send you the paper? I would like to do a
little — "

"Oh, you are too generous! We could n't afford anything expensive, but pretty and cheerful. There is an old-
fashioned Franklin in the study, and a high mantel with
pictures set round, just as they are beginning to do again.
Sarah was reading about it."

"Tiling," said Kathie. "Why, you make me quite

curious to see it. If you would n't mind, I think Uncle
Robert could send for the paper, if you will learn how
much is needed. And — is there anything else?"

" You will come up to the marriage, surely?"

" Of course." And Kathie smiled.

" We might go in and see the rooms then. I don't suppose the congregation want to do anything; but they may
get up a little home-welcome afterward. It takes away so
much of the tender joy to have people cold and indifferent.
There, I must not keep you another moment. Sarah will
wonder."

Kathie was quite thoughtful going home, but it was not
about herself. Presently she informed Uncle Robert of
the plans, and he readily agreed.

" Mamma," she said, the next day, " we must all go up
to Sarah's marriage. I mean to ask Emma, and Mr. Langdon, and Jessie. We shall be quite an imposing array,
and the disaffected at Middleville will see that there are
people to do her honor."

" Mrs. Alston smiled. She was glad to see her child
ready to do honor unto " the least of these." In all these
things she was fitting herself for the new life. Kathie had
always been a little different, and Charlie as well, and in
this matter there would be a perfect blending.

Charlie was very much interested when he came to hear
of the plans, and Emma wondered if they could not all join
and do something.

" I shall have to get back in the old ways and works,"
she said, with a tender, wistful smile. " We have just
been existing for ourselves, seeing, hearing, doing for our
own pleasure and benefit. But we cannot any of us afford
to narrow our lives and crowd out, instead of asking in to
the feast."

" Doubtless no one would take it amiss," returned Charlie, " and we ought to wind up our glad summer by making a bit of brightness somewhere; though it will be the

old story of the Fair, and Kathie putting the right grace just where it should be, and so surrounding it with all the little helps that it becomes a large blessedness."

" And that shows us how much greater one of the ' little deeds' often is than the penetration, and wisdom, and nice balancing of what we consider possibilities, proves. I don't believe any of us would have said that evening at the Fair, "Here is a girl who has strength and understanding, a sense of beauty and harmony, who can be made into a teacher, a musician, a potent influence in the world, by the proffer of a helping hand."

" But I didn't think so at all," said Kathie, between a blush and a little laugh of embarrassment. " I hated to have her and her mother made uncomfortable. And I remembered times when some pleasant word had bridged over a trouble for me."

" The doing unto others. But you see most of us wait to learn what measures others mean to deal out to us, and then make ours conform. You always seem to know with your nice instinct when some disturbance in the spheres needs to be adjusted, and to have the wisdom — "

"I wonder," began Charlie, filling in the pause Emma made, " if it is not just this : ' Whatsoever thy hand finds to do, do it with all thy might' ; not stopping to reason or analyze, or wonder about the end. God takes care of that ' If ye do His will ye shall know of the doctrine,' not the doctrine first."

" Quite an old-time talk," said Emma presently. " It makes us all feel like children again. I am beginning to get back to my proper self. And now can't we all go up to Middleville, and consult this cousin who has the matter in hand ? "

They drove up a day or two afterward. Cousin Ellen took them over to the parsonage. It did look gray and dingy. New paper and new paint for the rooms, and some modern additions. James and Ellen would see to the work.

"I suppose," said Emma, as they were homeward bound, "we could find one or two old articles that could be furbished up into prettiness, not glaring newness, you understand; that would look dreadful in such a place. I think I know of one old arm-chair that Mrs. Adams sent out to the barn yesterday. A little cretonne would make it cosy and presentable."

"And I'll add a study table," exclaimed Charlie. "I know of one that can be altered over to a charm. Perhaps I may find something else."

Mr. Meredith chose the papers, and sent them down from the city. They were soft tones and appropriate. They took them up to Cousin Ellen on the morning of the marriage, and she was to send word back as soon as the work was done.

Certainly the Brookside people made quite an addition to the wedding guests. The old sexton showed them to the seats of honor, and they filled the two middle-aisle pews. They were early, and it was quite entertaining, Emma declared, to see the air with which most of the assemblage settled itself. Disapproval was sternly written on many of the elder faces, and yet curiosity had conquered in several instances. The young people and the school children were full of diffident wonder. The minister's marriage was such an unusual occurrence. No one remembered any similar event.

They came in slowly, gravely, Sarah pale and self-possessed, ladylike in her soft gray silk, her reverent air, her earnest, serious eyes, the refinement in every line of her face. It seemed to Kathie that she looked greater, and richer, and finer than Mr. Truesdell, with all the years of cultivation behind him.

He was rather ill at ease. He saw the unfriendly eyes, even if they were not facing them; but she thought of only two things, the vows she was making to God, and her husband, till death parted them.

There was a little stir of congratulation afterward, but
they did not stop long. Those who carped and questioned
would have a fortnight to resolve upon their course. Mrs.
Alston's party paused for a little talk with Mrs. Strong.
Did it unconsciously sway opinion? All these things do
with weaker and more calculating souls. These refined,
cultured people, with their larger surroundings, had taken
up the girl, the whole family. It was not a question with
them whether *she* were worthy, but whether *they* could
afford to go against such a verdict. Many of the great
things of life begin with worldly reasoning. It is the
sowing beside *all* waters.

James Strong and Cousin Ellen had it all their own way
at the parsonage. The housekeeper looked on grimly; the
little girls were like shy, wild kittens. They did not go
beyond the two rooms. James was in a glow of delight.
After the paper was on and the painting done he touched
up the book-shelves with bits of moulding and an ornament
here and there. Sarah had bought a new carpet for her
own room, and they moved over her belongings. Then
they covered the worn study carpet with mats, and the
contributions from Brookside quite amazed them. Four
easy-chairs, and a study table, with its handsome ink and
penholder, racks for letters and pamphlets, a few well-
chosen books Charlie had added with his store, and the
place took on a cosy homelikeness, with the ripeness of the
lovely September world outside.

He was very glad to be in it all with Kathie. She was
living in the present and for her friend. What Sarah
would think, the glad, sweet surprise that would make a
sunshine in her face and a mist of tears in her eyes, the
hours of delight she would enjoy there. But his fancies
ran farther off, another home, a keener, sweeter joy, a
time when all things should be given to him richly to enjoy. And he was glad, with a touch of awesome humility,
that it was far off, that he should come to it by degrees,
as he was made fit and worthy.

With all this, and the preparations at home for Fred, Kathie was very busy, and she had no time to worry about herself. She put her letter to Bruce out of her mind. Then Charlie and Fred said their good-byes and were off, and Emma and Mr. Langdon were discussing a new home. Everybody seemed to take their plans and questions over to Cedarwood for definite shaping. In the midst of this a note came from Bruce. He had been greatly disappointed at the change of plans, and very busy with some perplexing frontier troubles. The two in California were having a most delightful time. Then a few lines called a bright flush to Kathie's cheek. ' Mother ' had written to him about her engagement. He wished her all joy, all happiness in a brief sort of way, as if at present it was a subject not to be talked of intimately.

12

CHAPTER XV.

THEY were not suffered to get lonely at Cedarwood, hardly to long for the boyish influences gone out from them. Rob's breezy presence had made a continual stir in the house, and his absence left vacant spaces everywhere. Fred was so much quieter, so full of his own projects and experiments, sufficient for himself, keeping much in his own room, or abroad, diving down into the secrets of nature; always ready and companionable if wanted, and, though tuned in a softer, tenderer key, not so dependent on sympathy and society as Rob had been. Perhaps even now his mother missed her first born the most.

But Uncle Robert was so identified with all the ways and the welfare of the little town that the house had come to be a sort of head centre; a cosier place than any hall or room for discussions. Often the ladies came over if their husbands had an errand with Mr. Conover, and then the young folks wanted to see Kathie. So all the larger living was in their midst. She was greatly interested in the talk about mills and factories and what was best for the hands, what was most entertaining and most profitable for the young men, what was to make the best citizens for the next generation. She had hardly time to miss anybody, even dear Aunt Ruth.

And right after Sarah's marriage came the engagement of Louise Collamore and the talk of a marriage in the spring. Mrs. Collamore had taken her delicate perplexities to Mrs. Alston. Louise was so young, so much less mature than Fay. Mr. Hunsdon was twelve years her

senior, and somehow she could not bear to have the young-
est go first. But the lover was very much in earnest, and
began to build a nest for his bonnie bird.

Kathie watched them with a great deal of interest.
Louise no doubt loved him, but she was not sentimental,
hardly as tender as Fay. Certainly there was much to be
proud of, and she wore her honors in that way, as if she
was not surprised at coming into a sphere of consequence,
and, indeed, believed it one of the things she had a right
to expect.

Through this time, when they were all brought into such
intimate contact, Kathie's promise gave her a certain
strength and decision. She was not her own any more;
she could secretly pity and sympathize with Eugene, but
when it came to a certain point she could assert her self-
reliance. What strange wisdom came with the knowledge!
She used to think of herself with a little awe, of that other
self which was not really hers any longer.

Fay was puzzling over her, still with a hurt feeling.
Why could it not have been, she asked of her secret soul.

"Eugene," she said softly, one evening, "I think she
shows that her heart *is* elsewhere. It may be all unknown
to herself. You know she was abroad so long with young
Mackenzie, and he is no real relation, but just near enough
to give a sort of piquant interest to the connection. If he
had come this summer, if we could have seen them together — "

"No," Eugene answered moodily. "I don't want to
see; I don't want to know. I am glad to have her
alone again, to feel there is no one very near. I had
rather love her all my life, as I shall."

Fay sighed. Would Louise so love against hope?
Would any one else?

The Langdons had their times of discussion as well.
What was to be done? Where would they go? For
Emma's sake they ought to be in a city, but he did not

love cities, and since he had enough for their humble wants why should he toil, and moil, and worry himself, he asked, whimsically.

His money had been largely invested in his brother-in-law's business. Emma had been quite surprised after her marriage to find how really wealthy her husband was ; indeed, no one had suspected it from his simple tastes and leisurely ways. And perhaps this was why the pure-hearted young girl, with no undercurrent of selfishness, had moved him so strongly in that past year, when many chords of his better nature had been touched.

"I am sure I could be contented here always," said Emma. "I am not half tired. And we might have our real home here, with holidays in the cities. I am not sure but we could do as much here as anywhere. Mr. Conover is always busy. I don't know what Brookside would be without him."

So they settled about the real home. It was to be pretty and artistic, so that, when Emma was very famous, people could make pilgrimages hither. They studied books, they drew plans, they talked over Mr. Hunsdon's ideas, and rambled about during the splendid autumn weather, always taking Kathie when they could get her.

The Merediths returned to the city. Mrs. Alston and Kathie would go up for a good long holiday visit, music, lectures, and other amusements. Aunt Ruth would be back then. Mr. and Mrs. Langdon would board for a while, and it would be home to them with the familiar faces.

They had not forgotten Mrs. Truesdell with all this of their very own. It was not their way to drop one out of daily living.

Sarah had come home at the appointed time, and gone quietly to the parsonage. Some sort of home welcome or tea drinking had been discussed, but none of the parties could agree, and the plan had fallen through. It was much more enjoyable to Sarah to come in and take her place at

once as a wife and a mother. And oh, the glad surprise
of the cosy rooms, the joy of the delicate little note lying
on the study table, with the best wishes of friends! It
could never be lonely or narrow after that.

"We will do our duty and our best," Mr. Truesdell said,
"and leave the rest to God. If it should seem that my
work is finished here, there are other fields. I might have
made a change, in any event."

Was there something real and vital in his Sunday's
sermon? Had his own soul been touched with the
sights and sounds, the new life he had entered into, the
depth and fulness? Surely there was no fault to find; one
and another pressed his hand cordially, as he came down
the aisle afterward, with his wife on his arm, and the men
gave him good wishes rather awkwardly. They had nothing against this fresh young girl by his side. The women
were a little more cautious. And yet it was done. Facts
must be accepted.

There were many little slights to take from "the best
people," the ones who considered themselves of most
importance in point of wealth and religion. But there
were delights on the other side for Sarah. It was not so
bad to stand between, after all. Brookside came up, and
they went down to it, and gathered new friends among the
clergy and various others. And when Middleville began
to feel itself crowded out, it made haste to assert its own
rights, to secure its own footing.

The most delightful of all was Mr. Strong's Christmas
gift to his daughter of a beautiful piano. He had considered it a long while. It was a good deal of money for
plain farmer people, but he had no fear now of Sarah outgrowing her place or station, or feeling ashamed of the
home folks. Hers was a wider sphere, a larger space, and
brought an increase, not a narrowing of soul.

He came down to consult Kathie, and was to meet her
in New York for the purchase. She and Mrs. Meredith

accompanied him, and, though he was sadly bewildered, he managed to acquit himself very well.

" Sarah has been a good girl and deserves it all," he said. " Miss Kathie, if there were more people in the world willing to share their good things with you, we should all get on faster, I 'm thinking And she 'll make hers go a good way. I think the Lord has put her in just the right place, and He made her good and ready for it. I do believe you and she would convert the world if you started out on a missionary tour."

Kathie smiled, with a dewy lustre in her eyes.

Mr. Strong went home with a great many new thoughts in his mind that would bring forth good fruit at the right season He was not given to hurrying Providence.

But Sarah's letter to Kathie afterward was one pæan of delight, not only concerning the piano, but the " pleasant visit father had with you all."

Kathie's holidays in the city were full of enjoyment. Something a little larger and deeper than before, new thoughts and opinions, graver questions to take hold of. Mrs. Garnier was forming a little circle where people dropped in two evenings a week, sure of finding her, and generally the doctor, and talked over the questions and ideas that were stirring the world, sifting theories and beliefs. Dick Grayson, who was now reading law, was a frequent visitor, and Fred was delighted beyond measure at being counted in.

Charlie came occasionally.

"After all," he said to Kathie, " it is the old, old story, the trying on of ideas and beliefs that the world used centuries ago. The conditions only are new, it is the souls that are fresh, and not the ideas, and yet the souls take them up as some new discovery, and try their utmost to disentangle, to find a way out by the many devious paths, quite forgetting that some one said, centuries ago, as well, ' Behold, I show you a more excellent way.' And yet we are so slow coming to the more excellent way."

Fred was quite caught and fascinated by it. He came
to listen always, he declared; yet he would sit with his
soft, bright eyes all alert as they tossed their brilliant talk
to and fro, giving the differing opinions that had come slowly
through the years and been proved as well as disproved
hundreds of times. Not because of no truth; there were
fine, solemn grains of truth in it all along; the stone
rejected at one time came to be the foundation stone at
another.

Dr. Markham went a little further than this one evening.

" I wonder," he said, " with all this science and meta-
physics, if they could do just what was done to her?"
nodding towards Ada. " If Dr. Garnier had come in and
tried to rouse her, and offered her the love of a true man,
not gilded over with wealth, would she have gone out of
that dismal room for his sake? Why, it would have
seemed so much Sanscrit to her; she would n't have known
what to do with it! Or if they had talked science, and
evolution, and brain, and nervous system, taken out their
souls, or what they thought were their souls, and analyzed
the component parts, would that have helped her? And
yet you did it that summer between you all, the little
touches of mother love and wisdom which she never had
in her own life helping and strengthening. There is
something simpler than the old philosophies, after all. I
don't know but we 're in danger of losing it again, only
it never has been wholly lost these eighteen hundred years.
Some one always holds the clew and guides the soul out
to day. I suppose it is natural to take a great race out
on the highway, but we do get tired of the dust, and the
heat, and the stir, and in the afternoon of life are glad to
come back to the shade, and the quiet, and the strength
not our own."

Yet Mrs. Garnier had grown into a very attractive
society woman, as one side of society was rapidly becom-

ing. She was in the centre again, and this brought out
her best efforts. It was not by self-assertion this time, but
the tact that had come from a finer breeding, the seed sown
in her soul through that dreary time of youthful despair,
and, though it had not brought forth its best fruit, it was
going on unconsciously. But at present it was the readiness and grace, the harmony that passes current in the
world for deeper wisdom.

Kathie's stay was not to be all in scientific or artistic
realms. The Collamores came down for Christmas and to
buy wedding garments. Mr. Hunsdon and Louise drifted
into Mrs. Garnier's circle, Fay and Kathie had lovely, long
evenings to themselves, and Rob made a flying visit of a
few days, having been sent on business. There were shopping, amusement, and gayety, and with Kathie's gift for
entering so wholly into the wishes and enjoyments of
others she scarcely thought of herself.

Charlie Darrell looked on, with a curious feeling at his
heart. Would she ever have any true life of her own?

Rob was very well, and almost restlessly energetic; a
good sign, his uncle took it, being more like the normal
state of his youth. It was not well to grow old too fast.
Charlie delicately stood aside and let him monopolize
Kathie, though it seemed quite odd for him to show so
much regard.

The bright party broke up presently. Jessie declared
she had had no good of it at all, and insisted on keeping
Kathie a fortnight longer, perhaps with a little sisterly
feeling that Charlie had not enjoyed quite his full share of
her visit.

Kathie thought at first she could not stay. Then word
came that Aunt Ruth was on her way, but could only
spend a few days in New York, as the General had urgent
business in Washington. So Mrs. Alston remained with
her.

They were all delighted to see Aunt Ruth again.

She was looking a little pale and worn, but sweeter than ever, it seemed to Kathie. General Mackenzie took Kathie in his arms and held her in a long, tender embrace, kissing the white forehead again and again with a strange solemnity that moved the child deeply, as if it touched an undercurrent of soul answering to something she could not quite understand.

"O Aunt Ruth," she began, one morning, "why was it Bruce could n't come last summer? Would he have felt awkward without you and uncle? It was such a lovely time. Rob was dreadfully disappointed. I think everybody missed him in a way, or wanted him."

"But you had so much on your hands, and there was the newness about Charlie," Aunt Ruth said very gently.

"I do not think it made very much difference, Aunt Ruth," was the slow answer.

"You know it is not *quite* an engagement, and Uncle Robert was n't willing; but then Charlie thought it right, too," she went on rather incoherently. "We were to go on just the same, and, indeed, I did n't have time for anything else," she continued, smiling through a rising flush.

The love of youth and association; was it anything deeper? Aunt Ruth wondered. Yet her heart ached for the other one, withheld by the finest sense of honor, a chain that could have no flawed link, that would hold another's right sacredly true through any pang. "It might as well have been," she cried in her secret heart, woman like.

Dr. Markham took her to task for languor.

"You have quite overdone the matter," said he. "When I consented to your dancing on the lawn I did n't mean you to turn into a fashionable tourist, and go galloping all over the world. The next thing we shall hear of will be a volume of travels"

"I think I shall leave the volumes and the experiences to younger people. I have been quite content to enjoy, and am fully satisfied with my rambles. The General expects to resign his commission this spring, and we shall settle down into quiet old people."

" Not so fast! not so fast!" cried the doctor eagerly. " You women run to extremes. There ought to be some grand middle life before one begins to go down the hill. The young folks must not crowd us out of everything."

" How lovely it will be for you to have a real home! " Kathie said afterward. " Only it seems as if Bruce ought to be in it."

Aunt Ruth's answer was a gentle sigh.

Kathie dreamed a little. If Bruce came, and married; everybody did sooner or later, and there were children growing up in the house. There was Fay and some of the new girls at Brookside, as well as several charming ones in the city that she had come to know, but out of them all she could not choose any one to her mind. For an instant she was back in Rome, saying her good by. If he could have stayed with them! A strange tide seemed to carry her swiftly out to unknown depths, a broad ocean she had not traversed before.

They went home presently and took up the old widespread living. Mr. Hunsdon's house approached completion, and the marriage took place. The Collamore house was full of cousins and guests, and Louise oddly entertaining with the importance of her new position, ruling Fay and everybody with bits of superior wisdom that were as new to her experience as if they had never been uttered. There was much gay talk, and jesting, and innumerable discussions on the æsthetics of house-furnishing. Queen Anne houses were coming in, and the old things were going out.

Even Eugene was drawn into it. Kathie could not help relaxing a little of her carefulness. It seemed quite absurd that one should go on caring with no hope. And soon everybody would know.

But he said to Fay, " If the Mackenzies are here this

summer the young lieutenant will be sure to come on if he cares for her. And a year will certainly convince Kathie that I do not mean to forget."

Fay had known so few unhappy loves in her short life. There were times when it seemed to her that this must come out right by the very force of its fidelity.

When Louise was gone, Fay and Kathie seemed to draw closer together. The spring days were growing so long, and there were bits of lonely evenings. They liked so to have her at the Alstons'. Then Aunt Ruth came home, and to Kathie it was a breath of the old-time sweetness.

" She is quite worn out," said the General, " and you must nurse her back to bloom and strength, Kathie, or we shall hear from Dr. Markham. There has been so much society in Washington, so much going about everywhere, that we shall be very glad of a little rest."

It was so natural to have Aunt Ruth, to see her lying on the sofa, to take her to drive in the pony carriage, to tell her little bits of the happenings and changes, and yet at first it seemed to Kathie as if they had drifted so far apart. The little heart things, the deep tendernesses, the real intimate life did not seem to glow within, although the outside was unchanged. Was it because childhood was over and maturity was coming? When one could walk alone one was no longer held up by watchful hands. She was left to hold herself up, to decide many things, to grow stronger by the exercise. If there was any other reason she could not see it then.

At Easter Charlie Darrell was ordained. Kathie and her mother went down for a few days' stay. To her it was a very solemn service, bringing before her the life and the work that were to be hers presently. Sarah had made it so large, and sacred, and was working it out in her sphere with an energy that seemed like inspiration in its wisdom, its tenderness. What could she do? In the shelter of her own home she might be brave, but in the great world — Well, there were times when she had taken up the cross and borne witness, only now it seemed to be from outside pressure rather than any of her own choosing. Could she make it her soul's earnest desire?

They had one little talk about it. They so rarely talked of their own selves that Kathie stood tremulous and abashed, as on the verge of a strange experience.

"I am almost afraid," she cried softly. "What if I should fail and mistake the way! O Charlie, it seems now as if you needed some one larger of soul, more in earnest, wiser —"

"'He giveth liberally.' It is not our strength, you know, and we are not to come to it all at once; that is, the blessedness. You must not worry over it; as you are I want you. And when we take up the work together, shall I not be there to help you bear any burden? We shall have the long, lovely summer to talk it all over, and you will be glad, Kathie, you will rejoice in my joy. Love could not do otherwise."

It was love; it must be. Kathie drew near in great awe, as to a sacrament.

"Mamma," she said, a day or two after, "when Charlie comes down to Brookside, would it not be better to tell the truth about ourselves, or at least let it be known. I cannot bear to be in a false position. It was very well last year, but now I want to think of it, to make myself ready for my future life."

Mrs. Alston pressed her to her heart. After all, it would come hard to give up her darling.

"Yes," she made answer softly. "It would be as well. But there need be no hurry about the marriage. I was to keep you two years, you know."

"I should like to stay always," and there was a little sob in her voice. Oh, why had she promised?

"'For this cause they shall leave father and mother,'"

Mrs. Alston returned in a tender tone. " It is right and natural, Kathie, and yet it seems a great parting, when you have always been so much to us. But you are sadly nervous and excited. You have had too much on your mind of late."

Charlie had promised to take some mission duty for a friend who was going away for a brief rest. But his first summons to Brookside was not the glad mission of joy.

And yet it was a peaceful sorrow. Grandmother Darrell, full of years and good works, went fearlessly over the swelling river. She had been rather poorly all winter, failing imperceptibly. Her great desire had been to know that her darling had been consecrated to God's work, and when this was done the silver cord seemed gently loosed. From afar she would see and know. Kathie's visits were a great pleasure, even to the last. Jessie and her husband and Charlie were sent for, and watched the tranquil death that was only another word for translation.

The funeral was a great tribute of respect paid to an honorable and useful life. They covered her grave with flowers, and wended their way back to the duties and responsiblities of the living.

To Kathie it had been a great shock. No one very near or dear to her had died since she could remember. She kept so pale and nervous that Uncle Robert insisted she should take a little journey with him, quite away from the cares of every-day life.

" It seems to me that I am going all the time," she made answer. " Perhaps, like Aunt Ruth, it is quietness I want."

" It is a little wholesome indolence, I think. We will leave everything behind us, and have one more rare holiday together."

They were gone a fortnight, and she came back much

improved. She had obeyed Uncle Robert to the letter and dismissed all her little perplexities.

"You are always so good and strong," she said. "I wonder what I shall ever do without you."

Why did she never count on the other strength that awaited her, that would be glad to serve?

CHAPTER XVI.

" I suppose we shall get used to the thought of her going away," Uncle Robert mused to himself, as he walked down to the post-office. There had been a little family talk on the subject. Somehow Ruth had not been at all enthusiastic, even though Charlie was one of her warmest favorites.

" We could not choose more wisely for her," Mrs. Alston had said with some decision.

" I suppose she chose for herself," Mrs. Mackenzie remarked, with the least emphasis of a rising inflection.

" Why, of course. And the life will suit her so perfectly."

Then it was agreed that the young man should come henceforth in the light of a lover. There would be no talk of a marriage until he was settled to his liking. Already the fervor of the young divine, and his extreme purity and sweetness, were making him a name.

Uncle Robert took his letters out carelessly, glanced over the unimportant ones, and paused at his nephew's. It had a small mark in one corner, ' Personal,' written very fine. No one ever opened his letters, and he smiled a little at the conceit.

But his face grew grave and pained as he read. It was very brief.

" DEAR UNCLE, — Can you come to me without creating any great surprise at home? I am in a terrible trouble, and need such a friend as you have always proved. I can only say it is no real crime on my part; at least nothing that transgresses the well-known laws of honor and honesty.

" ROB."

Then the trouble, whatever it was, had reached its culmination! Yes, it would be an easy enough matter to go. He need not mention any destination. Poor lad. When all outside surroundings were harmonious, even then there could not be peace.

"Dora," he said, walking up the broad steps, "I am compelled to go away to-night on some special business. I should not wonder if I took a run to Chicago and saw Rob."

"Oh!" The mother's face lighted up. "I wish you could bring him home with you."

"I suppose it is hardly his time for vacation," was the studied, careless answer. "Give me a little supper while I pick up a few articles."

It was not that he wanted to eat, but the curious impulse that leads us to observe little habits in any intense stress of feeling that must be kept hidden. Kathie came and chatted; he said good by to them all cheerfully, and took the evening train to the city.

It was evening again when he reached his destination. He had gone though with many phases of feeling during the journey, and settled at last to a tender pity. He could almost guess the secret of the trouble. Keeping it alone had become unendurable. Rob never could bear to be long shut on the outside of everything. It would be a great shock to the fancy his mother was cherishing. Ah, if they could have these children of their love back again to childhood!

As he stepped out on the platform in the gathering dusk of the summer night a hand was laid on his arm, before he could see the face.

"Rob," in a sympathetic tone.

"Dear uncle! I knew you would come. I was down to meet the other train, lest I might chance to miss you."

As they emerged from the crowd the elder drew the arm of the younger through his. There was something of comfort and confidence in the pressure.

"Let us go at once to the hotel; I have a room there," said the nephew.

Uncle Robert caught sight of the face then. It was very pale, and his eyes were heavy from lack of sleep. To the old resolute look there was added something stern, bitter.

"You are so good to come. There was no one else. I am always laying burdens on you." And the voice was tremulous with emotion.

"Since it is no disgrace like —" Dishonesty he was about to add, but Rob interrupted vehemently.

"I am not so sure of that! I have thought it over until I have gone almost wild."

"Rob, let us have done with the mystery. Something has been on your mind a long while. I think now you have married, unwisely, unhappily, but better that than any flagrant sin."

"O Uncle Robert! it brings back the errors of my boyhood to have you guess so unerringly. Did you mistrust, last summer or before?"

"I fancied at first you had contracted some debt that you resolved to work out of honorably. But last summer there were little things, and you kept so away from me."

"Yes, I was afraid. Wrong or sin always does make a coward of one."

"And your — wife?"

"We are here. I will order a little supper for us both, sent up to the room. It is a long story."

Uncle Robert asked no further question until they were seated at their meal, and he had a little time to study the face. There was something beside the bitterness, a certain vindictive force, long repressed.

"Rob, you have done her no ill?" he cried in sudden alarm.

"*She* has worked us both enough. Any one else would have paid the penalty with her life."

13

"Hush. Such a feeling is terrible. Rob, remember;
did you not choose her?"

He leaned his arms on the table and hid his face in them
for several minutes.

"I was such a blind, idiotic fool!" he began presently.
"I *was* warned, and it traversed all my plans, only I
hardly knew it until it was done."

"While you were in college?"

"Let me tell you from the beginning. I wonder now
how I could have kept it so entirely away from you all;
but I was ashamed, and it seemed such a poor return for
what you had done. I did n't seem to realize until it was
all over what I might have been to you at home. Are our
eyes always opened by these horrible contrasts, I wonder?
I feel as if I had cut myself off from everybody. No," as
his uncle offered him the plate of toast, "I don't want to
eat. I 'll talk while you are having supper. It is so good
to confess after this dreary time of secrecy.

"The last winter at New Haven I used to go to a house
where there were two bright, pretty girls, jolly and ready
for any kind of fun. Quite a number of the boys went
there; it was a regular free and easy, the mother seeming
about as young as the girls. They played and sang, and
were beautiful dancers. Some of the fellows used to send
wine and various things, and have gay little suppers. I
made up my mind not to be bantered into drinking, though
I did now and then take a glass of wine. Addie, the
younger girl, was very sweet to me, that sort of half-hidden, secret fondness that makes a mystery of a thing and
deepens its interest. I suppose she had gone through with
such fancies dozens of times; but I thought it was an entirely new regard that, somehow, she could n't help having
for me, and that it was n't possible for her to entertain for
any one else. Then she possessed one of the sweet, pleading, baby faces, and I suppose after a little, with all her
kissing and caressing, I did lose my head. I despise my-

self so for it now, that I could not be sure no really pure, high-minded, honorable girl would so throw herself at a man's head, or a boy's, for I was nothing but that. Two or three of the young fellows uttered warnings, but I set them down to jealousy

"Then Mrs. Weeks and Frances went to New York and were gone about a month Addie was at home with the girl, and she used to beg me so to come, and as I always found her alone it was very bewildering, fascinating. One evening she insisted on my drinking some wine with her, and when I refused the second glass she seemed so hurt, and cried a little, and said I didn't care for her while she cared so much for me, and would do anything to please me. So I drank a little more. We had fallen into the habit of saying silly things, making love without really meaning affection. I was a little startled at first by her way of uttering them, but she seemed so sweet and innocent about it; and you know I had never been spoony on girls," with a sad little smile. "I had never really cared for them, and I had no more thought of marrying Addie Weeks than of any one I knew at Brookside. Other boys were carrying on flirtations, and having no end of fun out of them. Yet I don't know as I ever settled it in my mind as a regular flirtation. She bewitched me when I was with her, and I never thought of any ending at all.

"Well, whether it was the wine or my own mad folly, or a something like love, or, as I have thought since, her deliberate aim to make me do it, we began to talk of marriage. I must have asked her to marry me, for she proposed that we should go to the house of a minister she knew and get married. How could I have been so crazy, you wonder! I can't understand it myself now, only then I was wild with a curious fascination, and I did it. It was two years ago last April.

"I felt strangely frightened after it was over, but I was not disenchanted. On the contrary, then I would have owned her as my wife anywhere in the face of the whole world. I thought her the prettiest, sweetest, dearest being upon earth. I was ready to do anything for her. For a week or two I was in Fool's Paradise. Then her mother came home. We were going to keep our marriage a profound secret until after I had graduated."

There followed quite a long silence. Rob was waiting for some word of condemnation or surprise, but presently his uncle uttered a soft, persuasive, inquiring, "Well?"

"The rest is so shameful, Uncle Robert!" And his pale face blazed crimson. "There was a little rumor that Frances Weeks had gone abroad with a rich New-Yorker in a questionable position. It made me furious when I first heard it. Addie denied it and cried over it, then admitted she had sailed, but that she was going to try the stage or do something for herself. But other ugly stories came to light about her, and there were hints concerning the mother. They lived prettily, dressed well, and always seemed to have plenty of money and quantities of presents.

"After a while my marriage grew to be an appalling certainty to me. I had to study hard to make up for a little lost time, and Addie went to Albany with her mother for a visit. I resolutely staved off the conclusion. She was pretty, and with a little toning down or refining might be made presentable. I was so glad to have them away over Commencement. I did have a nice time with you and mother, and I was glad to see you so pleased and proud.

"Of course I could not bring a wife home to you without any means of supporting her. I felt she was not the kind of girl you would approve; that it would half break mother's heart. That made me resolve to go quite away, to get in some business so far distant that much visiting would be out of the question. When Addie had been transformed into something a little more ladylike I would own what I had done. It was a horrible secret, and when I first came home I threw myself into all the pleasures and excitements with unwonted zest. I could n't comprehend all at once that I had really banned myself out. Of course Addie wrote to me. From Albany they had gone to Lake George, from thence to Saratoga, and she was having such a splendid time. I wonder that I did not feel hurt or jealous. If I only could get away before the time for explanations.

"Then you know I went to New Haven. They had returned, and Addie had admitted the marriage to her mother. Mrs. Weeks pretended to a good deal of indignation, and insisted that I should at once take Addie to my people and put her in her proper position before the world. She seemed to feel quite shocked that she had been taking her about as a marriageable girl. It was an extremely silly step, and she did not see how I could have thought of marriage, and blamed me pretty generally for it all. And then I found they believed, or affected to, that Cedarwood was in some sort mine, as I was your heir.

"I suppose I *had* come to my senses a little. Mrs. Weeks's talking appeared to me very much done for effect, and I could see what they thought of the money and position. When I said I would have nothing but what I could earn, and that it was my determination to go into business immediately, and that I would care for Addie to the best of my ability, she was desperately angry, and declared she would not have married me if she supposed that was to be her fate, and a great many other things that opened my eyes to her selfish indifference. They tried to compel me to bring her home to you, but I stood resolute, and when Mrs. Weeks said she and Addie would go without me, I declared then that I would go quite away, that I would never see her, never own her as my wife, and that from my own people she would get nothing. I was desperate enough for any step. But I did promise to take her out to Chicago, and to keep her as my wife if she would consent to that.

" I do think they were quite crestfallen when they found I would not go to you for any money, or take Addie to Cedarwood as a sort of *quasi* mistress.   We had two very stormy days, and my enchantment came to a dismal ending. It is a desecration to call such a sentiment love ! " And an expression of wearisome disgust crept over his face.   " In less than five months the romance or madness was ended, and I was tied to a woman for whom I did not care, and who would cling to me only for a support, or because the law had given us to each other.   I meant then to get a divorce just as soon as possible, and bury the shameful secret in my own soul.   I came back to Cedarwood ; you know we were all so happy about Kathie's return, and there was to be the party and all."

" Oh, my boy ! "   Uncle Robert began, " I don't know how you *did* endure it so bravely."

" I can't decide whether it was courage," and a wan smile crossed the face that was growing rigid with conflicting emotions ; " but don't you remember I always had a good deal of what the boys call pluck, endurance, obstinacy, and the sort of feeling there is no help and you must go through with the matter in hand.   And I had to do it without awakening any suspicion on your part, so I went into all the pleasures heartily.   I did n't even want to think it might be the last glad time.   There were hours when I felt wild, crazy, realizing bitterly how much of it I had thrown away.   Home never looked as lovely to me. Mother and Aunt Ruth were such sweet and gracious ladies, and the girls so pure, and refined, and wholesome. Kathie was so enthusiastic over Miss Collamore, and I liked her very, very much.   All the delights took a higher tone ; there was a repose and sweetness, a meaning to it all that came to me with a sudden, blinding light. And I was going out to eternal exile, it seemed to me.

There were moments when I wanted to put my arm around
your neck in the old boy fashion and tell you how grateful I was for everything you had ever done for me, for the
great effort you had made to keep me in the right way,
but I did not dare indulge in any sentiment. I should
have broken down, and the truth would have come out.

"So I went to Chicago. Addie and her mother gave
up their house in New Haven, came to New York for
a while, and I lived in a state of horrible suspense lest they
should appeal to you. They went to Baltimore afterward,
and did not reach Chicago until January. I had secured
a quiet boarding place in the suburbs. It seemed at first
as if Addie was quite glad to see me. She appeared tired
and worn out with dissipation, and looked so much older;
and I learned then she was some five years older than
she had claimed to be; that instead of being eighteen at
the time of our marriage she was twenty-three. All these
months I had been studying how I could get free event-
ually; but her coming rudely dispelled my plans. In March
her baby was born."

"Your child, Robert? Oh, my poor boy, what a dreary,
dreary time! It would have been better to have confessed
it all in the beginning. Where is the child; alive?"

"Yes," he answered moodily, "it is. It cried a
great deal, and she insisted she was not able to take care
of it, so we put it out to nurse. She did not get well very
rapidly, and I found she had made no improvement in
mind or character. The habit of using liquors had grown
upon her, and there were times — it is shameful to say it
— when she was not herself, but silly and disgusting. She
had quite made up her mind to stay with me now. Her
mother went off somewhere. I was glad of that. My
plans, therefore, must be changed. I could not shake her
off so easily. I had a strange feeling, too, about the child,
and whether I would be quite right to get free from the
mother, if I could.

"I redoubled my efforts to make money, doing copying at night, and keeping an extra set of books, and looking after expenses every way. She really seemed to have no idea about money. After the hot weather came in she grew stronger, and the last of July she wanted to go away for a month with some friends she had made, and I consented. I came home in August, you know.

"All this time I had been fighting with myself. Bruce and I corresponded frequently, and, without knowing the story at all, he seemed to understand that something was wrong, and his letters were so brave and comforting. I could see the right through his eyes, and all my own weakness and folly. I do believe if he had been at Cedarwood I must have told him. You know it would not have been as keen a sorrow to him as to you; it would not have touched him so nearly.

"Uncle Robert, I wonder if I was weak in so giving up my whole heart to the pleasure of home? I really had not made up my mind to anything until that first night; then I resolved to shut out my own misery, to be as happy, to make you all as happy as I could. And in a few days a curious knowledge or revelation came to me." And Rob turned his face a little, while he tried to steady his voice. "I may have misunderstood, but it seemed as if mother, Kathie, and every one had a secret feeling that — that Fay Collamore might be brought in our midst, and would be warmly, fondly welcomed. Suddenly, as if in a blazing light, I saw what it might have been to me."

Rob sprang up and began to pace the floor. Oh, what words could comfort! Mr. Conover rose, too, came and put his arm over the other's shoulder, but was silent.

"I knew then that I had admired Fay Collamore from the very first, that I had been pleased when Kathie wrote about her, that if all things were fair and right, I could bring such a complete happiness in the family; I could be happy myself. Here was a girl worth loving and hon-

oring, and I had promised my soul and body to the other.
While she lived I had no right to put her away except for
some great and awful crime. And if I did put her away
on any weak, flimsy pretext, a girl like Fay Collamore,
with so high and fine a sense of justice, would not marry
me, ought not. And so the training of my whole life, that
oftentimes seemed thrown away, I dare say; the companionship of such men as you, and Mr. Meredith, and Mr.
Langdon, of such boys as Charlie, and Bruce, and Dick,
and women like mother and Aunt Ruth, joined to save me.
I had gone into this thing by my own mad folly, and I
must bear it myself, not thrust it on other people's shoulders, not cry out for the joys I had missed by my own
heedlessness. And I vowed, with God's help, that hence-
forward I would be to you all it was possible for son, or
brother, or friend, and keep my own soul clear of any new
stains. I could not help being thrown with Fay, but I did
try utterly to give no look or word, to hold no thought de-
rogatory to her. Mother's delicate little plans were hard
to traverse, and I fancy Fay wondered at times. Yet difficult and painful as the path was, I hated so to leave you, to
come back to my own wretched life. I would not mar
your delightful hours with such gray shadows."

"But you might have told me," the elder cried, with a
touch of upbraiding in his tone.

"No, I could n't. My strength was in keeping still.
Sympathy, tenderness would have finished me. We should
have betrayed our secret."

"But now?" Mr. Conover asked in a tone of something
like relief. "Have you come to the end?"

Rob made a passionate gesture, as if he could crush
something out of sight. "If it could be the end," he
cried. "If you can decide —"

"Go on, then."

"I came back to Chicago, and she joined me a month
later. We had a new boarding place of her choosing,

among the kind of people she liked. They were polite enough to me, but I fancy they considered me a young fool, and they were right enough," bitterly. "I did try to awaken some desire of better things in her, and remonstrated, as I had times before, about her drinking, but it always ended in painful disputes. There was absolutely nothing I could do. She still kept her voice, but she used it to charm her favorites, with her other blandishments. I was not jealous; it is strange, but I never had been jealous of her from the first. I had to be away evenings with extra work, for the money was a necessity, but when I remained at home she was as likely to go out. And so we went on our way, the bond growing harder and harder to bear. I think she was really sorry she had married me; she did say now and then she was a fool for having done it. Oh, why *did* she? There was nothing in a home to satisfy her, and she might have taken some one older, richer, more like herself.

"I went home two weeks ago and found a note on the bureau directed to myself. Come to the light and read it, and you will hardly say that I have been bitter or unjust in this terrible story."

Mr. Conover took the crumpled missive and spread it out. It was poorly written and misspelled, and betrayed a sort of scornful animosity in every line. She had been altogether disappointed in the marriage, and she could endure it no longer; she had been a fool for ever trying to live with him. She had gone with some one who cared for her beyond a boy's silly regard; she would have all she wanted, and he need make no search for her or trouble himself in any way about her. She had never cared for the child or wanted it; so he might take the child, and get a divorce as soon as he pleased; it could not be too soon for her.

"There is no question, then, about freedom —"

The young face was turned to him with a strained, desperate longing, and yet a peculiar awe. His voice was hoarse with emotion as he cried : —

"That is not all. There was a terrible accident right in the beginning of their journey. *He* escaped unharmed. She was terribly injured about the head, and taken to a hospital. After a few days the doctors decided she might recover, but that she would never have her senses again. Then the word was sent to me. The lover, you see, could not take her at so great a sacrifice. O Uncle Robert, is n't it horribly hard ! What can I do ? "

He flung himself on the sofa and buried his face on the cushioned arm, while hard, dry sobs shook his frame. His uncle paced the floor in great distress. All this young life that should have been so bright, and glad, and promising, marred and blighted by one fatal deed.

He sprang up suddenly, his eyes fierce with despairing passion, his voice clinging to a last ray of hope.

"Ought I to keep to her, Uncle Robert? She went away for her own pleasure. She did not even care for her own little child. She has broken God's law, man's law, and a horrible, swift punishment has overtaken her. Is there any justice in making *me* suffer for it, years, perhaps ? "

"O my boy, we cannot decide this in a moment! You are worn out with excitement, and must have a little rest ; and I must think it over. Can I see her some time ? "

"Yes. She has been sent here. She is in the hospital. Every care and attention will be paid her."

"Then we will not settle that point to-night. Sit down here and rest."

CHAPTER XVII

In spite of Robert Alston's splendid physique and buoyant temperament, his night's vigil and the anxiety of the past week had begun to tell upon him. He looked worn and haggard; his lips seemed compressed to a thin, bluish line. His uncle had tried to make him sleep some through the night, but the greater part of it had been spent in restlessly pacing the floor, even if he refrained from impatient questioning. He had asked for leave of absence from the counting-house, so he could have the day to devote to his uncle and the sadder errands.

There were many little things that had not been related in the hurried story of the evening before. The young man did not spare himself, and yet it seemed as if the foolish girl had made fully as great a sacrifice, unless she had counted on the possible wealth of the youth. It was quite evident she had taken no special interest in any of his pursuits, neither had it been from any ardent regard for him.

They went together to see her. There was one cut at the edge of her hair, and the discolor from bruises had not quite disappeared. Seen there, in that strange life-in-death state, the face had come back to a curious, youthful beauty, the beauty put in marble when a soul is not needed. The skin was fine and soft, full of sinuous blue pencillings, the rounded chin had a deep dimple, the full, curved lips were closed even now with a coquettish half-smile, and the long bronze lashes shadowed the pale cheeks. Once, she opened her eyes. They were of that infantile, purple blue, and Mr. Conover, well versed in the ways and wiles of womankind, could readily understand how dangerous their snares might be for unwary youth. Yet it had seemed as if that would be the least of all temptations to Robert Alston.

They saw one of the physicians presently. It was merely an iteration of the verdict. There was no reason why she should not live; her physical injuries had not been severe, but the brain had suffered beyond any repair.

"She will be harmless," he said in a gentle tone; "never violent, and probably sink into mild idiocy. Of course she will need continual care. I think I should advise an asylum, unless she has friends, such as mother or sister. Even then it is a tiresome charge to one unused to such cases."

"Do you know anything about her mother?" Uncle Robert asked afterward.

Rob gave a shiver of disgust. "No," he answered; "they quarrelled bitterly the last time she was here, and they are not people one would care to hunt up, even if we could."

"Of course," the elder said gravely, "there is only one thing to do at present. When she is discharged from here she must be placed somewhere in safety, and provision made for her. An asylum will be the best."

If she had died! They could not but think of that simple ending to the tragedy, and yet God had not chosen so to make it. And how to take the next important step rightly and truly for this young soul was a matter of grave consideration to Robert Conover.

As they emerged from the hospital he said to his nephew, "Rob, will you take me to see the child?"

The young man flushed vividly, but assented. Uncle Robert made no comment, but presently his nephew broke the silence.

"I suppose you *will* think me heartless," in a kind of

15

justifying tone, " only you can't see all at once, Uncle
Robert, and understand how pressed I was on every side.
She did not want the child at home, and it was very troublesome at night. Then I needed my strength and ener-
gies for business. It was much cheaper to put it out, a
consideration I could not afford to despise, and it seemed
to me much better. I do suppose it weakened the tie ; I
never can make it *my* child. I feel as if I had no business with a child."

" And you surely have not, Robert, at your age. It is
a sad commentary on early marriages. I never imagined
you could be beguiled into such a step, and so this was one
of the points never discussed. There is too slight a
responsibility attached to it nowadays. I am not sure
but among our other studies we ought to educate young
men for marriage, train them to the gravity, the sacredness of the step, the awful solemnity of the vow, ' for
better, for worse.' "

" How could I have done it? I ask myself the question
over and over again. I had been drinking a little wine
that night, but that did n't take away my senses. And I
did n't care for marriage, either ; I had not been thinking
of it — "

" Just what I said. If it had been held as a solemn
sacrament, more important than joining a church even, or
any secular step in life, you could not have done it.
Did n't you say last night you *were* warned."

" Yes, two or three of the fellows talked about them in
a rather sneering manner, which always made me feel as
if I wanted to get up and fight. And yet they were
received in society, in some society, for Addie's music
made her a great favorite. And no one quite knew until
the sister went to Europe ; then a great deal of gossip came
out about them. But it was too late for me."

Uncle Robert understood more clearly than his nephew
how it had happened ; how a few moments of inconsiderate

imprudence had wrecked, if not a whole life, at least several years of it. A beautiful, designing girl, vain, selfish, with no thought beyond her own present pleasure and advancement, fancying, no doubt, this would be a road to wealth and indulgence. While he could not absolve the lad from a great share of the responsibility, he still felt he was not all to blame.

"It is remarkable how you kept her from making any overtures to the family," he said, a little astonished that it had been done so successfully.

"When her mother threatened so, in the summer, I took my stand boldly. I said you and mother would not receive them. Honestly, I did not think you would, and I declared if they did it I would go entirely away and take some steps to have the marriage annulled. I am not sure but I should have then and there, only the trouble and disgrace seemed so horrible! Then Addie suddenly changed and went at her mother in a fury. She loved me and she was not going to give me up, and she would wait until I was in some position to take care of her. She seemed so sorry and begged me to forgive her, and cried, and I did n't know what else to do. I thought something might happen to open a way out of it for me; she might get tired and obtain a divorce. I was almost crazy."

"You hid it very successfully."

"Is n't it strange how we can live such double lives? But there was everything to help. Kathie was the great interest, you know, and I tried to act natural, not to overdo anywhere. It was for such a little while. I could n't have kept it up very long. I think now Mrs. Weeks found during her stay in New York that it would be unwise to appeal to you. It was n't even as if you were my father. The law could not compel you to care for my wife. I made up my mind if they did I would fight it out to the end. They had relatives in Baltimore, some quite wealthy people, and it was not wisdom for them to remain in New

Haven. It was rather odd, but in a month I had found some quite profitable copying to do evenings. Uncle Robert, you would have laughed at my rigid economy"; and the boy smiled, even now. "I did not waste a penny, and had quite a little hoard when she came, although I think I had been saving it with the hope that she never would come. And then everything was changed."

"Yes." There was such an infinite tenderness and sympathy in the one little word.

"Bruce and I had been writing letters. I don't know why he seemed nearer to me than any of the boys through this time, but he was so strong, and manly, and earnest, that it did me good. I couldn't have written to you that way without telling you the whole story. I think he fancied I had a leaning or temptation for intemperance, and I let it go at that. Uncle Robert," and the young man's face hardened into marble-like resolution, "I think you know why I shall never touch even a drop of wine again in my life. Maybe, too, my rather solitary living and constant work had given me a sort of force and tone, and if Addie had loved and kept the child I should have felt quite differently. Afterward I realized that it was cheaper, and better for the child. Here we are."

A cleanly row of frame houses with tiny flower gardens in front, and at the open window of one sat a pleasant-faced young woman, sewing, who glanced up and smiled, then came to open the door.

Robert introduced his uncle to Mrs. Fleming.

"The baby is asleep," she said, smiling with a soft, motherly fondness. "She was late with her nap this morning. Will you look in and see her?"

In the next room the little one lay in her crib. There was not much in the baby face to remind one of its mother. A wholesome, chubby face, merry and cheerful, rather than specially handsome.

"She is the best little thing you can imagine," Mrs.

Fleming went on, with true motherly pride. " And I wish
you could see her eyes. They are something the color of
her father's, hazel, but just full of laughter and sunshine.
I think they are the prettiest eyes I ever saw. Shall I
wake her? She will not be cross; she never is."

" Oh, no ! " Uncle Robert stretched out his hand suddenly, and glanced at the child as if his soul had gone
past that to something else, a thought of her future, maybe. In his young-man days he had been fond of bright,
pretty, chatty, questioning little girls. His friends declared he always spoiled them. After the years of wandering he had come back unexpectedly to family cares and
sympathies, and the child Kathie had taken the love that
might have grown into something for an older woman.
True, he was not beyond marriageable age, but he was
settled in his habits, satisfied; nay, more, interested in his
work, suited with the home comforts. Yet one side of his
soul went out so tenderly to little children, especially girls.
He was the man to father a great house full of them, to
love, to direct, to enjoy their frolic and happiness. This
desolate little baby, not really wanted by either parent,
appealed to him powerfully, but he was thankful it looked
so little like its mother. Indeed, it was Rob over again in
his baby days.

He turned softly, as if a move might waken it. " We
will come in again, " with a pause, as if there were more
to say.

Mrs. Fleming glanced from one to the other, and a sudden anxiety crossed her face. You could see the real
mother love had been touched. Ah, that did not always
come with relationship.

" You are not thinking of taking it away?"

Her voice trembled, and there came a humid fear and
softness in her eyes.

" No," stammered the father, startled by the question.

" It would be better for me to keep her until fall, you

see. The summer is trying for such a little one, and she is used to my care and ways. It would be a bad time to make a change."

" Yes," was the satisfactory response.

They emerged to the street again.

" Robert," his uncle began presently, " how much of this disgraceful story is known or suspected. Have you been able to keep it within bounds?"

" It is very little known," and he gave a somewhat bitter laugh. " You can hide almost anything in a great city. You understand now that I have not gone into much company. I did allow myself one little luxury, the membership of a debating club. I could not afford to get rusty in everything. Last year we lived quite in the suburbs, and the people with whom we boarded have gone farther west. Our other home was most uncongenial. Whether any one there was in her confidence I do not know. I said nothing the night I found the note, and had all arrangements made for a change when the accident occurred, two days later. Consequently I have not seen them. Even the most exciting stories do die out soon."

They went back to the hotel for lunch, and then retired to their room. Rob threw himself on the sofa. The reaction from the terrible strain had come. Giving up the secret, he had also given up much of the tense strength that had borne him successfully so far.

" Try to get a little nap," proposed his uncle, kindly, " though if you will answer me one more question?"

" You have only to ask it."

There was a sad little touch of penitence in this; the tone that implied all manner of reservation was forever at an end.

" Robert, have you gone through all this without getting in debt? Your expenses must have been beyond your salary, it seems to me; beyond anything you could earn."

" But I have earned it, or nearly all. A week ago I

took up a hundred dollars. I have been deadly economical with myself," smiling faintly. "I put some of the lessons of my boyhood in practice. I was resolved not to come to you, and not to get in debt. Uncle, it was almost like fighting with wild beasts at Ephesus, if I may be allowed to use the simile."

"You have shown a great deal of bravery through it all." And Mr. Conover felt really amazed.

"Thank you." There was a wistful pleasure in the heavy eyes.

The quietness of the room, the drowsiness of the warm summer air, and the fatigue of weary days and nights had their influence presently.

Robert Alston fell into a light slumber, and his uncle, watching him, revolved many points in his mind. He was too experienced in the world's sad wisdom to blame unreasonably, and the vague suspicion of the past year had in some degree prepared him for the blow. Had there been any negligence or wrong in the lad's training? Could there have been a warning, counsel, anything to save him? Yet what availed going over the past? The blindness and madness of the hour had wrought their terrible woe, and the cure was not looking backward and picking out a hundred different courses that would have saved it all.

And withal he gave thanks fervently, devoutly, that it had not hurried him on to ruin. He knew how swift and easy the path could be made in a moment of horrible discouragement. Yes, the good seed had sprung up and borne fruit; manful endurance that an older soul might have wavered in, a clinging to truth, and honor, and right, in spite of adverse circumstances. The clean and wholesome boyhood, the pure ideals, the graces of higher life, the training of all those years, were not without a certain recompense. He was glad to have his boy back again, unstained by any gross vice, unpolluted by an association that might have dragged him down to shameful depths.

The thought of home and friends had held the wavering balance. In time there might come something higher, the greater strength, the perfect peace. All wisdom was not in youth, not even in middle life. It was going on, stumbling and yet rising, imperfect, and yet being made perfect in the end by the divine love and patience. If that could so forgive, so stretch out a helping hand, were we to judge, and weigh, and condemn?

And yet he hardly knew what step was best. The shock would be very great to Mrs. Alston, with her clinging, tender fancies that had grown into other plans. And there was a path out of it. Worldly wisdom and prudence would approve of it.

When Rob stirred the afternoon was almost gone. He woke with a sudden start, as if he could hardly remember, but his uncle's face reassured him.

" Suppose we put by the perplexing questions for a while," he said, " and go for a pleasant drive. I have just written a note home that I shall stay with you several days. We will begin our visit now."

" How good you are ! " Rob pressed his uncle's hand, and the tears of gratitude shone in his eyes.

" I thank God that he has kept your love and trust for me through it all "

Rob started a little. Had there been, unconsciously, a higher power ruling, guiding him? Many a time in his agony he had cried to God, feeling himself so helpless, so despairing ! Had there been an answer? Was this what was meant in the text that flashed suddenly into his mind, "My grace is sufficient for thee " ? Not take thee out of the depth, or set thee up on high, but just " suffi-cient." Not even any left over to glory about, or for the days to come ; to-day and here, — that was all of the promise. But when we get at to-morrow, is it not to-day already?

They had a delightful drive out through the suburbs and

by the edge of the lake. The sun dropped down in his gold and crimson splendors, and the moon, a silvery bit of crescent, floated along on the edge of a blue-rimmed cloud. They talked in bits and snatches of old times, of the boys and their aims, of the past pleasures, now doubly dear.

"I ought to tell you about Kathie," Uncle Robert said in a soft tone. They had been discussing Charlie Darrell's pure and gracious youth, with its refined and exalted ideals. "It was spoken of last summer, but they were so young. The faith has been kept, however, and your mother is extremely happy. It is now an acknowledged engagement."

"Not Charlie?" There was a peculiar unwillingness in Rob's face.

"Why not?" Why could there be secret dissatisfaction here?

"Oh, if Kathie cares — loves — " And Rob glanced away.

"She could not have done it without caring."

"I suppose not," lingeringly. Yet it seemed to him he held a clew to another "caring." "Did no one know of it last summer but just you and mamma? I never suspected."

"No one. It was hardly more than a fancy. At least Aunt Ruth was told, and Charlie's family on his part. You must not feel hurt; we were afraid you might tease her."

"Oh, I was not thinking of myself." Some sudden impulse checked him, and he understood then he had grown finer and more considerate than in that heedless boyhood.

It was another's secret, guessed at, and he had no right to betray it. But he held a clew to sentences in Bruce's letters that had puzzled him as greatly as the sudden resolve of not coming East.

"And have you no word of approval?" Uncle Robert was a trifle perplexed.

" O Uncle Robert, it seems so queer for Kathie to be engaged! Yes, I suppose it is just the life for her, and they have always been such friends. I do believe Charlie has loved her from very boyhood, and he is good, and noble, and tender. Any one cold or hard, or even carelessly indifferent, would break Kathie's heart."

And yet Rob gave a little sigh. How lonely it must be out there, with nothing to keep the heart warm and glad. Robert Alston seemed drawn to Bruce at that moment with a deep and wordless tie, a sympathy no one else could feel, he thought, not knowing of the bitterer disappointment in the two older hearts.

" Dear little Kathie, I hope she will be very happy," he said after a while. " She has been such a comfort to you and mamma, while I have brought nothing but sorrow and disappointment."

" Yes, Rob, many hours of pleasure as well."

" You are very generous to say so ! " he cried with deep emotion. " It would be just right, Uncle Robert, if you gave me up altogether."

" No, not *just right*."

He understood the allusion. It was divine love that went after the one sheep astray, and meted out a tenderer mercy than worldly justice.

The following day Rob went back to business for several hours, promising to get off early. Uncle Robert visited Mrs. Fleming and made acquaintance with his little grand-niece. A bright, cunning baby she proved, beginning to run about, and saying pretty little sentences, with her glad, laughing face in an eager glow of interest. Full of mischief, too, and winsome ways that were not allowed to degenerate into disagreeable habits. A wiser, tenderer foster-mother could hardly have been found, though she was a plain body and a poor man's wife. Her vague explanations corroborated what Robert had said, that the mother cared little for her child.

" It seems a pity for God to send them to fashionable young folks who only care for dressing, and company, and pleasuring," exclaimed the honest woman. "They waste their health and strength on other things, and have nothing left for their children. She was such a poor little baby when I took her, and she fretted all the time, they said ; but no one knew how to take care of her, and she 's the best little thing now you can imagine. I should be sorry for them to take her back now ; not for the money's sake, either, though that comes good, but I 'd rather care for her for nothing the rest of the summer. I 've lost two little ones of my own, and it seems almost like having one of them lent to me a while again."

Uncle Robert smiled and assured her there should be no change made for the summer.

But some step must be settled upon. After a conscientious talk with the hospital physician he decided upon the asylum. It was physically impossible that she should recover her senses ; indeed, there might come presently a gradual paralysis.

" It seems a hard fate for a handsome young woman like that, and with a fine fellow for a husband. There is many a sad romance in a hospital ward, and sadder ones still shut inside of asylum walls," the grave doctor said slowly, thinking to comfort his hearer.

The days passed so quickly that Robert Alston grudged them, as if the sunshine were grains of gold. He almost forgot the keen edge of wretchedness in having this tender friend with him again. Oh, how was he ever to spare him ?

" Robert," the elder began, one evening, " we ought to make some plans about the future. You are content, satisfied with your position in a mercantile house? "

Robert was silent.

" It was your choice, you know."

" Oh, Uncle Robert ! " he cried vehemently, " it was

the result of that miserable, mad folly. I could not make you suffer for the misdoing, and so I gave up my choice. And now," his face settling into resolute lines, " there is nothing but to go on for the present."

" You did have another fancy?"

" Well, I may tell you now ; chemistry always interested me so much. Maybe I should not have had the patience, and it is too late to wish about it. But I would like to ask one favor, if you think it best."

" Well?"

" That I may come back to New York some time. You see," with a sad smile, " I have not taken root here. The place will always be full of miserable memories for me. And I have learned to care a great deal more for the old friends."

There was a lingering tremulousness in his tone that touched the elder deeply.

" We must also decide upon your standing with them. Robert, how much of the truth are you willing to face?"

There was a great struggle in the young man's mind. A mad desire to leave it all behind, to start afresh, possessed him.

" How much *must* I face?" he cried passionately. " Uncle Robert, I kept my truth and honor under temptation ; you must confess it was that. I did not love my wife, and yet I did everything. I would not be pushed or thrust out of any right line. I tried, yes, I think God will bear me witness that I *did* try faithfully to give her all the happiness in my power. Her ways were not mine. I could not drink and carouse, even to please her ; but she openly, flagrantly transgressed and outraged all laws. There is the proof, her own admission. Am I bound to her? She had decided her course before this fearful accident. I should have been free."

It was man to man now. The tender regard, the penitence and sorrow, were put aside. He was ready for a desperate struggle. The matter had been brooding in his brain for days, though it had been so quiescent.

Robert Conover's sympathy was on the side of freedom as well. His affection for the young life just coming to understand itself and its needs; his admiration for the brave manner in which he had taken up the sad results of his great mistake, his boyish unwisdom rather than flagrant sin, worked powerfully in his behalf. And yet, just here would be the turning-point of character, the firmness of truth and higher living, or the volatile desire of what was most pleasant, after a brief repentance. Yet it was so hard and bitter to remand him back to the old chain.

"Robert," and the voice was unsteady with conflicting emotions, "I do not think either of us is in a condition to decide so important a question; we cannot take in all its bearings."

"But we *can* take in its main points. Uncle Robert, you have never toned down or softened sins that I committed, even when you loved me best, and no one could have loved me better; now why can you find palliation for her? It is not even as if she were going to realize any disgrace. The punishment came swiftly to her; why should that, the result of her sin, be made to reach me? I have been over and over the ground. I don't see any right. any justice — "

Rob bowed his face in his hands. To have all things remain the same; why, he might as well die at once!

"Yes," returned Mr. Conover with grave sweetness, "all this seems the side of justice. It is too wide in its significance to be hastily settled. There is another life to consider. There is a little child that did not ask to be born to a blighted heritage. Robert, suppose I was to tell you to-day that the husband your mother loved so well, the father you children had been taught to revere and honor, even after he was in his grave, had been a forger, a thief, dishonored his name and that of a family, and just by death escaped a prison cell! Could you ever throw off the terrible shadow? Thank God there is no such thing to say. He was the soul of honor and integrity, and I am not sure but his example, though I used to think him a little rigid on some points, has made me more thoughtful, led me in some doubtful cases to see the finer right. It seems to me here is an opportunity to come out of the affair without any open disgrace. A boyish imprudence can be excused, forgiven. You are not the first lad who has made a secret and unwise marriage. Some women, well loved and sheltered, have lost their reason and spent whole lives as she must spend hers. Your share in it can step now from a fault to a misfortune. The people who know or have known her may never connect her with you or your child. When you have gone over all this ground patiently you can decide whether you will suffer a wrong, or do a wrong and harm to right yourself."

"Then there is no hope for me!" He sprang up and began to pace the floor with passion in every step. "All my life I am to be bound to her! I can do nothing, be nothing for my very self. Why," with a bitter laugh, "it is harder than if she had not gone. The punishment is greater for me than for her, since she is relieved from all mental suffering. There will be no use trying for any future."

"Robert," his uncle said kindly, "this is why we older men try to restrain and advise youth. We know of so many snares and pitfalls, and the disastrous consequences. This is why I have so desired to keep your confidence; it seemed as if you could not take any fatal step if you came and discussed it first. Did I make the terms too hard? Where did I fail?"

"You are not to blame," Rob said sullenly. "It is my own doing and I must bear it, that is all. I suppose I have been a blind fool and thrown away all my chances.

There are only the husks left. It *is* hard to be condemned to them years and years, perhaps always."

"As I said, we cannot decide the matter now. There are some legal aspects ; in any event you will be answerable for her maintenance, I think, and we had better see what must be done and what can be done."

"It will not matter much to me now. Good night," he said abruptly ; and, going to his room, threw himself undressed on the bed, and, burying his face hard in the pillow, gave way to bitter, desperate tears. He had dared to dream of freedom, of being in the old home just the same, of having a new chance for right living, happiness. He was so young, so young! He *had* tried to be just, and fair, and honorable ; *she* had never tried for anything but her own enjoyment, and to-night her fate looked the best, he said, in his sullen misery.

CHAPTER XVIII.

ROBERT ALSTON was gravely quiet the next morning, with that baffling, polite reserve that shut him out as effectually as the obstinate determination of his boyhood. He made a pretence of eating breakfast and went to business, leaving his uncle sore at heart, puzzled, and anxious. It certainly was a critical time in the young man's life, and on this decision would depend much of his future character. Home and love were such strong ties, Uncle Robert knew well. The lesson was a bitter one, and it was hardly likely any other great temptation would assail him in an active, contented life. But dissatisfaction, unrest, no safe anchorage, the gloomy despair of youth; what then?

"Robert," he said that evening, "I must return home for a short time, and make some explanation of matters. Your mother ought to know. Some safe and proper home must be provided for the baby. The poor thing at the hospital will remain a few weeks longer. I have visited two asylums, and find she can be kept very comfortably at no very great expense. In the mean while you must consider upon your course. I have resolved *not* to attempt to bias you. I only ask you to take plenty of time to decide."

"Uncle Robert," the young man replied in a cold, even tone, "suppose you lay down the burden of it? I have always made you trouble and sorrow; give me up now, cast me off. I have a good situation, and Addie will not cost as much in an asylum as elsewhere. I will look after the child."

" O Robert! After the years and confidence! What have I done that you should cast *me* off? For it is thrusting aside love, sympathy, help. Are you so strong you can stand alone?"

"If I can't I deserve to go under, that is all. I shall always be grateful to you for what you have done, only I am not worth any more."

"If God thinks we are always worth more love and pa-. tience, if he is willing to take the wrong and evils upon himself, to deliver us, to strengthen us, can we not do something for one another? Or must his grace be in vain?"

"But the evils are there; no one can remove them," the young man replied, with stubborn apathy.

"If it were best, He could. Rob, I am not going to preach to you. I think you know so many of these truths yourself; but if your eyes are blinded, a more powerful hand than mine must give them light. There are so many things to stumble over. I cannot see why God did not take her out of the world when he deprived her of all mental power and responsibility. She can never repent, she can never be conscious of any retribution, hardly of physical suffering. It would be so much easier to have it all ended here."

There was a sudden gleam of interest in the stoical face.

"Yes, that is it. If—"

"Rob, did you ever wish her dead before?"

"No, Uncle, God is my witness that I never did. I never even thought of her going away as she did. It was a desperate living on day by day, wishing for you, for some friend, some comfort. And, when it came so near, oh, why, why was n't there an end?" And he studied his uncle's face with feverish intensity.

"That is one of the things we cannot tell. I have learned to leave it just there, with God. He has not made us our own pardoning or condemning angels. He gives

us states and conditions to live through, the sort of outcome of something that has gone before, some mistake, or
negligence, or failure. Out of it may come redemption.
The why is his, the work is ours. We get confused and
transpose them ; but he never gives us up, and as he loved
us, so we are to love the brethren."

"It is very hard."

Rob's lip quivered with the suppressed sigh, but he
could not keep the shiver from running through his frame.

"You can make it harder. You *can* have help to bear
the burden."

There was a long silence.

"You feel that you must make some explanation at
home?" the young man inquired presently.

"It is not absolutely necessary now. You can make
your decision first, if you like. There is one thing I want
to say ; nay, I shall ask it as a favor. You will have
heavy enough burden on your hands. You are very young,
and the mere fact of parentage does not always bring wisdom or love. When it is best to make the change, I want
you to give the child to me. She will need oversight,
training, and home tenderness. When Kathie goes we
shall all need a new interest," with a faint smile.

"You are very generous."

"You will write every few days and keep me informed
of any change. For the rest, I can only commend you to
your own patience and God's wisdom. I can trust you
not to take any rash or desperate step. When this matter
is decided, we will attend to other plans and changes."

Robert Alston sat in silence by the open window, very
heavy hearted, very despondent, shut out of everything
that would make life worth having, home and love such as
he could fancy now. There was just endurance. He felt
secretly that he should accept his uncle's views and act
upon them, not from any high motive of expiation or resignation, but because he would be ashamed, partly, to ill-

requite such tender devotion. They must know at home, and the least disgrace the better for them all.

The parting was not as warm and tender as the meeting had been. Rob seemed frozen into utter indifference. Nothing could hurt him; there was no further struggle; he had nothing to gain. His life was wrecked; that was all of it.

At home Uncle Robert found them going on much as usual. There was a promise of less absolute gayety, Georgie Halford, the moving spirit in all this, having succumbed to woman's destiny, her troop of admirers settling itself to one lover. The Langdons were busy and interested in their house, as they had decided upon the summer residence at Brookside and winters wherever they chose. Emma had disposed of several pictures through the winter and taken orders for others. Mr. Langdon was very proud of her success.

The new bride, Mrs. Hunsdon, was quite a central figure already. They had little intellectual clubs and gatherings, and discussed progress and the new phases of art, the true and the beautiful, leaving the good to get crowded in. There was music, and talking, and research. It made Kathie think a little of Ada Garnier's evenings, only there every one was desperately in earnest about the great questions, the vital pith of life; here it was culture and grace, ease and pleasantness, harmony; the kind of living that a little knot of people in a pretty country place invariably settle into when there is education and refinement, instead of ostentation and striving to outshine each other. There were some who voted these things a bore, and could only be roused on the subject of new gowns, dinner parties, and diamonds; but this class was apt to seek the congenial society of fashionable watering-places in the summer.

When Kathie wanted something plainer and more stirring she went up to the quaint old parsonage at Middleville. It seemed now as if Sarah must have been there always. The sour-visaged housekeeper was gone, and in her place a cheerful young girl, stout and strong, who held her mistress in a kind of wondering awe and joy. The little girls were still shy of strangers, but they made friends with Kathie, and clung to their new mother as if they were afraid some untoward fate might spirit her away.

Mr. Truesdell was much changed, improved. He seemed to have gone into an ampler, more generous and vivifying way of living. He read and talked with his wife, they visited together, they studied the wide out-of-door world, and his sermons showed the added breadth and vigor. The narrow animosities and objections were dying out, as such things invariably do when left to themselves. For the younger people the parsonage was a rallying point. There were music, books not too good to lend, pictures and photographs that whetted one's mental appetite to know more about the great world outside.

" I can sympathize with them so," Sarah said. " There is a side that cannot be quite satisfied with the every-day work of clearing up a house, washing, ironing, and mend-ing. It is the ' clause,' the ' making things divine,' the more than raiment, the unfolding of the seed implanted by a divine hand. It is what He puts the husbandmen in the world for, to watch, and care, and tend, while he jour-neys."

Kathie always wondered a little. This was to be her life. How could she grow into it, to be a very part as Sarah was !

They were very glad to get Uncle Robert home again, and asked questions innumerable about his namesake, easily enough answered, since none of them trenched on the main point. And then he was so busy with town work, streets, and mills, and drainage, temperance and sobriety, and schools, that Kathie seemed left altogether to Charlie in his frequent visits.

It seemed the most natural thing in the world to be

engaged. They talked about the kind of place they would
like, they planned church music, and services, and sermons, gatherings that should include rich and poor, work
and worship, and the lovely, saintly life, the larger holiness that would grow out of it

"If I only can be good enough," she always said, and
he invariably replied : —

"But you are. It is only your exceeding humility that
makes you fearful."

She used to pray in these days, and was careful about
a great many things, questioning with a very tender conscience, trying to shape her soul in a satisfying mould, and
never quite succeeding. Perhaps it was so everywhere.
God did not mean that here on earth there should be perfect satisfaction.

Mrs. Langdon expressed some surprise at the admission.

"Are you really in love, Kathie?" she asked one day.
"You take it all so much as a matter of course. It doesn't
seem to be strange or wonderful in any way. Why, it
appeared to me at first as if I had gone into some enchanted country. In the morning when I woke up I was
sure it was a dream, that nothing so entrancing, so absorbing *could* ever come to me. I was so afraid, yes, I
really was," blushing at the remembrance, "that Mr.
Langdon would come in and say it was a mistake, that he
had changed his mind. And oh, I *was* afraid he would die
or something happen to take him away from me, and when
he did come I was all in a tremble and hardly knew what I
said. I suppose you think it all very silly," with an expression of piquant deprecation.

"Perhaps we are different," hesitatingly.

"But you are a young girl with a first lover. And love
is ever a ' sweet madness.' Only, you and Charlie have
known each other always, and, well, I was going to save
you for Fred, you know; so no wonder I am a little disappointed."

Fay Collamore had appeared surprised as well. Kathie felt the awkwardness ; there had always been a secret consciousness between the two, a curious little rough place now and then in spite of the tender friendship. It never was allowed to work any harm. Indeed, the two girls were quite inseparable. Mrs. Alston had a way of claiming Fay that was irresistible.

Eugene rebelled passionately at first.

" I don't believe it. I can't make it so," he cried vehemently. " They look just like friends, not lovers, and I 'm sure she does n't know. It is just because they have been together all their lives, and girls are always foolish over ministers."

" Kathie is n't foolish over anything," said Fay, " and Charlie does love her. O Eugene, if you had not cared ! " in a distressful tone.

" But I have cared ! I shall always care ! There is n't another girl in the world like Kathie Alston ! "

Eugene was very thankful for another business trip, this time a long one, westward.

Dick Grayson had rejoiced warmly with the young couple.

" I half envy you, Charlie," he said, wringing the slender hand in his own broad palm ; " I 've had a suspicion now and then, and you are both so much alike. But for you I think I should have tried myself; I always had a fancy that way," laughingly. " I 've envied you Kathie, and Rob his uncle. There never was such a bright, enjoyable place as Cedarwood, or such delightful people."

General and Mrs. Mackenzie smiled on the young lovers. How could they help it? but both were sore at heart. It might have been but for a little punctillio of honor. And yet would Bruce have been satisfied with so calm a regard? But it was done past recall. The brave boy had uttered no word of blame to his father, but accepted the loss, the shadow that stretched gray and desolate in his path, and without knowing Rob's sorrow he had been tenderer from the pain of his own grief.

Bruce and Kathie had kept up an infrequent correspondence. There were a great many impersonal subjects to write about. Once Kathie had repeated Charlie's hopes and wishes. Bruce had answered cordially, yet he supposed their lives would always be widely apart.

Uncle Robert waited for some sign of relenting on his nephew's part, but the weekly notes were brief and cold. Once he apologized. "I know it is hateful in me," he admitted with boyish impulse, "when you have always been so tender, but I cannot write what I do not feel. I am stranded on a rocky shore after a shipwreck, and the waves have even refused to drown me."

Uncle Robert had made arrangements for his nephew's wife to be removed to an asylum, and he received tidings from the physician in charge as to her health, which was now quite restored, except that a slight paralysis of the spine had been remarked. She would have the best care and treatment, and he felt nothing more could be done for her. It afforded a certain sense of relief to know that in this money could do all, and there was no occasion for deeper anxiety.

The lad, for Robert still seemed so, was never out of his mind a moment. Sleeping and waking the pale, defiant, despairing face haunted him. He longed for a word of recall, for even the faintest sign of the need of sympathy.

"Robert," Mrs. Alston remarked one day, "you have quite too much business on hand. You look worn and worried. Can no one else attend to these matters?"

"Am I really pale and thin?" he asked, with a poor attempt at a smile.

"Yes; Ruth has remarked it as well. If home was not so delightful, we might take a trip somewhere. Robert, you must not put the whole strength of your body and soul into the joys and cares of other lives; think a little of yourself, of us."

" It *is* pleasant, and I believe home becomes dearer to us as we grow older ; jaunting around is not a perfect panacea, and Ruth has improved greatly."

" Kathie is so thoroughly satisfied that it seems the wisest and happiest course to remain at home. Is not Rob coming ? When have you heard ? "

" A few days ago."

" I must write to him myself." She gave a tender little sigh that did not signify care. She was so prettily important in her motherly ways with young people, and beginning to live her life over again as mothers do when the care and the responsibility of childhood is at an end, and the little jealous feeling of not being first, is overlived. A new phase was opening before her, new claimants, new interests, a higher heart-to-heart communion ; a sympathy dearer, finer, in that all the young souls, in their reaching out, were glad with a great joy to meet hers.

How would she, how could she bear what was to come ? Robert Conover used to ask.

In this summer lull, when everything was tranquil, General Mackenzie had gone up to the city for a few days. He could not settle readily to his new life ; the vital energy and interest had gone out of it. His son's sorrow, his own secret misgiving that he had turned the branch aside to blossom for another, gave him a restless, questioning mood. As he watched Kathie, bright, ardent, and so purely innocent, a coveting pang would sweep over his soul. Aunt Ruth tried to minister gently, but she could not dismiss the belief that it might as well have been.

Fred came rushing breathlessly into the breakfast-room one morning, after his constitutional on horseback, his eyes startled, his face indicative of strong agitation.

" Where is Aunt Ruth ? " peering cautiously about. " O Uncle, there is some terrible news here in the paper."

" Hush, Fred ! " And Mr. Conover came forward with his hand raised in entreaty. " Be careful ; is it the General ? "

" Oh, no ; come out here. A telegram ; another Indian massacre, and Bruce badly wounded. Dick saw it
first ; the news had just come in."

Uncle Robert had not been very eager of late for daily
news. He took the paper, but Aunt Ruth and Kathie
came down the stairs at that moment, and the breakfast
was brought in.

Kathie was devoting herself to Aunt Ruth, with pretty
delicate attentions, " For," said she, " it is so seldom that
I have you to myself that I mean to make the most of it."

" What makes you all so queer and still?" she asked
presently. " Fred, what has happened?"

The young man flushed redly and turned a half-fright-
ened face to his uncle.

" It is Fred's secret and mine," said his uncle, coming to
the rescue.

Mrs. Alston gave her son a hurried, questioning glance.

" You have n't lamed Hero?" cried Kathie. " I want
to take Aunt Ruth out. I can count on this day without
a rival." And she smiled.

" Try and be back by ten. Will that give you long
enough drive?" asked Uncle Robert with gentle gravity.

" Oh, yes ; will you want the horses?"

He let her think so. They must have had the news last
night in New York. There was a train at ten, and he felt
sure that would bring General Mackenzie.

When they were gone he told Mrs. Alston, who was
greatly shocked.

" Oh!" she declared, " Ruth will want to go unless the
General started last night. It is very real motherhood to
her, Robert."

" He would not go without seeing her. It is an exquisitely tender marriage bond as well," smiling gravely. " I
hope the real news may not be as sad. We are so little
used to anything of the kind now. I shall walk down to
the station and meet the train."

As he supposed, General Mackenzie came. The two grasped hands in heartfelt sympathy.

" You have seen the word? My poor boy ! "

"'Just the briefest telegram."

" Badly wounded in the hip and the lung. Conover, these outbreaks are a disgrace to civilization. They must be fought out in a different manner if ever we are to have peace. Ruth — "

" She does not know."

" Let us hurry home. Of course I must start at once. Every moment seems an age to me."

As they reached the gate they saw the phaeton winding up the drive.

" I am afraid we have grown cowards," General Mackenzie said, with a sad, absent smile. " How will she bear it ? "

It was a high tribute paid to her motherhood, real only in the diviner part, love.

She saw at once that something had occurred. After her tender greeting, they went up to the chamber of confidences, Aunt Ruth's room.

" What *has* happened? Oh, you *do* know, Uncle Robert? " And Kathie studied him with painful interest.

" Bruce has been wounded in an Indian skirmish, very badly, they fear."

Kathie turned and went quietly up-stairs. Some time after — it seemed an hour, but it was not more than ten minutes — she heard Aunt Ruth's voice and went to her, to them, standing tenderly in the midst of their sorrow, yet oh, sad irony of fate, quite outside, sheltered in another love !

They were going West immediately. The one comfort in his cup was the exquisite wifely sympathy.

By noon they were gone. How sudden and strange it seemed ! Kathie read the papers and then wandered about in a lonely mood, until she bethought herself that she owed Rob a letter.

In the evening's mail came one for Uncle Robert, that caused him anxious study.

"I wish I could see you," the young man wrote. "I feel sometimes as if I should go out of my senses in this blank, dreary loneliness. I have given up fighting, everything! Let fate take its course. For the child's sake it is best to keep the wretched secret. Have I shut myself out of home, all love, all sympathy, all trust? When I think of mother and her bitter disappointment in me, harder to bear than any that have gone before, I feel as if I ought to stay quite away from you all. What shall I do? I am so tired of thinking. Decide for me. Whatever way, I shall be quite content. I am not sure but that I can bear the burden better when I know exactly what it is to be."

It was not the yielding Robert Conover had wished for him. Perhaps that was asking too much. It was not penitence in the greater sense, only sorrow and weariness. He must go to him at once, for hours like this were subtly alive to temptation. It was not full salvation, but it is a long way from the city of destruction to the heavenly city.

It would be better to tell his mother now, and let her have the intervening time to get over the shock, yet that would commit Robert to a course without his own volition. He wanted him to choose for the sake of after years. It was a sad puzzle, and he could not sleep, thinking it over, so when morning dawned he rose unrefreshed.

The papers came with fuller details of the massacre, a cruel, cowardly, planned affair, in which several brave lives had been sacrificed. Lieutenant Mackenzie was reported dangerously wounded.

"I am going out to Chicago," Uncle Robert announced. "I think our boy is homesick, and may bring him back."

"Let me go with you," cried Fred eagerly.

"But we cannot leave the house alone."

"Why not take us all, then?" inquired Kathie. "Somehow we should be nearer Aunt Ruth."

" I don't know that I could just now," pausing as if to consider.

In old times Mrs. Alston would have been quick to take alarm. Now, she seemed to turn the matter over in her mind leisurely.

" I couldn't go on so short a notice," she said.

" And I shall travel rapidly. We may go somewhere else, Fred, before the summer is over. Cities are not always at their best in heat and dust."

Kathie alone appeared to have a misgiving.

" I hope nothing will happen to Rob," she said. " It seems to me the world has turned gray with trouble."

CHAPTER XIX.

CERTAINLY these few weeks had wrought a great change in Robert Alston. The bright complexion had grown pallid, the eyes were heavy with purple shadows underneath, and the eager, joyous vigor changed to a kind of stolid apathy.

"O my boy!" Mr. Conover exclaimed in genuine distress, "have you been ill?"

"No." But the grasp of the hand was lifeless. "That is, I don't sleep much and have wretched headaches. I have n't given up business, though I have been offered a month's vacation."

The tone indicated an impending change, even if he had no distinct plan in view.

"You have never been out of my mind for a moment," said the elder in a tone of warmest sympathy. "I have wanted to come, but I did not know whether I should help or hinder. Robert, you must know by this time that nothing can change our love for you. It may be wounded by coldness, it may stand silently aside when thrust out of confidence, but it is always waiting for you. We can give, but we cannot force you to take. That is your own part, your own work."

He gave his head a little impatient toss and frowned. "Shall we go to a hotel?" he asked. "I have changed my boarding place and have only a little box of a room."

"Yes, that will be better. I am afraid you have not been taking very good care of yourself."

"What does it matter," wearily, "when everything has gone out of life?"

"Robert, you are making a fatal mistake," began his uncle in a decisive tone. "Life is just opening before you. You are too young to give up in this hopeless way, to wreck yourself for one sad misstep. You made such a good, brave fight at first; you kept in the right path so steadfastly that I can hardly understand how you have let yourself drop down to this level. It is unlike you."

"I had not come to the dregs then," bitterly.

"I do not think you have now, or, if you have, remember there is, or should be, a wholesome tonic in the bitter. If you had loved her I could see how horribly dark and dreary all the years to come might look, unless you turned to God's light and strength for grace. But here we are. Let us take a room, and while I am freshening up a bit you may order supper."

Robert Conover felt that human wisdom and strength were vain, and he cried to the Lord for that diviner grace to guide this young soul aright, to save him from imminent wreck and perishing. For he must come out of it rightly, or all the after life would be weak and flawed, rendered dangerously susceptible to other temptations.

The young man ordered the supper and glanced over the evening paper.

"Of course you know all about Bruce," he began. "Isn't it terrible? And his father and Aunt Ruth have gone out to him. He loves her so; I don't know as he could love an own mother better." Then a flush quivered over the pale face, thinking of *his* mother, and how he had never seemed to know quite all the sweetness and depth between mothers and sons until last summer.

"How did Kathie take it?" he asked abruptly. "She and Bruce were such friends; but I suppose the new love crowds out everything else."

"She wanted to come out with me. I think she has been deeply touched and stirred, but your mother needed comforting." Uncle Robert's thoughts were not in what he was saying; a new idea had crossed his mind, perhaps a path out of this dreary tangle, — a little way, at least.

" It is rather critical."

" We have had no direct word, although I suppose there is some at home now."

Their supper was an extremely silent meal. Evidently Robert was not in a communicative mood.

" Have you seen *her* since she went to the asylum?" his uncle asked.

" Yes, once." A shiver of repugnance crossed the pale face.

" How is she?"

" She goes about and is well, I suppose, but is like a silly child. She does n't remember anything, or any one, and is not much trouble. But it is all horrible! I almost feel as if it were quite another person; she looks differently, even, and is handsomer, except the strange expression in her eyes."

" Have you formed any plans?" was the gentle inquiry.

There was a long silence. Rob was resting his elbow on the table and his chin on the palm of his hand, while his eyes seemed fixed on the far corner of the room, yet were seeing nothing. To Uncle Robert it brought back some of the old pictures of boyhood, when he had tried to bring the lad to confession, and waited patiently, as he must now.

There was a low, husky answer presently.

" Yes."

" Will you tell me?" in a tender, persuasive tone.

" I can't stay here!" Rob broke out suddenly, with the force of a long smouldering flame. " It will kill me or drive me crazy! It would n't be fair to shift all these burdens on you when you have done so much," pausing to steady his voice. " I can get employment elsewhere. I will do my best and care for her. You spoke of the child; I would rather have her nearer home and you."

" Where will you go?"

" I don't know," drearily. " I thought of trying California. You see my life can never be anything again."

" It *can*, Robert, unless you wilfully throw it away. I think your manhood so far has been honorable. You have allowed yourself to drift into one sad mischance, but I dare say you know of others who have gone madly into flagrant sins. You should have kept away from Miss Weeks if you did not want to marry her. Still, I do not hold the marrying an irreparable sin. You did not love her ; you did not really know what love was, and you yielded to a dangerous fascination. Since then you have honestly tried to repair your mistake. I think you have been unusually prompt, brave, and decided. Your course through that hard time goes far to redeem it all with me. Now you throw away all the patience, experience, and steadfast virtue of that time, just when God has opened a way to still higher living, to a manliness and honor greater than any that went before. He has given you one chance to come out of it without absolute disgrace. The fact of her travelling under an assumed name at the time of the accident happily shielded her from any scandal as your wife. The little talk and surmise here will soon die out, as you have said. I, too, believe a change is best. I want you to come out of this with your real manhood unscathed, your soul pure and honest, and ' of good report.' Do not look at the long years to come, but the to-day, in which you must act. God gives the strength like the manna of old, for to-day only, and never fear but he will provide for to-morrow as well. It is a hard thing to learn. The Israelites in the wilderness saved it up and found it useless."

There was no answering light in the young eyes, no softening of the tense lines about the face. He replied coldly : —

" I told you I had given up the struggle. Whatever you think best — "

It was not the concession Mr. Conover wished. He was

patient, remembering his own youth, and too wise to lose
his opportunity by striving to convince. One must act in
many cases and wait for the justification of time.

"Thank you from the bottom of my soul, Robert. I
believe you will never regret this. The awful secret we
two will keep; rather, we will put it in God's keeping.
That the marriage was unwise, infelicitous, it would be
wrong to deny. I think you will find love and sympathy
awaiting you at home."

"But I can't endure any of it just now," he answered
passionately.

"No; it is best that I should make the explanations.
You have gone round in the little circle, girt by fire on
every side, and see no escape; but God holds it out, and
I think you will accept it in time. And now, suppose you
go out to Aunt Ruth? That will take you quite beyond the
depth and despair of your own soul, and not leave you
alone."

A sudden flash illumined the young face. Then he said,
"Suppose they should not want me? They may bring
him home."

"They will be glad to have you in either event. And if
they return you must come home with them."

"Uncle Robert, I—" And a flush mounted the very
edge of his forehead.

"You have given the matter into my hands, and until
my method fails you have no right to take it back."

There was a quiet decision that had always gained the
victory in the old boyish days. Perhaps, too, he was weary
of his fruitless wandering through tangled ways, physically
weak and rather liking the proffered strength. It was not
what Robert Conover desired, and yet he accepted, with
a grateful prayer to God, and resolved to use his utmost
efforts for the larger result.

They retired quite early, and for the first night in a long
while the young man enjoyed some refreshing slumber. It
was visible in his face the next morning.

It had not fared so well with his uncle. His soul was full of anxious questioning. Had he taken too much responsibility in his fear for the lad? The buoyant temperament, the ease with which he laid down burdens, the almost forgetfulness of past suffering, might be doubly dangerous here. He could but watch and pray.

The baby was well and gleesome. Mr. Conover went alone to the asylum, and found Robert's statement entirely correct: the poor creature was in the best of hands.

Then they discussed business, and it was decided that for the present, at least, Robert would relinquish his position. His employers spoke of him in terms of highest praise, and would welcome him back at any time. They telegraphed to General Mackenzie, and received word that Robert would be most welcome. When the lad was started on his journey, Mr. Conover turned his steps wearily homeward. Robert had thrown off so much of the burden already. True, he had been deeply grateful, affected even to an unusual show of tenderness; but what would be the result, — any clearer sight or greater strength?

They were all glad enough to get him back at Cedarwood. The news from Aunt Ruth was not encouraging. Charlie Darrell had gone to Connecticut to take a month's duty for a friend, ordained the year before and now absent on a bridal tour. He had spoken tenderly and sympathetically of Bruce and tried to cheer Kathie with bright hopes; then his heart had gone back to his own dreams. This pretty little town, with just business enough to give it a brisk air, framed in with mountains and outlying farms, a small church, ivy grown, a cottage near that had been modernized into a gem of beauty by the taste of its possessor; a quaint, artistic study, with pictures and a well-chosen though not large library; rooms cosy, inviting, peaceful. Charlie Darrell read and dreamed, mused through lovely, soft evenings, with a vague shadow at his side, of the time that was to be. And to Kathie, whose tender heart was full of another's sufferings, these things seemed to speak of self, of a narrowness in life, instead of the generous sympathy she craved. She could not think now of beautifying rooms, or discussing the respective merits of Palmer's or Thorwaldsen's "Night and Morning," or the most exquisite tint for photographs.

"Dear Uncle Robert," she cried, "we have been so lonely without you. I shall never let you go away again." And her soft arms were folded tightly about his neck.

"But you —" There was a suggestive inflection in the tone.

"Oh, I do not know!" with a weary little sigh. "Suppose I never did go? What if the boys were married, and I stayed right along here with you and mamma?"

He kissed her gently.

That night, after the rest had retired, Uncle Robert had his sad confidence with his sister. Mrs. Alston was shocked, incredulous, kindled to a fire of passionate unreason. Nothing could be too bitter, too harsh to say of the girl who had tricked and inveigled her son into such a marriage.

He let her anger spend itself. From indignation she went to tears, and this mood was still harder to relieve. He had been through the bitter hurt himself, and was patient. He, too, had seen the large and perfect possibility awaiting the youth, but not with a mother's heart.

She came round to this presently.

"Robert," she said, "it was shameful to be keeping such a secret last summer. Think of the pleasant times, of the love he seemed to show as never before, of Fay, — I can't understand; he *does* like her, and we should all be so glad! And yet he is bound to that thing! Can he not get free, Robert?" she cried in an agony of grief and desire.

"Not to marry Fay Collamore, much as we all love her. Think, Dora; human laws are made for the preservation of society, divine laws for the preservation of the soul, and we have no right to help another to overstep the bounds, no right to lift him out of the gulf of his own folly and set him in a large room where he shall not suffer or miss anything."

"Then he had no right —"

"He had no right to keep the secret, but it was a difficult place to be in. I can imagine that if she had been different it would have been easier to tell. And yet I am glad he did not bring her home. He saw the utter incongruity, and that is something for him, for any man who goes beyond the pale of propriety in marriage. There is this to be said in his behalf, she was dangerously beautiful, utterly unscrupulous, older and wiser in the world's ways than he. Still we must not forget that he had no right to throw himself into temptation ; and I think he was very brave and discreet last summer. To have avoided Miss Collamore when she was brought in our midst would have been rude, but the many delicate little evasions he practised made me fear there was some entanglement, though I did not suspect a marriage. And when he had in a measure shut himself out of home sympathy and love, I think he began to realize how sweet a thing it was. I only wonder that he kept it so rigidly."

"O my poor darling! My boy, my boy! Must he always wring our hearts? O Robert, what a heavy burden yours has been !" And her tears flowed afresh.

"There ought to be something after thirty odd years of selfish living," he replied in a tone of deep emotion. "And, Dora, I have a hope for him. His sins have not been those of viciousness or real weakness, but that headlong thoughtlessness. And, my dear, God takes so much from us all, even the best, that we must be patient and long-suffering with these our brethren."

"Yes," she answered drearily, "we shall be patient with him, how many times ? "

"We have not reached the full measure, the gospel measure." And he gave a tender little smile.

She buried her face and wept softly. It was such a bitter disappointment. The mother's pride, and love, and trust had been cruelly slain just when it believed all danger past. Other mothers had sons who never brought them a pang, and she thought of Charlie Darrell, of Dick Grayson. Why had this come upon her?

She said this presently to her brother.

"I wonder," he returned in a soft, vague tone, "if there is not sometimes a sacrifice, a sort of slain right in these things that brings a remission, a bearing of the cross for another, rather than any judgment for ourselves. The innocent suffers for the guilty to teach us all that no sin or weakness is ever quite alone in its consequences, that ours may react on another. And when we do learn it we shall have the care for others that brings us up to the divine love."

"Robert," she asked, after a long while, "what about the child and her relations?" with a shiver of disgust.

"Robert will never be troubled with them, I fancy. After all, people of that class have a tendency to stay where they belong; they do not enjoy higher and purer air. We can and shall dismiss them forever. The child I shall care for."

"You will not bring it here!" she cried suddenly, in a tone of distress.

"Certainly not, if it would pain you. It is very well cared for with a good woman who is fond of it."

"And as long as that creature lives, Robert must provide for her?"

"We could hardly turn her over to charity."

Mrs. Alston rose with a kind of grave, injured dignity that showed how deep the wound had gone.

"You must excuse me any further talk," she exclaimed brokenly; "I feel half crazed with all this. If I have not

16

borne it as I should, pardon me, for it is so hard, so hard. Good night."

Oh, what of the boy? Would he be saved, as by fire, if the flames scorched even here?

Kathie was not long in guessing that something had transpired. She helped Fred get ready for a little fishing party, then she went up to Mrs. Alston's room to find her mother weeping passionately.

" O mamma! Is Bruce — "

" You can think of nothing but Bruce," said the mother in a wounded tone, that filled Kathie with dismay.

"O mamma!" with a long, quivering breath.

" My darling!" the mother's arms were about her. " Kathie, my heart is nearly broken. Go to Uncle Robert, he will tell you; you must know sooner or later. Let me remain alone with my sorrow."

Kathie stood quite still a moment, in utter amazement; then she turned slowly. The comfort with her was that she obeyed without stopping to discuss reasons.

Uncle Robert was slowly pacing the wide hall; her awe-stricken face startled him.

" Mamma said I might come to you. O Uncle Robert, what great sorrow — is it Aunt Ruth?" with a strong, apprehensive shiver.

" It is a sorrow time may mend. Put on your hat and let us go out under the trees; I can tell you better there."

Many a time in after years Kathie recalled the scene like a picture. The soft, wandering air, the sun sailing through fleecy drifts that toned its blazing rays, the little nooks of shade made by the wide-spreading spruce and firs, the tasselled larch, where a tiny wren came and sang its song, flew away, and returned with the same dainty little burden that it must unfold to sun and air. It seemed at first quite as if it could not be their own Robert, but a story about some one else. But her mother's grief; ah, yes, that made it all real.

Her tears dropped silently

"O Uncle Robert!" she said, with a great, pitiful sob, "can she never come to sense and memory again? May be she might have learned to love and to care. And the little baby, — Rob's baby?"

He knew then it would have one friend; but he almost grudged the tender tears for the other, knowing well the worst part, that would have shocked them with horror, and perhaps entirely rehabilitated Rob, had been withheld. Was it right and just? For an instant he felt quite uncertain.

There followed a quiet interval at Cedarwood. Kathie spent her time in trying to comfort her mother. She was glad in those days that Fay Collamore had gone to Lake George with Mr. and Mrs. Hunsdon. Emma was her only friend, and they two drew nearer in a tender spiritual communion.

Once Kathie had spoken of having the baby, but her mother had answered with a sharp, sudden pain. Charlie came home full of joy and hope, but he tempered it sweetly to the sorrow he found. Every day or two they heard from Aunt Ruth. Robert had come, and they were so glad to have him. Bruce lived, but it was a doubtful question. They all hoped, they could not give him up.

The whisper floated about that Robert Alston had made a secret, unfortunate marriage, and that his wife through an accident had lost her mind.

Dick Grayson knew more about her, though he made no comment to any one save Mr. Conover.

"They were a bad lot," he said; "I don't see how Rob could have been fooled by them; but the girl was very pretty. And, somehow, I'm not sure but I would rather have her in an asylum, out of harm's way, than to do as her sister has done. But poor Rob! We must all try to make it up to him."

CHAPTER XX

THE very brooding over her sorrow worked a partial cure in Mrs. Alston's case. She saw the suffering, the shame, the fear, the brave resolve to eat the bitter fruit he had gathered, to make no outcry at the sting, since he had grasped · the nettles of his own will and pleasure. She longed for a first word from him, and yet she admired the strength that could wait and accept the sentence.

Yet he was hers, and nothing could weaken that bond. She could recall so many little remorseful touches of the summer before ; once when he had stood with his arms clasped about her neck, and said, to some little word of hers, " I wish I were more worthy of your love, but the duty of my coming years must be to make myself so." And the little thoughtful courtesies that had never been much in his way before, how they touched her now.

So she wrote a brief note, blotted by tears, and he answered. They knew it had come, but its contents were sacred to her. Then he wrote to Uncle Robert : —

" During one of the long night-watches, when the General was quite used up, I told Aunt Ruth my story, all that we decided had better be known. Uncle Robert, I think I must have behaved brutally to you during that last visit ! I was almost crazy with loneliness and despair, and fighting for the thing I wanted. I see some of it now. Aunt Ruth has been so sweet, so lovely, and, though I can 't accept it all now as you would like me to, I have come to my senses a little. I can never make amends for your love and patience, and I have broken poor mother's heart.

O Uncle Robert, why don't we have a little sense, a little sure faith in the inexorable laws of right and wrong? We cannot overstep them and go scot free. Every wrong way has its penalty.

"Comfort my mother. I shall not ask you to forgive me until I have in some sense earned it by my endeavors in the future: as if I ever could earn it or repay you for what you have done."

Bruce was better. The wound in the lung was under control, but the hip was not doing as well as they wished. There was a great deal of anxiety lest it should settle to permanent lameness, but they were all coming home. Jessie Meredith and Kathie had orders to find a cosy furnished house for winter quarters. Aunt Ruth was anxious that Dr. Markham should have her boy under his care. And again she said: "I hardly know what we would have done without Robert. I think him truly brave and noble. He lacks only the 'one thing,' and I am not sure but the discipline of living out of this sorrow will lead him to it."

Fred returned to college and the family went to the city for a visit. Hunting a house was a new and perplexing, as well as absorbing interest. There were enough of them, as Jessie said, but some were all up stairs and down, others all style and show. Mrs. Garnier came to the relief at last, with a pretty home, whose owner, a young widow, was going to Cuba for the winter. The lower floor had a cosy reception and dining room, with a spacious kitchen, and up stairs a lovely parlor, taking in the whole front, with two alcoves, and two sleeping-rooms beside, and apartments farther up in abundance.

"This will do admirably," Jessie decided. "Bruce can have the range of this floor, and there will be very little going up and down for Aunt Ruth. Then the furniture and adornments are neat and harmonious, which is a great thing for an invalid, and is just far enough from the avenue to afford quiet."

Mrs. Alston had brought Jane Maybin with her, and engaged a nice tidy country woman for housekeeper.

They had just completed all arrangements when the telegram came. The party would reach New York the following morning.

Mrs. Alston had meant to accompany the family to receive them, but at the last moment her courage failed, and so the four went without her. Mr. Meredith had planned everything for the invalid's comfort, so there would be no confusion or delay. They watched eagerly as the long train wound its way slowly in.

Kathie and Jessie stood a little back, and the crowd kept surging between them and the gentlemen. Then Rob stood on the car step and grasped his uncle's hand, and General Mackenzie followed him.

"Jessie and Kathie are here," said Mr. Conover. "Bring Aunt Ruth and let us send them home in a carriage, and attend to the rest afterward."

It was a good plan. Rob had just a moment to come and clasp their hands, and see that Aunt Ruth was safe between them all.

"Wait a moment; I think I will go in the carriage with you," said Mr. Meredith.

While the horses stood still Jessie asked a few questions. It seemed to Kathie she could only look at Aunt Ruth and wonder.

"Bruce stood the journey very well," Aunt Ruth was saying. "Until last night he did not show any special signs of fatigue, but he is extremely weak. He does not gain strength as we hoped he would, and his father is afraid the hip may settle into a permanent lameness. We were so anxious to see Dr. Markham." And she smiled over to Kathie. "I am not sure but it would have been better if we had brought him at the very earliest possible moment; but we had to guard against the strain and hemorrhages."

"How dreadful it has been!" Kathie sighed softly. "And we thought the war was all over. You know Bruce used to laugh about being a peace soldier."

"The war never seems quite all over," Aunt Ruth returned gravely.

"Now," exclaimed Mr. Meredith, springing in, "the rest of the procession is under way. Kathie, do you remember what a lank, white fellow I was when Jessie brought me home? There will be some nursing for you, to keep your hand in. I think we can both answer for her, Mrs. Mackenzie?"

Aunt Ruth smiled faintly again as she pressed the hand that clasped hers so fondly. Then the carriage rattled over the stones and there was no more talking. They reached home a long while the first, and Aunt Ruth had time to lay off her wraps and take a view of her new domicile.

"Oh, how very pretty!" And a soft pink flush overspread her face.

Mrs. Alston held her in her arms many moments; then there was a stir in the street.

"Send Robert in here to me when you have done with him," she whispered, and disappeared in the adjoining room.

The strong arms formed a litter, and bore Bruce up to the parlor, where Mr. Meredith had arranged a large and comfortable reclining chair. But as they laid him down they saw he had fainted quite away.

Kathie looked on curiously, awe-stricken. She had never seen Bruce but in the highest state of physical health. She could not remember that he had ever complained of a pain. He had gloried so in walks and climbs up dangerous mountain-sides. He had rowed and driven like an athlete. And always the splendid coloring of youth and vigor, of ambition and hope, — hope in the seen and unseen ; and now the dark edge of hair framed in a thin, transparent face that bore the marks of high suffering, a heroic struggle somewhere, that at the first moment dazed and confused her, when it seemed as if she ought to hold in her own hand the clew. She could only think of one thing distinctly.

He opened his eyes suddenly, and drew a long, shuddering breath, as little shadows of returning animation quivered through the translucent veins. His lips moved, his hand was outstretched, and a tender light gleamed in his eye.

" Kathie ! "

He had seen her for an instant, as in Heaven. When she clasped his hand, when she stooped over and kissed the marble brow, he had lapsed into forgetfulness.

" Kathie," — Rob touched her. " Mother," — and there was a tremulous quaver in his voice.

She led him to the door and opened it softly, just uttering "Mamma " in her gentlest tone.

They went straight to each other's arms : the one, knowing how it must be, because he understood the great love ; the other, having found her lost piece of money, was content. Not the prodigal who had gone down to the depths of the husks and swine, but the one who had squandered and betrayed love, who had gone astray and was found.

Kathie wandered around in a strange state of awe and loneliness. Mr. Meredith had gone for Dr. Markham. Uncle Robert and the General were trying to make the invalid comfortable and picking up the travelling wraps.

"Jane," Kathie exclaimed, " I think there ought to be a sort of breakfast luncheon for them. I dare say they ate very little this morning. Make some tea and coffee, and I will arrange the table."

That gave her a connecting interest with the world again. It seemed as if she had been in some strange country, had half known or seen something she ought to know wholly, and now she was on the outside rim again.

"It is the excitement and confusion," she thought. "And oh, poor Bruce!"

Dr. Markham had been holding himself in readiness for the summons. The General and he were closeted a long while with the invalid, but presently they rejoined the others at the table, where he gave Kathie numberless orders, and teased her a little about donning a black gown and white cap and becoming a regular Sister of Mercy.

"Of course the poor fellow is dreadfully worn out by the journey, and weak from loss of blood," explained Mr. Meredith. "Markham thinks the treatment of the hip has n't been quite the thing, but the other was all right, and, though the lung may require a little carefulness, there's no trouble to be apprehended from it. People rarely get . over these things in a day or two. I did n't myself." And he smiled humorously.

"But it's a kind of fight for life, after all," Rob said, later on, to Kathie. "There was one night that I wished I could die in his stead, and I understood then what a comfort it was to pray," with a low, reverent intonation. "And I know how he feels; he wants to get entirely well. He's so young, and he has always been so strong. Kathie, I don't know but Bruce is the bravest hero of them all. It was a good thing in Uncle Robert to send me out there. And when I found him bearing a life-long sorrow — "

"Oh, he will get well!" cried Kathie in a passion of tender pain.

Rob stopped and colored. This was not the fidelity he had promised.

"We all hope so. But he may never be as strong, and possibly have to change his whole career."

"Rob, I do not think Bruce cared altogether for military glory, or as much as he used at West Point," Kathie answered, with a vague consciousness of some change.

Mr. and Mrs. Meredith left them in the afternoon. Bruce had been put in the middle room, and was quite comfortable, but, oh, so ghostly wan, and white, even to his hands!

"Quite fine, is n't it, old fellow?" he said to Rob. "Civilization has its advantages, we must admit, and it is extremely pleasant to the eye. Ought we to class these among the pomps and vanities?" glancing around.

"Not a bit. The best of all things could never be too good for you, and you 'll never hoard them up or crowd out any one else!" was the earnest rejoinder.

"And I made quite a Miss Nancy of myself fainting away and all!" with a wan little smile. "I did get so horribly tired last night, and then jolting over the stones was excruciating. But Dr. Markham thinks it may all come out right in the end."

"It will, it must," declared Rob vigorously. "God won't give you anything harder to bear, when you 've been so brave, so —"

"The thorn in the flesh! St. Paul suffered all his life long. And coming nearer home, mother is a little lame, and it adds a sort of piquancy; she never complains."

"But Aunt Ruth always was an angel!"

"And a six-footer without petticoats might make a guy of himself. It does n't add any romance to a man, does it? Where is mother?"

"Gone to lie down."

"Poor, sweet mother. O Rob, I 'm so thankful for my share of her."

"And how like a brute I 've been all my life to an own, real mother!" Rob said in a remorsefully passionate tone. "O Bruce, I thought of your grand verse to-day, about the heights and depths, and powers and principalities, and I could n't help saying a little of it to mother, for nothing ever *can* separate us again. It has been so horrible these years, when I had the bitter realization that I had put such a gulf between."

The thin hand stretched out and found the other so plump and warm.

" And if that love is so great, what about the other, Rob? If it is so sweet to get home to the heart of human affection, what of the Divine? "

" I can't see it all — "

" I believe you will presently. The mistake is, we do not any of us see it all, or all the time. There are clouds, and storms, and wanderings. And in our slothfulness we are not looking out continually."

" Rob," he said again, after a long silence, " did I see her ? "

" Yes, no ; you had fainted away."

" And I dreamed she came and kissed me."

" Oh, she did ; that was n't a dream ! And she is frightened half out of her wits."

" Do you know if she is going to stay ? "

" She is here yet. Dr. Markham said she was to help Aunt Ruth nurse you. I don't know what mamma thinks, but it shall be just as you wish. No one shall make you suffer a needless pang."

Several changes passed over the pale face. He thought he had fought it all out, given her up, but the renunciation was one thing out there, alone, and here quite another.

" Bruce — I don't think — and Kathie — she does n't know," incoherently began Robert, but the hope in his face pieced together the broken sentences.

" Oh, Rob, hush," the feeble voice entreated. " You are so strong, so full of vigor, and life, and health ; let me lean on you a little now, and do not tempt me to covet my neighbors' joys. If I cannot see her without desiring, longing, I have no right to see her at all. I must take a coward's place and skulk in the rear, along the hedges."

" But — "

" He that hath used no deceit in his tongue, nor done evil to his neighbor — "

"O Bruce, you think of it all." And he hid his face repentantly on the pillow. "I never can, and that is why."

"We must do a little pulling in the same boat, old chap!" And the words came with a quivering sigh. "Don't you remember how He lay and slept in the boat until they came and called him, and he is always there to say 'Peace.' You know we settled the other matter."

"But you never had a chance, at least not a fair chance, and that is what bothers me so. If she had seen you together. Oh, forgive me, Bruce, I never will pain you so again! Oh, don't faint," besought the lad, pitifully, his eyes swimming in tears.

"No, I am not going to faint; but I am so weak to-day. Suppose you read a little, Rob, the dear old 'In Memoriam.'"

Rob found the book; he had put it in his satchel. He had read a good deal to Bruce in the last fortnight, and found it very soothing. There was so much in the poem to comfort them both.

They heard Kathie's voice presently in the adjoining room talking to Aunt Ruth.

"Rob," he said, in the little pause, "suppose we have it over; I must see her some time."

Rob opened the door. "You have not been in to visit our invalid, mother," he said, as he caught sight of her by the window. "And you, Kathie, unless he frightened you out of your stately composure."

"Oh, no, indeed"; and Kathie smiled. "Come, mamma," holding out her hand.

"How is he, Robert?" asked Aunt Ruth.

"He wanted to see them," Rob made answer, including his plural with a slight hesitation, for though the subject had never been spoken of between them, he understood the fear implied in Aunt Ruth's tone.

Mrs. Alston was much shocked. It hardly seemed that one could change so greatly. Kathie came around and took the thin hand.

" It does n't look much like fighting now," she said,
" or climbing Alps."

" No." He smiled faintly. " I am glad we had all that,
and our grand winter in Russia, and all the delights.
But you have all been very good to me to-day ; and Rob
here thinks I behaved quite like a baby."

" Because he had been such a hero ! See what it is to
exalt one's opinion."

" I think you have managed to tone down my boisterous
boy a good deal," said Mrs. Alston. " I never fancied
nursing his forte before."

" Rob and I have been good comrades." And the
look told the rest.

" Oh, you have drifted in here," said Mr. Conover, entering the room and casting a quick glance at Kathie
" Well, Bruce, my lad ! "

" I expect to be the centre of attraction ; I shall feel
quite hurt if any one slights me. Will you all sit down?"

" We must not disturb you. It has been an exciting
day, and rather hard on your little strength."

" I think," began Rob, " that I might be spared. I
want a good walk before dinner. Will you go, Uncle?
and we might hunt up Fred."

" We shall not have far to hunt ; both boys are making
their home with the Merediths. I am quite ready for the
walk. We might go down there to dinner, unless you are
wanted."

" I 'll be generous and give Rob a holiday," declared
the invalid.

There was so much to say between the two who went.
Rob had recovered his strength and elasticity, much of his
bright coloring, although thinner than of yore. What if,
after all, that deep anguish was evanescent and bore no
real fruit.

But the effort Rob had been compelled to make in Bruce's
behalf had brought him out of his gloomy despair. He

was able to see something beside all the long stretch of years, how they were to be lived; and the use he was to make of his one talent or many. He was beginning to learn that the austere Master exacted something beside not losing. There was a growth and work, and if he had plunged himself into the slough of despond he was not to lie there, not to disdain the help of friendly hands, not to feel that the great aims had dropped out because he had lost for a while the right clew. He could live out of, but he could not go back and begin again. The flawed and spoiled must be taken out patiently.

He had learned a little of it, dimly, wonderingly. The truth had always been there, but in the heedlessness of youth he had leaped quite over it, and now he must retrace these steps that he hated, that shamed him, that had cut him off from so many things he was beginning to desire.

They had a delightful time at dinner. Charlie and Fred gave him the warmest of welcomes, and unfolded so many plans. They sympathized with Bruce as well, and hoped all things in the future. Only it seemed to Rob they were very young, and he felt old beside them.

"Uncle Robert," he said, as they were walking home, "I have about made up my mind to one of two things, if you are willing. I should like to go in the Merediths' business house or some other here in the city."

"Rob, do you remember what you said about chemistry?"

"O Uncle!" Rob's heart gave a great leap of joy, then he sternly brought it under control. "You are so good to think of that. You have all been so good to me, but I have incurred some expenses that I ought not to lay off on any one's shoulders. If I could n't think when I was crazy enough to — to marry, I *must* think now. I must earn sufficient to take care of the two whose comfort, to say the least, I became responsible for. I shall make that myself, beside my own living. Why, I need not work as severely as I have. Then if I have any time, or energy, or money left over, I shall feel free to spend that on myself. I was talking a little to Mr. Meredith to-night; he thinks it can be brought about."

"Robert," his uncle said gravely, tenderly, "I honor your resolve. It is simple right and justice. It will do more toward strengthening your character than any assistance from friends. I think you can be trusted, and I shall be glad to have you here."

"And I must learn to be my mother's son. After all, she may have me more years than she ever dreamed." And he choked down the sigh for the chain he must wear. "And I want to say," a little tremulously, "that for the child's sake, for the family's sake, your proposal was best. In any event I owed it to you to accept it. It is my business to render my life the better for it."

He felt the approving pressure on his arm.

They found Bruce comparatively comfortable. He did not need a watcher, so Rob brought in the reclining chair for his bed, to be at hand at a word. General Mackenzie seemed quite worn out, and the promise of a night's sleep was extremely refreshing.

"I don't know what we should have done without your boy," he said, with his good-night to Mrs Alston, "and I think very few would have passed through such a terrible ordeal as well. Poor lad."

The mother's eyes filled with tears.

The house grew quiet presently, and all the lights were out save the one turned low in the parlor. The door was left open, for Bruce liked the shadowy suggestiveness better. Rob uttered a happy good-night, he was so at peace, and in a few moments Bruce heard the regular breathing of healthful slumber. He could not sleep, partly for pain, bravely borne while the others were looking, partly because there was a tumult in his soul.

He had come into *her* life again, so differently from anything he had planned. He was to wait until they were married and in their own home, and she was hedged about with pretty wifely and parish duties, the bright, generous, outflowing woman, infusing the spirit of her Master in ever-widening circles, taking in the poor in heart, the weary and worn, and feeding them with some living bread of holiness and redemption. Like a pilgrim journeying on to the same far country he might stop and break bread, and exchange greetings of cheer. He would have over-lived the pain and longing; the comfort she could have given would have been held out by a higher hand. He should see her there and rejoice with her in her work, diviner than any he could have brought her.

But it was not so to be. He had met her to-day, rather she had come to meet him, with the old friendly fondness he once fancied meant love. The same sweet, generous graciousness, the pure, upward look. Yes, he *had* been mistaken. Even if he had won that, it would not have brought supreme satisfaction; he would have wanted more, a depth and richness, a woman's love, such as Aunt Ruth was giving his father daily. Could girls love like that, or was it the larger awaiting of full womanhood?

And now he must see her daily and keep himself from any coveting, from any envying. He turned to God for strength; there had been many times in his young life when he would have fainted but for this help.

CHAPTER XXI

It was a lovely, glowing autumn, full of long, dreamy days, with Indian summer skies; just the time for delicious country rambles, and yet the city seemed to hold the most interest for Kathie. Mr. Meredith had offered Rob a very fair position, and he had gone to work with all his olden energy. There was one heavenly precept that would never have to be instilled into the young man. Whatever his hand found to do he did with all his might. Ned Meredith often smiled, recalling the Rob of old days at his play.

He was to board through the winter with Aunt Ruth. Bruce wanted him; that was sufficient.

"But I have made an arrangement to spend every other Sunday with you," Rob said to his mother. "Mr. Meredith offered to give me off the Monday morning, but I shall make it up. Only I shall have the house astir catching the early train. Shall I prove a nuisance?"

She kissed him to hide her tears, touched by the devotion. He had begun in the path of duty. If he did not understand, if he could not see the certain evidence, still he would not abate, but persevere to the end.

And while she was holding him to her heart another thought entered it. The little child alone was an innocent outcast from their love and sympathy. They had forgiven him; why should they be so cruelly hard to her?

"Rob," she said, with a soft tremble in her voice, "your uncle once spoke of the — the baby. I am not sure but we ought to have it. I was so surprised and hurt then, that my heart was steeled against it."

"Oh, no!" he cried, with sudden shame and repugnance. "Do not bring it here!"

17

"Your child, Robert!" She thought of the warm welcome her own little ones had received on every hand.

A deep flush suffused his face.

"It seems so strange," half impatiently. "I have never known much about it. I never had Kathie's fondness for babies."

"I think it had better come," in a tone of grave reproof.

"As you like," he answered quietly.

She discussed the matter with her brother, and they decided to go out to Chicago. Perhaps. too, she had a half-confessed curiosity to see the woman who had made such havoc of her boy's life.

Kathie was left with Aunt Ruth. She was such a bright, useful, and entertaining body. Her very face, full of exquisite hope and tenderness, said so much without a word. Perhaps it was because she was so free from the platitudes often used in a sick-room, well meaning, but frequently extremely trying to sensitive nerves. She breathed patience and fortitude in her very aspect, she brought hope in her quick smile. Then she had so many expedients ; the comfort and solace of to-day was a little changed to-morrow by some added grace.

The "boys" came in to see Bruce when he could enjoy company. Charlie had some of Kathie's ways, Bruce was forced to admit, almost unwillingly. He brought in a handful of flowers, not a regular-made bouquet ; or a paper that had a fine article Kathie must read aloud ; another day it would be some deliciously ripened fruit, or a set of fine photographs, borrowed from a friend. Bruce schooled himself to watch them together, to think of the time when their lives would be irrevocably blended.

After two weeks of suffering patiently borne, Dr. Markham found that, in spite of all his efforts, an abscess was forming. Dr. Garnier did not take the matter so seriously ; the patient had youth, a good constitution, and excellent habits for the groundwork of hope. And when

he recovered from the fatigues of the journey he really
made some improvement. If he could get through without
any permanent injury; to save him from that would be
their work.

Dick, and Charlie, and Fred were glad to have Rob back
in their midst. Ada Garnier welcomed him, too, but he
was a little shy of her at first.

"It is as good as a school," declared Dick, "to meet
the people at her house and hear them talk."

And but for the child Robert might have almost forgotten the miserable episode of the past.

Mrs. Alston went on her journey with a half-sense of
unwillingness, although she considered it her duty. The
many changes and the brilliant autumn scenery interested
her and diverted her mind in some degree from the sad
aspect of affairs. They would see the child first. She
was not quite certain she could take this alien to her heart,
even if she did pity its lonely condition.

They found Mrs. Fleming bright and tidy, and her little
charge in riotous health. She stared at the new-comers
with her large, laughing brown eyes, and then half shyly
hid her face in her foster-mother's dress.

"This is Mr. Alston's mother," Mr. Conover announced.

"Bertha, Bertha, you must not be naughty," said the
gentle voice. "She is not usually afraid," in apology.

"And she has quite forgotten me," declared Uncle
Robert. "We became very good friends in the summer.
Bertha."

The child peeped out in such a pretty, piquant manner,
showing a face strangely like, yet mysteriously unlike her
father. There was a great struggle in Mrs. Alston's soul,
and perhaps it was more from duty than love that she
stooped and held out her hands.

"Little Bertha," she said softly, "will you not come to
me?"

The child studied her a moment with grave intent, then, breaking into a merry peal of laughter, ran to Uncle Robert to be caught and lifted in his arms. Her satisfaction was but momentary, however; the next instant she struggled to get away.

" I want my mamma ! " reaching out her dimpled hands ; " I want my own, own mamma ! "

Something in the bright, bird-like tone touched Mrs. Alston's heart, brought back the by-gone years.

" She is a little strange," said Mrs. Fleming, coloring. " But she is very good, so merry and cheerful, and I think quite forward for her age. She can say nearly everything, and has so many cunning ways. As for her health, that is perfect. Don't you think she resembles her father?"

" Yes. You have seen her mother?"

" She came a few times. She owned that she did not care about children. I can't understand why the Lord sends them to such people, when there is many a hungering soul that would welcome a baby. But young people rush into marriage without thinking of the sacred responsibility." And Mrs. Fleming checked herself suddenly, coloring. " Is the poor thing any better?" she asked.

" She can never be restored in mind ; otherwise she is well, " Mr. Conover made answer.

There was a brief pause, and then Mrs. Alston said in a low, gentle tone : —

" We have decided, my brother and I, that the proper place for the child is with us, since its mother will never be competent to care for it. But she is so fond of you, I hardly know how we will be able to get her home. Robert, it will tax your ingenuity." And she smiled.

" I should like to keep her always." The tears came in Mrs. Fleming's eyes. " If the parents had been very poor, I should have proposed it, but I could only bring her up plainly."

Mrs. Alston felt self-condemned. Not that she should

ever grudge the child anything money could procure, she
was not selfish in that respect, she was even sympathetic,
but she could not instantly open her heart to love. In her
soul she had blamed her son for this hardness, and she
must struggle to overcome it. Simple duty was not all
that was required ; there was a higher point. And how
teach Robert to see it if she evaded it herself?

"It is right and best that the child should be brought
up among her relatives," she answered kindly. "I think
we shall be able to manage. When will you be likely to
return?" glancing at Mr. Conover.

"Oh, you will want to see the city before you leave it !
There is no hurry. We can come in and visit the little
one again."

He managed to coax a kiss out of her before he went
away.

Then they started on their sad and distasteful errand.
It was one of the poor creature's quiet days. She sat by
a sunny window turning the leaves of a child's picture-
book in gaudy colors. There was a lovely flush on her
cheek, yet hardly the tint of health, and her vacant face
had a curious, unearthly beauty.

Mrs. Alston looked and turned away with a sigh.

"Poor thing !" said the nurse. "She gives very little
trouble. My opinion is that she's not so long for this
world as they think, though some of them do live beyond
everything; but that's more likely when they go insane
naturally, without any accident, I mean. There's something wrong with her spine, the doctors say. Mercy
grant that she may not lie helpless years and years !"

They both echoed the prayer. Mrs. Alston turned
away and her brother followed.

"I think," she began, after they were in the carriage
and driving slowly along, "that in some respects we can
excuse Rob. He has always been hasty and impulsive. I
can imagine the fascination this girl's beauty exercised

over him, and no doubt she did lay a trap for him, if she
fancied him the heir to a fortune. Evidently there was
some object in marrying him ; it was not merely the love
of flirtation. Still, it seems to me she might have done
better, taken some one whose fortune was secure."

" She had no doubt seen a good deal of the world, and
on her part, I fancy, there was no very deep sentiment.
But in the first place Robert should have kept away from
such people. It serves to lower any young man's respect
and regard for womanhood. He had been taught better,
nay, he *knew* better. Then, as Mrs. Fleming said, there is
too much careless taking on of the most solemn vows of
life. Marriage seems so easy, so delightful, that our
young people take it up with about as much deliberation
as going to an opera. They do not ask if it is the thing
they want for thirty or fifty years, that they are not to
thrust lightly aside, but endure with patience, realizing
that it is an obligation of their own choosing, or their own
haste and unwisdom. Then the ease with which these ties
are sundered seems to offer a premium on thoughtlessness,
and does weaken the sense of responsibility."

" It is a bitter lesson. I fancy Robert will feel it more
keenly as time goes on. But you thought he accepted it
bravely," as if she could not bear to have him so
severely blamed.

" Yes, I think he displayed a great deal of courage and
true manliness in his course, even to keeping the secret.
He might have come to us then with his burden, and I
shall always respect him that he bore it in silence as long
as it was possible. The true test now is his living out of
this, the kind of man he makes under this discipline. He
has always been thoughtless as to consequences ; the present want has dominated him. He will have time now to
ponder over the impatience of youth."

" But, Robert, if she — "

" Hush, Dora, we must not allow ourselves to think of

that," he answered solemnly. "With God alone belong the issues of life and death. It is the now that we are in, the present, and our work is to do the duty of the present."

She did not make any immediate answer; but after a considerable silence, said in a low, awed tone, "There is one thing that I shall feel thankful for always, that she did not openly disgrace her child. A misfortune can be borne with dignity, but a scandal is never entirely over-lived."

Robert Alston had saved his mother this bitter sorrow.

They spent several pleasant days in going about the city that Mrs. Alston had not seen in years. Uncle Robert managed to make quite friends with Bertha, but at the last they took the little thing away in the evening, asleep, to spare the sad scene of a violent parting. Mrs. Fleming was deeply moved at separation from the little one who had become so like her very own.

Their first day and evening were exceedingly trying. Bertha could be amused for a brief while; then her sense of loss and strangeness would overwhelm her. Uncle Robert proved an admirable nurse, and before the journey's end Mrs. Alston's heart had gone out to the little one, who displayed so many reminders of her father. She was large of her age and brimming with vitality, piquant rather than beautiful, and so little like her mother that it was a positive relief.

They were watching for the travellers at Aunt Ruth's. Kathie saw the coach stop and ran down.

"Oh!" she cried with eager delight, "is it really Rob's baby? How pretty! O mamma, how wonderfully like Rob! Why, she hardly looks like a girl."

Bertha was growing accustomed to strange faces. Something in Kathie's glad voice attracted her, and she stretched out her hands at once.

"O you sweet little darling!"

" Republics are ungrateful," declared Uncle Robert, with an air of injured dignity.

Kathie took her up to Aunt Ruth's room, and stood her on the floor while she was unfastening her cap and cloak. Bertha glanced around surprised, then startled, and stretched out her small hands with unforgotten longing.

" I want my own mamma ! " in a pitiful, quivering tone that went to each heart.

" O baby, we will all try to be your mamma." And she kissed her with tender fervor.

Bertha leaned her head on Kathie's shoulder and gave a few sobs. They were fast friends then.

It made a great diversion in the house, and baby soon settled to two prime favorites, Kathie and Uncle Robert. In a few days she recovered her wonted equilibrium, and proved herself a bright little mischief. Rob studied her with a curious feeling of awe, and secretly confessed to Kathie that he could not make her seem his, but he was deeply grateful to his mother for the love she gave her. In fact, the advent of the baby made Rob more of a hero than ever with the boys. He had a pathetic history, an unusual misfortune, and even at this early stage he felt his uncle's wisdom had proved invaluable.

Among the baby's many gifts and graces Kathie discovered one quite charming. Her laugh was like the ripple of softly shaken bells, but she had a quick ear and unusual voice, and could sing the melody of her little cradle songs in a remarkable manner.

Bruce, too, was much interested in the little creature.

" I find I have a powerful rival," he said to Kathie one day, quite in the old tone.

A quick color came to her cheek. Bruce had accepted the state of affairs quietly. He had even congratulated Charlie in one of their pleasant talks, but to Kathie he made no reference to the tie between them.

" Mamma thinks she must take her home ; she is getting

rather spoiled, but to me she grows lovelier every day. I shall hate to give her up."

"Give her up?"

"Yes. Mamma and Uncle Robert will return the last of this week."

"And you —" His heart seemed to throb up in his throat, and he felt the flush in his face, but he could not quite ask the question.

"Don't you care to have me stay?" she inquired, with girlish frankness and honesty.

"Oh, you *must* know, only I may be keeping you from some greater pleasure!"

"No, it could not be a greater pleasure if it was a comfort to you."

"It is." Then he tried to think that her staying would give her more of Charlie's society.

"Dr. Markham thought I had better, on Aunt Ruth's account. You see he does not consider me of paramount importance to you," laughing brightly. "But I shall hate to give up Bertie."

And Bertie proved almost inconsolable again, going back to the longing for her "own mamma."

"The little thing has a most affectionate memory," said Uncle Robert, as he comforted her.

There was quite a stir at Brookside at the advent of Robert Alston's baby, and much sympathy with the unfortunate marriage.

"My dear Mrs. Alston," Mrs. Adams said one morning, during a call, "I think one has need to feel more anxiously on the subject of sons' marriages than of daughters'. The girls can be counselled and restrained, and their own desire to do well helps a little. I used to feel so anxious about Maurice, and if ever I saw a designing girl laying out her charms to entrap him I was in a fever. I can never be thankful enough that he found the flower of all in our own little place, for Emma does make the loveliest of

wives. And, though I have no children of my very own, I
can understand from Maurice and Georgie how anxious
one may feel."

Mrs. Collamore, too, proffered a delicate sympathy. To
Mrs. Alston, Fay's presence brought a great pang of self-
condemnation. She had coveted her. She had brought
her into intimate contact with her son, and showed her in
many tender ways that she would be welcome to the
mother's heart, as well as the son's. What if she had
learned to care, allowed herself to dream? True, she could
remember no overt act or attention on Robert's part.
They had all been young people, having a good time
together, and oh, how devoutly grateful she felt that Rob's
sense of honor and manliness had restrained him from
foolish freedoms he would be ashamed to remember, from
any dangerous intimacy that would call a blush to this fair
young cheek. Yet, if it *could* have been! Ah, did other
mothers often covet sweet, lovely girls and find the wrong
ones in their places?

"How very much the baby is like its father?" Fay said
at length. She had been studying it; Miss Bertie, by
some rare condescension, coming to sit on her knee. She
did not make friends with everybody, or in a hasty manner, with some notable exceptions, and evinced quite a little discrimination.

"Yes," Mrs. Alston answered, with a smile; "and I
find a few traits of disposition, though she has Kathie's
sunny nature "

"I suppose she will almost be a second Kathie to Mr.
Conover."

Then they talked a little about Louise and her pretty
home, and Eugene's prospects now that his father had
taken him into business.

"You must come over often," Mrs. Alston said, holding Fay's hand at parting. She could make no difference
now, retrace no steps, only guard the future. "I shall miss

Kathie very much, but I suppose I must learn to do without her some time."

"O Mrs. Alston, there is no such happy time as when our children are grown into companionship and we have them around us!" exclaimed Mrs. Collamore. "Only," with a sigh, "it is so brief."

Fay Collamore walked home beside her mother, answering trifling observations. It was a late October day, and the strips of wood over beyond the lake were all aflame with autumn splendors: scarlet, brown, gold, and the massive green of the firs and spruce. There a long arm of Virginia creeper flung out a defiant banner that the sunset only would dare match. Barberries were hung with coral bells; sumachs were in the glory of brown and crimson, and the deep wine tints; while golden-rod was turning pale and grayish bronze. There were purple asters and late cardinal flowers with sentinel spikes, courageous, daring. How beautiful it all was! To-morrow she must get Mrs. Langdon and go for a walk. Presently this splendor would fade, the trees would be bare and brown, the little shrubs shrivelled up, the grass dry, and the wind blowing dismally. Winter always came, everywhere, in every life, an echo seemed to add to her thought.

It was rather chilly in doors, and a cheerful fire was burning in the grate.

"How blue and cold you look, Fay!" her mother said. "Sit down here and get good and warm, while I look after the dinner."

She dropped into a low rocker and shivered with something more vital than cold. For a long while she did not think at all; there was only a formless, slow-moving consciousness, a vague pain that she would not let come to light. Some "might have been" had gone out of the world for her, something she must grope after or long for, a part of herself set aside to be passed by quickly and quietly as one passes a little child one must not take up. lest the small hands might be too soon outstretched. They had been so happy, — *she* had been so happy since their first coming to Brookside, two summers ago. The neighbors proved so generous with their friendly living, Mr. Conover among the very first. And Robert Alston, with all his new college honors and his bright, fascinating ways, his vigor, and joy, and gayety; Kathie's return, and the lovely ball, and all the rich friendship in which the year had sped away, bringing him again, curiously changed, she had noted, but with a depth, and tone, and gentleness, a touch of some subtle experience.

This was what it had been. An unfortunate but perhaps not altogether an unhappy marriage She had made a terrible mistake. She had come so near a thing not intended for her that its glory, all wrongly translated, had illumined her for a brief space, lulled her into a sweet, happy content. She must gather it up and put it quite out of her life, this half-joy she had watched so tenderly. It was not meant for her then, it never had been, never would be. She must not even recall any day that had been the happier for the something akin to hope, the gladness to meet him, the remembrance of a graceful little turn or a flower, or a walk when he and she fell a little behind the others.

She was thankful as only a pure, right-minded woman can be that there were no stings in memory placed there by his thoughtless enjoyment. No word, no look but of friendliness, yet she knew if such a thing could have been, she of all the girls would have had it for her very own. The mother's preference and her own leaning had made a sad mistake. If she could go away somewhere, if he were to be always absent; but they must meet all along the years to come. The sorrow had given the mother her son again, and made between them a wide gulf, over which she must walk now and then, sure footed, clear eyed, and unflinchingly. She could not stay away without giving

pain to the mother, without betraying her own mistake ; it
must all go on just as before, that was the hard side of
it. Eugene, in his hurt, had wanted to. linger about, to
watch, to gather some little gleam of hope, but with her it
was quite different, from nature as well as necessity. How
strange they four should have come so near, just to miss
and wound! She could not understand the tangle.
Eugene had given up to a stony despair when his loss became certainty, and yet he was growing out of it, over it,
coming to a man's fortitude and sense. Some other sweet
heart would cure his wound in days to come ; and for her?

There was a cure, but not that way. She should never
want that, she said with an indignant protest. She must
gather up her self-command and go straight onward, living
out of it in the daily duties, taking earnest hold of the
" next," the work set her to do by a greater will than her
own. She must make no confused lines or tangled paths ;
she must not linger near the flame for her garments to
even have the faint scent of the burning, and yet she must
stand in the light.

They talked of the matter a little at the tea-table.

" It is a shame for a young life like that to be thrown
away," declared Mr. Collamore. " The girl may live
years ; insane people often do. And he seems such a fine
fellow ! Fortunately, he has the best and noblest man in the
world for his uncle. They are all delightful people."

" She may live years," Fay Collamore said to herself
under her breath ; " and in all that time it will be a sin for
a woman to think of him in any way but that of the
merest friendship."

CHAPTER XXII.

KATHIE missed her "little darling" greatly. The baby had been such a source of amusement, and the night after it was gone she felt almost homesick for them all. But she had to rouse herself and do double duty, as Aunt Ruth had a slight touch of fever.

In spite of the doctor's efforts the abscess had formed. There had been days and nights of constant and excruciating pain, relieved occasionally by morphine when the sleeplessness went beyond bounds. Bruce bore it bravely and with very little complaint. The silent heroism touched Kathie almost to tears, and was not without its effect upon Rob. Sometimes he would start in the night, hearing a soft sound, half groan, half sigh, and rising, use his best efforts to alleviate it. Or he would read half the night, until Bruce bade him close the book.

"You are such a dear, generous fellow, Rob; but you must not forget the work of to-morrow."

"Why, you see I thrive on it," Rob would exclaim laughingly. "I have actually grown fat under the regimen."

And so he had. Regular living and duties not very onerous, social life and enjoyment, and the horrible burden he had borne so long rolled away; safe without any further questioning of duty or harassing secrecy; his old, blithe buoyancy returned. The ringing laugh of the boy, toned and mellowed a little, was good to hear. The gleam of merry mischief in his eye was so exactly like the baby's, that Kathie could not but smile at it.

She, too, had her hands full ; but they would only let her do day duty. And even then Dr. Markham took her out for an hour's airing, or she ran around to Jessie's, and had a romp with Robin and Marjorie. During the most trying hours General Mackenzie remained with his son, who bore his suffering with much patience and fortitude, and a courage that fascinated Kathie. It did seem at times as if he could easily let himself drop out of life.

Kathie spoke of this one day to the doctor. "Well, why should he want to die?" asked the doctor a little gruffly. "Seems to me you young people nowadays make a great mistake about this dying business. God puts you into the world to live, and to make a fight for it. It is the survival of the fittest, after all ; but your work is to make yourself fit to survive, fit, even, for some other life, some other world. It looks cowardly to me to give up at the first hard blow, to want to get out of the pain and suffering to ease, and call that resignation. What does your old apostle say? 'Having done all things, to stand.' Not to cry to be taken out of the world when you have n't done more than half the things. There 's too much weakness, too much irresponsibility, too much fear about using one's will. They talk a lot of stuff down there at Ada's ; but there is strength and substance in it, after all. They go back to the seekers in the dark, ignorant ages, when the little knots of philosophy lighted a few feet from the centre, when the strong, earnest, pure-minded men interpreted the secrets of nature, and came so near to the other grand secret. We have been losing them both, throwing out the ballast and calling on a curious, soft, sweet mysticism to save us, and when the mysticism has failed, cry out that there is no salvation. It is a grand old fight, and it is sheer indolence to be swept out of it. So my hero," with a little twinkle in his eye, " is making the fight for life, quite confident God wants him to live until he sends the other message. He has his father and your sweet aunt, and a work to do when he gets about it again ; and he is going to get about it, though it may not be soldiering in the future. But," and Dr. Markham's voice fell to a reverent tone, " if he *was* called, I think we should all see how a hero could die."

The tears stood in Kathie's eyes.

" You know, my child," he continued, " it is not always the great deeds that make a hero. The fine, pure, wholesome, every-day living has something in it as well. We can squander that, but extravagance of vital or spiritual forces is not courage, but waste. I go over these things a good deal now, and wonder why we are so willing to throw away the best of our lives instead of living them out in a true and honest fashion, or moaning that the days have no pleasure in them. It is our rightful business to find the pleasure."

Dr. Markham was correct about his patient. There were several days when the balance almost trembled, when there were fears of various kinds, but they proved fears only. The abscess had not touched a vital part, and it was nature's way of casting out useless matter. By Christmas the young hero was out of danger and on the high road to recovery. He would be weak and perhaps a little lame at first, but there was no permanent injury to the joint.

It would be a glad, joyful Christmas. Where to keep the feast was the next consideration

Mrs. Mackenzie wanted them all to come to the city, and not be divided, since Cedarwood must be shorn of some of its members. Mr. and Mrs. Langdon were down for a month or two, so the holiday in the city was most promising.

Rob had kept his word to his mother steadfastly. The alternate Sundays had been hers alone. No restless roaming around for companionship, no outward show, at least, of the days being long. They were, sometimes, in spite of his best efforts. He missed the stir and interest of the

every-day life. He went to church with his mother and
his uncle, he played with or oftener teased the baby, who
was a source of amusement. Mrs. Alston had come to
love it devotedly. For a long while Bertha had been rather
shy of her grandmother, as if in some way she understood
the want of perfect accord, but both had outgrown that.
Mr. Conover had made known to her his intention of ulti-
mately adopting the child.

"We shall need something when Kathie goes," he said
gravely. "Bertha will keep us from growing old too fast."

Kathie was a most important personage in the Mackenzie household during this time. She lifted half the burden
off of Aunt Ruth's shoulders; she infused strength, and
brightness, and sunshine everywhere. Bruce once said
there were no cloudy days or storms, at which she laughed
gayly.

"Well, there may be in China," he answered. "But
when we get around to China it has cleared away."

He was so sure he had over-lived the passionate want
and longing. She had been lent for a little while to bridge
over this time of pain and suffering, but she belonged to
another; so he let himself rejoice and be glad with a
greater joy, a possibility of satisfying and peace, a height
which lifts one above the desire for self and rejoices truly
in the happiness of another, and all heights bringing one
nearer the great glory. He was so thankful, too, that he
should get entirely well.

"I think we often have good tidings of great joy," he
said to Kathie, "if we could only stop and view them
rightly."

So "the feast was set, the guests were met," and no
one enjoyed it more than General Mackenzie. He had
rather envied Mr. Conover his many occasions of playing
host, but now he had the full glory, with Kathie at his side,
almost as a daughter. Oh, why could it not be?"

Charlie, and Fred, and Kathie had hung the house with

18

evergreens. Rob had scoured the city and ruined himself, he declared, in holly berries, and brought up from Cedarwood some trails of glistening bitter-sweet. They had emblems and flowers ; the whole house was fragrant with them. The parlor looked lovely in its adornments. It had been a great enjoyment to Bruce as he lay in bed and saw them at their pretty work through the open door. Then they had invaded his room with the fragrance of spruce, and pine, and hemlock. They were to have a little Christmas-eve service there.

Mrs. Alston and the baby came down the day before, and then Kathie's heart was quite divided, but brimming over with happiness. She kissed Uncle Robert tenderly.

"Do you know," she exclaimed, "I feel almost like Tennyson's little May queen, as if to-morrow would be not the merriest, perhaps, but the happiest of ' all the glad new year'? There have been so many times in my life when I have not had anything more to ask, and now it has come over again, and I shall have all the people I want together.

Yes, she was very happy. There was no need of doubting, wondering.

Their dinner was at four during the short winter days. Aunt Ruth went up to keep Bruce company during his meal, leaving Kathie free for her mother and baby Bertie.

Bruce had not much appetite yet. His mother fed him the dessert, with a playful smile.

"Two babies in the house at once," he said. "Mother, I think God's best gift to my father and me has been your tender love, yourself. What would my life have been without it? And with it his is so blest."

"I am glad, thankful. And — you are quite resigned, Bruce?"

There was such a soft, sympathetic falter in her voice that he was much moved. He pressed the hand he held to his lips.

" Resigned ; that is just the word, mother. I don't know as we are expected to be glad to give up our greatest happiness. I can never imagine being glad that I have not Kathie, but she is another's, and I can see her now without coveting. I can even rejoice that she will make another life happy, that she will do a noble work and be in all things a helpmeet for her husband. It was very hard when I first came." And his voice dropped to soft, slow inflection.

" Oh, I was afraid of it ! "

" Mamma, dear, I was not educated for a soldier to shame the profession. I shall always be thankful that my father was a Christian gentleman, as well as a soldier. And now, though we can't quite see the haven, we are coming to it. You and father will have your son, no poor lameter," with a smile ; " and as the years go on he will try to comfort and cherish. I think we shall never be very much separated again. I have been considering a new calling, and if my plans should work, — but that will keep. And to-morrow will be a white day, I was going to say the happiest of my life. I have more, really, you know."

Just what Kathie had said.

He drew some short, quick breaths.

" You are tired," she said apprehensively. " Will not the service be too much to-night?"

" No, dear. It will not be until quite late, and I can rest between, you know. You may even keep Rob away, though he will be too busy to come, I dare say. I may fall asleep ; I often do at the edge of evening.

" Thank God you are so happy ! " And she kissed the brow, pale to transparency.

They were busy, though they would all have rushed to his room but for Aunt Ruth's prohibition.

But baby went to sleep, Uncle Robert sauntered out to make a few purchases, Kathie added some finishing touches, and then came down in her white cashmere with its swan's-down trimming, that all the boys liked so well. Fred and Dick Grayson dropped in. They had been helping to adorn Charlie's mission chapel, and reported that the young man would soon be on hand.

Bruce was rested and awaiting them. A reverent group of young people who had passed so much of their lives together, who had been drawn into the great chain of fellowship by little links of pleasure, enjoyment, and pain, and cemented by love, standing on the threshold of life with high ideals and brave purposes.

Charlie entered in his white robe. Bruce seemed to realize the exceeding spirituality of his refined and idealistic face as he never had before. True, and gentle, and tender he had always thought him, but this placed him in a new light; the soul, strong in the might of a high work, strong in the faith of the living Christ. The man and his work centralized suddenly, and Bruce bowed in unconscious reverence.

Kathie sat at the piano and played. To Bruce her face was the face of an angel. Her soft white robe fell about her in billowy folds, and the light made a halo around her fair head. One sentence went floating through his mind with the recurrence of tide beating up on the shore, — "Whom God hath joined together." Was it designed from the beginning?

They had their carols, their reading, their prayers. They all kept the feast in peace and good-will, in new resolves and purer faith. Last of all they sang the evening hymn and listened reverently to the greater benediction.

Charlie and Fred were going out to a midnight service. They all gathered about Bruce's bed for a little chat of good wishes and gratitude, and then dispersed.

Bruce was calm and tranquil with heavenly peace, and yet he could not sleep. There was a stir in the street after the house became quiet. Then the bells pealed for midnight, and the chimes rang out their message : —

" Peace and good-will, good-will and peace."

Yet there lingered last of all one verse in which the remembered sweetness of Kathie's voice haunted him : —

> " Teach me to live, that I may dread
> The grave as little as my bed ;
> Teach me to die, that so I may
> Triumphing rise at the last day."

Christmas morning dawned gloriously. Kathie and Uncle Robert went to early service while their souls were still " unvexed by care." The Merediths and the two children came, but Bertie stood her ground boldly and bravely.

" Kathie, I believe ever so long ago you promised to endow Robin with half your fortune and all your love, was n't it?" and Mr. Meredith shook his head with a half-comic gravity. " I begin to fear for his undivided estate."

But Robin seemed very much taken up with the second of the name, and relegated Kathie to the girls, in his imperious boy fashion.

They had almost persuaded Aunt Ruth to let them bring Bruce down stairs for dinner, but Dr. Markham quenched their project. They might wheel him out in the parlor on the reclining chair, but he was on no account to sit up.

He thought that a great treat. They had dinner rather earlier and a pretty tea up-stairs, Kathie making it over the spirit lamp, and the boys passing the plates and refreshments. The gifts had all been ranged on a console in the alcove, in lieu of a Christmas tree, and in the evening they had another delightful time singing.

Dr. Markham said to Bruce, " Now you can address yourself to the task of getting well; there is nothing in the way."

The young man went at it with great vigor and earnestness. It was good to live. There were many things to do. The whole fascinating realm of science lay before him. Dr. Garnier, young, enthusiastic, and fervent, used to drop in for a talk; Dick and Rob brought him news of the outer world and its progress; he had long discussions with his father on philanthropical problems; and when he was too tired for these there was chess and music. Kathie used to sit at the piano and play "songs without words," until his soul was stirred to waves of rapt melody. She had taken her brother's place in the poetry reading, and they went over volumes together, culling the choicest flowers.

Then he could begin to walk about a little with a crutch, for the hip joint had still to be tenderly guarded. The days were bright and pleasant, sometimes with a hint of spring in the air, and occasionally they spoke of the summer days and Cedarwood.

Kathie went home for a little visit.

"I've about half adopted Fay," said Mrs. Alston. "I don't know what I should have done but for her. Georgie Halford is to be married presently, and Mrs. Adams wants you and Emma. I think she is afraid things will go wrong if you are not here."

Fay had made no positive difference, nothing to remind Mrs. Alston of any little mistaken hope that had sprung up too soon and been nipped by an untoward frost. She came over frequently. Rob was never home on week days. She played with and petted the child, she listened to little fragments of the sad story until it seemed she had it all by heart, and pitied profoundly the life that had been so wrenched out of proper symmetry.

And then Kathie must go up to see how Mrs. Truesdell's life was widening out and bearing fruit, the fruit of the spirit, patience, gentleness, and charity; to note how much richer the man at her side was growing with the stir and freshness of her soul.

Aunt Ruth wrote every day or two: "Bruce went down

stairs"; "Bruce went out with Dr. Markham"; and one
evening they ventured to Mrs. Garnier's, where they found
Ada quite a little queen, set about with brilliant stones,
that flashed, and sparkled, and emitted strange lights as
they were rubbed and stirred by the friction in the atmosphere. But to Bruce there came another vision, a fair,
sweet girl, a Una, not with her lion, but with her loyal
young knights.

He thought of her daily, nightly, I was going to say, for
she often was his last remembrance. All her sweet, un-
selfish joyousness, her out-giving, her never saving up bits
and choice delights, and oh, never finding any lack.

Charlie Darrell was sitting by his reclining chair one
evening, while the General and Aunt Ruth had gone to
hear a famous singer.

"Don't you miss Kathie terribly?" asked Charlie with a
sudden irrelevancy. "The house seems so strange and
still without her! quite like another place. Kathie is n't
ever noisy, but there is a curious sort of pervasiveness
about her. She seems to fill every place. She is like the
scent of heliotrope. You can tell from ever such a little
bit that the real bloom is there."

"Yes — I miss her — very much," Bruce answered
slowly.

"Is she coming back, do you know? If not, I must
take a run to Cedarwood; I have something of importance
to lay before her. Do you mind my telling? Lovers
prove bores so often that I have resolved never to be
obtrusive." And a bright color flushed his face. "It is
about a call. You know I have been doing mission
work here in the city and waiting. I promised her mother
I would n't really ask for her in two years, and that will be
next summer," with a softened, lingering accent, and
a dreamy flush of anticipation. "But I have received a
call to one of the prettiest towns up the Hudson. The
salary is very fair, the society above the average, the

church beautiful, and the loveliest rectory imaginable. A Mr. Dinsmore, one of the wardens, does business here in the city. I went up once and exchanged with the clergyman, and now he is going abroad. I think Kathie ought to have a voice in her future home."

There was a long silence. Her future home. She had come into his life, but she must go out again. She could not remain the bright, eager friend and companion!

" I should think it might be very delightful," Bruce made answer slowly.

" It is a lovely place. I wish you were well enough to take a day's journey up there. Perhaps you will be before long. You know we have counted on you for a steady friend, and this episode has brought us all so much nearer together. But for all the terrible suffering to you, I should rejoice that it had happened. And that is just the sphere Kathie could grace so well, though she would be charming anywhere."

" You like it; the work, I mean?" Bruce's voice was a little husky and strained.

" It will be delightful in many ways, but there is something — See here, Bruce, you are not the one to shirk a square ordeal; help me with a little clear sight. I ought to do this for Kathie. No doubt I shall soon be content and satisfied. But, oh, what of the perishing souls here? What of the young men with no homes, no hope, rushing madly to ruin on every side? There is enough to save them if they would come, but they will not; the way is a strange path to them. And just here comes the Divine mandate, 'Go into the highways and hedges.' They will listen sometimes to youth when they would laugh and jeer at an older person. There are so many ways; and I'm not sure but a man who has had a clean, wholesome, love-appointed home knows better what these have lost. My heart aches for them. My whole soul goes out in strong crying. And yet it is hardly the place or the work in which to take a sweet young girl like Kathie Alston."

Bruce placed his hand softly on that of the other, but his face was partly turned away. There was the ring of the true soldier. He could never think Charlie rather weak and idealistic after that certain sound of the trumpet. He *had* undervalued him. The poetical ideas, the exalted reverence, the diviner life of self-consecration that seemed to stand a little out of the common work, the extreme purity and almost girlish sympathy and tenderness: if it could take its white robes down to the mouth of that seething pit, if it could hold out its clean, dainty hands unshrinkingly to that wretchedness, there was the truth and strength of the Almighty in it. The brave young soldier felt humbled, self-condemned. He longed to ask pardon, to show the other how high he did truly exalt him.

"I must think a little of her. There is work to do in the other place as well, and sometimes I believe the rich are as much in need of devoted missionaries. They make their lives narrow and cold, and wrap themselves up in indolent, dreamy music and fine preaching. So I would not need be idle."

"Dear friend," and the clasp tightened, "can any one answer for another? Ask her. Tell her truly."

"There, I have quite stirred you up by all this vehemence. I forgot you were not as strong as Dick or Rob. I feel the excitement in your voice, in your hands. I'll go and play a little while. That is a trick I have caught from Kathie."

He seated himself at the piano. He was very fond of improvising, and now it was something in the soft minor chords, tranquillizing rather than saddening. Bruce listened. He did not want to think just then. He would wait for that until the lights were out and all was still.

They said good night after Rob came in, and, as the young man had not quite given up all his duties, he saw Bruce safely in bed.

"Seems to me you look a little pale, old chap!" he said gayly.

And then, in the silence of the night, Bruce confronted the phantom he had thought laid forever. He had been fancying, feeding his soul with friendship, and out of it had arisen the old love. But if ever there had been a dream it must be put away, sternly, wholly. The coveting regard was a snare and a delusion; he had called it by another name, but now he dragged it out to the pitiless light. His soul should not be stained with it; even if it took a lifetime of effort, it should be done. He had not designedly gone into temptation. He did not see how any of this could have been helped, but he had overrated his own strength and discipline of mind. The fancied security had been built upon false premises. All the rich and sweet associations, all the deep and tender memories, the past and the present, had been leading his too willing feet over into his neighbor's beautiful fields until he desired, with the mad, passionate desire of covetousness, to gather the fruit, to pluck the blossoms, and carry them quite away. A little more and he might have spoken, or smiled, or looked, and told the whole story. Her infinite pity would have been touched, perhaps won, for people in a moment of mighty temptation do not always consider if it is the true, unflawed pearl they are reaching after. Always there would have been a shadow of wrong and stain on both lives, an uneasy sense, a hiding away in the garden at the voice of the Lord.

He prayed a little by snatches; it was so hard just then to desire to be saved, even though he knew it was the right thing. Now and then the other course seemed so possible, so plausible. What was in her soul? If he could know! Had God really joined them together in that completest of all love?

"Save me," he cried. "I am weak and worn with the tempest, but do Thou bring me to the haven where I would be."

CHAPTER XXIII.

THERE followed a week of warm, rainy, and foggy weather, and with it a pause in the vital forces of Bruce Mackenzie. He could not sleep; his appetite fell to a mere nothing. Yet in his patient submissiveness no one could guess the wearying inward strife, the temptation resisted so silently that its existence was not suspected. He compelled himself to speak of Kathie in the most cheerful of tones; he allowed himself to be lulled and soothed by his mother's playing, so like hers. He fought Rob at chess with no outward diminution of valor, but inwardly it was weariness of soul.

"We shall have to send for Kathie again," declared his father, " and compel her to disclose the secret of her unfailing panacea."

Upon this hint Rob wrote, in a funny, melodramatic manner, quoting from " Lord Ullin's Daughter," on the very first line, with a change of pronoun : —

> "Come back, come back, they cried in grief
> Across the stormy water."

The house was desolate; Bruce was sinking fast. Charlie was in a state of awful uncertainty about something or other, and he, Rob, would expect to bring her back with him next Monday morning."

He said nothing to the others, so again Bruce had no choice.

Kathie laughed over the letter. There would always be some fun cropping out in Rob. The healthy buoyancy of nature would assert itself.

"I suppose I shall have to go," she said. "Charlie spoke of something, but he has two very sick people on his hands, and it does seem as if I never stayed at home any more. Bertie is so fond of me, too," with a remorseful touch to her tone.

"You might go for a little while," rather reluctantly.

"Mamma," eagerly, "I 've just had a bright thought. Dr. Markham says Bruce must have change of air; that he has exhausted New York." ("Just imagine the immense receiver," Rob had appended.) "Why should n't they come down here for the summer? We have this great house and lovely grounds, and only so few people now; then Brookside is really cultivated and artistic. And, oddly enough, Bruce begins to design such pretty little things. Emma says he has a real artist's eye. She will be here."

"I am sure I would be only too glad to have them do it," returned Mrs. Alston.

"Then I should n't be running hither and yon forever. It would be terribly lonely for Rob, though."

Always ready to think what any change might bring to another, and desiring the other's happiness.

The Mackenzies were surprised and overjoyed by having Rob march in Monday noon with Kathie on his arm. General Mackenzie kissed her tenderly, and Aunt Ruth seemed to lay down a burden at her entrance.

She was a good deal surprised at the change in Bruce; indeed, for days an unseen something baffled her. He was gentle, grateful, ready to be entertained, but he seemed holding back a secret pain or resolve, as one does a breath in a moment of agony. He would not let himself enjoy the full, long respiration of relief.

Then a little cloud shadowed the exquisiteness of Kathie's flawless sky. It brought back the sort of pain and secret shame of Eugene Collamore's love, though why it should unconsciously connect itself with that she could not understand.

They had the pretty reception-room at Aunt Ruth's to themselves one evening, and Charlie explained to her the call and its many advantages, and the necessity for some kind of a decision.

"Rob went up to Mr. Dinsmore's with me one evening to dinner: I suppose he told you? He was wild over the rectory and the grounds. This Mr. Copeland is quite a middle-aged bachelor, and very artistic, over much, I fancy," with a little smile. "But it made me think of you and Emma. We never could find anything so near our ideal."

"I am afraid I have n't had any — much — of an ideal," Kathie said hesitatingly. "And it seems so sudden. Must you give an answer immediately?"

"I ought to have told you before. Mr. Dinsmore spoke of it a month ago. I thought it over a little myself, then there were so many things, and this poor fellow who had just died! Kathie, there was some similarity in his history to that of Rob's. He belonged to a wealthy family, and married a coarse, designing girl, and his people would have nothing to do with him. He must have been very much infatuated, for after his wife showed him how utterly heartless and unprincipled she was, and left him for evil ways, he still clung to her. I dare say he had drank some before, but then he threw himself into the awful gulf of intemperance, and became worse than a brute. I found him in all the horrors of delirium tremens, and had him nursed and cared for, but it was too late to save his poor body. That was worn out at the age of twenty-seven. I think he saw at the last, but he was so afraid to face God with the broken fragments, and he could not bear to have me leave him. Kathie, we must all be thankful that there was enough true manliness and true godliness in Rob to save him. I think he will see some day just where the strength lies. Everybody does n't come to the full knowledge at once."

Kathie drew a long, shivering breath. "Oh, if it had been Rob —"

"There, do not think of the dreadful picture. God kept him for us all, especially, I think, for Uncle Robert. He always had a rather curious, honest, rough courage. Perhaps God has given him just the measure he needs. But, my little darling, we must think of ourselves."

"Oh, is it right, when there is so much work in the world?" she cried hastily, but with the utmost fervor.

"To a certain extent, yes. You know our Saviour said, 'The poor you have with you *always*,' and I believe he designed to teach us patience as well as sympathy, patience for ourselves, that we should not rush at the great work with superhuman efforts, and fall away discouraged because we could not accomplish it all, cure all the harm, and sin, and wrong. Mine is only a very little piece. And beside, He made homes, He set them in families, and showed them 'the better part'; He bade them love one another. I shall not be idle in the other place." And there was a certain bright hope in his voice.

"But —" How explain the strange unwillingness? "I do not like to be hurried into anything. I like to look it over, to consider. Must you decide soon?"

"Yes, I ought. It is not fair to keep them waiting."

"Which would *you* rather do?" She asked it with a great fluttering of soul.

"The work here interests me deeply. Still, it will not give me the home I want for you, the place where we may work together. It would break your tender heart to see the sights, to hear the groans and cries, that remind me of Dante's Inferno, here upon earth. And it may be a long while before any home as lovely as this comes to us again."

"I am not a coward," she said bravely. "I am not thinking of the fine raiment, or the high seats, and sometimes in parishes like that there is pride, and coldness, and obstacles of all sorts. You can't get to people's hearts,

you can't do any real work, and if it was this way would
you be satisfied?"

He was silent. It had been his one fear.

"And —" Her bravery was all gone now. There came
a white flickering in her face, a great tremble seemed to
shake her very soul. "Oh," she cried, "are you quite
sure we are right? that I ought to have taken what I
did that summer night? For it seems so strange to go out
of my own life into another's. After all, I have been so
little with mamma, and to go away from them all!"

She paused, with a piteous sob of excitement in her
breath. She stretched out her hands as if she would cling
to some sure anchor.

He caught them, clasped them in his own, and held them
firm and strong.

"My dear Kathie, my darling, you are so excited. I
suppose it does seem sudden to you, but we would not
come to the real separation until next summer or fall.
And there may be other chances."

"There will be. I don't know why, but that seems so
cold and far off, so finished, and hemmed about, and polite,
as if one would never get out of the polished rims. It
catches my very breath. How foolish!" with a sudden
gesture of disapproval. "Charlie, promise to do what
you would like as if I were not in it at all."

"But you are in it, even here." And a smile of heavenly
content illumined his face. "You are always with me, in
my soul, so you cannot escape. I am not sure, however,
but that I *would* rather stay here a while longer. So we
will let it go for the present. When I have served my two
years we will plan for it. And I should be sorry to go
away from Rob."

"Stay," she said then. Some flashing inner consciousness impelled her.

He kissed her reverently. He was more than content.
She would never strive for the gauds of this world, the
pride of life.

Rob was surprised at the decision. Aunt Ruth wondered and discussed it a little.

"I am afraid it would be like getting among the patricians at school." And Kathie smiled faintly.

Bruce said, "You were very brave to give it up."

"I am of the opinion it would have required bravery to go," she made answer simply. And he asked himself if she understood *all* that it meant. Try as he might to put it out of his mind, some vague questioning would creep in.

The weather came off oppressively warm, May instead of March. Bruce went about a little, but he did not gain strength. He would not confess to suffering any intense pain, but there was a worn and anxious look in his face, and his eyes were heavy.

So they began to talk in good earnest about a change. Brookside was discussed; then more bracing seaside places, as it was rather early for mountains. "A sea voyage," said Dr. Markham. That set them all to thinking. There was Europe and the Mediterranean, Egypt.

Bruce settled it at length, as he and Rob were poring over the map.

"I should like to go to the Azores. Fayal is said to have such a perfect climate. Since I am to live I should like to get thoroughly well."

They considered a little and then agreed, since Dr. Markham thought they could not do better.

"I'm not going to have any sad good-byes," said Bruce one evening. "I want all the boys to come in as for any other call, and wish me 'bon voyage,' and you and Mr. Conover may see us off," nodding to Rob.

"Thanks, old fellow, for being remembered in your will." And Rob made a funny face.

"It is n't as if I was in the last stages of consumption —"

"With the sands of life nearly run out," interrupted Rob. "The Indian bullet missed its deadly mission."

" O Rob ! "

It was Kathie's tender, upbraiding voice.

" Well, if he will not let me be pathetic, I must be tragic. There is a great fund of unused material lying about my massive brain."

" O Rob, it would be jolly to take you."

" As jolly as our first tour together to the camping-ground of the brave red men of our school days." And Rob laughed.

They settled about giving up the house. Mrs. Alston came up for a few days. Bruce held receptions and took the good wishes and love. The boys were not over-sentimental, yet it had been a kind of glorious winter, after all.

So they came to the last evening. Kathie had been playing some old songs, and Bruce was stretched out in the reclining chair ; Rob was looking over several little matters, and the three were by themselves.

Kathie rose presently.

" Oh, we shall all miss you so much ! I should not want the suffering over again, but — " And she came nearer Bruce.

" It will be sweet to remember the sympathy and tenderness all my life long. Yes, it *has* been a happy time " ; as if he had to convince himself of the happiness that should have been there.

Then he suddenly held out his hands.

" This is our good by," he began, taking both of hers, and drawing her to him.

She bent over, and there came a strange light in her face, a little flush, a swift tremulousness that she felt in her very finger ends.

" No — " He would not let her say anything, but the sweet face came nearer, the lips touched his, pure as a child. He could not even kiss his parting that way ; every pulse was in a flame. He moved the face a trifle,

19

and the brow received the secret of the lifelong love. Then he just murmured : —

> "Say not good night, but in some future time
> Bid me good morning."

She went quietly out, as in a trance. He lay back on the pillow, and a sound like that of waves surged in his ears.

"Bruce, old fellow, dear old chap! let me call her back! You have n't learned to unlove her all this time. Oh, it has been this —"

"Hush, I shall be better; I *am* better," rising in an excited manner, his eyes burning with an intense light. "It was miserable cowardice on my part —"

"No, it was n't!" vehemently. "And I don't see why you should not have your chance! I don't believe Kathie knows, or thinks. Let her compare the two loves and choose between them. Come, that will be only fair!"

"She has no right to compare his love with that of any other! She must take it or leave it, but to balance or weigh, to analyze —"

"I don't mean that," passionately. "If there is anything greater, tenderer, better — "

"Not even then, Rob. If I had *not* known of this I might plead for my chance. But it would be the one little ewe lamb over again, the friend treacherously supplanting the friend. I can't help loving her, but I *can* help being false and selfish. And I think we undervalue Charlie. He has a grandly simple nature, the unconsciously noble, the tender sweetness and truth of a woman. I don't wonder that a man would love to have him near when he came to die; and if God gave her to him, no one has a right to tempt her away. It would be a sin."

"But if God did *not* give? If you are all wrong?"

Rob was confused and troubled, and his eyes were filled with fear.

" It has the semblance of giving. Neither you nor I have the right to remove the seal. If there is any mistake," and his voice shook visibly, " I think God will bring it to light, and I am going to stay until there is nothing more to tempt me, until I can come in and sit down by their fireside, a true, strong friend, and look them both in the face with clear eyes. I have been weak."

" I couldn't do it if I loved a woman as you love Kathie." The words seemed almost wrested from Rob.

" When *you* come to love a woman placed out of your reach," and then he remembered the chain that might last for a lifetime, " you will go to God, then, Rob, for nothing else will be strong enough to save you."

Bruce dropped back on the pillow, deadly white, and shivered as if chilled through. Rob chafed the hands.

" You are a loyal friend, Rob," said the other, " and you must be true to the end. Promise me that you will never disturb Kathie's faith, *their* faith. Keep my secret; otherwise you may hurt and hinder some fine, choice work of God."

Rob winked the tears out of his eyes, but did not speak until Bruce said again, " Promise."

Then he bent over and kissed him, and was still sitting quietly beside him when the General entered.

The ladies said their good-byes at the house the next morning, but Rob and his uncle went down to see the travellers off. Mrs. Alston had a few articles to pack up, and some boxed to send to Brookside. Rob was relegated to Mr. Meredith's care. Charlie was to go on with his work, and when Kathie was quite rested up they would talk over matters.

So Kathie returned to Cedarwood with her mother. There seemed a little lull in merry-making. Georgie Halford was married and gone. Mrs. Hunsdon had a wonderful baby. Eugene Collamore was coming to a graver and higher manhood, and, like Bruce, putting away the joy that was not for him. A more serious tone seemed settling over the young people. Kathie had hours of quiet revery, long walks by herself, from which she sometimes came in with a curiously disturbed face. It seemed as if there had never been time to think of herself until now.

A very quiet summer it proved. They heard from the voyagers, and all was well. What was to come next?

CHAPTER XXIV

THE period had at length reached Kathie Alston when the personal responsibility of living could no longer be evaded. The happy childhood, full of love, the bright, radiant youth, with friends and counsel on every side, tenderest care bridging over the rough places, wise thoughts smoothing out little perplexities, until now, when she must make the great decision for herself.

What had changed the placid current, what troubled her with importunate asking? Why she should not go forward gladly to the new life? The "girls" each in her time had been so happy, so full of little palpitant joys that shone in their eyes, trembled on their lips, and fluttered up and down broken, incoherent sentences. She was grave and calm when she talked with Charlie about his work; they joyed over the pleasant happenings to their friends; they took pride in Rob. In all these things they could stand side by side. But when it came to the more intimate life, the "thou and I," she drew back with a shiver as if some phantom looked out at her with fearful eyes.

One summer night, when she sat holding Bertie asleep in her arms, loath to lay the sweet little thing in her bed, they talked about Rob.

"Uncle," she said, "if it had been merely an engagement, would Rob have been right in giving it up?'

"I think he would, if his family had advised such a thing. I am not a believer in very young engagements. A fancy can take time to grow into strength and richness, to reach out to a glad and hopeful awaiting of all that is best, even where all is right and proper. But it seems to me a young man owes it to his family not to choose or bring any one in their midst who will make disunion, or shame, or sorrow. And the same with a girl. I am not speaking now of unreasonable objections. If Miss Weeks had been a proper sort of person to marry, we should have received her, and still thought Rob unwise or injudicious. If he had been engaged and learned any shameful secret about her or her family that had been purposely kept from him, he would have been justified in giving her up."

" Suppose she had been — suppose he *had* tired of her, and she had loved him very much ? "

" Those are hard cases, little Kathie. *I* should give up a woman who did not love me, no matter how much I cared for her, but if the case were reversed I think she would have the *right* to hold me to my promise. It would be my duty to love her all I could, to honor her, and make her life happy. I would have no right to throw back a heart I had tried to win, and I ought to accept the result of my thoughtlessness."

She made no answer, but presently rose and carried Bertie up-stairs, laying her softly in her dainty crib. If she could stay here always and watch this little girl as her mother had watched her ! Why did she not want to go?

Did she love Charlie Darrell with the great, true, honest love of womanhood? She would have to answer the question to him shortly ; she *must* ask it of herself.

There was no moon, but the stars were coming out slowly, rims of gold in the pure blue ether. How wonderful the world was ! How strange it was to live, to do, to suffer, and make others suffer. She leaned her soft chin on her folded arms and glanced out as she knelt at the window, and the fragrant air toyed among her soft curls and soothed her throbbing temples. What was love? She had read about it in romances, she had seen its fruit in real life. Could anybody make a palpable thing of the grace of God? And had not the mystery of human love been likened to that great mystery? "If a man love not his brother whom he hath seen, how shall he love God whom he hath not seen?"

Did *she* love? Yes, in a relative sense. She could go out in any field and work side by side with Charlie Darrell, she could even keep his house as a sister might, but all that sweet interchange of heart, — no, she had not been shown the mystery. Why not, when she had prayed and striven to learn? Not endeavored to win, — she was guiltless there. She had not dreamed that night of what he was going to say, any more than she could have imagined Eugene Collamore's love. Why was she so sure in the one case, and so at fault in the other? And having promised, would it be her duty to go on, to honor him and make his life happy? She *could* make him happy, a bitter knowledge. If both were tired, or had outgrown it, but there had never been anything to outgrow. She remembered back in the old school days, when all the children were telling what they were going to wear to Charlie's party, and she had nothing but her simple Sunday dress, how he had taken her part in their teasing, and cared for her, and how in her mind he had surpassed the rest. There was something that held him higher than all others now, he would always be the Sir Galahad in the quest of the Holy Grail. Perhaps this was why he seemed above every-day fancies; but why, then, could she not reach up to his height?

Could she not learn? Ah, if she had not learned in two years, was there not some fatal blindness or hardness of heart?

She had never been used to trying on loves. She had never speculated how it would seem to be dear to this one or that one. She had been dear to everybody. Was it because she had had so much love? She felt humbled, self-rebuked. The slow tears gathered in her eyes.

" Kathie," called the kindly voice, " do you want to walk over to Mrs. Adams's with me? I promised your mother I would come for her."

" Yes," she answered down the stairway, and went for her hat.

She seemed to be growing so womanly in these days, Uncle Robert thought; yet he was not quite at ease about her. He had wondered a little when Bruce first went away. Everybody had kept the secret well, yet sometimes he had fancied there *was* a secret. Not with her, though. The clear, untroubled eyes could not have hidden that.

He meant to continue the talk about Rob, but she took up quite another topic. Her voice had a clear coolness; she was not in the stress of agitation. The trouble was that she did keep so outside of it.

Rob and Charlie came down on Saturday, the latter for a brief vacation, as he was quite tired out. Was it her fault, she asked herself, that he was in all this depth of misery, and care, and suffering. The pleasant, restful home he had given up, and yet this work *was* nobler.

Rob seemed a little restless, too, some way, and rambled off by himself Sunday afternoon. Fred was planning a journey to the White Mountains.

" Can't you get a week off and go with him, Robert? asked his uncle. " Would n't you like it? "

" Like it! Why, it would be royal. You think I might?" And he gave a quick, delighted glance.

" I dare say you will have years enough for work."

" But I should like to go on Wednesday," said Fred. " How will that suit? "

" Well, I can telegraph to you. I think there will be no doubt about my going, though."

The telegram came in due time.

" Is n't it odd?" said Kathie on Monday evening; " Mrs. Collamore and Fay are going to the White Mountains.

Eugene goes to Boston for several days, and then joins
them."

"Jolly!" declared Fred, "I'll see Eugene. He is a
capital good fellow for a tramp, and I would like to be in
Boston with him. Rob won't mind, I guess."

They all went, and Kathie was left alone with her lover,
without even Fay's brief calls to break the daily round.
Bertie was a bright, winsome little mischief, and she
amused Charlie greatly and seemed to take away any
sense of awkwardness between him and Kathie. But
there were long evenings, there were walks she could not
refuse, there were talks, coming nearer and nearer, that
filled her with a blind, dull terror, as if she had no strength
to fly, and could not see the way if she had. And then
she tried to make herself quite content. She had taken
the life in her hands hoping, meaning honestly to do something with it, and now had she any right to thrust it out
of hers after having allowed it to grow alongside?

It came to him presently that she was not her olden,
joyous self. She had been so bright and happy all winter,
and now, when nature was all astir with life, her gravity
seemed amiss, the little distance such a wide, wide thing.

"Kathie," he said one evening, "let us talk of ourselves, our own lives. Are we coming nearer the time
that should be to us a great joy? I am not impatient, but
yet it is something to think of. I should like to know
where you would choose it, what kind of a home or work.
Have we lost our first glad ideal?"

He reached over and took her hand. It was cold and
trembled in his.

"Kathie?" There was a vague wonder in his tone.

She *must* speak. She could not go on without trying
to rectify the mistake, if it were that, or the wrong, if she
had fallen into one.

"You know what I said that night last spring," — and
her voice had a strained sound, even, — "if we were quite

sure — if there was no mistake? Are our lives the two to be set together in God's sight? I have been considering; it troubles me so."

She wanted to lean her head down on his shoulder and cry. He was her nearest friend, save Uncle Robert. It always had been so.

"Kathie, you do not mean, you cannot mean that our love — "

"I think that your love is true, and sweet, and strong in its perfect honesty. I feel as if it were too holy a thing for me to take."

"But it is not. O Kathie, you surely have no foolishly exalted idea — "

"Let me tell you all," she interrupted, "and you shall be the judge. You only have the right. When you spoke that summer night, two years ago, I only felt that all my life I had loved you, with a child's love, it was true. Some one else had asked me," and her voice faltered, "and because I had shrunk away then, and did not now, because it seemed such a lovely thing, and did not surprise me, I — Did I drift into it unthinkingly? It is always so vague to me, like the music heard in a dream. Mamma was pleased."

"Kathie," there was an almost breathless halt in his tone, "was it Bruce?"

"Bruce! No," she cried sharply, as if some quick pang had pierced her.

"I can guess; Eugene. But if you did not love him, and knew it, could you not judge?"

"I had loved you. I did not know. It is all sore confusion in my mind, as if I had stopped with the child's love, somehow, and never could grow to anything greater."

"But I will take the child's love. I will trust it to grow, to thrive on the tenderness I shall bring," he cried, drawing her nearer to him.

It was the same as in years agone. She was as dear to
him then in her school dress as in the pretty silk; she was
as dear now in the old love. But how could she pro-
fane God's sacrament with it, so poor a thing to be offered
on so high an altar? And how could she make him understand, without too great a pain? She was not sure she
wanted to be given up; but to be set straight, some way,
to see her duty clearly, to be shown the path wherein she
must walk.

"Kathie," he began slowly, but the tone was one of
great, searching inquiry, "is there any other thought. or
what might be a half-hidden hope; any love refused to
yourself, that might come with an asking?"

"There never was up to that time; and if anything
came afterward, I would have no right—" in a tone of
unflinching honesty.

Was there anything put away between her and Bruce?
He could not ask it quite like that.

"No word with a meaning, Kathie, that might have
been answered differently if you had been free?"   .

She could answer clearly, and she was proud to do it.
Not a word or look on Bruce's part returned with any misgiving.

"Then I think you have been vexing your gentle soul
with some high ideals, and because you cannot make
everything fit the pure and perfect picture you feel
nothing should be there. But there is a good deal of
every-day to life, — six days to the one Sunday, you know,"
with the tender, encouraging smile lighting up his face.
"So many plain and common things, keeping a house clean,
eating, resting, talking over the A B C's to people who
never can get beyond them to the great sentences. You
have been doing this always, and we can't put it out of
the new state any more than the old. I suppose it is natural
to idealize a clergyman's life, and yet it is not all up in the
mountains of joy with God. Are you not desiring to be

there, to have the assurance perfect, so there shall not even be a shadow?"

Was she asking too much?

"I ought to be glad to come to you," she said out of her high, self-judging mood. "I can think of the work, of the trials, and they do not alarm, but to go into another life, to hold it reverently, tenderly, so that no bruise or wound shall ever come to it, to *desire* this —"

"You have not quite come to the desire?" If there was a little ache he kept it out of his voice. "I do not wonder at that; I can readily understand it. Your life has been so full and rich that you have felt no need of the shelter of love, no lack, and it is hard to go out of this little Paradise. You have been hedged about with all the blooms of care and affection, and you have a mind of such sweet content that you don't care to stray out of your pasture. Kathie, darling, I think it is that you are not quite ready for love. Don't trouble or worry any more. I can wait until the time comes. It will come, I am sure."

She drew a long breath. She knew how a man felt who had been reprieved from a terrible doom. Yet she told herself she had no right to experience this relief.

"And we are both young. I like my work; I am not sure but it would please me best to remain in it another year. We can wait and see. You shall belong to Uncle Robert until you do want to give yourself to me."

There was a great revulsion in her soul. She loved him with the old love again, and was at peace. He read it in the clear, exultant tone of her voice when she spoke.

Yet to the man was coming a larger outlook than had been visible to the boy's eyes. There were so many delicate mixed motives, so many surprising conclusions to the impressions one had felt quite sure about. The hidden meanings must all prove themselves before one could hold fast.

The old tranquil happiness returned to them. They

did not worry at the wound to see if it was healing. If there was to be any change from the old interest it must come from clear seeing.

Uncle Robert understood that the something had been made up or laid aside. There was no word about a marriage.

Once Mrs. Alston said, " Kathie, do you think it was a wise thing to give up that lovely parish of Edgewater? Mrs. Treherne has a sister living there, and she says the church society is delightful, and the house a perfect gem. Charlie is so refined and cultivated that I should fancy it would have just suited him."

" He decided himself," in a gentle, apologizing tone.

" But the home will be a great deal to you?"

" I am not homeless, though." And she ran to catch Bertie, who was trailing over the flower beds.

The boys returned, brimming over with enthusiasm, and for a few days the house was quite as of yore. Even Rob admitted that Eugene Collamore was a capital good fellow, and asked him over to tea, which invitation somehow was made to include Mrs. Collamore and Fay.

" It was so delightful to have your two boys," Mrs. Collamore said to Mrs. Alston. " I have always wished Eugene had a brother. He admires Robert so very much, and I don't see how one could help feeling proud of him, and Fred is a real mother boy. It will do the young people good to be together, for we think Eugene rather too grave for his years."

They all knew Rob's story. Mrs. Alston, too, understood what could never be, and bridged over her longing with delicate, motherly ways that accepted the hard fact of fate.

Fred Lauriston had stayed four years in South America, instead of three, and brought home with him a pretty, dark-eyed wife, whose gift of music and piquante brilliancy attracted them all. Rob's Sunday at home was the great

treat of his life, and Saturday evening there was always
some social engagement for him.   He could not help
being very happy, and no one felt quite like checking the
exuberance.

A long, glowing autumn that went almost up to Christmas, with little incidents, but no great event.   Comings
and goings, friendly neighborhood life, musical evenings,
often on Saturday night, intellectual gatherings, interest
in churches and charities, and homes for the poor; there
were few outcasts in Brookside.

Fred Lauriston obtained a fine position in the city, and
added one more to the group of friends.   Emma was delighted and happy with the pictures and little son added to
her household.

Just after Christmas another offer came to Charlie Darrell: the assistantship in a church whose rector was his
warm, admiring friend, and not less earnest in mission
work than the young man.

Rob brought the tidings first.

"I hope he will take it," was the earnest exclamation.
"The salary is very fair, and Charlie has some means of
his own, so you won't be reduced to a meal a day, Miss
Kathie; but I do not believe he could be induced to leave
the other work.   You would be surprised to see the influence he has over those half-drunken wretches; and he
never puts himself down to any lower level.   He seems
just to draw them up to himself.   I don't understand."

No, he had not come to the understanding yet.

Kathie waited for her letter.   She had not been to the
city all the fall, and, though strongly urged by Jessie to
come for Christmas, found herself too deeply engrossed with
home affairs.

Deeply engrossed, also, with herself, searching, asking,
comparing, with great humility.   She did not truly know
of anything else she wanted, and a less conscientious
woman would have resolved once for all, would have taken,

and lived it out afterward. Another lover might have urged, hastened. He was too noble to be satisfied with anything less than her perfect giving; he had seen so many mistakes already. He could satisfy himself in making her happy; but if he could not satisfy her? And with her the case was reversed.

She could come no nearer. Sometimes for a few days she said she did, then fell back to comradeship. The very calmness of the awaiting startled her, as if, somehow, the end was planned from the beginning, and she had to go on before she could see.

Yet it gave her quite a thrill of joy when Charlie wrote that he had accepted, and found much pleasure promised in all that pertained to it.

He had not appealed to her this time for a decision. Something had moved him to a clear certainty.

She had been reading her letter in the library. Uncle Robert was in his arm-chair beside the glowing grate fire, a little indisposed with a cold. He watched her face lighting up, the satisfaction that shone a moment in her eyes.

"It is good news?" he said in soft inquiry.

"I think it is good. Charlie is so satisfied about the position. He has taken it. I *am* glad, for now he seems to have a friend and a home."

"A home?" There was a grave, questioning smile. Mr. Conover leaned back in his chair, studying the young face.

"My little girl," he began, "have you no confidence for me? It seems so long since — and I am a rather jealous old fellow. Is there to be a home for two?"

The old, grave expression returned. She came and seated herself on the footstool and put both her hands in his.

"I have been trying to decide," and the voice had an undercurrent of tremulousness in it, "what I must do, what is best and right. It has perplexed me sorely, but I have been keeping it between God and my own soul. Uncle Robert, is it right to marry a man with anything less than the greatest love?"

She did not know how much of her soul she put unwittingly into her eyes. It was, then, as he had feared. Oh, sad, sad mistake!

"Kathie!"

She buried her face in her hands on his knee.

"I am not going to blame, my child; so let us look at the trouble calmly."

She gave a long sigh, but she was not crying.

"How did you come to find out this mistake?"

"I can't quite tell. I feel now as if I had been trying all the time to fit myself where I did not entirely belong, but where I *wanted* to belong. And I cannot get in to the very heart of things. It has all been sweet, and tender, and lovely. I think I must be wicked, or hard-hearted, or cold. Do you suppose there ever was any one, a woman I mean, capable of friendship only?"

Her face, as she raised it now, was full of such simple, genuine distress, that, though he bowed to kiss it, he smiled.

"How can she tell if she never compared it with a love?"

There was no color, no dropping of the eyes.

"I don't quite understand," she answered slowly. "If everything had been friendship, and they were all alike —"

She was innocent then of any double meaning in her soul.

"I am afraid friendship is not *quite* the foundation-stone for marriage, although excellent structures have been reared upon it. I cannot tell why, yet I have felt afraid of this from the very first, that you did not know your own heart sufficiently. You were too young."

"Yet, why could I not grow into it? I have tried, so hard. And now what ought I to do? For the heart I have taken is *all* mine. How can I reward it with a half-love? And yet how dare I give it up? Will not the pain of his life be as great a suffering in God's sight as any pain of mine? Ought I not use my utmost endeavor?"

The tears gathered then and beaded her long lashes.

"My dear," he said gently, "go over it from the beginning, the first doubt."

She had not been much given to introspection. He could see the surprise to herself when the truth had dawned upon her slowly, at no precise epoch, but made itself manifest at length. The tender conscience had striven up to every point of duty. There has been no going after forbidden gods. And, though there was sorrow and penitence, there was no shame.

"It is because I know what it will be to him," she cried, with remorseful tenderness. "He loves me so! He would take the half-love and be content, trusting for it to grow and blossom. How can I make myself fit and worthy? What must I do?"

She asked it in all earnestness. He knew how resolutely she would go at her task if he decided it was her duty, but she could do no more than she had already done out of her pure heart. It was a sad mistake for both. He seemed almost unable to counsel

"There is only one thing," he said presently; "waiting. Some light may come. But it would be a sin to marry this way, unless it were an expiation. If you had tried for this love, if you had detached it from some other joy it might have had, you would owe it a solemn duty. Such debts have been paid, and the soul has come to a higher living through sacrifice. But I cannot see that this would be your duty."

She was weeping softly now. What havoc these young people had made with their lives!

But he comforted her and bade her be patient with what was to come. The way would be made plain.

Charlie Darrell waited as well. If this would bring her

20

nearer; if the outgrowth of it all could be such love as a man had a right to expect! But her answer, touching and tender as it was, gave him no thread for a nearer hope.

What if it was a greater thing than a love to hold for his own comforting and delight, — a love to give away some time?

He said at first, as youth is prone to cry out in the darkness and sense of bitter loss, that he could not, that God would not have placed this lovely blossom in his garden only to be transplanted. Some other thing, some other cross to bear; another duty to test his ready obedience, not the sacrifice of the first dear object.

But she gave no sign of drawing nearer. Tender, sympathetic, interested, saying so many comforting things to make up for the loss of the one thing she could not say in highest truth to herself. He read through the lines as well, missing keenly what was not there.

CHAPTER XXV.

" Robert," Mrs. Conover said one evening, as she sat sewing some dainty trifle for baby Bertie, who had come to be a great favorite with her grandmother, " have you any idea that matters are not quite as they should be between Charlie and Kathie?"

Mr. Conover glanced up from his book, then down again, rather perplexed for an answer.

" I fancy something is wrong. Kathie will not talk about it, but seems to evade it at every turn. I think," in a slightly wounded tone, " I am entitled to my child's confidence in this matter. Has she said anything to you?"

" We discussed a few points of duty, one morning," in a slow tone. It was a delicate matter. He could see just the lack of fine agreement on which Kathie and her mother would miss.

" She has grown so — so different; I should say grave, only she is bright and interested in all other matters. Yet a young girl's marriage one would think might be a great event to her, touching, as it does, all the deep chords of the soul."

" It will be to her."

He was thinking how he could smooth the way for his darling, for he could foresee there would be rough places.

" Has it been put off for any cause?"

" I do not know, Dora, that they have come near the real thing, the marriage."

" But Charlie is settled, as one may say. And he could have been before if Kathie had cared."

It must come some time The mother would be sadly hurt, angered, perhaps. Since the engagement, and the coming of baby Bertie, she had held her own child with a loose clasp, so to speak, ready to transfer her rights to another, the other she loved so well.

"I believe the young people have made a mistake, and time only can right it. I was a little afraid from the beginning."

"The engagement is not broken?" Mrs. Alston let her work fall, and her hands held themselves nerveless, while varied expressions seemed to flash over her face.

"The engagement stands just as it did, for aught I know. But it seems to me Kathie is coming no nearer the vital joy and anticipation. I doubt if she is as near as on that first night. I suppose the question with her, with any thoughtful person, would be whether this is the love with which to prove a lifetime, to make the sum of all joys come right."

"You never did cordially like it, Robert, and you will encourage her to give it up. Why, ' wonder?" And the tears stood in Mrs. Alston's eyes.

"My dear Dora, you are mistaken in some points. I *was* surprised, and a little afraid that it might be nearness, the tender feeling of the boy and girl who had always been friends, and whose hopes, beliefs, and aims were much alike. I think she could choose no better man if she searched the world over. And if it had gone on to complete fruition —"

"You don't think the winter with Aunt Ruth, with Bruce, changed anything?" she interrupted.

"I do not think it consciously changed anything. I do not believe Kathie has any thought of Bruce in her heart that she could not show the whole world, and if Bruce cared deeply he kept his feelings well under control. Besides, he grew very fond of Charlie; but we will let all that alone. The only point to be considered is, whether

Kathie loves Charlie sufficiently to make a happy, contented marriage."

"But, Robert, are these feverish, extravagant loves to be preferred? Look at poor Rob's sad mistake; yet I suppose he thought he loved Miss Weeks madly."

"I have no more faith in mad loves, certainly." And a rather sad smile crossed his face.

"What do you want, then? What does Kathie want?" she asked rather sharply.

"What Kathie wants is to love with her whole heart and soul, which she has not done yet. Think a little of all this time of probation. Even that first year a girl in love would have found many shy, sweet ways of seeing her lover alone a moment."

"But they were both very true and honest. I liked it in him," she answered decisively.

"It was extremely honorable in *him*. Yet we should have forgiven Kathie some little aside, a quick blush, or a girl's longing. This troubled me, I must confess. And when they came to the time of declared lovers it was just the same. They are near and tender friends, but her heart does not beat or her pulse quicken when he comes. No sweet, tell-tale blood flushes her face. There is no stealing away into corners for a word, no lingering as if the moments were precious. Dora, go back to your own girlhood and remember what it was to you."

Her face softened and a delicate flush stole over it, while the eyes drooped almost girlishly.

"But Kathie is different."

"What should make her so different? She is a sweet, fond, ardent girl, quickly moved by her emotions, tender, responsive, capable of much that is highest and best in life, in joy, in enduring happiness. Why should she not taste the brimming cup of that sweet satisfaction?"

"And if she should be deceived in her ideal? In Charlie she cannot be deceived. His life is open, and pure, and

sacred.   *Why* can she not love him when the life with him
would suit and satisfy?"

"I suppose a woman must love a man for what he is to
her, not what he is to other people.   Kathie has loved her
friend all her life, and loves him still.   We give to others
the measure of love they are capable of creating in us.
Why is it that some will kindle in you a fine and exalted
enthusiasm, and yet you never quite fuse spirit with spirit.
I think Kathie's entire nature has never been kindled.   She
misses in some dim way the sacred fire on the altar.   Yet
so slightly does the balance vibrate that if she was advised
to make herself content, to believe this were all, I think
she would act unshrinkingly.   It would always be beside,
never within the holy of holies "

"But if she *had* married him?"

"She would grope about pained and confused awhile,
then settle herself to duty, and leave the perplexing mysteries to be cleared up at the last day, when all crooked
things are made straight.   It is just here where she
stands.   She has a vague, beautiful vision of something.
Shall she follow it until the angel really does appear, or
shall she give up the intangible thing here and now, and
take the duty work that comes first."

"But Charlie, does no one think of him?" cried Mrs.
Alston, with a pang.   "Has he, too, made a blind and
ignorant mistake?"

"She thinks of him constantly.   Instead of going forward in joyous anticipation natural to one so young, she
halts in fear lest she shall pain him as much if she takes
the life as if she leaves it.   She might sacrifice herself for
his sake if it was clearly her duty, but do we dare tell her
that it is?"

Mrs. Alston gave a long sigh.

"Then I think the engagement might as well be given
up if she feels this way about it.   It is a great disappointment to me, and certainly to us all.   The Darrells have

been so perfectly satisfied with it, and they always were
so good to her. I do *not* understand why she cannot love
him when she likes him so much, but it is unfair to
him."

" I am not certain but the settlement of the affair
ought to be left to him. He is sufficiently clear-judging
to understand, and he is daily witnessing the issue of so
many mistakes as well as sins. We have no right to hurry
either of them."

Mrs. Alston wiped away a few tears and took up her
sewing again, but it was only a pretence. She was bitterly disappointed. Her son's fate had its tragic side,
but in her estimation there was nothing to redeem this.
A simple confession that a foolish girl had not known her
own mind, and accepted a wrong love.

And, though no word was exchanged on the subject,
there was something in her mother's wounded demeanor
that pained Kathie and filled her with a peculiar sense of
shame. Why could she not make this matter seem right
and joyous, as Emma's marriage had been, or as Sarah
Strong's? She should never shrink from the work. She
was in some measure fitted for it by all her life-long experience.

She went up to spend a few days with Sarah, who was
always so glad to see her. She could not drag her soul
out for her friend's inspection, or ask if any one knew why
this must be so. But in the simple, truthful atmosphere
she did gain some strength. They two were growing in
knowledge, in tender, reverent wisdom, and exquisite happiness. One day the friends spoke of this.

" I think it is because we just suit," said Sarah, with a
bright glow in her eyes. " I can take his best without
any misgiving because I can give him mine without any
reserve. It is the one perfect soul that marriage should
be, the faint, imperfect type of the other great love.'

Could Kathie compare hers with the other great love?
No, it was blurred and imperfect.

After this there was quite a diversion. Fay Collamore went to the city to be bridesmaid for a cousin. Jessie came up on a brief visit to her mother, and insisted that Kathie should return with her.

"I think I had better go," she said, with a curious decision quite new to her. For her duty must be plainly and clearly settled. She could not go on living between, with the ache and misgiving so near the surface that every little touch made her shrink.

Everybody was glad to have her back. She and Fay went to one of Mrs. Garnier's evenings, — Rob had told Miss Collamore about them, — and out of this grew other little meetings, and a grand concert for which Rob bought tickets. He was so ready to take her anywhere, and somehow she always found herself inviting Fay.

Charlie saw it in his quiet way, and yet it had no real meaning for Kathie, being mostly of Rob's planning. She was thinking of him always. How could she give back the life that had so shaped itself to hers? how could she go on and perhaps mar both?

The friendliness was still friendly. The grief was that she could come so near and not belong, heart and soul. Her very trying gave him an exquisite pain, the blended joy and bitterness of a possibility he had taken to his heart, a live and real thing, and watched it growing dimmer, not dying, but living by some high, self-judging resolve.

She should not so torment and vex her soul. He would set her quite free. If any late regret or repentance should blossom into a new trust for him, God would surely return it fourfold.

He told her this one evening, one of the rare times through the visit that they were quite alone. She was not to speak of it to Jessie; he would make that all straight and pleasant. They would go back to the old friendship, and have no break or coldness. He had schooled

himself to this for her sake. Only a high, passion pure
love could have done so, but his soul was too purely noble
to be satisfied with anything less than a perfect self-for-
getting.

She sobbed out her sorrow in tender, broken sentences,
but he would not listen to her condemnation. There was
a better ordering in it than they could see to-night. God
had some true lesson and meaning in all this that would be
made manifest in the years to come. She was not to
shadow her life with vain regrets, but to go on with her
duties and her pleasures until God should send peace.

But the first one after her return to Cedarwood was
very painful. She must explain all to her mother; she
owed her this respect.

"Mamma," she began the morning afterward, "there
is something I must tell you." And the voice struggled
against the great throbbing in heart and throat, while the
sweet face crimsoned with abasement and genuine grief.
"Charlie and I — that is, I mean I have — O mamma,
pity and forgive me for paining you so much, but I *did*
make a great mistake! I could not go on; and Charlie
gave me back my freedom."

Her arms were around her mother's neck, and the soft,
wet face pressed close against her cheek in fervent penitence.

"Kathie," her mother made answer, "you have pained
the noblest, sweetest soul that ever loved a woman. You
had no right to treat it so. You should have known," in
a tone of remonstrance.

"But it was so strange and new that evening. Because
nothing in my soul warned me then, I thought it was quite
right. And he was so good; you all liked him so well.
When I tried with all my heart, why could I not make
myself come nearer to him?"

The pitiful asking touched the mother. Had she been
blameless? Had not her satisfaction been one important

factor in the engagement. Ought she not have guided the
youthful heart to its own sure examination?

" I am very sorry, and there will be some other judg-
ments to meet, Kathie." The mother could not soften all
at once. " I don't know what the Darrells will say, and
Mr. and Mrs. Meredith will be bitterly disappointed.
Think of Jessie's goodness to you, years ago! Why, it
will seem — "

" Ungrateful! Yes, mamma," in her meek, touching
way. " I have hurt everybody, and now it seems as if I
had better have wounded only myself. But Charlie understood. He would not let it be anything but perfect freedom ; only, if I should see my way clear in the years to
come, I have only to go back."

" I don't understand it at all," said Mrs. Alston, wearily.
" Perhaps we had better not talk it over now ; it is too
near and too full of pain. Of course I shall always love
you, Kathie ; a mother's heart is not easily turned aside.
Only I do not seem very fortunate in my children in this
respect."

Kathie kissed her, realizing how deep the pain had gone
in the kindly heart. Why must she have given it a stab
as well as Robert?

She turned slowly from the room, but instead of going
to her own, walked up to Fred's little den, where Uncle
Robert often amused himself with scientific experiments,
and she had seen him go thither some time before. Kathie
paused in the doorway, and he caught sight of the flushed
and tearful face.

" O my darling!" he exclaimed in quick, tender sympathy, folding her in his arms.

She had the rest of her cry out on his shoulder. Now
and then he kissed her throbbing brow with his cool lips,
but did not speak again until her sobs had ceased a little.

" O Uncle Robert, what shall I do? I have been so
weak and selfish, and made everybody so unhappy!"

" We will talk that over presently. I suppose, then, it
is all settled between you and Charlie? Of course, Kathie,
your mother is sorely disappointed. I think," with a
little smile, " most mothers would be. But old-bachelor
uncles are in no hurry to have their little girls go away, and
are always jealous of these attractive young men."

She clasped him more closely. It was so good to be
taken fondly back to one heart, even when she had been
so much at fault.

" I think we all feel very sorry," trying to soothe the
tense, aching nerves with his most comforting tone. " We
should have liked Charlie in our midst, and your mother
will always love him as a son. No one else will ever be
so dear."

" But suppose there should be no one? I wonder if you
would get tired of me?" And a faint misgiving trembled in
her voice.

" We should never have tired of Aunt Ruth, you know.
Some of the loveliest women I have ever met did not marry
until middle life."

" I cannot see how I could have made such a painful mistake. And it does seem sometimes as if I should have set
my small self aside, and rested in his love, grown larger
and more tranquil of soul. It is not even as if I had loved
some one else. That might have been an excuse."

" I am very glad you did not," was the grave reply.
" Such mistakes have been, as well, but I would rather
have this clear seeing for you than any pure want for self.
I think Charlie came to understand the larger satisfying
and peace. And now, Kathie, you must be patient and
tender with mamma. Remember you have been carrying
the burden quite a long while, but it has newly come upon
her, and mothers cherish so many pretty hopes of their
daughters' marriages. It is like living over their own girl
life."

" And Rob, too," cried Kathie remorsefully, quite disregarding her sentence. "Poor mamma; we ought to be very devoted to make up all this."

"It will be made up presently with tender, earnest affection," he said hopefully. "Robert goes on so well that I sometimes think living out of such a trouble is the best discipline he could have had. He has grown more careful of consequences to others, and he has evinced great steadiness of purpose. I do believe his nursing and caring for Bruce brought out the tender side of his nature, the side most boys are ashamed to show, and not infrequently assume a sort of roughness to hide it, quite forgetting what the term "gentleman" includes. I hope we shall have many happy years together."

"You are so good. Oh, what should I do without you?" cried Kathie impulsively.

Uncle Robert smiled.

It was not an easy task, Kathie found, living out of such a mistake. A less noble lover might have made it harder, but Charlie generously took upon himself much of the burden. She might easily have been over-influenced by circumstances. He remembered on the night he had first spoken there had been simply girlish awe and wonder, no great throb of joy, no exceeding gladness any of the time. He had failed to touch the depth of her nature, to awaken the keenest bliss. For himself, he might be satisfied to do and to give, but her life ought to be wider and more outflowing than in mere passive recipience.

He explained the matter first to Jessie, who was really hurt and angry. It seemed a slight put upon Charlie.

"No, Jessie," he said; "it would have been a worse thing for her to have married me and never know of her own sure experience the highest joy of life She would have made herself content, but it would not have been a wholesome, happy life."

"Are you quite sure she is not in love with Bruce Mackenzie?"

"She could not love a finer man."

"You are as good and noble, and more self-sacrificing," cried Jessie vehemently. "Charlie, why should you stand aside for any other?"

"If Kathie loves Bruce it is all unknown to herself, and then it would be God's sure seal that her love was not for me. And if he loved her — "

"Let them find it out then," said Jessie resentfully.

Mother Darrell was the greatest comforter to Kathie.

"My dear," she said, "we all regret it so deeply. I am not sure but we have coveted you. And yet it has seemed to me that you were always too near to be the nearest, for friends do not always make lovers. I want you to come just the same, to be to us what you were before. We old people can't aford to let a pleasure slip out of our lives because it may take a different turn from what we hoped. God knows best."

They had all been so engrossed through this time with Kathie that Rob had gone his way, straying in pleasant fields unnoticed. He and Miss Collamore had settled into a steady kind of friendship. Uncle Robert remarked with pleasure the touches of reticence in certain directions, the little fence of propriety she placed about herself and never overstepped, as if she understood what might have been but was not to be. Fred's intimacy with Eugene brought them all nearer together in many ways.

During her visit in New York Robert had made himself chief cavalier to her and Kathie. Mr. Gartney, who had stood with her at her cousin's marriage, had not proved insensible to her charms, and made delicate advances toward a closer acquaintance. His business standing and character were excellent, and he was received by the Collamores with the refined cordiality that told him under any circumstances he was a welcome guest.

His visits startled Miss Collamore out of her wonted tranquillity. The young men of Brookside had at times shown preferences, but these were easily turned aside. This man had a definite purpose ; he showed it in his bearing, in the peculiar grace of his attention. He was refined, chivalrous, well informed, quite fit to be set beside Mr. Hunsdon. There was no reason why a girl should not like him, or let herself drift into the swift, pleasant stream of interest and caring until it came to more, and the meaning proved itself to both.

There was another side. Fay Collamore could not, would not look at this when she could help. Sometimes it seemed to get sharply thrust under her notice ; there was a pang and a long, quivering breath, but it was soon over.

Only of late there had come a troublesome shadow, a secret knowledge that however successful she might be in putting away any thought or temptation for herself, she could not so put it away for another. Now and then there came a flash of a " might have been " in Robert Alston's eyes, a touch of something in his voice that startled no one else, but struck a vague terror to her soul. It would be a sin to let it settle into any unhallowed longing. In her eyes he had been so brave, had borne his sad trial with a fortitude hardly belonging to youth, had made it no excuse for throwing away his bright young life. Even now he was studying between whiles with the boys, in case the step higher should come to him in the future. Could she let him mar his life a second time with any fondness for her ?

They were not the people who could keep to the level of a friendship ; she would not blind herself by any specious half-promises. He was ardent, impetuous, strong, and passion might carry him like a whirlwind for a brief space, but if even a word took him over the boundary, it could never be brought back with any repentance.

And the woman who held his freedom might live years. Every one said so. To wish it otherwise were a crime.

What if she placed an effectual barrier between. Could she not make herself happy in another life if she knew she had put temptation quite out of his way?

CHAPTER XXVI.

It was the soft lapsing of the spring day into evening The windows were open, and the fragrance of the evergreens, the delicate moisture of the young grass that had drank in the sunshine all day and was now giving it out to the dew, made the air sweet with promise. Robert Alston had taken a holiday, partly to attend to a little business for Mr. Meredith, which would have made him too late for a day in the city. He had been out rambling, and returned with a great bunch of wild flowers, Kathie and his mother were so fond of them. Kathie was not in, and Mrs. Collamore sat with his mother in the parlor, so he stepped into the library and threw himself in an easy-chair by the window.

Uncle Robert came up the path, pausing to look at the hyacinth bed. In his hand he held two or three letters, and, catching a glimpse of his nephew, came across the piazza to the window and stepped in. Mrs. Collamore was taking her leave now. She seemed to pause in the hall and said quite distinctly, though in her low, even tone, —

" We all like him very much, and think it will be a good match for Fay. I shall have only my son left. I think I should rather keep her nearer, but I must comfort myself with Louise and her baby."

Rob sprang up with a sudden, decisive impulse, and his face was like marble. "It is Mr. Gartney," he said in a hoarse, strained whisper.

" Yes, Robert." The voice was sharp, decisive.

The young man dropped back in his chair. In his

momentary madness he hardly cared how much he had betrayed.

"Robert, you would have no right in any event; rouse yourself and think a moment."

"Of what shall I think?" in a passionate, despairing tone. "That I have lost my chance with the only woman who could have helped me to live a perfect life? That all the years to come —"

Mr. Conover closed the library door, and, returning, stood in front of the young man.

"Robert," he said sternly, "has it come to this? Have you allowed yourself to dream over this young girl until it has led to the verge of sin? Better a hundred times that she should be removed from your reach."

"You think so!" in a bitter, hollow tone. "As if I could not dream over her and covet her anywhere! And if she stayed, if she waited —"

"Rob, my boy," and the voice was infinitely tender, the touch on his arm strong, yet gentle, "you have forgotten yourself and your duty. No madness can quite convince you that you have a right, that you are free —"

Robert Alston sprang up and stood straight, strong, and daring. Every pulse within his body had mutinied. There was a blaze of defiance in his eyes and a white line about the lips.

"I should have been free! I _can_ be free!" he declared in his madness.

They glanced at each other steadily, and neither seemed to breathe.

"If you were free," the elder said, "what would it avail, since she will belong to another?"

"She would not. Uncle Robert, have a little pity on me. I can't tell you how I know it, but I do believe as firmly as I can believe anything, that if I went to Fay Collamore and told her of my love she would wait years. She would not marry. Why should I give up my chance?"

"Because it would be a sin and dishonor. It would
stain your soul and sully the pure whiteness of hers. No;
you could not win Fay Collamore that way, and I thank
God that it is so. Rob, when you have made such a brave
fight, when you have won back respect, honor, will you
throw them away in this mad endeavor? I thought you
were to be trusted to the uttermost. And I have news
for you. See here!"

He lighted the lamp on the table and took the letter
from its envelope, handing it to his nephew. A scornful
smile crossed the scarlet lip, as if the first impulse were
to fling it away.

"Read it. It *is* your business."

It was from the asylum physician, concise yet comprehensive. "They had remarked a great improvement in
the patient for the last month. Some faint remembrance
had returned. She had asked for her child, and seemed
gratified when a babe had been brought her. Her youth
and her good physical health gave them a slender hope
that there might be some restoration in time."

Robert Alston went over and over the letter, though he
was not thinking at all. A horror seemed to have possession of him. Moments passed before he spoke, then he
said, almost savagely : —

"You believe I ought to have forgiven her? Well, I
never, never shall. I might if she were dead."

"O Robert!"

He strode up and down the room in a tempest of passion.
Then, as if suddenly bethinking himself, he said : —

"It is nearing train time. I must go to-night."

"Let me drive you down."

"No, I will walk; I want to go alone. Say good by to
my mother. There is your letter!" And he threw it con-
temptuously on the floor.

"Robert, we cannot part this way. Stay—"

But he flung off his uncle's arm and made a snatch at

21

his hat from the rack in the hall. His steps echoed on the gravel walk an instant, then all was spring-time silence and softness again.

Should he follow him? What would he do in this desperate mood? There would be the long ride to the city, but the reaching there almost at midnight, the fierce struggle within himself. Ah, how would it end?

"God help him," he cried. "Save him from himself."

It had all been so sudden that now Robert Conover wondered if he had done his best, had acted with wisdom and prudence. Surely the mad boy would not dare to go to Fay.

When he could reason himself to a state of calmness he went up-stairs. Kathie had just come in. He took with him Rob's flowers and a tenderer farewell than he had left.

"Oh, how lovely!" cried Kathie. "Dear Rob! I did try to get back in time, but old Mrs. Boden had so many last messages."

"And I have some news for you, Kathie," said Mrs. Alston. "Mrs. Collamore was here. She thinks Fay is very likely to marry Mr. Gartney; but of course she will have to go to New York to live. You will be left quite alone presently."

Kathie colored softly; she never answered when her mother made comments like this. They were gradually coming back to their old love and confidence, and if she could have the tender patience to win all.

Robert Alston went his way in a mad, blind fury. It came to him with the unreason of youth,— what if he threw himself here under the car wheels! Of what avail was life, and strength, and manhood, only to make the loss tenfold more bitter? *She* would go away out of his life, and what would be left? Only the hateful reminder of that boyish idiocy? But no repentance could atone for the wrong *she* had done. No ; if she came and pleaded on her bended knees, he would never forgive her. She had blighted the man's promising career, she had kept him from the man's dear and tender love !

He turned to the image of Fay Collamore and revelled in the vision of what might have been. Not a sweet would he miss, even if it turned to tenfold ashes and bitterness afterward. He let fancy have full play. Up to this time she had been sacred to him ; he had not even dared to dream of her. In this reckless mood he would stop for nothing. And all the years to come he must miss this glowing, enchanting happiness.

He bowed his head and groaned in his misery. He had the seat to himself, and could indulge in a little weakness without prying eyes. From this mood he went to sullen despair. The night dropped down, and still he peered out in the darkness with hot eyes and throbbing brow. Of what avail had been all the struggle, all the resolving? He might as well have stayed in Chicago. There he would not have seen Fay. She would be at Brookside,—in the city. She knew all the friends in the little circle and would meet them. He should see her another's man's wife. That woke all the passion of jealousy within him.

The tumult went on, fierce, eager, sullen, and despairing by turns. They ran into the station. How strange it looked in the yellow-red glare, and the voices seemed like something heard in another world ! Yonder was a train steaming up. If he were to take it, to-morrow morning he would be far away. Would it not be better ? Away from temptation ! He laughed bitterly.

Should he go home to the Merediths'? They would be sitting up for him, — Fred and Mr. Meredith. To go in there, screne and pleasant, and answer questions, — ah, it would madden him ! Better roam the streets all night.

Something came to him suddenly, and he stood quite still, as if stopped in the way.

"When you come to love a woman placed out of your reach you will go to God, for nothing else will be strong enough to save you ! "

Bruce had said that to him. He, too, had seen a love placed out of his way.

At first Robert Alston had a dim, awful impression that he did not want to be saved, that he was in some uncomprehended way quite strong enough for himself, or that no salvation could comfort him for the tremendous sacrifice wrenched up out of his life. Not made freely, not given.

Where should he go? The night was growing chilly and the streets beginning to look deserted.

He had tramped around unthinkingly until he found himself in Charlie Darrell's vicinity. Another who had sacrificed all. What a mocking, illusive thing love was, — a sweet madness !

He glanced up. There was a light in the window. Was this hero calm and tranquil after his fight? Ah, he fancied *he* had fought it all out, but he did not think then this might come. Had not some one said in a sermon that it was a life warfare? Was Charlie Darrell fighting always? What if *he* knew Kathie was about to marry another, could he still wear his high, heavenly smile? Or was there a strength he, Rob, knew nothing about? Life had been so pleasant since that terrible time, and he had gone bravely onward, believing the great storms over-past. Why should this have come?

He paced up and down the street. Curious bits floated through his mind in a sharp, electric fashion ; texts heard long ago, it seemed, almost in another life : " God is faithful, who will with the temptation also make a way to escape, that ye may be able to bear it." How many had escaped? how many wanted to escape?

The window above him was raised and a figure leaned out a little. Rob dropped his head and drew up his shoulders. He could not make up his mind whether he desired to see Charlie or not, but the light from the opposite lamp betrayed him.

"Rob, wait until I come down," said an entreating voice.

The young man strode fiercely away, then paused. The door opened and a light step came flying after him.

"Rob, are they all well at home? What has happened?"

"Nothing," pulling half away.

"Come back with me; I am all alone. Let us talk it over, for something has happened to you?"

"You cannot help me."

Charlie was leading him back. The hall lamp was out, but they groped up-stairs, guided by the long ray of light from the open door. Entering, Charlie pushed a chair forward with a cordial invitation, but Rob stood stupidly. His hair was blown about, his face set and pale, and his eyes were aglow with the wild light of passion. Had he been drinking?

"Sit down and tell me," gently. "Perhaps it will not be as hard as you think."

"I don't know," Robert Alston said unsteadily, drawing a long, quivering breath. "I suppose," laughing mirthlessly, "I've been tempted of the devil; murder, and all the long list of crimes mentioned somewhere. You all supposed I was going on so well."

"So you were." Charlie sprang up beside him. Something in the pure, high face seemed to touch Rob dimly. "But a soldier may be surprised at his outpost, and it is his duty to be ready. The surprise is not a sin, but cowardice or negligence would be. Even *there* 'Thy hand shall hold me.'"

"Why does n't it, then? Oh, why should we live at all, Charlie? It seems such a useless, unmeaning, blurred, and wretched thing! Nothing comes out of it all that you really want."

He had wanted some denied gift, then. Charlie's intuitions were rapid and sympathetic. A few days ago Rob was gay and glad; he had been unusually bright during Kathie's visit to the city and afterward. Ah, had he a clew?

" If anything true, and right, and honorable has been put out of your way, Rob, it is only held in the larger awaiting of by and by."

" It was the one chance, the one glimpse of a lovely, satisfying life, and I think I *have* a right. You do not know; as a clergyman, all secrets are sacred to you; but I *could* have been quite free from that hateful marriage, that boy's folly; I can be now. Must I let all the great joys of life slip out for a mere figment of honor? And *she* is better. We heard this very day. Suppose she recovers? Would you all send me back to that old existence? Why, I might better never have left it!"

It would be better to go back than to stain any new life with a sin. Rob, you said one glimpse; was it another?"

"Yes," he flung out sullenly, " you may as well know all. I did not understand it myself until I heard to-day that *she* might go to some other love, not knowing, and I *could* win her, I am quite sure. I believe when I first met Fay Collamore I knew just the kind of woman I needed, high, honorable, gracious, true as steel, and as unflinching. Then I understood the madness I had yielded to and that had blurred all my life. I had no right to complain, and I did not. I kept to my own miserable path, shutting out my vision, making no comparison. When the time came that I might have been free I gave it up for others. And now she, who could so bless my life, will blight and wound her own, taking something less than she might have had, *making* herself content when there should be a sweet, spontaneous joy. It ruins both! Will it do that other miserable, negative existence any good? It discrowns love to apply it to any such *dis*union as ours was."

A strong shudder ran through Robert Alston's frame,

and the eyes were heavy, like one half asleep. But in the other face there was a strength and steadfastness not to be gainsaid.

"Rob," he began gently, but in a firm, ringing tone, that gave no uncertain sound, "you *were* heroic through all that time. I think God helped you then. Some of the boyhood lessons lingered in your mind. It was a perilous way, and you came out of it morally unscathed, clearer-eyed, stronger, for every temptation overcome adds strength. And you know this night, as well as I, that yours would be an unhallowed love to offer to any woman. You are *not* free."

"Do you suppose I should offer it until I was?" he asked almost savagely.

"No, I have that much faith in you. You will not do it until your conscience is clear and clean, until your duty is done, until you can meet the eyes of every one, and how much more the one thus set above all others, in truth and honor. You said, back there, it was murder and all the long list! You will not stain your soul, Robert Alston. You have not fought your way up to this to slip back!"

"What shall I do?" in a hollow, broken tone. "Why does n't God save me?"

"Will you be saved? Will you be snatched from this fiery temptation? Remember there was just one who met the Lord Jesus in the way, and who afterward carried about with him the 'marks' in his body. To the others He said, 'Follow thou me.' Rise, you are able. Follow. Obey. Come to me."

"Then I should save myself."

"Well, can you? Have you come off victor by your own might? Are you so strong that you can pass by this thing without a longing? Will you never shrink when it meets you in the way?"

"There is no use," gloomily.

"There *is* use. See, Rob, you may have been betrayed

into a word or look; you and Fay may have seen for a
moment a blinding, dazzling glare, but if you put it away
before it has had time really to belong, it is all God asks.
He might have made us insensible to all these things, and
we should never have sinned, never even have seen the
temptation. But it is braver, yes, I think it is better, to
see and to resist. That, then, is not mere negative goodness. That is accepting, using the divine strength, sup-
plementing our weak desire with his greater aid, which is
always sufficient if you will try it to the uttermost. The
trouble is we so often try it only half or a little way."

The midnight clocks were striking twelve. Rob dropped
into a chair. He was suddenly tired, worn out. The face
was ashen gray, the eyes lost their fire.

"You will not throw away the victories of your life in
this evil fashion. When it comes to deliberate choice you
cannot."

Could he do such a thing deliberately? Robert Alston
paused to think. In a moment of selfish madness he might
rush headlong, as he had been wild to do this evening, but
seen here in all its wrong and wretchedness —

There was a long, long silence. Rob's temples throbbed
like the blows of ceaseless machinery. He could not think
clearly. Was there *any* ark of safety?

"You remember our old hero, Rob! 'It is necessary
for me to go; it is not necessary for me to live.' It is
necessary for you to be pure, and strong, and resolute.
Other men have given up dreams —" And his voice faltered a little.

"Oh," cried Rob, "it was cruel to come to you!"

"No. I think you were led thither to see the salvation of God, for he will save you from yourself. And
perhaps He showed me it had a wider significance, that I
might comfort some one tried and tempest tossed."

"Well, let it be given up, all of it. Let me come out
of the horrible slough. For I could have wished the

other dead to-night; I am not sure but I did. How is it that one can never desire to do right first of all?"

"Because life must always be a warfare, to strong natures, especially. It is the old warring of the two natures, and even St. Paul, resolute and earnest, comforts us here. 'That which I would,' 'that which I would not,' and they are always present."

"I make a poor soldier!" Robert Alston buried his face in his hands. And then he thought of another soldier who had fought as hard a battle, who had thrust out unlawful desire before it became blighting sin.

"No, Rob, I think it is very fair. We are gauged by the strength of the temptation, and what might almost sweep you away would just touch another, who could not feel it so keenly."

"Because I am so weak?"

"No. You have shown your strength in many ways. You might have rushed into intemperance."

A shudder of disgust passed over him. "I shall always hate drunkenness!" he cried vehemently.

"And you will come to hate and shun other things. It is not all done in a day. The vow is 'a faithful soldier and servant to my life's end.' You have only begun."

"Charlie," he said in a low tone, many moments afterward, "could you have given up Kathie so readily if you had known another stood by to take her, that she was going quite out of your life?" He must test the temper of this grace.

"I did not give her up readily," in a lingering tone. "I think I understand. If Miss Collamore *can* go to another, Rob, it is quite certain that this is not, could not be the true regard of her life. And perhaps that is the cross for you, and the saving knowledge."

And then an old thought came back to Charlie Darrell. They so seldom spoke of her in this connection.

"Rob," he said softly, "did you ever imagine Kathie cared for, loved any one?"

"I don't believe Kathie knows, and it is queer, too," brightening up a little; "but you see you all were so ready to do her honor. I can't understand how you all came to love her so! She is not wonderfully beautiful nor regularly fascinating as some girls; but she has been a little queen, with all her knights about her."

Should he ask the question that he had more than once asked of his secret soul?

Charlie turned his face away a little, that it might not show its anguish.

"Did you ever fancy that Bruce——"

There was a silence that seemed almost deathly, in the room. A color fluttered up in the other's pallid face.

"Rob!" He came and stood over his friend, took his hand, studied the shrouded expression.

It was drawn suddenly away. "Don't make me cruel to you of all others!" cried Robert Alston, with a pang of remorse.

"I fancied afterward—— Do you know when they mean to return?"

"Not until—— But I have n't any right to betray him. He would have cut off his hand or plucked out his right eye rather than have swerved a line——"

"Ah, you see it there!" cried Charlie Darrell. "You cannot help honoring it, Rob! Bruce Mackenzie is a Christian soldier."

A Christian soldier. That had given the lovely grace of patience and steadfastness through all that trying time. That was what had interposed, when Rob first went out to Bruce, in his own behalf. He seemed to have found the clew, faint, wavering, but not uncertain. These two possessed something he had not. His own strength, manly and robust, was not enough; there was a diviner grace. Yes, he must be saved, even if as by fire. His longing love might not desire it——

He rose then, almost overshadowing the slenderer figure. His step was uncertain, groping.

" I think I have been a madman ! " he said in deepest humiliation. " I have gone to the very brink of destruction, trusting in my own might. But I shall never rest until I have found the greater strength. You need not be afraid to trust me."

He started as if to go. " No, you will stay with me to-night," Charlie said. " It is late, and I want you to help *me*. If Bruce knew Kathie was quite free — if I wrote — they are going to Egypt soon, I believe. But he had bet-ter come home."

" I wronged you a while ago. I said you did not know."

" I do know. We both know that a love given away may grow into something higher than a love kept for one's self."

" But you have the right to give," he cried, bowing his head in an agony of shame.

There was not much sleep for them that night. Robert Alston's thoughts would have kept him awake if it had not been for the almost intolerable headache. And he had been shown himself the thing he might become if left to his own devices, his human side, with no interposition. But he believed now that Fay Collamore could not have been tempted into any specious waiting, any wrong step, only he knew she *had* seen, and put away, like these other brave souls. There was a great deal of it to do in this world.

Mr. Meredith rallied him somewhat the next day on his paleness, little dreaming of the struggle. He had one more duty before the new life could quite begin, and that was a letter to Uncle Robert, who came to answer it, in person. And Robert Alston realized then how easy it was to make the innocent suffer for the guilty. No one ever bore a crime or a shame quite alone. Some other heart was always wrung with anguish, often the one who should be nearest and dearest, first considered.

CHAPTER XXVII

THEY were in the glow and throb of mid-summer again. Kathie Alston stood on the wide balcony, nodding to baby Bertie below, who was making imaginary visits and coming back for cunning good-byes. Then espying Uncle Robert, she ran like a sprite to meet him, and he caught her in his arms.

Kathie ran down as well. She was radiant in health and brightness. All the cares and perplexities seemed overpast. She had simply to live, to take up the nearest duty.

"I am jealous!" laughingly. "I don't even have one arm any more."

"But I must have one hand. Stand down a minute, Bertie ; I have a load of letters for Aunt Kathie. Does n't that sound staid and ancient," smiling. "Here is one from Mrs. Truesdell, from Miss Fay ; and oh, what will you give me for my news?"

"A kiss used to be sufficient," with a piquant sparkle in her eye ; "but you have so many from my rival —"

"Take me up, Uncle Robert, take me up," said the imperious little queen.

"A spoiled child! What would become of her but for mamma and me? And the news?"

"It is funny how many times we have said it. Aunt Ruth is in New York ; she is coming home to-morrow. I had a telegram."

"Oh, how lovely! So they gave up Egypt. Or did Bruce go on alone?"

"The telegram says ' we.' "

"Oh, I do wonder— The boys will be delighted! Rob is fairly homesick for a sight of him."

"Some letters for me?" demanded Bertie, as they sat down on the wide step.

"There, this will do; oh, no, this," giving her the telegram. "There was a letter from Chicago."

"Uncle Robert," said Kathie seriously, "suppose she," nodding toward the letter, "should quite recover?"

"That does not seem possible."

"I have thought of it sometimes. What would Rob do? He has begun to be so curiously conscientious of late."

"Why curious?"

"Unusually, then. Do you know I think Rob singularly attracted by beautiful women. He always admired Fay Collamore greatly. And you all say *she* is so handsome."

"Her beauty alone could not win him back."

"But duty might," Kathie returned gravely. "Still, we never could give up Bertie. It always seems to me as if her mother must be dead."

Uncle Robert stooped to kiss the baby lips. "She is mine," he said, "to comfort me after you all go away."

Kathie smiled. She had been glancing over Fay's letter. Miss Collamore's episode had not culminated in an engagement; why, she knew best. Just at that juncture Louise had been taken seriously ill with a fever, and Mr. Hunsdon had called on Fay's sisterly offices. On her partial recovery they had been sent to the mountains.

"Mrs. Hunsdon is doing beautifully," Kathie announced; "and oh, Dick Grayson is up there! How odd they should stumble over each other!"

Then she opened Sarah's letter, and before she had read a dozen lines she uttered another exclamation.

"Uncle Robert, listen to this. Mr. Truesdell has an excellent call to Westport. The church is quite large, united, and flourishing, the salary very fair, and a house. Two

of Sarah's pupils are married and settled there. It seems
like such a splendid opportunity — "

" Well? " filling the pause.

" To live a broader life. For, after all, there is just so
much of a round in Middleville, and no more. They have
conquered their place and a peace, I might say respect, for
I do think Sarah's wise patience has served to unite and
raise the very ordinary congregation. I should like to
see her at her best estate. And Charlie has a high opinion of Mr. Truesdell."

She could quote Charlie again quite comfortably. He
would not let the break make a difference. Mrs. Alston
had become quite reconciled, though he had said to her,
" I cannot give up my old love for you ; it has in it all a
son's reverence."

Oddly enough Charlie and Rob had been great friends
of late. They all discerned a gradual change in the latter.

" Rob is growing wonderfully like uncle," declared Fred
daily.

" I think Mr. Truesdell well fitted for a much larger
sphere. I wondered at first how he could resign himself to
the place, though there is a work everywhere."

Mrs. Alston came out presently, and was delighted with
the news.

" I do think Ruth is very tired of rambling about," she
said. " I hope now they have come to stay."

Kathie arranged the guest chamber again, and made it
sweet with flowers. Would Bruce come or not? How
oddly quiet it would be this summer. Emma was away
painting some seaside views that had been ordered. The
olden, merry group were scattered far and wide ; even the
Merediths were going elsewhere, and would not spend
more than a fortnight at Brookside.

Mrs. Alston and Kathie went over in the family carriage.
There was dear Aunt Ruth. grown a little older, but sweet
as ever, and the General, looking much better than last
year.

"And no Bruce!" Kathie said. There was not a very keen disappointment in her tone.

"Oh, the boys took possession of him at once! I began to wonder if I had any rights in my own son," said the General with an assumption of injury. "I shall have to come to you for comfort, as I have times before."

Kathie slipped her hand into his. It seemed almost like going back to the happy childhood when she first knew him. And she remembered how he had asked permission to bring Bruce to Cedarwood, that long-ago summer.

"Am I to be left quite out in the cold?" she asked.

"I am learning that the boys can do very well without me; the end of youthful admiration, I suppose."

They took up Uncle Robert at the post-office, and Bertie was running about the lawn watching for him.

"How wonderfully like Rob in his babyhood!" Aunt Ruth said.

"She is the happiest of all happy children," said Mrs. Alston. "I wonder at it sometimes; but I think much of it is due to Mrs. Fleming's judicious nursing and training. I am thankful she fell into such good hands."

Cedarwood was so quiet and restful. It had that well-used home look, nothing obtrusive, nothing that had been thrust in, but the general growth of needed things, of beauty thought and planned year after year. The great porch now was rich in vines, that gave shade by day and sweetness at night. They went out in the evening and talked over the many happenings of the year and more since the last parting.

Bruce was quite recovered in health and strength, but there would always be a little weakness about the hip joint that would need thoughtfulness, if not care, and would not admit of a life of hardship. He had sent in his army resignation and turned his attention to literary pursuits, in which he had done a little at the West. They would always have him now.

Kathie listened with a thrill of interest. She wondered she had not suspected Bruce's penchant the winter of his illness, when they used to read and talk so much.

He was to be down in a day or two. Rob meant to get a holiday and come with him.

" I must congratulate you on your fine and manly son, Mrs. Alston," the General said. " If I had none of my own I should want to adopt him."

The mother smiled, pleased with a deeper joy than mere satisfaction in a handsome presence.

They enjoyed another day resting up. A telegram from Bruce saying he would be down the next evening with Robert.

Kathie was in a curious little maze of excitement, innocent, glad, and girlish. Their coming seemed to have taken her out of the rather grave present. Everything appeared fresh, and bright, and hopeful.

They were planning some pleasure the next morning when a messenger came with another telegram for Mr. Conover. He opened it and looked rather disturbed.

" Not bad news?" said Kathie.

He hated to damp her joy. " I hardly know," slowly. " There is some change at Chicago. I think I shall have to go, and it might be better to take Rob. I must go to the city immediately," rising with unwonted alacrity.

She misunderstood, and he did not correct her, but he told Mrs. Alston the full import. There had been so many little improvements that a partial recovery had been spoken of, and Kathie took this as an indication of it. There was a brief hurry and no time to ask questions.

Late in the afternoon Mr. and Mrs. Adams came over to call on the Mackenzies.

" You will have to drive down for Bruce," said the General smilingly to Kathie.

" Yes, I will honor him with my pony phaeton. Oh, can you really believe that Bruce has never been here since his return from Europe? Why, it will seem quite a new place to him."

A slight flush touched the father's face. He knew the reason so well; she was so innocent of it. Ah, if Bruce should fail this time!

She drove slowly down; there was plenty of time. As she sat there in the phaeton she wondered if she had better get out on the platform. If he was watching he could surely see her.

The train came whistling and crunching on the rails, and all the air was hazy for a moment. Then a confusion of forms and faces, and yes, a wave of the hand that brought the bright color to her cheek.

" Kathie ! "

" Bruce ! "

It was all they said for the first instant. Then Kathie's expectant, uplifted eyes wavered, trembled. She made a pretence of turning aside the robe and giving him the seat. There was a curious rushing consciousness, a surging of blood at her heart, a sort of deep sea ringing in her ears, and her hand trembled.

He took it in his so fond and warm. He almost knew. Her fingers had never throbbed under his pressure before, and her breath came in a great gasp.

" How awkward ! " she said. " You are in the driver's seat and must do duty. Every rank in life has its corresponding penalties."

" These are not very severe." He straightened himself up. How brown and well he looked, and how softly bright his eyes were, as if some fire was veiled in their depths.

" We were all so surprised," she said at length. " You did not go to Egypt."

" No, my next tour will be straight around the world, I think," laughingly. " But I should like to stay at home five years, at least."

22

Five years. Why should it seem so brief to her? And then —

"Which way? You see I am a stranger."

"Hero would know, anyhow," with a bright smile. "But it has changed wonderfully since you were here."

"That was so long ago. What a lovely avenue! And there is the lake. And Cedarwood! Why, it is like some beautiful dream."

"I have brought your son home to you," Kathie exclaimed as she sprang out of the phaeton beside General Mackenzie.

He bent and kissed her tenderly. Once he had said almost the same words to her mother.

"Then Robert went on to Chicago?" Mrs. Alston asked, as she shook hands with the distinguished-looking young man.

Kathie blushed vividly. How could she have forgotten everything?

"Yes," Bruce made answer. "Mr. Conover thought it better, I believe."

They all walked in together. Kathie ran to her room and tried to bathe some of the troublesome color out of her face. What had happened to her? Surely she was not used to this much excitement over so simple a thing as the coming of a visitor.

They had a strangely quiet evening. A sense of satisfaction pervaded them all, and, after the first few inquiries about absent friends, Kathie went to the piano and played some of the old things that had been such a rare pleasure to Bruce that remembered winter. Ah, why should she think of them now? Was it comfort again? He sat and listened as if in a trance. There was only the light in the hall and the moon flooding the room through the open windows. All was so mysteriously sacred, as if he had gone into some dream country and was listening to the flow of soft, winding streams, of silver bells blown about by the wind.

She was there. She was free for him. Honor had held
her so securely before, that there had been no temptation.
And the grand, generous heart that had given her up,
the dear friend of her childhood and youth? For an instant
it seemed to Bruce as if he ought not to accept the sacrifice.

The soft flow of music ceased. She came over to the
sofa with a curious, half-unconscious nearness.

"Have I played you asleep? I used to do that, you
know?"

He took both hands in his and drew her nearer. His
love was such an old familiar thing to him, but quite new
and strange to her, he could see that. Yet was it awakening?

"You were so good to me through those days of pain."
The voice was tenderly suggestive. She drew her hands
softly away again. What was this coming upon her?

"Let us go out and walk," he said. "The night is so
lovely."

It was stifling here, she thought. The others sat at the
lower end of the room, talking in a low tone. They passed
them and went out on the porch, down the steps. The
wide, warm night lay all about them, the stars glowed softly
overhead, and the very grass at their feet quivered as the
tender wind swept over it. It was so new to her, though
she had seen it hundreds of times before. An enchantment
transfixed her.

"Kathie," he cried suddenly, and his tone seemed to
penetrate every pulse with its sweetness, — "Kathie, do
you know, can you think, why I have come back? I cannot wait for the tardy hours to whisper my secret. I love
you! I have loved you always, it seems to me, and now
that you are free I have come to win, if possible, the great
joy of my life!"

"Oh!" She uttered a sharp, pathetic cry. "I wonder if
I would have the right to take the joy at so high a price?

For I have wounded the noblest heart, and it seems as if my life could be none too long a penance — "

" He gave you to me, my darling. His great love was not content with merely setting you free, he wrote. I can almost guess how he learned my secret, and bade me come back and try. For I should not have come otherwise for years, unless you had been his wife. I did not mean to be tempted with the portion put aside for another. I waited at first because my father thought it best, and all that long winter I wonder if I sometimes appeared unthankful to you ; but God was keeping me away from the temptation I could so illy bear, on the safe, sweet side. I am so glad I never wronged Charlie in word or deed. But now, *now*, Kathie? "

What was this sudden thrill of desire, this great wave of intense satisfaction that flooded her heart like a high tide and floated her toward him with no doubt or question? She could not ask if it were love, she was simply and supremely content.

He drew her toward him and kissed the dewy, throbbing lips. She remembered then so many little events, flashes, something shown and withheld at the same moment. Why could she not have seen? And if she had seen, would she not have believed it her duty to uproot every fibre of an unlawful longing? Yes, her right to take this love now, lay in the fact of truth, perfect and entire ; she had never made any kind of barter with her own soul.

" Kathie ! " The tone was so soft, so entreating, so lover-like, impatient.

She put her hands in his, for she could not speak just then. It was so new, so delicious, so overwhelming. Ah, she knew now.

They walked up and down the path in happy silence. The fragrant wind, the rhythmic stars, the satisfaction of the whole world, told their story for them. Was it moments or a lifetime?

" We must go in," she said in timid entreaty. The girl's delicate sense was returning. There was a flutter in her face, in every pulse.

He turned and led her back, up the steps, her hand in his, her face shyly averted with the strange, new knowledge, the girlish abashment.

" Truants ! " her mother exclaimed.

Kathie was thankful for the shaded lights, the fragrant dusk, the carelessly unconscious tone.

" Yes, it is getting late," she said in a rich, tremulous voice that missed her mother, but caught Aunt Ruth's longing ear.

She rose hastily. " I suppose it is time we broke up our conclave," with a little smile. " Kathie, my darling, good night," with a tender kiss.

She went to her mother, and then held out her hand to the General, but she had no courage to raise her eyes to Bruce. They all went up-stairs together, and said another good-night.

Kathie hurried to her room. She made quick work with her toilet, for she wanted to be in the dark and the silence to think. She buried her face in the pillow as if to stifle its heat and blushes. Was this great happiness for her? Could she, dared she, feel at home and rejoice in it?

She lingered the next morning until she heard them all go down. If Uncle Robert were here.

Bruce was waiting for her in the hall, his eyes luminous with happiness, his face full of grand content.

" They all know," he whispered ; and then she seemed in the midst of them, receiving approval in their tender kisses. But she could not talk about it. Aunt Ruth saw that and came to her rescue, shielding her from obtrusive demonstrations.

" I hope you have made no mistake this time, Kathie," her mother said afterward, gently, yet as if she could not quite forget.

"O mamma, I wonder if I have a right to take so exquisite a happiness!"

"Yes, you foolish little child." And with the kiss she gave, vanished the last remnant of bitterness.

"But I do not want to make any real promise until Uncle Robert comes. And oh, if —"

"It will be well with them," Mrs. Alston rejoined hurriedly. "That must not mar your delight."

"And so I shall have my little girl," the General said with deep emotion. "Kathie, the first time I saw you, a strange little girl in a box at the opera, you went straight to my heart. I wanted you then, and if you had not been so well loved and sheltered I should have begged to adopt you. But how do you suppose Uncle Robert and I will ever get it settled?"

Uncle Robert telegraphed when he reached Chicago. The poor invalid was living. More than that he would not say, for he had a faint presentiment there might be a sacred joy at Cedarwood that he would not disturb.

But they had found Robert's wife unconscious, slowly breathing her last. There had been two strokes of paralysis in rapid succession. Up to the time of the first seizure they had considered her improving, and began to hope for partial restoration.

One side of her face had been a little drawn, but she lay calm and still beautiful. There was no change through the hours, and death came so silently at last that the trained eye of the nurse hardly told when the little flicker of life went out.

"It seems very sad," Robert Alston said, when they returned to the hotel. "I cannot pretend to any deep grief, for her utter indifference destroyed what might have been affection on my part, and yet to-day I give thanks that God kept me from any wild, desperate act. I might have made myself, in my madness, the very thing I so hated and despised in her. O Uncle Robert, I believe I *did* learn at last to be patient in God's time, to do the work appointed for my transgression, and until you came, a few days ago, I had no thought of her dying, of my freedom. I had so resolved to live that I should not be ashamed or confused at the last, to ask for nothing."

He bowed his head and wept silently. Uncle Robert laid his hand affectionately on the shoulder.

" It has been a hard fight, my dear boy, but you have come off conqueror."

" ' Thanks be to God, who giveth us the victory.' " He rose as he reverently uttered this. " And, Uncle Robert, I think no boy, no young man, ever had a truer, stronger friend than you have been to me. All that is fine and noble in me I shall owe to you and Charlie Darrell."

" There was some good soil, Rob." And the elder smiled in his old, meaning way. " It was a rich soil, and the great struggle was which should grow the fastest, the wheat or the tares."

" And you have been a faithful gardener. My whole life from this time must be an endeavor to repay you. For you took all the burden, all the trouble. What if I had been left alone?" And he shuddered, remembering many bitter hours.

" God never leaves us quite alone unless we place ourselves outside of help, and reject it because it is not what we want, paying no regard to our real needs. But I had my reward the night Charlie Darrell helped you to decide."

Robert Alston's wife was buried in a quiet corner of the cemetery. The one name on her headstone, "Addie," would tell no story to the passer-by. Her mother had been once to the asylum, but had left no address, and with the notice in the paper Mr. Conover considered their duty ended.

He had written to Mrs. Alston, but he knew he would reach home almost as soon as the letter. He came by himself and walked up from the station, finding Mrs. Alston quite alone, to his great satisfaction.

"Robert wants you very much," he said after the first news was told. "The boys are all at the Merediths, with the housekeeper, and it would be more agreeable to Rob to have you to himself awhile, if you would not mind going."

"I think I can be spared, and I must see my boy," she answered with deep feeling.

It was arranged that she should start the next morning. The others came back from their drive, and the evening was spent discussing graver subjects than those of love; but Uncle Robert was quite satisfied. His questions were answered by the deep joy in Kathie's eyes, and the color that mantled her cheek at a thought, the quick flutter in her voice, and the many little signs that told how deeply her heart had been touched.

"Conover," the General said, as he was pacing the long drawing-room that evening, "you and I of all other men must give thanks for the blessing vouchsafed to us in our boys. I think you can hardly have a doubt about the future. And it is the young men of the present who are to be the statesmen, rulers, and fathers of the next generation. Can we, dare we turn them adrift with no firm principles and ill-regulated wills, no strict sense of honor, integrity, and manliness, no definite purpose of fighting and conquering the temptations on every side? If we fail in our duty, and what is more, our example, what shall they believe? And our country's future welfare depends upon them. It has a wider significance than our own small lives."

CHAPTER XXVIII.

KATHIE ALSTON'S marriage was set down for Christmas. She chose the day, because there were so many sweet and sacred memories connected with it.

"And you know, mamma," she said, "I was reading my Christmas fairy book the day that I first began to think what I ought really to do, that I wanted to be a fairy for your sake, when we were so poor and Aunt Ruth was ill."

Mrs. Alston smiled. She was enjoying her daughter's happiness without stint, and surely the fine-looking Lieutenant Mackenzie was enough to gratify any mother's pride.

But Kathie did not lose interest in her old friends amid the new anticipations. She was glad to welcome back the summer strays, and find Mrs. Hunsdon quite restored to health and Fay sisterly sweet. Then, too, Sarah's affairs called for some attention.

Mr. and Mrs. Truesdell came down for a day. Mr. Truesdell wished to consult Mr. Conover, for he relied greatly on his judgment.

"My people are all very united now, and I think would be truly sorry to have me go," he said, "but the social life is narrow, and there can be no great gathering in. Some young man or some elderly shepherd could fill my place, while it seems to me I am fitted for the heat and the burden of the day. I want to do a wider work. And Mrs. Truesdell would be of so much service in the great world. It seems like wasting time and energy, although nothing, I suppose, *is* really wasted. But I do not want to feel that the larger salary draws me. Although we could

have as many comforts at Middleville on the smaller sum,
I dare say, Westport is wider. There is a class of young
people, mill hands and in shops, that ought to be reached
and interested. They are too often left out between the
wealthy and the class on which we expend sympathy and
charity, and they go to ruin by scores. Mrs. Truesdell
could be of great service in such a work."

" I think there is no question," Mr. Conover returned.
" The world needs constant, steady workers, and every
man ought to deal his best blows where they will tell.
There is too much waste of positive material in your spending both your lives in a little place like Middleville."

Sarah and Kathie discussed it as well, with the fine,
strong conscientiousness of the former. And yet Sarah
was deeply interested in Kathie's prospects, a little disappointed that it had not all come to pass as first planned.

" You would have been drawn so closely into my life,"
she said. " I used to think how we would compare, and
plan, and strive to the utmost. And yet my first fancy
was that you would marry Bruce Mackenzie."

Kathie blushed brightly.

Fay had said the same thing. The first time she had
heard of Bruce she had set the unknown hero beside Kathie.

They were all well satisfied when they heard, a week
later, that Mr. Truesdell had accepted, and would remove
as soon as possible. James Strong had married a nice,
tidy, sensible girl, one of his sister's pupils, and his
parents were much pleased.

There was a great deal of planning and going to and fro.
After the wedding the Mackenzie family would settle
themselves in New York, but in the spring they would
return to Brookside permanantly and set up a household
of their own. Rob was delighted. No brothers of blood
could be nearer or tenderer. His regard for Charlie Darrell was something sacred and reverential, and, indeed, on
this ground Bruce's warmest sympathies met and blended

with his. The deeper side of both natures had been stirred
by this gentler spirit which had taken fast hold intellectu-
ally and spiritually upon the deeper things of God.

Robert Alston was a little more grave, perhaps, yet when
the first shock was over, of the event he had never allowed
himself to imagine since that fearful night, could be, and
he was somewhat accustomed to a sense of freedom, he
settled readily into the new sphere. He was the elder
brother, the stay and comfort of his mother. Out of all
the wild waves beating upon the shore this gem had been
rescued. He would always have a broad, genial nature, a
quick eye, and a keen sense of fun, he would be strong of
will and desire, just as he was strong of brain and limb,
the sort of man who at middle life leaves an impress on
everything he touches, and is always fascinating to the
young out of the abundant vitality and sympathy of their
natures.

He had consented that Uncle Robert should legally
adopt Bertha.

"It will be much better," the uncle had said to Mrs.
Alston. "Robert may marry; it is right that he should,
for a nature like his needs the tie and interest of a family,
the warmth of feeling, and incentive to the highest of all
motives, love for others. Bertha would never seem a real
child to him, and might suffer a little from being uninten- ·
tionally put aside. I shall like her for an interest in my
own life after Kathie has gone."

"O Uncle Robert!" the young girl cried with deep
emotion. "Why did you not marry and have a house full
of girls? You make such a lovely father that daughters
ought to rise up and call you blessed."

A luminous tenderness filled his eyes.

"I shall have two daughters," he said softly.

They approached the marriage gradually. There was
a sacred mystery about it to both Bruce and Kathie that
could not be dragged about and inspected, or robed in the

gear of common talk. It seized and held them with a touch of deep and vital joy, a blessedness that was to set them a little apart from the old life and old friends, to give them an insight into that greater mystery, that living completeness. They were happy with all the joy and sweetness of youth and undisturbed love.

Cedarwood was made beautiful again. All without was covered with white, new-fallen snow. There was a sacred hush in the very air, and when the sun came out, with its warmth and glitter, the whole earth seemed attired as a bride.

The bells were ringing Christmas peals as she came down-stairs in her white array, her soft veil falling to her feet, enshrining her in a still, mysterious temple of girlhood; her fair hair twined about with lilies of the valley; and her sweet face a little startled perhaps, but reverent in the unseen sacredness of the blessing to be given and received with a pure, untroubled heart.

Bruce Mackenzie took her from her uncle's hand. They bowed their heads, the solemn questions were asked, the irrevocable answers given, the blessing pronounced. He put aside the soft enfolding draperies and kissed her, his wife, and she glanced up to the proud, manly figure with a great tremble of awe and content. They were quite still for many seconds, before any one spoke, as if they were silently entering into the profound mystery of the new relation.

There was much joy and many tender wishes from friends and relatives. Kathie moved around in her wraith-like cloud, her face touched with a luminous radiance. Well that she was not to give up these dear ones forever, that the distance between was only the spiritual sacrament, not any actual separation.

She kept the feast with them until mid-afternoon, then the two went out to try one small glimpse of the new life with only each other.

" It was so lovely," Fay Collamore said afterward.
" Just that quiet serenity, with no haste or disturbance.
Kathie Alston never hurried any sure awaiting, and she
has come to the right joy, to the certain peace."

It was summer again at Cedarwood. There was the
same wide, hospitable life ; Uncle Robert would not let it
flag. Almost before they knew it Bertie would be growing up to girlhood, laughing, loving, caressing little Bertie,
who had kept them from missing Kathie too sorely. The
Mackenzie home was not far distant, and the General was
slipping into a delightful, restful evening of life, taking
pride in his son's new venture, and enjoying the praise the
world accorded him, and loving Kathie with all the fervor
of a father.

They had a bright, genial, neighborhood life. There
were pursuits and children, joys and anticipations. Mr.
Meredith was growing stout, but kept his olden laughing
vivacity. There were three babies now, and Jessie was
charming in her matronly ways. Emma Langdon had
added a lovely little girl to the group, and still found time
for her art, as Louise did for her needle-work. Fred had
come home a newly fledged physician, but Rob adhered to
his old plan of making a fortune before he devoted himself to science, though he and Fred had many a good
study between them.

But it was not the fortune he was thinking of now. He
had been walking along the edge of the small lake that had
been such a pleasure and comfort to him in boyhood, and
now he had the arm of the tall, fair girl beside him linked
in his, and was holding her hand in a fond clasp when it
was not pressed to his lips. For he had asked and she
had answered the great question of his life, of both lives.

" No, Fay," he was saying, " don't make a hero of me,
I do not deserve it." And for a moment his voice was
husky with emotion. " It is an easy thing to be brave,

and happy, and high-hearted when everything goes well, and there are friends to hold you up, that you dash not your foot against a stone. And I think you ought to know — you have so much of my life in your keeping — that there was once when I had no right to think of you, that I went mad with passion, that I could have taken any step for freedom! It was when Mr. Gartney was coming. I was afraid to lose you." And his clasp tightened. "I did not ask what right I could have in you, whether you would be likely to accept a love flawed and stained with a wrong. It was like fighting wild beasts. We never know the utter barbarism of our natures until in times like these. Uncle Robert put up the first bar, and between him and Charlie Darrell I was saved, after I had been let to see the thing I might become. And then, my darling, I placed you resolutely out of my soul. I would not covet or desire. If God meant that all the rest of my life should be spent in atoning for the other mad moment, that I might have helped with just one thought of my mother, or Uncle Robert, or my duty, I would accept it. And I did truly. I thank God, who gave the victory," bowing his head reverently. "I did not see you again until I *had* conquered. I said to myself, 'God bless her with that other, wherever she may go.' Fay," suddenly, "what happened? Why did you not—" And she knew by the tremor that shook him how hard it was to put the rest into the sentence.

"O Robert!" she cried remorsefully, "I am afraid I made it harder for you, meaning to be true and upright, but in my carelessness, not thinking how I might hurt and hinder the best. I *was* afraid It was while I was in New York at my cousin's. You were so ready and kind, and many little trifles occurred between us that sometimes filled me with wild apprehension. I could see the wickedness of our growing to love each other. I put Mr. Gartney between. I was a coward to save myself so, but I *did*

try to love him. And after a while I saw the wrong and
shame of it, so when Louise was ill I resolved it out by
myself. I would not take any love for which I could make
no fair return; and if the opportunity never came I would
stay single. It would be a horrible thing to put one's self
into bonds that would presently become a wearing, drag-
ging chain!"

It was a sweet knowledge to know she, too, had realized
the danger.

"You shall not take the blame upon yourself. It was I
who had no right so to act. And that is my besetting sin,
that awful, obstinate wrong-headedness, that trying for the
thing I want, right or wrong. I have gotten the upper
hand of my 'familiar' a little, I think, and you must help
me, Fay. I want to deal justly and walk humbly, but it
seems as if Fred and Kathie took the graces, and I have
to make a hard fight for the small, sweet virtues."

"You will conquer." She uttered it proudly.

"Let us go up to my mother," he said. "Fay, you
must not be jealous, but I have a good many years of
mother-love to make up to her. What a cub of a boy I
used to be in the old times! No, dear; there are heroes in
the world, but I shall never be one of them."

She turned and kissed him through her tears. Was it
not "the least among these" who should be greatest?

They passed the gentlemen on the porch, deep in old
army reminiscences, and saw the gleam of Mrs. Alston's
dress in the dining-room.

"Mother," Rob said, with a proud, uplifted look, "I
have brought you my love, the one sweet, true love of my
life. Will you take her as a daughter? Shall we three love
each other and keep to each other as long as we all do live?"

It was the sacred solemnity of a troth plight. She had
her son and her daughter. God had given her the oil of
joy for mourning. A proud and happy mother, she placed
her arms around them both and kissed them; but there
were tears shining in her eyes.